UNLEASHED

Books by Crystal Jordan

CARNAL DESIRES

ON THE PROWL

UNTAMED

PRIMAL HEAT

EMBRACE THE NIGHT

PROWL THE NIGHT

NIGHT GAMES

UNLEASHED

SEXY BEAST V
(with Kate Douglas and Vonna Harper)

SEXY BEAST 9
(with Vonna Harper and Lisa Renee Jones)

UNDER THE COVERS
(with Melissa MacNeal and P. J. Mellor)

NIGHT SHIFT
(with Kate Douglas and Lynn LaFleur)

Published by Kensington Publishing Corporation

UNLEASHED

CRYSTAL JORDAN

APHRODISIA

KENSINGTON PUBLISHING CORP.
www.kensingtonbooks.com

APHRODISIA BOOKS are published by

Kensington Publishing Corp.
119 West 40th Street
New York, NY 10018

All Kensington titles, imprints, and distributed lines are available at special quantity discounts for bulk purchases for sales promotion, premiums, fund-raising, and educational, or institutional use.

Special book excerpts or customized printings can also be created to fit specific needs. For details, write or phone the office of the Kensington Special Sales Manager: Kensington Publishing Corp., 119 West 40th Street, New York, NY 10018. Attn. Special Sales Department. Phone: 1-800-221-2647.

Aphrodisia and the A logo Reg. U.S. Pat. & TM Off.

ISBN-13: 978-0-7582-6157-1
ISBN-10: 0-7582-6157-8

First Kensington Trade Paperback Printing: October 2012

10 9 8 7 6 5 4 3 2 1

Printed in the United States of America

This book is dedicated to my fans. Most especially to the Smutkedettes who always keep the Smuketeers Yahoo group laughing. You ladies (and maybe even a few gents) are the best!

Also, no dedication page would be complete without mentioning my best friend, Michal, and my boyfriend, Frank. Love you both.

CONTENTS

Hunting Temptation

I

The scuff of a boot on the ground alerted him to the fact that he wasn't alone. It was the lightest of sounds, almost indiscernible from the loud bustle of humanity on the thoroughfare only a few meters away. But if anyone sensed the danger, they looked the other way. It didn't pay to be a Good Samaritan in this part of New Chicago.

Kienan Vaughn suppressed the growl that threatened to rumble up in his throat. The gray wolf inside him didn't care to be hunted, wanted to take control of the man, shift forms, and rip his stalker's throat out. He felt his fangs slide down, and he ran his tongue down to the sharp point of a tooth. Instead of confronting his stalker, he ignored him.

No need to encourage the local color.

A low hiss sounded just behind him and to his left, indicating the other man had moved, but Kienan continued at his steady pace. Until the other man took direct action, he wasn't going to engage.

"Sooo, tasty." The reptilian hiss was fuller this time, low and

ominous in the way only a snake could manage. "I've never seen you on my street before, tasty. How much?"

"I'm not a jade." Nor did he look in any way like a man who prostituted himself, so this sidewinder was trying to take advantage of someone he thought had stumbled into the Vermilion District by accident.

This steaming cesspool of humanity was the worst that the city had to offer, the crumbling remains of the Third Great War festering with criminals and degenerates. Kienan sighed. His cousin couldn't have mated himself to a woman who lived in the affluent Lakeshore District?

"If you don't sell it, maybe I take it for free." His stalker's scent drew closer, and Kienan's muscles tensed. The wolf waited to spring, while the man just snorted in annoyance. This was going to go south. Fast.

Fuck.

Turning abruptly, Kienan caught the other man off guard, and he stumbled back a step, his eyes widening. Kienan let a lupine grin form on his lips, an expression only a suicidal fool would call friendly. "I don't want to play. Go away."

"You're not from here if you don't know Niso's rep." Another hiss rattled out of the man's throat, angrier. "My district, my game, my rules. You'll play if I say so. Won't he, boys?"

Two more men slid from an alleyway that was more like a dank crevice between two buildings. They were in front of Kienan, blocking his path to freedom. He'd sensed them, sensed the menace from them, but until they'd been called by their master, it had been no stronger than the average citizen's in this part of the city. Now it was. Now he knew he was their target.

"No, I've never heard of you, Niso." But he'd remember the name from now on, which was unfortunate for the reptile and his goons. They just didn't know it yet. "I'm not interested in fighting you off."

Triumph shone in Niso's gaze, and he licked his lips, looking Kienan over. It wasn't that he minded the idea of fucking another man—he'd slake his lust with whomever was convenient as long as everyone was willing. But he wasn't willing. The snake-shifter palmed his erection, a cruel smile twisting his mouth. "You don't have to fight, tasty. Just do what I want. Nice and quiet. We won't hurt you much."

Much. Kienan ground his teeth together but rolled his shoulders to loosen his limbs. His pack shifted across his back. He'd do better to drop it, but he'd rather not part with his possessions unless he had to. If he dropped the bag, it would probably be stolen.

A quick glance around showed no easy escape route. The buildings on either side were several stories high with no windows in reach. Except for the alley the two goons had come out of, there was no direction left to go. So fighting his way out was his best option. Three against one didn't make for good odds, but he'd faced worse. Many, many times. And he was still breathing. Others who'd faced him couldn't say the same.

He welcomed the adrenaline that coursed through his veins, let it heighten his awareness even more than normal, but controlled it so it wouldn't control him. Years of training had sharpened him too much for that.

Turning back to look at Niso, he found the snake had pulled a gun. The muzzle was a few centimeters from Kienan's nose. His heart rate bumped up at the sight, though he kept his voice even. "You know the problem with firearms?"

The evil grin grew wider. "What's that, tasty?"

"They're best used from a distance. Up close they just give your opponent something else to grab on to."

"What?" Confusion darkened Niso's gaze for just a moment, a split second of wariness that his prey wasn't reacting with the terror he'd expected.

Too late.

Snapping his hand out, Kienan caught the snake-shifter's wrist, breaking it before he could even squeeze off a shot. Screaming, spittle dribbled from Niso's lips as he fell to the ground, curling in a ball around his injured limb. The other two were on Kienan in milliseconds, and time seemed to stretch, become fluid. Every sense intensified until he could hear their every breath, their pounding hearts.

Goon One launched himself at Kienan's back; Goon Two came at him from the side. His pulse hammered, sweat beading on his forehead. Throwing the gun, he nailed Goon Two in the nose and blood sprayed out as he stumbled back, his hands over his face. Goon One slammed Kienan forward into the ground, and he heard claws tearing at his pack. The goon was going for his possessions rather than trying to kill him. *Fuck.* He wiggled under the weight of the other man, working his arms free of the straps.

Dragging himself out from under his bag scraped the flesh off of his palms, but he rolled and kicked out a foot to catch the man looting his belongings in the gut. The air whooshed out of the goon's lungs, but he lunged forward, his fist catching Kienan in the jaw. Kienan fell back a few steps, coppery blood filling his mouth from the blow.

A leonine roar echoed down the narrow street, and the goon bared his fangs, coming at Kienan again. He growled, but froze in place and made himself an easy target until the last moment. Turning aside, Kienan sliced the side of his hand into the base of the other man's skull.

He went down.

Kienan didn't pause, didn't look to see if the other man would get up. He knew he wouldn't. Goon Two had recovered from the blow to the nose, though blood still flowed from his nostrils, and his mouth and eyes were swollen. Kienan didn't underestimate the danger—he'd been as injured before and come out the victor in a fight. The man was huge, someone who expected to use his size to intimidate, to overwhelm. It was going to fucking hurt to take a hit from him. They circled each other, looking for an opening. Goon Two grew impatient, and Kienan knew he had him. The big man charged and Kienan stooped to grab his pack off the ground, swinging it between them to block the other man's hit. Kienan thrust the butt of his hand up to slam into Goon Two's already damaged nose, and his eyes rolled back. Unconscious.

It felt as though an hour had past, but his chrono said the fight had been over in mere minutes.

Energy hummed through Kienan, and he spun in a tight circle, waiting for the next challenge. His fists clenched and unclenched, but the only other person moving on the street was Niso, who whimpered and crawled away from the fight.

"Who are you?" His broken wrist was tucked up to his chest, and he dragged himself across the ground with his good hand. Toward the discarded gun. "You said ... no fighting ..."

Sighing, Kienan walked over and kicked the weapon away. Niso flinched as his revenge spun out of reach.

"I said I wasn't interested in a fight." Kienan spit the blood out of his mouth. "I never said I didn't know how."

A quick tap to the temple and the man was drooling and insensible like his goons.

Brushing off his clothes, Kienan went to retrieve his bag. His heart rate and breathing began to return to normal. Only then did the aches and pains from the battle begin to screech. His palms stung, his muscles twinged, the side of his face ached. He doubted he'd have a bruise, but it didn't feel good.

He grabbed the bag, and as he lifted it, his senses shivered, alerting him to the fact that he was being watched. By more than one person. Another welcoming committee? He gritted his teeth and straightened, glancing around. There were people who peered out of the shadows, waiting to see who lost the struggle, waiting like so many carrion to pick apart the scraps.

He snorted, weariness crashing down around him. He shrugged to resettle his kleather jacket before he slung the bag over his shoulder. Likely, the bone pickers had been hoping he would lose for the prime kelp leather coat alone. It was his one indulgence, and would have gotten the scavengers quite a few creds.

He shook his head and strode toward the larger street ahead. Not that it would be any safer, but it was the direction he needed to go to find his cousin. What was he *doing* here? He hadn't seen Pierce in years. Decades. He had no idea if the other man even wanted to see him. But it gave him something to do, since he had no clue what to do with himself now that he was a free man.

Free. Was that how he considered his years in the government's black ops? A prison sentence? No. But it had felt like one the last year or so. Dissatisfaction had closed in around him until he could barely breathe. He was burnt-out, married to his work in the shadows, living every day as a lie where he played cat and mouse with criminals and operatives like himself from enemy countries. He'd sacrificed everything for his mission, and it was too late that he realized the darkness he lived in was eating away at his soul.

He'd had to get out before there was nothing left of his humanity to be worth saving. Now he just wanted to see someone who knew his real name, who'd known him before. So here he was, hauling his ass through the shittiest part of New Chicago in search of the last of his family. Everyone else was long dead, and he'd rarely been home except to attend a funeral.

Home. There was a word he hadn't used in a while.

Dragging in a deep breath, he shoved the past away. There was no hope there. He had only now, had only that slender thread that still attached him to abstract concepts like home, family, love. Things other people had, things he'd left behind long ago. He didn't know who he was without his job, but he had to find out. Another deep breath and he nearly gagged on a wave of the stench coming off the street.

Deus, the Vermilion had gotten even worse since the last time he'd been in town.

A woman sitting on a heap of garbage bared her fangs and hissed at him. She reeked of cat piss, so he didn't have to wonder what species of shifter she was—feline of some kind. Everyone was a predator here. Everyone, everywhere in the world was a predator. The Third Great War had seen to that— it had left its touch on humanity as much as it had on the crumbling buildings in this district.

Biological warfare early in the twenty-first century had ripped the planet apart. Their scientists had never anticipated the effect long-term exposure to their weapons would have on humans. It twisted their genes, morphed them into shape-shifters—jungle cats, bears, wolves, birds of prey, every possible predator.

No one had ever uncovered why, but the chemicals brought out the most feral instincts in humankind. Dark, rough, and dangerous, just like the world they now inhabited. Nearly a century later, people simply accepted that inside each human lurked a beast who might take control at any moment. It had made Kienan's job as an operative that much more deadly. At one time, he'd loved that. Loved the adrenaline rush, the challenge of pitting himself against another predator. All of it.

Now, he was just tired.

The weariness hadn't let up in more years than he could count. It wasn't so much a physical issue as it was a state of mind: tired of life, tired of death, tired of himself. Just fucking tired of it all.

He inhaled a breath and coughed as the stench of rotting waste and human filth hit his nose. Laced in with the stink was the scent he sought. Following it, he worked his way deeper into the Vermilion. Here, what was left of the pre-war buildings clustered together in all their dank, moldering glory. He could feel eyes on him, and his shoulders twitched, but he kept walking.

Keeping to the shadows he'd lived in for decades, he ghosted down the streets and through twisted alleyways littered with refuse, until he found himself in front of a building that made his eyebrows arch. He checked the locale against the intel he'd received on his cousin. Yes, this was the place.

His cousin lived in a jadehouse.

Curved windows belled outward into the sidewalk, and his brows rose higher as he strolled toward the door. Inside the windows were naked, masked people, women and men who dangled from clamps attached to their nipples, their vaginas, their cocks. Some had lighted stim-probes inserted into their pussies and asses, and each time the probes lit, they undulated against their bonds. Still others were mummified in black kleather and hung upside down like wriggling corpses.

He stepped closer to one display. A woman and two men were bound together, clamped, probed, and had fluorescent blue wires attached to each probe and clamp. The men were chained on their knees, one piercing the woman's pussy, the other filling her mouth. Their muscles flexed as the men thrust their cocks into her, fucking her hard. All three arched together, writhing as the wires flashed blue.

Kienan swallowed as one man threw his head back, obviously reaching orgasm. Stepping away, Kienan turned toward the door, ignoring his body's reminder of how long it had been since he'd gotten some trim. He pulled his ident card out of his jacket pocket and swished it in front of a vidpad beside the entrance. The word *Tail* was etched into the surface of the massive iris door. The vidpad beeped and the middle point of the door split into nine curved slices, retracting into the walls.

Loud synthrock pulsed from inside, and he stepped into the most notorious technobrothel in the world. Where his cousin, Pierce, now made his home with his two mates. One of those mates, Lorelei Chase, was the owner of Tail. She was supposed to be the most beautiful woman alive, and a notorious madam whose jades specialized in any wild pleasure a person could dream up. From what Kienan had seen through the windows, he believed it. What would he find inside?

He shook his head. It was difficult to believe Pierce lived here. Kienan could only hope his cousin was home and willing to see a long-lost relative. Some of the weariness fell away as Kienan moved forward.

This should be interesting.

Sex with Gea was some of the hottest he'd ever had in his life. And he'd had plenty.

Quilliam North grinned, reveling in the feel of soft female curves and raw hot fucking on smooth microsilk sheets. If there was anything better than this, he hadn't found it. She straddled his lap, her back to his front, and he slid his hands up to cup her pert little breasts. The nipples stabbed into his palms, and he couldn't resist them. He pinched, twisted until she moaned.

"Quill!"

"That's my name, dearheart," he purred.

She stiffened a bit at the nickname, one he knew she wasn't comfortable with. But that was why he used it. Because she reacted, because he couldn't resist pushing her buttons. Because in the year they'd been having sex, she'd continued to shy away from anything that might be called affection, intimacy. She didn't cling like other women when she got near a man with as much money as he had. She didn't demand more. She just used him for his body, fucked his brains out whenever she happened to be in the mood, and then she disappeared again.

She fascinated him.

Shoving deep into her pussy, he ran one hand down to tweak her clit, just the way she liked it.

"Move on me, Gea." He let his fingertip slide in to tease her slick flesh, stretched around his cock.

Leaning forward to brace her palms on his thighs, she did as he wanted. Her hips rose and fell, her wet pussy taking his dick deep. They moved together, the carnal sounds of mating making the leopard within him purr. Blood pulsed through his veins, hot and fast. Every micrometer of her soft skin that rubbed against him just served to stimulate his senses. Her scent, her touch. He dipped his head forward to bite the back of her shoulder. A flavor that was uniquely Gea's filled his mouth. His fangs scored her flesh and a moan bubbled out of her, her sex flexing on his cock.

A groan tangled with a hiss in his throat, and his claws slid out. He used one to flick her hardened clit, oh so lightly. She cried out, her sex clamping down on his. Deus, she was close to the edge. He could sense it, smell her dampness, feel the way all those delicate little muscles gripped and released his cock. It turned him on, made him pant for breath.

Her hands tightened on his legs and she worked herself on him harder, faster. The friction was enough to drive him wild. He hissed, his fangs scraping his lower lip, the leopard warring with the man for dominance. Only Gea had ever brought him this close to feral during sex since he was an untried youth. Even then it hadn't been this intense. Arching his hips, he thrust into her, meeting her halfway.

"Quill!" She froze over him for just a moment; then her movements grew frantic and she pumped herself on his cock while she reached orgasm.

The contractions of her pussy around his shaft were enough to send him spinning. His mind emptied and he thrust into her again and again. He held her tight to the base of his cock, grinding his pelvis into her until his come exploded from his body in shuddering waves. Ecstasy rolled through him and a feline roar ripped from him.

She collapsed forward and he caught her, pulling her back into him and rolling them onto their sides on his wide mattress. Sweat made their flesh glide together, and his teeth locked at how good it felt. He ran his hand down her side, enjoying the feel of her silky skin.

Shivering a little, she sighed. "I have to go."

"I know." It irked him, and it amused him that he was so annoyed. How long had he wished for a woman just like her? One who didn't give a damn about how many creds he had in his bank accounts? He suppressed a snort. Well, he always got what he wanted, didn't he?

She scooted to the side of the bed, sitting up to stretch. "I have to meet with someone soon."

"Ah, I wondered what brought you down to my part of the city." He folded his hands behind his head, watching her nude form move around the room to collect her discarded clothes. All of them were black, the better to blend in to the night. Now the color just accentuated her creamy coloring. She really was a beautiful woman, made even more so by the fact that she cared even less about her beauty than she did about his money. It simply was—she didn't play it up.

Wisps of white-blond hair danced around her face and brushed her chin, but tapered to a sharp point at the nape of her neck. The pale color nearly matched her fur when she shifted into an arctic fox. So lovely, so cagey. A mystery that constantly intrigued him. She thrust her fingers through those shiny locks. Experience taught him exactly how soft and silky those thick strands were. Wide brown eyes dominated her face, but it was the curiosity and mischief that often filled her expression that made him come back for a second look. She wasn't short, but couldn't be called tall either. Her body was toned and athletic, with just enough curve to fill his palms. Perfect.

She slid her shirt over her head, covering the small nanotat of a hummingbird that fluttered back and forth across one shoulder blade, the delicate wings in constant motion beneath her skin. The shirt also hid her lush breasts from view. A pity. She cast a glance at him. "This part of the city doesn't belong to you, despite what you might think."

"Give me time, Ms. Crevan." He let an easy grin spread across his face. "Just . . . give me time."

Snorting, she shook her head. "Should I be impressed now?"

"Do I impress you?" Where had *that* question come from? It had been years since he'd cared what anyone thought of him. One didn't survive a childhood like his and come out on top without stepping on a few toes in the process. Or stepping over a few dead bodies. Such was life in the Vermilion.

"Why would you want to impress me? I'm nobody in your powerful world." She rolled her eyes. "I'm in this part of town for a job, but you've already figured that out."

"Of course." He kept his smile in place. "Why else would you come over here?"

"It isn't exactly what attracts the tourists."

He chuckled. "Depends on what they're looking for. There are a few *attractions* that can only be found here."

"Too true." Her nose wrinkled.

Drugs, weapons, whores who'd fulfill any fantasy or fetish one might want to indulge in. For some, this patch of sin was as close to nirvana as they'd ever come. Ironic, but he made a tidy profit from all those depravities. "Who's your client this time? What dirty little secret are they having you unearth? Pity the unfortunate soul they've set you upon."

Her white teeth flashed in a smile, and he saw a hint of fang. "I take that as a compliment."

"I meant it as one." He quirked an eyebrow, crossing his ankles. "Details, dearheart."

She growled, the fox even more evident. "Don't call me that."

"You don't want to be dear to me?" He clapped a hand over his heart. "You wound me."

"Ha!" Her tone was scornful, but her lips twitched in a grin he knew she didn't want to show him. The feline in him couldn't resist taunting her. She reacted so nicely.

"Maybe you'd be dearer to me if you told me a little about you. Come on, what was your mother's name? Where did you grow up? A tiny clue about the mystery that is Gea." Partially he was yanking her tail again, but partially he wanted to know. If he really needed the information, he could pay to get it, but he enjoyed the game too much to end it easily.

Her grin was quick, a spark of wickedness flashing in her gaze. "Now, what fun would it be if I told you?"

"Perhaps I should guess..." He pretended to consider. "You're a Tahitian princess exiled from her homeland?"

She pulled a lock of her pale hair in front of her eyes. "Hm. Yes, Tahitian. That's likely."

Releasing her hair, she stooped over and picked up a small pack to sling across her shoulder.

"What's in the bag?" It was a standard question, one that he knew she wouldn't answer.

She stuck her tongue out at him. "Quit being nosy."

"Coming from you, that's rich." He chortled and she had the grace to flush, but she still didn't give him an answer.

The woman was a private investigator, a specialist in digging into other people's business. That she was so guarded and protective of her own privacy made excellent fodder for him to tease her.

"Fine, keep your secrets." Sobering, he sighed. "At least tell me who's hired you this time. Perhaps I can help."

Her work was how they'd met in the first place. Someone had hired her to ferret out information about a colleague of his, and her meddling had brought her to his attention. He'd developed a soft spot for his fox and had occasionally fed her intel to assist in her investigations. It behooved her to tell him what he wanted to know.

Hesitating for a long moment, she shrugged and capitulated. "Who hired me isn't important. Who I'm looking for is. Do you know Felicia Tamryn?"

"Tam? Yes, I know her." A grifter of the first order. She was a cheetah-shifter who could make a man fall in love with her with a single glance . . . and rob him blind before he could blink.

Gea's brown eyes locked on him. "Have you seen her?"

"Not recently." He frowned, groping through his memory to find the last one he had of Tam. "Not for a few months, at least, but we don't always move in the same circles."

Gea hummed in her throat. "If you happen to see her, don't tell her I'm looking. Or that anyone might want to find her."

He chuckled. "Scared she'll outrun you?"

"She *is* a cheetah."

"Touché." His chuckle turned into a laugh, and he wrapped an arm around his stomach. For some reason, the thought of his little fox trying to run down a big cat amused him to no end.

"She might be fast, but that doesn't mean I can't catch her." Huffing, she picked up a pillow and threw it at his head. "I'm leaving now."

Getting his laughter under control, he couldn't resist a last dig. "It was lovely seeing you again, dearheart. Do come again. And I'll make you come again. And again."

Her body stiffened, but heated awareness flashed in her gaze. She crossed her arms to cover hardened nipples that thrust against her shirt. "Good-bye, Quill."

He grinned and shook his head as she darted out the door, but any desire to linger in bed went with her. Rising, he moved to the window and pushed aside the curtain. From here, he could see the gleam of her pale hair under the streetlights until she pulled a black cap on and was engulfed by the darkness of the Vermilion.

Forcing himself to look away, he glanced out over the rest of the city. New Chicago at night was all towering mercurite skyrises and glittering lights. The Lakeshore District and downtown had been built over the rubble of the old city after urban riots had destroyed everything in the last great war. As close as it was in kilometers, that gleaming elegance was a world away from where he grew up in the Vermilion.

Now he was somewhere in between those worlds. His headquarters were right on the edge of the Vermilion, far enough away that his legitimate business associates felt safe coming here, close enough that his seedier contacts didn't have to stray far from their own territory. It had worked out well for him, and he liked that his penthouse flat took up the entire top floor of the building. Work was always close by if he needed to take care of something, but he could lock himself away if he required some peace.

While he was glad to have clawed his way out of the gutter, a part of him would always belong in the Vermilion. It was in his attitude toward business, cutthroat and unapologetic. He'd use whatever advantages he could to ensure he was never at anyone's mercy again. Now he had the power, and he'd do whatever it took to keep it and ensure his fortune thrived.

He shook himself out of his reverie and stretched. Perhaps it was time for a run on his old stomping grounds. He'd been too long in civility. Besides, he had an investment opportunity to offer Lorelei Chase, a friend he'd known for years who still lived in the heart of the district. The Vermilion was the only place in the city where one could find their famed technobrothels. Politicians had decided it was best to give their constituents a place to "let the wildness out," and they looked the other way at the rampant crime and poverty in that district as a result. It was just the price the city had to pay for people being half-animal.

Of course, Quill had seen more than his fair share of those same politicians taking advantage of the attractions of the Vermilion. Taking a hit of bliss while fucking a muscular jade up the ass was just the start of a night when they let their feral nature run free. As long as they paid their bills when the night was done, that was all Quill cared about.

He rolled his shoulders. The leopard within him wanted to prowl. Turning for his 'fresher, he pulled out a clean set of clothes. All black, to blend in to the night, and topped it with a jacket that had a nanosheet built into it that hardened into an impenetrable layer if it was pierced with a bullet or blade. It didn't look like much, but it had taken a load of creds out of his accounts.

Worth it for the protection it offered, especially considering where he was going.

2

It was a dangerous game she was playing.

How long could she expect to keep fucking her mate without telling him what they were to each other? Gea could only be grateful that he couldn't sense it himself. Only shifter species that mated for life could tell when they found their mate, and leopards couldn't. Arctic foxes, however, were not as lucky. Just a handful of species could sense it. Even then, not all of them had a mate they were supposed to spend the rest of their lives with. It was a crapshoot, and she was on the losing end. Deus, after what her mother had been through, she'd thought there was no way that fate would land her with a mate.

She'd been wrong. So very, very wrong.

When it came to Quill, she stayed away as long as she could, but when the need grew too strong, she had to have him. Touching him, tasting him, feeling him thrust deep inside her fed a craving she didn't even want to admit she had. She licked her lips, savoring the flavor from his kiss that still lingered.

Tonight's trip into the Vermilion had given her an excuse to show up on his doorstep. His place was right on the edge of civilization, right before it gave way to the dangerous wild side. A perfect metaphor for the man himself. One foot still in the shady dealings of the Vermilion he'd grown up in, one foot in the upstanding world of legitimate business. The dichotomy intrigued her, and she wished it hadn't.

She wished she could resist him, resist the draw he had on her, but she hadn't once been successful since the night she'd met him and sensed what he was to her. If she was close enough to touch, she did. Her insides twisted tight, and she clenched her fingers to still their shaking. Now was not the time or the place to show weakness.

But she was weak, wasn't she? As weak as her mother had been, addicted to her mate. Dependent. Pathetic.

No. *No.* That would not be her. That would never, ever be her. As long as she never told him, never claimed him, she was safe. It was just sex. She never gave him more. Her only lucky break was that his upbringing had made him just as wary as she was of tying himself to someone.

Next time, she'd fight harder to stay away from him. Next time, she might even manage not to knock on his door.

It was unfortunate her investigations took her into the Vermilion as often as they did. But where else could people hide all their filthy little secrets? Or so they thought. So far, not one of her investigations had been fruitless. The information was there, if you knew whom to ask. If you knew whom to pay.

Suppressing the pain and fear and self-loathing that always followed the high of being in Quill's arms, she focused on the task at hand. This was what mattered. This was her life. This was who she was. She needed to remember that.

Another block of skirting through the darkness and she was in front of the warehouse she wanted. Slipping around the side into the unlit alley that separated it from the next building, she faced a wall with no door. Or so it appeared. Squatting down, she pressed her ident card to a tiny vidscreen hidden at the base of the wall. A small click sounded and she pushed in a rough square of staggered bricks that was level with her hip. She hopped up and shimmied inside. The bricks swung shut behind her.

"Ziegler?" She squinted in the gloom, waiting for her eyes to adjust to the total lack of light. At least outside, there was the hint of moon and stars. "Ziggy, where are you? Since you called to set up this meet, you'd better be here!"

Never mind that she needed the information he claimed to have, it was usually better to keep Ziggy on the defensive. The blisshead wouldn't hesitate to make the most of any situation that could get him more creds to feed his addiction.

She shoved aside a dusty tapestry that covered a doorway in the narrow warren that ran the length of the building. It was doubtful the owners of the warehouse even knew Ziggy had his hideout back here. The tight space always made her antsy and claustrophobic.

"Ziggy!"

"Here." The skinny man slinked through a door, his fingers twitching the way they did when he was coming down off a high. "You got my creds?"

"Depends on whether you have the intel you promised." She crossed her arms and jutted her chin.

"I got it. It's prime." His yellowed teeth flashed in a smile that was supposed to be ingratiating but wasn't. "Just what you wanted about Tam."

The last place anyone had seen Tam was in a technobrothel. A very public area in a technobrothel. The question Gea wanted answered was why the cheetah had been there in the first place. Hardly a way to lie low after pulling a job. Her client didn't know what Tam had been there for, only that she'd disappeared shortly after and hadn't been seen since.

Gea figured that if she wanted to know were Tam had gone, then she needed to know where she'd come from. And why.

The *why* was always the hardest question to answer, but usually the most crucial and most revealing. People did all manner of stupid and insane things, but unless they were completely bent, they had their reasons, and it was a lot easier to do her job when she knew the motivation behind the action.

She made an impatient gesture at Ziggy. He always claimed his information was prime, but he'd say anything to get his next fix. "Let's hear it."

His smile grew wider. "She was meeting with someone, a buyer. Wanted something her mark had."

"What's that?" She kept her expression bored enough that he knew she was still interested, but didn't give away just how interested.

"Some old book." His shoulder jerked in a shrug, the muscles throughout his body starting to twitch. "Called it a Gutenberg."

"The Gutenberg Bible?" She arched an eyebrow. Now, wasn't that intriguing? Her client hadn't said a word about anything that valuable going missing. She'd have to do some checking to see if he'd had a Gutenberg or if Tam had nicked it from someone else.

"Yeah. Yeah, that was it." Ziggy's head bobbed in a nod.

She chewed her lip for a moment. "You got a name on her contact?"

Eyes narrowing, his grin turned sly. "Maybe. Cost you extra to find out."

"Don't mess with me, Ziggy." She hardened her voice. "You like our arrangement, so don't start jerking me around. I can always get my information from somebody else. Is that what you want?"

"Need it bad this time, Gea." His tone rose into a screeching whine.

"Take that up with your dealer. Maybe he'll give you a discount." She flashed her fangs at him in warning. "What was Tam's contact's name?"

"Meier. German guy. Bear-shifter, big and scary." His fingers twitched, flicking against each other in a spasmodic movement. "Wouldn't want to mess with him."

"I'll keep that in mind." She pulled out her palmtop computer, keyed in a few codes, and heard a beep from his pocket. "You've been paid."

Retrieving his palmtop, he glanced at it and giggled like a delighted child. "Prime."

He walked her out and sped away the moment his hidey-hole sealed shut behind them, no doubt on his way to his next score. Blissheads.

Her muscles relaxed a little at being outside again where she could see the slice of sky overhead. Not that anyone could relax much in this part of town, but she'd take exposure over enclosure any day. She'd never enjoyed being caged. By anyone or anything.

She sighed and straightened the cap that covered her hair, tucking a stray wisp away, her mind returning to the puzzle Ziggy had given her to work out. Tam had been trying to fence a stolen artifact. One that could go to only certain buyers, who were willing to have an illegally acquired relic in their possession. It wouldn't be impossible to move an item like that, but it would take knowing whom to contact. Gea knew someone who used to be in that game but had recently retired. Perhaps that would make for a more pliable source of information.

The piece of the puzzle Gea couldn't figure out was why her client hadn't mentioned anything about Tam stealing from him. But he had to be tracking the cheetah down for a reason. Maybe that was it. Maybe it wasn't. The man was in love with her, that was clear. But love and hate had a very thin line between them.

Shouting at the end of the alley had Gea pressing back into the shadows. It sounded like two rival gangs were getting into it. Shit. That was not a mess she wanted to get tangled up in. She hoped Ziggy had disappeared before the fighting started, but there was nothing she could do about it either way. Shots rang out, and she gritted her teeth to keep from flinching. Time to get out of here. Now.

She eased her hand behind her and into her knapsack, trying to move slowly enough that no one would notice her. Doubtful they'd be paying attention, but she wanted to be gone before anyone suspected she'd ever been here. Her hand closed around the butt of her grappler gun and she eased it out. A quick peek showed no one looking her way, so she aimed at the top of the building and fired. The thing had a silencer on it, so only a whispery *pop* sounded. She winced at even that small noise.

A gossamer-thin strand of mercurite shot out of the gun to form a molecular bond with the building ledge. If she couldn't walk out of the alley, she had to go up. She engaged a setting on the gun so it would pull her up the wire. Her heart jolted at the initial jerk that yanked her off her feet. Every muscle in her body tensed and she clutched the gun tight as wind sped past her in an exhilarating rush. A howl rent the air below her, and bullets exploded into the side of the building, spraying debris in her face. She sputtered, her grip slipping on the grappler.

"Shit!"

She kicked her feet against the wall, hoped she was close enough to the top to make it, and used the momentum of the grappler to flip herself up and over the railing to land on the roof. She dropped to her haunches to keep her balance, a triumphant grin spreading over her face. A quick tug and the mercurite strand disintegrated into silver dust that left no trace of her passing. Deus, she loved her gadgets.

The triumph was short-lived. She heard the distinct sound of claws scrabbling against brick and peeked over the edge.

Bullets exploded into the railing, forcing her back, but she caught a glimpse of a massive Komodo dragon climbing up the side of the building. Fast.

Adrenaline flooded her system, fight-or-flight instincts warring within her. She could stay and fight, but a smart fox knew when to run, so she hoisted her pack and ran as if her ass had been lit on fire. A short leap and she was on the next rooftop, but the dragon-shifter wasn't far behind her. She could sense him closing in, his reptilian speed giving him the advantage. Her muscles burned, but she kept sprinting. She'd rather not be gang-raped before someone put a bullet in her brainpan. That thought sent energy coursing through her and she shot forward. Sweat poured down her face, searing her eyes. She wouldn't last much longer, and the dragon wasn't slowing.

He was gaining on her.

A building loomed before her, higher than any of the others around it. She didn't know if her grappler could reach high enough to get her to the top, but she'd try. Swinging the gun around, she fired and the mercurite hit about a meter below the ledge.

She'd take it.

Switching the setting so it would pull her up, her senses howled that the dragon was there, upon her. *Hurry!* She leaped forward, launching herself off the side of the building. His claws raked across her calf, slicing through her clothes and flesh. She screamed, one hand slipping off the gun. The wind rushed by at dizzying speed as she spun wildly through the air. She gagged when she slammed into the side of the taller building, the breath exploding from her lungs. Dangling for a long moment, her arm screeching from the abuse, she reached her free hand up and grabbed for the ledge. Shimmying forward, she slowly hauled herself up to the rooftop.

Tumbling over the railing, she lay there, panting for breath, still clutching the grappler. She was more grateful than ever that she'd dropped the load of creds it took to buy the gun. Kissing the grip, she let it clatter to the rooftop. The cold blast of air from Lake Michigan was welcome in cooling down her sweaty flesh. She closed her eyes, sucking in oxygen as fast as her lungs would allow. It took long minutes before her body stopped shaking from the adrenaline. That was a far closer call than she cared for. She tested her limbs and drew in a sharp breath as the sting from her leg made her wince. Rolling into a sitting position, she put the grappler away and pulled out the small med kit she carried with her. The occasional tremor in her fingers made it take longer than she would have liked to slap a nanopatch over her torn flesh. She flexed her calf. It wasn't too bad. She could still walk on it, run if she had to.

Which meant she could still do a bit more information seeking before she called it a night. Normally, she'd seriously consider taking her ass home right now, but her client wanted Tam tracked down immediately, if not sooner, and he was handing over a lot of creds to make that happen. A client as wealthy as he was could send a lot of prime business Gea's way if she made him happy. Plus, she was too tenacious to scurry home just yet. It was a trait that made her good at her job.

She dug out her palmtop computer, keyed in a code, and waited. A woman's face appeared on the vidscreen, her green eyes wide with curiosity. "Gea."

"Delilah, I was wondering if you have time for a meeting."

"Tonight?"

Gea wiped at the sweat on her brow and made her voice nonchalant, though she knew the other woman would see through the façade. "Tonight works for me, but whenever you have a free moment."

"You look a little out of breath." Delilah's eyebrows arched and she leaned closer to her screen.

"Just taking a constitutional stroll through the district." Gea shrugged. She didn't care to show any weakness to the other woman. Delilah might have dropped out of the thieving game when she mated with a man richer than Deus, but she wasn't someone people wanted to show their underbelly to. Gea let a little grin quirk her lips. "You know how it goes."

"Yeah, I do." Delilah chuckled. "I'm on my way over to my sister's place now." The gleam in those green eyes said she was amused by the exchange. Good. No one ever wanted to deal with her in a bad mood. "I'll be there most of the evening, if you want to stop in."

"Perfect." A glance over the edge of the building confirmed Gea's location and that she'd lost the Komodo dragon-shifter. She didn't have far to go to reach her destination. "I'd like to talk to your sister anyway."

"Well, lucky us."

Gea paused for a second as she realized Delilah might have a connection to her client that could complicate things. "Your husband isn't with you, is he?"

"Hunter? No, he's got a meeting with an associate of his tonight. Breck hasn't been up for entertaining in a while, so I left them to their business."

Breck. As in Constantine Breckenridge, Gea's client. She winced, but there was no hope for it. She could only hope Delilah knew how to be discreet.

And maybe if she escorted the other woman out of the Vermilion on her way home, she could resist the temptation to stop by Quill's place for a second round of hot shagging.

3

Kienan sat at a small table, facing the last living member of his family. His cousin, Pierce, stared at him for long moments before he spoke. "What's the occasion, Kienan?"

He looked around at the enclosed balcony that overlooked the main floor of Tail. The polyglass windows muted the synthrock, the sound of people shouting or groaning at the gaming tables . . . or at some of the other, more sexual offerings of the technobrothel.

"I retired." Neither of them were chatty men, so this conversation might be even briefer than he'd imagined. Then again, he wasn't sure what he'd been expecting. The Vaughns were hardly the type for heartfelt family reunions.

Surprise flickered in Pierce's silver gaze. "I figured you'd die in harness."

So had Kienan. He'd never imagined a life for himself outside of covert ops. If one assignment or another didn't get him, he'd expected to be kicked upstairs to an admin desk job.

He shrugged. "I got tired of the game, so I got out."

Every moment had been spent in a dark game of wits, lying to everyone around him, infiltrating crime organizations, terrorist cells, enemy governments, whatever was necessary. He'd realized there were only a handful of people in the world who knew his real name, who knew him at all. It had been an unsettling thought. He didn't say that to his cousin.

Pierce grunted. "Never expected to see you again."

"I thought the same with you." Kienan rubbed a hand over the back of his neck. "I don't have any plans in place yet, but I just wanted to reconnect, see how you were doing, since we're the only ones left. That's all."

Connection. Something to link him to reality rather than the world of secrets and lies that had been his existence for so long. Maybe coming to Pierce for that was a bad idea. The two of them were too much alike. Too dark inside. Too used to dealing in death and tragedy. His cousin was an agent for the FBI and had the same edge to him that all operatives did.

Pierce rubbed a thumb over the condensation on his glass. "I'm mated now."

"Oh yeah?" Kienan's intel had already told him that, but when he'd heard, it'd surprised him. He'd never have guessed his cousin had a mate.

"Two of them, in fact." His cousin snorted, as if he knew how ridiculous and unlikely that sounded. "Nolan and Lorelei."

Nolan Angelo was an assassin for the FBI, one Kienan's superiors had tapped before to do their wet work. Not that the other man knew it, but it was something else Kienan didn't say, so he focused on the other mate. "Lorelei Chase, the owner of Tail, is your mate."

Pierce waved a hand around at the wild activities taking place below them. "The one and only."

"Huh."

"That's what I thought, too, at first."

Kienan chuckled and startled himself with the sound. When had he last laughed and meant it as something more than a part of the charade? "Congratulations."

"Thank you." Pierce tapped his finger against the gleaming mercurite table. "Why did you retire?"

"It was killing me."

The words were abrupt, startling them both. He didn't have to explain, though; his cousin understood. Pierce had been an agent for decades. They'd never been close, but he knew the lifestyle, knew what it cost a man. Kienan was grateful for that, at least.

"You can stay here with us for a few days, until you decide what to do with yourself."

Kienan blinked, surprised by the offer. "Thanks, I think I'll take you up on that."

Pierce left their private balcony and went down to speak to the woman behind the bar, who nodded and tapped her fingers over a vidpad. He ran a single fingertip down her cheekbone, more affection flashing in his gaze than Kienan had ever seen from his cousin. Interesting. So that was Lorelei Chase. She was even more gorgeous in person than she had been in the holopics he'd seen in the intel file on his cousin. She was probably the most beautiful woman he'd ever seen, with auburn hair cascading down her back, wide green eyes, high cheekbones, and a body that could make a man beg to touch.

It took no time at all to get his one bag transferred to a room in the technobrothel. He was staying in the private quarters, where the jades lived, not where they entertained clients. He'd expected to hole up in a hotel for a few days or weeks, but this worked out better for him. If Pierce had mates, that meant Kienan had . . . in-laws wasn't the right term, but if they were mated to his cousin, they were family. Part of the Vaughn pack, though neither Lorelei nor Nolan was a wolf like Pierce and Kienan.

He'd wanted some connection to people. It looked like he had it. Or something.

He left his room to wander around Tail, learn the lay of the land. Pierce had been called away by a case, Nolan was apparently out of town on assignment, and Lorelei was busy, which meant Kienan had the chance to look around. Many of the doors were locked—taken by Lorelei's jades and their clientele—but the main floor was crowded. And loud.

The gaming tables were on one side of the room, and a long, curved polyglass bar took up the other side. He wended his way through the raucous gathering. It felt odd not to have anything he had to do, had to plan, had to think about. He didn't have to worry about money for a while, didn't need to hurry to find some other kind of employment. He was at loose ends for the first time ever.

The very concept was unsettling.

He wasn't the type to remain idle for long, but he didn't feel the need to rush into anything either. Slipping through the crowd, he stepped up to order a drink, but his gaze was transfixed by the display behind the bar.

There were massive iris windows that opened and closed at intervals, revealing people doing every imaginable carnal deed. One had a man getting fucked up the ass while a woman sucked his cock. Another had two women paddling a man wearing a leash. Kienan arched his eyebrows and settled onto a barstool. Voyeurism wasn't usually his kink, but he doubted anyone could resist watching.

A bartender in a tight microsilk-and-kleather corset approached him with a saucy wink as a greeting. "Hey, handsome. You looking for Lorelei?"

He shook his head, pulling his gaze away from the show. "Just looking for a beverage."

"What'll you have?"

"Synthbrew. I'll open the bottle myself, if you don't mind." Too many years with too many people trying to kill or disable him meant he didn't take chances with ending up drugged or poisoned. He might not live that life anymore, but old habits died hard. Besides, this was the Vermilion.

She grinned and didn't look insulted, thank Deus. "Sure. In the bottle, we have German falsch-hefeweizen or English simu-stout."

"Hefeweizen."

She dipped down behind the bar and came back up with his order, sliding it across the polyglass to him. Her gaze went to someone behind him, and a dimple flashed when she smiled. "Quill."

A man walked up and propped one elbow on the bar, facing Kienan. Black nanotats laced up the side of his neck to his jaw, and a thick mercurite hoop pierced one ear. More nanotats peeked out of the sleeves of his jacket, wrapped around his wrists, and covered the tops of his hands. He smiled in a way that said he was good-looking and knew it. Tall and muscular, his brown hair cropped short, his golden eyes alight with interest as he looked Kienan over.

"What have we here?" The man all but purred, and Kienan could smell the feline on him. "Hello."

Kienan nodded a greeting, feeling heated awareness skitter down his flesh.

"Are you enjoying the Peep Show?" The feline gestured to the windows behind the bar.

"Is that what it's called?" Kienan didn't bother to look, keeping his focus on the other man. There was something . . . different about this one. Something Kienan liked.

The golden-eyed man waited a beat before he spoke again. "I'm Quilliam North. Quill."

"Kienan Vaughn." Deus, when was the last time he'd used his real name to introduce himself? A downward rush, a horror tangled with a sense of utter liberty. He took a deep drag of his beer. "I'm Pierce's cousin."

"You're a gray wolf, too, then?"

"Yes." More information than he'd offered a stranger in one minute than he had to anyone else in years. It was heady. "And you are?"

"A leopard." A slow smile spread across the other man's face and attraction sparked inside of Kienan. He held out his hand to shake, wanting to touch. The craving was sudden, sharp, an unexpected bonus to his first night of freedom. When was the last time he'd allowed himself to just *feel* without considering the ramifications to whatever mission he was on? Not since he'd joined the military at eighteen. Not since he'd been recruited into the murkier organizations of the government.

Sexual interest shone in the taller man's gaze, enough to make Kienan's muscles tighten, his cock begin to stiffen. The moment their flesh touched, instinct exploded inside of Kienan's head. *Mate.*

A shudder ran through him, and he clenched his jaw as the attraction turned into hot, wild lust. Unstoppable need. His cock went harder than mercurite, and his hand tightened around Quill's.

The other man's eyebrow arched, and a little smile kicked up the corner of his mouth. "I had a meeting with Lorelei before her sister arrived and kicked me out of the office. She mentioned Pierce's cousin was staying at Tail for a few days. You'll be in town for a bit?"

"Come back to my room." Kienan couldn't care less about meetings or anything other than the fact that this man was *his.* His mate. The blood rushed through his veins as his heart raced and his breathing sped. His dick was so hard, he ached. The scent of other people annoyed him, kept him from smelling Quill and only Quill. It was exhilarating, this feeling. Powerful enough to make him shake.

Quill blinked, but didn't hesitate. "Yes."

He ran his thumb over the back of Kienan's hand, raising gooseflesh in the wake of his touch. When hard claws scraped his skin, sweat broke out on Kienan's forehead. Deus, he'd never been so hot in his life. *Mate.* The word drummed through his head. Mate. He wanted. He craved. Leaning in, Quill "accidentally" brushed up against Kienan's heavy erection and purred in approval as he trailed one finger up the hard length of it.

Fangs grazed Kienan's bottom lip, and he realized how close he was to feral. His voice dropped to a barely audible growl. "We go now or we fuck right here against the bar."

Shuddering, Quill dropped his hands, stepped back, and motioned toward the private area of Tail. "After you."

Kienan pivoted, striding toward the correct hallway while he felt the heat of the other man searing his back. Soon. Soon he'd be fucking his mate. The thought was almost enough to make him lose control. He stopped in front of his door and fumbled into his pocket for his ident card.

Hissing, Quill grabbed his shoulder from behind, spun him, and shoved his back against the door. Kienan snarled, the wolf close to breaking free. Quill just laughed and kissed him. It was rough and wild, the two biting and sucking, fighting for control of the encounter. Kienan thrust his tongue into the leopard-shifter's mouth, felt the scrape of fangs, but didn't know if they were his or Quill's. It didn't matter. What mattered was tasting his mate. Quill's hands moved down Kienan's chest, one settled on his nipple while the other trailed down to his cock to fondle him through his pants.

Deus, yes. He arched his hips, thrusting into those talented fingers that stroked him so perfectly. He tugged at the other man's clothes, wanting them gone. He managed to wrench open the seal on Quill's pants, drove his hand inside, and pumped his dick in his fist. When Quill twisted his nipple, dragging a sharp claw over it, Kienan nearly came in his pants. He jerked back, reversed their positions, and pinned the leopard to the wall beside the door.

Quill's cock was out, hard and twitching with need, and Kienan was beyond caring if anyone should see. He wanted to suck and fuck his mate. He sank to his knees, wrapping his hand around the long shaft and using his grip to pull the other man forward. Quill hissed at the rough contact and snarled when Kienan took him into his mouth. He sucked hard, his teeth scouring the sensitive flesh while Quill's moans rang through the empty hallway.

Kienan's cock throbbed as heat flowed like lava through his veins. His hips rolled in time with his sucking on his mate's cock. The head of Quill's dick hit the back of his throat, the salty tang of his pre-come sliding over Kienan's tongue. The low sound of his mate's groans drove him onward, and he gripped the other man's thighs, felt his talons dig into Quill's muscular legs. Urgency ripped through Kienan's system, the need to fuck, to claim, to mate tearing into his very soul. He'd never felt anything like it before, but he wanted more. He sank down on Quill's cock, sucked him in as deep as possible until his throat contracted around his mate's dick.

"Deus!"

Kienan heard Quill's claws scrabble against the wall, his other hand fisting tight in Kienan's hair. In retaliation, he let his fangs drag lightly over the other man's cock.

A feline scream ripped through the air, and Quill jetted come into Kienan's mouth.

Gea knocked on the back door of Tail, knowing there was always a staff member in the kitchen who would answer. It was her job to know when and where information could be found. The kitchen of the most notorious technobrothel in New

Chicago was where prime gossip could be found. The newsvids would never get wind of anything as juicy as these people knew.

It helped that this was also the last place that her target had been seen alive, and that Delilah's sister Lorelei owned it. All roads led to Tail.

A wide smile creased the scarred face of Sienna, the retired jade who ran Tail's kitchen. "Good to see you, Gea."

"You too." She walked in and dropped a smacking kiss on the old woman's cheek. "Got any tidbits for me?"

Sienna laughed and handed her a pastry filled with rockfish. "This is the juiciest thing I've got for you tonight, but Lorelei and Dee are waiting for you in the office."

"Mmm, thank you." Gea's stomach rumbled and she realized she was famished. She hadn't eaten anything since before she'd been to Quill's, and she'd burned off a lot of energy since then. She took a bite, and the mellow flavor of the fish combined with spices exploded in her mouth. "You're the best, Sienna." She spoke around the food. "I'm looking for a woman who was here a few months back—Felicia Tamryn. You know her?"

"I've met her once or twice, but I wouldn't say I *know* her."

"The buzz on the street was that she left here in a hurry." She stuffed the last bit of pastry in her mouth.

Sienna snorted. "Grifters sometimes need to make a quick exit." She shrugged. "Lorelei would have been the last one to talk to her, so you might want to ask her about it."

"I will. Thanks for the meal." Gea felt a lot less shaky now that she'd eaten, and except for the occasional twinge, her leg seemed to be doing fine. All in all, it could have been a much worse night for her. Now, if she could get the intel she wanted, she'd be all set.

"Anytime." The old woman waved her off, already back at

work. "And, yes, I know. If anyone asks, you were never here asking too many questions about people who don't want you to find them."

"You really are the best." Gea skirted around the prep table that dominated the kitchen and took the staff hallway to Lorelei's office. The staff areas weren't gilded in the finery of the public areas, but they also granted privacy and quiet from the raucous customers.

The door to the office popped open before she reached it, so she swung it wide and stepped inside. Delilah sprawled across a red kleather chaise while Lorelei sat behind her polyglass and mercurite desk. She motioned to a wall of vidscreens behind her that showed angles of every room in Tail. "I saw you coming. Mooching for information in my kitchen again?"

"And food, naturally."

Lorelei's green eyes—so like her sister's—twinkled with amusement. "What do you want to know about this time?"

"A few months ago, there was a couple in here, caused a small commotion." Gea moved to the chaise, dropped her bag on the floor, and sat sideways next to Delilah, propping her feet up on the rolled arm of the couch. Her leg ached, but it felt better after she elevated it.

"What'd you do to your pants?" Delilah leaned in to look at the shredded cloth.

"There was this guy earlier—during my constitutional stroll—who just couldn't get enough of me, Dee. He wanted to take home a souvenir, so I let him have a bit of my pants." Gea grinned as sweetly as she could, which wasn't very. "I'm nice that way."

"I bet that's exactly what he thought, too." Delilah settled back into her seat with a chuckle.

Gea glanced at Lorelei, but one of the vidscreens behind the desk caught her attention. A woman arched in ecstasy, her mouth opened in a silent scream, riding out her orgasm on top of a polyglass stand with a phallus built into it that thrust into her body.

"You got the updated version of the game," she noted.

"Space Race 6000. Just installed it yesterday. My jades love it." Lorelei's gaze swept the screens, checking her establishment.

The game always amazed and appalled Gea. It wasn't her style at all—she liked her pleasure a little more private. Two contestants stood on motion-sensing pads with controllers attached to each hand. A massive vidscreen on the wall was split in half, with each side trying to blow up the other's animated spaceships. It was innocent enough, until one looked at those polyglass stands beside each player. A male and female jade were mounted on the stands, and each time a contestant destroyed a ship on the screen, the stand vibrated and thrust the phallus into their jade's body.

Gea shook her head and refocused on Lorelei. Time to get the info she needed and get on with her night. "The woman in this couple was—"

"Tam." Lorelei pushed her coppery hair back. "Yes, she was here and Breck found her. She demanded I make him leave, he made a few threats, and Pierce set him straight. There were a few *I hate you's* thrown in with a few *I love you's*, and they spent the night in one of the Peep Show rooms. That's the last time I saw either of them."

Delilah slanted Gea a glance that made her look every bit the lynx-shifter she was. A cat, ready to pounce. "So, Breck hired you to find her? Is that what you wanted to see me about? You want the buzz on your client?"

"No. You, I'll get to in a moment." Gea stayed focused on the elder Chase sibling. "You have no idea where she went after she left here?"

"I don't. Breck asked the same questions the next day, when

he woke up alone. I can tell you what I told him—she snuck out the staff door you came in tonight just before dawn. I only know that because my vidmonitors picked up her escape. No one here saw her leave."

Which was her intention. Sneaking out was pointless if you left a bunch of witnesses behind. A dead end, though. Unlike in the Downtown District where Gea lived or the posh Lakeshore District Delilah and her husband called home, the Vermilion didn't have vidmonitors on every street. There'd be no surveillance to help Gea track her target. She managed to repress a growl. Barely.

She turned her attention to Delilah. "A source of mine said Tam was in here that night to try and fence something to a bear-shifter named Meier. He's from—"

"Germany." Delilah shuddered. "Yeah, I know him. Not one of my favorite people to work with. He's a mean bastard, but he's got connections to some very selective Eurasian buyers with deep pockets."

His mean streak might explain why Tam had chosen such a public place for a meeting. Also a place with a lot of exits one could use, if the need arose. "I wonder if she ever managed to meet with him."

It was more a rhetorical statement than anything else, but Lorelei answered her anyway. "She wasn't here long before Breck found her, and she hasn't been back since. If she met with Meier, it wasn't at Tail."

Gea nodded. "Thanks so much. Your standard fee for information?"

"As well as the understanding that you were never here, and we never spoke." Lorelei was very selective about whom she gave intel to, and what she was willing to talk about, so Gea was grateful when she could pry information out of the madam. Which wasn't often. More than likely, she'd only offered up the goods because Breck had already done the asking, and what had happened occurred in the public areas where other people could report on what transpired. Gea was just grateful that, unlike other sources, Lorelei hadn't felt the need to include details about what the couple had done in the Peep Show.

A knock sounded on the door and Gea slid to her feet. "Is there a private exit from here?"

Delilah flapped a hand. "It's just Hunter."

A tall man with dark hair stuck his head in the door. His eyes lit when they fell on his wife. "Hello, kitten."

"Hey, birdie." Delilah rose and moved to his side. "Finish your business?"

"Yeah." He nodded to his sister-in-law and to Gea, wrapping an arm around his wife's waist. "I came to say hello to Lorelei and to see if you'd like an escort home."

"How could I resist?"

His eyebrows arched. "*Why* would you resist? Don't I always make it fun for you, kitten?"

"You two can go now." Lorelei shooed them out. "Pierce will be back soon, and I want him to myself." She shot a glance at Gea. "You too."

"I'm gone." Gea grinned, grabbed her knapsack, and sped out the door first. All the lovebirds could take care of themselves. She was going home and she was not stopping by her mate's penthouse on the way. Absolutely not.

With that in mind, she spun resolutely for the kitchens, winding through the staff hallways she'd become familiar with over the years. She turned a corner and what she saw made the breath freeze in her lungs. It felt as if she'd been kicked in the stomach. She covered her mouth as horror punched through her.

There was another man sucking off her mate.

Deus. *Deus.*

Ecstasy molded his face and she knew from experience he'd just come, spurted into the other man's mouth. She hated that someone else had put that look on his face. She'd known he had other lovers. Probably many of them. A man like him could twitch his finger and have women—and men—fighting for him. He was handsome, young, rich, sexy without being a twisted pervert. Of course he slept with other people. Their arrangement wasn't exclusive, and that was her choice, wasn't it? She had no one to blame but herself.

It was only her who sensed the mating instinct. Only her who couldn't bring herself to let anyone else touch her. She'd tried. Deus, she'd tried, but she couldn't go through with it.

She swallowed the bile that burned her throat, spinning away from the scene that sent pain and jealousy knifing straight into her soul.

"Gea."

She closed her eyes, cursed under her breath, and then faced them. Her eyebrow arched, and she tucked away all emotions to offer up a lopsided smile. "Sorry for the interruption, gentlemen."

"Don't worry about it." The man who'd been sucking Quill had risen to his feet and faced her. She focused on him rather than her mate. Anything not to think about what she'd just witnessed. It was one thing to assume he slept with other people, it was another to *know* it, to see it with her own two eyes.

"I didn't know you'd be here." Something close to guilt flickered across Quill's face, but he covered it with a teasing grin. "I might have asked you to join us."

"I was just passing through. Excuse me."

"Your name is . . . Gea?" the other man asked, frowning. His hair was black and edged in silver at the temples, his eyes were a deep gray. He was tall, though not as tall as Quill, but broader. He had the kind of leashed strength that said his body was a weapon he knew how to wield. Deadly. There were shadows in his eyes that spoke of seeing too much and keeping too many secrets. This was not a man to cross. Ever.

Wariness slid through her, and she moved to skirt around them. "Yeah, I'm Gea. I'm on my way to the kitchens, so don't mind me."

The sooner she got out of here, the better. What she'd seen would be seared into her memory forever, but that didn't mean she wanted to stick around like some masochist fool. She jolted when the silver-eyed man's hand closed around her arm and pulled her to a stop.

That inner wrenching that she always felt whenever Quill was near hit again, only in double. Mate. Both of them. Mate.

Deus, no. *No.*

Awareness flared to life in that silver gaze, and panic bolted through her. She blurted out, "What kind of shifter are you?"

Please, please, don't let it be a species that mated for life. Please.

"Gray wolf."

Fuck. He knew. He knew what they were, what she was to him. Her stomach turned and she had to swallow hard. "Oh."

"I'm Kienan." The pad of his thumb rubbed over the inside of her wrist, and tingles raced down her skin. She fought a shudder as emotions collided with each other. His gaze searched her face, inclining his head toward the door Quill stood beside. "This is my room. Come inside and have a drink with us."

"Yes," Quill said, and what could she do? If she ripped herself away from Kienan and ran the way her mind told her to, Quill would come after her, want to know what was wrong. He'd ask questions she couldn't answer.

"I'm tired. I should go home." She tugged away from Kienan's grip, but his fingers tightened just enough to let her know she wouldn't escape so easily.

"The Vermilion is no place to run around when you're tired." Quill pushed away from the wall and set his hand on her shoulder, concern in his gaze.

Heat spiked through her at his touch. Her body was well trained after all these months, and her muscles loosened to ready her for something that logic told her to retreat from. Kienan drew her toward the door, swiping his ident card over a vidscreen to unlock it.

She shouldn't. She knew that, but her instincts didn't want to listen. They sang from having two mates touching her at once. She was caught between them. Her sex clenched when Kienan stroked his thumb over her skin again, her pussy dampening. She closed her eyes and told herself to leave. Right now. Save herself while she could. Kienan's scent intensified as he leaned close. "Stay the night with us, Gea."

He rolled her name on his tongue like it was fine wine, sweet to the taste. His warm breath brushed the side of her neck and a shiver passed through her, her heart racing with panic and lust at the same time. What would he say to Quill? That the wolf wanted her to stay the night with both of them told her one thing—he felt the mating urge with Quill as well. It wasn't just her with both of them, it was a true three-way bond. Or so fate intended. Deus help her. Quill slid his hand down her back and urged her forward.

Mate. Mate. *Mate.*

The knowledge pounded through her, the need to rut breaking her logic. She allowed herself to be drawn into the room, feeling a death knell toll when the door shut behind them. Kienan kept his grip on her, as if he sensed she might bolt. He lifted her hand to his mouth and kissed her palm. Just that simple touch sent ecstasy coursing through her. Her nipples went tight, and she clenched her thighs together to still the ache between them. It didn't save her. Nothing would.

Quill engaged the lock on the door and closed in on her other side. He kissed her shoulder. "I didn't think I'd have the pleasure again so soon, dearheart."

She opened her mouth to protest the endearment that always sent sweetness winging through her, and she hated that, but he bit the spot he had just kissed. A jolt went through her, pain mixing with her pleasure, sharpening both. Her pussy flooded with juices, and it was all she could do not to drag both men to the ground. The fox within her writhed in mating heat, demanding she do just that.

A moan broke from her when Quill's lips brushed the side of her throat, his fangs scraping the sensitive spot that connected shoulder to neck. He took her hand and drew it to his renewed erection. The erection that Kienan had been sucking when she found them. The memory flashed through her mind, and this time it didn't horrify her. This time, it titillated, added to the passion that flamed to life inside her. She'd like to watch them again, just like that. One filling the other's mouth with hard cock. Her pussy throbbed at the thought.

She closed her fingers around Quill's dick, stroking it in the slow rhythm she knew would drive him to madness. His deep groan made her grin.

"Lovely," Kienan whispered, and the look he sent her was filled with a reverent worship that made her chest tighten.

She slammed her eyes shut and refused to think about what his expression meant. "Kiss me."

Distraction, that was what she needed. Something to keep her mind from focusing on things she never, ever wanted to consider. Like mating. His mouth closed over hers while Quill's lips and teeth and tongue teased her sensitized neck. His hands were busy opening the front of her shirt while his hips plunged his cock through the ring of her fingers. Kienan swept his tongue between her lips, and her brain emptied of all thought. The taste of him burst into her mouth, burning into her psyche forever. *Mate*.

She bit Kienan's lower lip, then suckled it. The hot masculine flavor of him made her moan. He growled low in his throat, his hand moving around to squeeze her ass. Lust made her sex fist on emptiness, and she welcomed the heady feeling. Anything to keep from acknowledging her instincts. She tightened her grip on Quill's cock, pumping him faster while he closed his hand over her breast. He toyed with her nipple, sent heat streaking through her that arrowed straight to her pussy and made her even wetter for them.

Both of their hands on her was intoxicating. She'd never had two men at once, never thought she'd enjoy it. But she did. Oh, she did. She broke the kiss and threw her head back. "Now. I want it now."

Quill hissed, stepping in behind her. He lifted the single strap of her pack over her head and dropped it on the floor. "You don't need this right now."

His thick cock rubbed over her ass, nudging at the cleft of her cheeks. He reached around her and wrenched open the seal on her pants, working them down her thighs. "I was inside you tonight, but I want more. I want to fuck that sweet little pussy of yours."

A sound of pure need issued from her throat, and her knees threatened to give out. "Quill."

"I want you between us." A small smile curved Kienan's mouth. "I want your mouth on me."

Yes. Deus, she wanted that, wanted to taste him. He tugged her shirt off and, within moments, they had her naked. She quivered at the way they looked at her, gazes hot enough to set her aflame. "Now the two of you. Clothes off. I want to watch you strip."

Quill's chuckle mixed with a purr, and he unsealed his boots and kicked them away. His jacket and shirt were next, then his pants, revealing every solid micrometer of him. She'd always loved his body, long and lean, black tattoos scrolling from his calf all the way up to his temple on one side. It was one of the few things that showed his rougher upbringing when he had such an urbane, polished surface now. She'd licked her way from one end of his nanotat to the other on more than one occasion, and her pussy slicked with cream at the remembrance.

"You too." Quill gestured to Kienan. "Strip. Now."

The wolf's eyebrows arched, but he obeyed. His fingers danced over the seal of his kleather coat, revealing a dark gray shirt underneath. He pulled both off and tossed them aside. When he bent forward to unfasten his boots, she saw a large nanotat across the back of his shoulders. From upside down, she couldn't tell what it was. He pushed his pants down and stepped out of them and his shoes. A black nanotat banded one thigh, and it looked like tribal-style sea creatures swimming in a circle around his leg. He straightened, and his chest rose and fell in bellowing breaths, a flush of lust running under his skin.

When they were both naked, she absorbed the masculine beauty of them. Kienan was darker, broader, a triangle of hair stretching from one nipple to the other and arrowing down to a thin line that bisected hard abs and expanded again to a thick thatch around his jutting cock. Beads of pre-come slid down from the head of his erection. He was broad there, too, his dick wider than Quill's. She wasn't sure she'd be able to get her mouth around it, but she wanted to try. Quill's cock was longer, could slide deep inside her and make her scream. Her pussy spasmed, and the fire within her threatened to consume her.

Quill reached out a hand to both of them, one slid between her thighs, two big fingers pushing inside of her while his thumb brushed over her clit. He closed his other hand around Kienan's cock, used his grip to draw the wolf nearer, and then pumped the thick shaft in rough strokes. Kienan's head dropped back and he rocked his hips forward, groans spilling from his lips. The sight made Gea burn hotter, and Quill dropping to his knees to slide his tongue up the length of the wolf's dick did nothing to assuage the lust rising like a tsunami wave inside her.

Letting Kienan's cock slip from his mouth, Quill continued to stroke the wolf. He looked to her, curled his fingers inside her, and dragged her closer. A cry broke from her throat at the rough treatment, and the sound rose to a scream when his lips closed around her clit. She rose up on tiptoes, trying to escape the overwhelming ecstasy that exploded through her. But there was no escape, and her hips pressed into his mouth of their own volition. He thrust his fingers into her, suckling her clit until she thought she'd die. He switched back and forth between Kienan and her, flicking his tongue over their needy sexes, driving them both wild. Sobbing for breath, she quivered right on the edge of orgasm. Tingles rippled up and down her limbs, her inner muscles fisted around Quill's fingers.

So close.

And then he stopped. She moaned a protest, but he withdrew from her pussy and yanked her down to her hands and knees. "I believe Kienan wanted *your* mouth on him. And I want to fuck you."

He didn't need to tell her twice. Kienan knelt in front of her, and she took him deep into her mouth. The essence of Quill lingered on his flesh, so she could taste both her mates, and it sent a jolt of utter need straight to her core. Then Quill plunged his cock into her pussy, and she screamed around on Kienan's dick. He groaned, sliding his fingers into her hair to grip tight. She rolled her tongue around the thick head, taking him as deep as she could. It was difficult because he was so big, and she had to concentrate on relaxing her jaw. Not an easy task with Quill fucking her. Her sex clenched each time he filled her. It was the most erotic experience of her life—both her mates taking her at once. She loved it and she knew she shouldn't.

Shifting her weight to one hand, she slid the other up the inside of Kienan's thigh, pausing for a moment to stroke the nanotat circling his leg. She cupped his testicles, rolled them between her fingers. He groaned, his thrusts into her mouth picking up speed. But she wasn't done with him. She slipped her hand farther between his muscular thighs, caressed the sensitive flesh behind his balls, and moved to tease his anus. His body tensed, his thrusts faltering, but she pressed a finger into his ass, curling it until she stroked just the right spot. He jolted, his cock expanding between her lips. She rolled her tongue around his hard shaft and pushed her fingers in and out of his anus, making sure to rub over that sweet spot inside him.

"Deus. Gea!" Kienan choked on a breath; then his big body went rigid. A rough shudder racked him, and his fingers tightened in her hair. He fucked her mouth hard, his cock hitting the back of her throat as he came. The salty flavor of him filled her mouth.

"Swallow it, Gea," Quill growled, reaching around to flick his claw over her clit. She moaned around Kienan's cock, swallowed his come, just as Quill had ordered.

Heat flushed her face, skittering through her body. She could feel the scrape of Quill's talons on her, the clench of Kienan's hands in her hair. Their breath rushed out in pants, Quill's skin slapped against hers, Kienan groaned out his climax—a carnal symphony that ratcheted up her excitement. Quill pinched her clit hard, and it was too much. She hit orgasm in a hot rush that exploded through her body. Her pussy flexed around Quill's thrusting cock, and each time he entered her, her sex spasmed again. And again.

He pounded into her, and she knew from the roughness of his movements that he was close to climax. The thought sent heat spiraling through her. He sank deep, grinding against her ass, his fingers working her clit in time with his thrusts. When he spurted into her, another wave of orgasm shuddered through her, and they both groaned. Her pussy contracted tight, milking his cock until she thought she might faint.

Kienan slipped his cock from her mouth, sliding his hands down from her hair to her jaw and massaging the tight muscles there. She sighed, shut her eyes, and relaxed. Not a single thought went through her mind, which was a blessing she'd take and not ask questions about. She was ready to just curl up and sleep. One of the men lifted her into his arms, cradling her close. She drew in a breath, then opened her eyes. Kienan. The hair on his chest rubbed against her cheek and then a soft mattress gave beneath her.

Reality would return soon to bite her in the ass, but for just a moment, she drifted, boneless and content. Each of the men settled on opposite sides of her, surrounding her in solid warmth.

"Sleep," Quill said, his purr a sound of deep satisfaction that lulled her into doing as he commanded. She closed her eyes again, just for a moment. She'd wait for them to pass out and then she'd go. Just a little nap.

When her eyes popped open again, she knew it was morning, that she'd stayed all night the way Kienan had wanted. The three of them were tangled together and she eased away from the men, praying exhaustion kept them from waking. She stood, turning to look down at them.

Their breathing remained the steady cadence of deep slumber, Quill with an arm thrown over his head, Kienan facedown with one arm flung across Quill's stomach. She'd never seen him sleep, never allowed herself to stay long enough for that. The sweetness on his face was unexpected. He was usually so in control, so aloof and mocking, so willing to yank other people's chains to get the reaction he wanted from them. The vulnerability nearly broke her. She wanted that. She wanted it so bad she could taste it. Forever.

No. Deus, had watching her mother's life melt around her taught her nothing? What was wrong with her? She knew better than this. She'd been so careful.

Until last night. Until Kienan. Until there had been two of them overwhelming her ragged willpower.

Everything in her wanted to stay, craved it like someone blissed out on a bender.

She didn't even take the time to grab her clothes. She just shifted to her fox form and ran like hell.

4

Quill awoke in a bed that wasn't his own, but sheer feline lassitude sapped at his will to care. Or move. The oddness of being so relaxed and replete was enough to make him open his eyes. Mellowness was not his strong suit. He yawned and stretched against the mattress, his hand encountering the warm flesh of another human body.

Turning his head, he met the gray gaze of Kienan Vaughn. "Good morning."

The wolf's eyebrow quirked upward as he cocked his wrist to check his chrono. "It's closer to afternoon."

"It was an active night." Heat rushed through his body as the memories flipped through his mind, starting with Gea at his flat and ending with Gea and Kienan here at Tail. Definitely one of the better nights he'd had in recent memory, maybe ever.

Kienan waved a hand around the room. "We seem to have lost our third party, though."

Yes, Quill had already sensed that, and it made his gut tighten to realize she'd run out on him. Again. "When did she leave?"

The wolf shrugged. "I saw a fluffy white tail darting out of here a little while ago."

"Arctic fox. That would be her." It stuck in Quill's craw more and more that she ran from him. He shook the feeling away. He liked his lovers with few strings attached, and Gea gave him just that. It shouldn't bother him. He refused to let it.

"So I assumed." Kienan rolled to his side and propped his head in his hand with easy lupine grace. His chest rubbed against Quill's arm, and even that simple contact made his body begin to stir. The wolf-shifter's brows drew together in a frown. "Do you think she didn't enjoy herself?"

"She seemed to. I'll call her later and make sure she's all right." If she bothered to answer. In the last year, Quill had left her messages before that she'd ignored. It didn't matter. She didn't matter. He'd long since learned that letting anyone in exposed the soft underbelly of a person, and that was asking to be gutted by another predator's claws. "Likely, she's off hunting down a clue on something she's investigating."

"She's a cop?" The wolf grunted, an expression that might have been surprise flitting over his features. He wasn't the easiest man to read.

"Private investigator."

"Ah."

Not a conversationalist, this one. It didn't matter much when the wolf-shifter dipped a hand under the sheet to encircle Quill's morning erection. His breath hissed between his teeth, his fangs sliding down when the other man put just enough pressure on his cock to have pleasure and pain streaking through him. "Deus."

One of the things he loved about fucking other men was the rawness, the roughness. There was nothing soft about this man, and Quill was more than ready to test his stamina.

Pulling his cock free of Kienan's grip, Quill wrapped his hand around the other man's arm, flipping him neatly onto his stomach. He came down on top of him, nudging his erection between the globes of the wolf-shifter's muscular ass. A purr rumbled in Quill's chest. "I like to be on top."

"I got that sense from you last night. Maybe I can change your mind about that." Kienan grinned over his shoulder, and Quill had the feeling it was rare to see a genuine smile from the sober man. He didn't say much, but he had an intensity that drew Quill like a magnet.

"You can try." Unlikely, though. He didn't like feeling out of control. It was a weakness he never allowed himself. Dipping down, he bit the nanotat on the other man's shoulder, using his fangs on the skin. "Some other time. Right now, your ass is mine."

Kienan groaned, rocking his hips back. The pheromones wafting through the air were enough to make Quill clench his jaw. His cock was harder than mercurite, wet with his precome. He wanted to slide inside the wolf's ass, make the quiet man beg for him. A shudder went through Quill at the thought. The head of his cock nudged the tight pucker of Kienan's anus.

A low growl came from Kienan, a hint of the predator within. "There's lubricant in the wash closet. Let me up and I'll get it."

Chortling, Quill flicked his tongue across the other man's nape, making gooseflesh break down his skin. "Take that with you when you travel, huh?"

"No, a new container was already in the room." Kienan dropped his head forward, allowing Quill all the access he wanted. "It *is* a technobrothel."

"Point taken." Quill nipped and sucked at the wolf's neck, savoring the flavor of him and the anticipation that built higher and higher inside of him. When Kienan bucked upward, his claws ripping through the sheets beneath them, Quill grinned and knelt up on the mattress to release his hold on the wolf-shifter. "Get that container, Vaughn. We're going to need it."

"Yes. Now." Kienan moved with silent speed and was back in a moment, handing over the lubricant to Quill.

He unsealed the container and poured a dab of the contents into his palm, looking Kienan over. The man's chest was heaving for breath, his fists clenching and unclenching at his side while he watched Quill stroke the slick fluid onto his cock. "On your back. I want to see your face when I slide inside you."

Kienan's dick jerked, stretched even farther, until it danced just below his navel. A muscle ticked in his cheek, but he nodded and slid onto the mattress in front of Quill, face up, just as he'd been told. A purr soughed from Quill's throat, the leopard inside him loving the erotic image before him. A sexy male, primed for fucking, willing to do anything to get the surcease Quill could grant him. Deus, it was better than a hit of bliss.

Pressing Kienan's thighs open, Quill used the lubricant on his fingers to slide inside of the wolf-shifter's anus. The muscles were tight, so he added a second and third digit, stretching the other man for his penetration. Groans spilled between Kienan's clenched teeth, and Quill loved the power coursing through him.

"Deus, Quill," Kienan gritted out, his hands bunching in the sheets. "Quit teasing and fuck me."

Quill wished he could make him wait, but it wasn't going to happen. He wanted what the wolf wanted, and he wanted it now. His heart hammered in his chest, his lungs burning as he sucked in each breath. His cock was so hard it ached. Grasping his erection, he pressed the head against Kienan's anus, leaned his weight forward, and began impaling the wolf on his dick. Both men groaned, the sound loud and obscene in the small room, which just spiked Quill's excitement higher. The feel of Kienan's ass closing around his cock was maddening, the ring of muscle scraping at his shaft, squeezing him so tight it was almost painful. Almost.

"Try to relax." He set his hands on the wolf's thighs, digging his fingers in to massage.

Kienan grunted, the tension leeching from his body, though his hands went white-knuckled on the sheets. "More."

Withdrawing one slow micrometer at a time, Quill shuddered with the need to come. Deus, he hadn't boiled this close to losing control so fast in damn near forever. The thought should have bothered him, but he couldn't focus on anything other than taking the man beneath him. One sharp thrust and he was back inside Kienan, deeper than he'd been before, making both of them growl, fangs bared.

The feral display made the leopard within Quill fight for supremacy, wanting to rut with abandon. He clenched his jaw and held on to his restraint by the tips of his claws. Pistoning his cock in and out of another male was amazing, the heat and friction shoving him right to the edge of orgasm. Moving his hands to Kienan's hips, Quill lifted the other man so he could drive deeper with each plunge of his cock. The wolf rocked himself upward, meeting Quill's downward thrusts. Their skin slapped together, the scent of sex permeating the air.

Kienan's eyes were wild, his chest heaving. "Harder. I need it."

So did Quill. He wasn't going to last much longer, the speed and roughness of his rhythm enough to topple him in another few nanoseconds. But he was taking the wolf with him. Quill groped for Kienan's cock, relentlessly working it in time with his thrusts.

"I need to come," Kienan grunted. Desperation reflected on the man's face, his normal stoicism dropping away.

"Then come." Quill's muscles drew taut, impending orgasm gripping him tight. "Come now."

Kienan's back bowed, an animalistic howl ripping loose from his throat, and come spurted from his cock, bubbling between Quill's fingers as he continued to stroke the wolf through his orgasm. Letting go of his own control, he exploded inside of

Kienan's tight ass, ecstasy rushing through his body as he hammered out his climax inside the other man. A long groan spilled from him and he slammed deep one last time, froze, and shuddered.

They stayed that way for long moments, and only the ragged sound of their breathing broke the silence in the room. When Quill's heart slowed from its racing beat, his sigh tangled with a purr. A smug grin curved his mouth. In terms of sex, the last twenty-four hours had been superb. The wolf looked a little dazed, just as he had the night before after Gea had sucked him off. There was nothing innocent about this man, but somehow the sex seemed to have surprised him. It was good to know that Quill wasn't the only one experiencing this level of intensity.

Slipping backward on his knees, he slid his cock out of Kienan. "You all right?"

"Yeah." The wolf-shifter blinked, his gaze coming back into focus, his expression going inscrutable. "You?"

"Never better." Quill's grin spread. It was a little late for the other man to pretend he was impervious and unaffected by what they'd done, but Quill wasn't going to call him on it. He knew the truth, and so did Kienan. "Shower?"

Kienan nodded and crawled to his feet, leading the way into the wash closet, and Quill licked his lips as he watched the other man's ass flex as he walked. Prime-grade muscles there. He definitely wanted to get his hands on that again.

"So, how long are you going to be in town?" Whatever time there was, Quill was going to take advantage of it. It might help distract him from his irritation over the fact that Gea had bolted again. That it bordered perilously close to anger just irritated him more. It was a kick to the gut and the ego that she ran, even though it shouldn't bother him. With any other lover, he didn't think it would. Clamping down on that dangerous thought, he focused on the lover before him.

The wolf glanced back, the lines of his face somber as death.

"What?" Quill asked, reaching around him to start the shower's spray.

Shrugging, the wolf stepped under the blast of water. "So, you came here last night to offer Lorelei a business proposition, is that right?"

Wariness slid through Quill. Where was this question coming from? His business and his sexual affairs were things that he never mixed. Ever. "Yes. Why?"

"Just curious. What kind of business offer was it?" Droplets slipped down Kienan's face as he stepped aside to let Quill get under the spray. "Or is that confidential?"

Something in Quill wanted to trust this man, and that sent a hint of panic through him. He trusted no one, not really. It was safer that way. He let water sluice down his body before he answered. "It's not confidential, but I don't make a habit of discussing business with strangers."

"Just fucking them?"

"Touché." He let a small smile touch his lips. Dealing with the people he did made him justifiably paranoid about being a target for industrial espionage or insider trading, so he flipped the questioning around. The best defense was a good offense. "Lorelei said you were some kind of operative. Not for the FBI like Pierce, but some other government organization."

"I was. I recently retired."

"Why?"

"I burned out. It can happen in that line of work." He spread his hands, but his gray eyes narrowed. "What was your business with Lorelei?"

Instead of answering, Quill grinned. He wanted to play cat and mouse? There was a game a leopard excelled at. He almost purred with the challenge. "Afraid I'll lead her astray into nefarious, illegal dealings, Vaughn?"

Lathering his arms and chest, the wolf didn't look away.

"Would you? I may have only just met her, but she's still family."

"No, I wouldn't." He saved offers like that for people who were interested, and Lorelei liked to keep her hands clean. Part of his success was knowing his market and his competition. "She wouldn't allow it anyway. She's careful, conscientious, and smart. All things I like in people I deal with. She wouldn't take my word on anything—she'd want details, records. She'd probably have Pierce do a little background checking."

One of Kienan's dark eyebrows went up. "And that wouldn't bother you?"

"Only if I had something to hide. Which I don't." This time. He'd gotten his start in every illegal pleasure this city had to offer, so his hands were far less pristine than Lorelei's.

The wolf-shifter's other eyebrow joined its twin, a look of skepticism crossing his face. "How often do you have something to hide?"

"Often enough." Quill soaped up and rinsed off with quick efficiency. "Is that a problem for you?"

"No." The other man snorted. "I've hidden a lot over the years, just for different reasons."

"How noble."

He barked out a laugh. "Hardly. It was dirty and exhausting."

Interesting. Quill tilted his head, finding himself as curious about and fascinated by Kienan as he was by Gea. It made him want to push to know more, especially since the wolf seemed less recalcitrant than the fox. For the moment anyway. "You must have liked something about it to stay there for so long."

Kienan let his head fall back against the wall of the shower, sighing. "I did like it. For a long time. And then I didn't. It was a challenge, and I liked that. It was risky, and I liked that, too, liked the rush of *almost* getting caught. I liked winning."

"Sounds like all the reasons I got into my line of work." Which was even more interesting, and unexpected.

"Surprised we have anything in common?"

"Yes." It was the truth, something he normally weighed before he gave it to anyone, so it stunned him to have it come out of his mouth so easily around this man. When had he last tried to find common ground with anyone if it wasn't to gain the upper hand in a business negotiation?

"You still like your work, though. I got damn tired of lying to everyone about everything, never knowing where I'd be sent to next, who I'd be trying to deceive or kill." Something close to shock crossed Kienan's face, and Quill would guess he was even more stunned to have revealed anything to a virtual stranger.

Neither of them was the type.

Quill nodded. "Though, like you, I grew weary of the web of deceit that was waiting to catch me, so I transitioned into more legitimate lines of business a few years ago. I still keep my interests . . . diversified . . . but that's just good business. Keep my hands in every pie I can reach."

"I could see that." The wolf pushed his hair back from his face. "There's not a lot of ways to diversify in my line of work. My former line of work. I guess I'm looking for a new challenge."

Quill cocked an eyebrow. "I assume you're not angling for a job."

That made the wolf-shifter break into a rare chuckle. "Not even close. I'd be a terrible businessman. The bureaucracy was bad enough in government work."

"True enough. Though a well-placed cred can slice through some of the red tape."

Kienan blinked. "Bribery."

"You disapprove?" Why he felt the need to ask, Quill would never know.

The wolf squinted through the steam, his gray gaze focused on Quill. "Is that what you're hoping for or just what you're used to?"

"I gave up caring what people thought of me a long time ago. I did what I did to survive." He shrugged but couldn't meet that piercing gaze. Something tangled in his chest that he didn't understand, so he pushed it away. "Growing up in the Vermilion doesn't leave you with a lot of *legal* revenue sources outside of prostitution."

"Were you ever a jade?"

"No, I own interest in a few jadehouses now, but I never worked in one, never sold my body for money." He grinned. "Though some might argue I sold my soul instead." His smile faded and he cleared his throat. Why had he said that? Why did he feel the need to explain himself to this man? The wolf was a temporary distraction, nothing more. It was of no importance whether he understood Quill's motivations. He turned off the shower and stepped out, turning his back on Kienan. "The truth is, I never knew my father and my mother was a blisshead who sold the drug to feed her addiction. I took over in order to keep a roof over our heads and food in our stomachs. My incentive was money, not drugs, and after I made my first few creds, I wanted more."

"And you always will." The words were quiet, as unassuming as the man himself.

"I like to be in control. In my house, everything revolved around my mother's addiction. It controlled our whole life. Worse was when she had a man around who tried to 'teach me some respect' or father me in any way. I usually ended up getting my ass kicked." Over and over again. Quill had the scars to prove it, too, inside and out. Only the most tenacious bastard would have made it out of his childhood alive, and he was nothing if not a survivor. He laughed, the sound harsh. "There was always someone bigger than me on the street, so I had to be smarter and faster. And I decided that someday I'd be the one making the decisions. *I'd* be the one dictating my own life."

He didn't like to think about that time, rarely let himself. He'd learned long ago to look forward, not back. But the memories swamped him now, those ugly moments that shaped who he'd become. How many times had he been beaten so badly he couldn't stand? How many bones had been broken before he'd even turned ten? How many times had his mother stood by and watched, so out of her mind with bliss she didn't know or care what was happening? His gut roiled, and he swallowed hard. No, there'd been no control for him then. He lived by the whims of his mother's habit.

If he didn't want to starve to death, he'd had to deal the drug she craved so badly and figure out how to keep his stash out of her hands. Seeing what it did to her had probably been the one thing that had saved him from diving into that same stupor. His friends back then had fallen prey to it, one by one, but Quill wasn't going out like that. He fucking refused to give his life to a drug, to spin so far out of control he didn't give a shit if people he loved were beaten to death in front of him. He'd scrabbled and scraped and fought, done things he never wanted to think about ever again to get out. He'd do it all again if he had to. Never again would he live like that. Never.

Kienan hummed. "My work taught me I can only control so much, and in the end, there was always someone I answered to, always someone yanking on my leash and calling the shots. I controlled myself and my part of an operation, everything else was out of my hands."

Seizing on the chance to talk about something besides himself, he faced Kienan. "And you were okay with that?"

"I didn't have a choice. That was what I did." The wolf shrugged. "It's who I am. Who I *was.*"

"Then who are you now?"

Kienan sighed, shook his head. "I'm trying to find that out. I didn't . . . I don't know how to be anything else."

"Good luck figuring it out."

"Thanks." A rueful smile flickered on and off his lean face.

Quill wanted to know more. Perhaps it was sheer feline curiosity, but he'd never met a man who affected him this way, who intrigued him for reasons that had nothing to do with business. So he asked again, "How long are you going to be here?"

That gray gaze grew shuttered. If he was difficult to read normally, it was impossible now. "Here in Tail? Not long. Here in town? Like I said before, I'm not sure. I hadn't planned beyond stopping to see my cousin."

Quill cocked his head. "While you're in New Chicago, why don't you let me show you the town?"

"I'd like that."

Well, this was a first. A lover he actually wanted to spend time around, who wanted to spend time around him. With Gea, that street went only one way. Which was how Quill liked it, of course. Kienan was just a temporary distraction until he left. Nothing was any different than it usually was. Quill would get back to his business and his solitary life soon enough. He would end it when he decided it was over, as he did with all his affairs.

Gea shrugged out of her pack as she jogged up the stairs to her flat. Lorelei had had one of her jades deliver the bag the day after she'd left it in Kienan's room. Nothing had been missing from the bag, though there had been a note from the wolf requesting that she contact him. She'd ignore that, as well as the two vidmessages Quill had left for her. A week later, and her willpower was still holding. Barely, but it was holding. She took one day at a time.

Flashing her ident card at the panel beside the door, she let herself in and dropped her bag on her desk. Her home was also her office. She was on the second floor of a downtown skyrise, a few blocks from the old piers that jutted out over Lake Michigan. The rear of the flat held her bedroom and kitchen, and the front room served as her workspace, with a large antique wood desk that was the only thing her father had ever given her.

After a trip to the wash closet and then the kitchen to get a bite to eat, she sat behind the desk and pulled her bag toward her, digging out her vidcam. She interfaced it with her home system and downlinked the vidpics she'd taken for one of her clients. A cheating spouse, which was her bread and butter. Another case closed. Her client should be satisfied, if not entirely pleased to be proved correct about his wife's dalliances. But that was how her business went. Not all news was good news, but being right offered its own vindication.

She sat back in her kleather chair, tapping her fingers against the desktop. Her newest case was the one troubling her, namely, the information she *wasn't* given. A bit of digging in the last week had confirmed that Breck had owned the Gutenberg that went missing. The bible had been scheduled to go on auction for charity just before Tam disappeared. The auction had been canceled suddenly, and rumors had gone around that it was because the Gutenberg was stolen. However, her client had never reported it to the police nor had he filed an insurance claim.

While the vidpics downlinked, she accessed her messages from her palmtop. She grinned at the first one—an informant letting her know where she could find the elusive Meier. About damn time that intel came through. She'd been putting out subtle feelers for days and come up dry.

The next message was from Quill, the last one from a blisshead who was hoping to score more creds, but she'd already had his information for a week. She deleted everything but the message from her informant. The stupid female part of her wanted to keep the one from Quill and savor the concern in his voice, but even on the small screen of her palmtop, she could see the irritation in his gaze that she was ignoring him. There was nothing she could do about that that wouldn't get her in deeper than she wanted to be with her mate. Her *mates*. Deus, she still couldn't believe there were two of them. She had the worst possible luck.

The large vidscreen embedded in the wall across from her desk beeped, informing her that she had an incoming call. Quill wouldn't attempt to contact her office, would he? The thought barely had time to form before she saw the code was attached to Breck. Her erstwhile client.

She tapped the vidpad embedded in her desk to accept the call. "Prime Investigations."

"Hello, Gea." The man looked tired, lines bracketing his eyes and mouth as if he hadn't slept in a while. The screen showed him sitting in the same office where he'd interviewed her ten days before.

She nodded in return. "Mr. Breckenridge."

"Call me Breck, it's less of a mouthful." He ran a hand through his blond hair, mussing it. "I'm calling for an update. What do you have?"

Deciding not to beat around the bush, she got down to business. "Why didn't you tell me she stole a Gutenberg Bible from you?"

He blinked, then looked aside. "It wasn't relevant. It was a write-off I was auctioning for charity."

Bullshit. An artifact like that going missing was always relevant, so she called his bluff. "Then why are you searching for her, if not for that?"

A muscle ticked in his cheek, and his blue gaze cooled as he met her eyes again. "That's not your concern."

"It may help me find her. It *would* help to know what she's running from." Gea brought one knee up to her chest, bracing it against her desk. "People react differently depending on the severity of a situation. I need to know how dire she thinks her circumstances are. What did she take from you that you want bad enough to have her hunted down?"

His jaw worked and he rolled his shoulders. "I hired you to investigate where she went, where she is now. That's what you should concern yourself with."

"I *am* investigating, and what I'm finding is that my client is withholding valuable information that's keeping me from doing my job." She made her voice as chilly as his. Client relations be damned. If he wanted to fire her for doing her job, then she didn't need to be working for him anyway. She ignored the fat retainer she'd have to return to him if he canceled her contract. "Do you want me to find her or not? If you do, you need to be straight with me."

"She's my mate." His gaze was clear and icy as it drilled into her. "I trust that information will remain private."

"Of course." She swallowed hard. "Does she know?"

"No. I've never told anyone and cheetahs can't sense it." He spread his hands and leaned toward the vidscreen. "Let me be as straight with you as I can—I don't give a shit what she's stolen, I just want her back. So find her."

"I will." She gave a sharp nod and ended the call.

Mate. Deus, did everything in her life revolve around how warped mating could be for people? She slumped in her chair, dropping her forehead to her desk. She wasn't hunting a grifter who robbed a powerful man; she was hunting a thief who happened to be a powerful man's *mate*.

Why, Deus, why?

She beat her forehead against the wooden surface in three slow thumps. "Fuck. Fuck. Fuck."

"Does that really help?"

Her head jerked up and she spun her chair toward the window. Kienan stepped through the opening that had been firmly closed and locked when she'd gotten home. "What are you doing here?"

His eyebrows arched. "I came to talk to you, since you're not speaking to me. Or Quill, apparently."

"Did you eavesdrop on my call?" she demanded. The last thing she needed was information she'd promised to keep confidential getting leaked out just minutes later. Her personal life already blew, she didn't need her professional life to go the same way.

He slid his hands in his pockets, one shoulder rolling forward in a shrug. "No, I just got here to see you hammering your head against your desk."

She searched his gaze, looking for a lie, but she couldn't tell one way or the other. He was too hard to read. It stuck in her craw that she'd just have to trust that he was telling her the truth.

"What do you want? I'm busy."

His gaze strayed to the desk. "Yes, you looked as if you were working hard."

"Your time to talk is running out. Fast." She tilted her wrist up to check her chrono.

"Fine. I'll get right to the point." He stepped closer to her desk, and she fought the need to shrink back. "You, Quill, and I are mates. You know it and I know it. Don't bother denying it."

Her eyes closed and her throat tightened. "I'm not denying anything."

"Why are you hiding it from him? Why haven't you claimed him?" The questions were voiced quietly, but they battered against her soul. Her instincts screeched, reminding her for the millionth time that her mates were within reach. She ignored them. Again.

"It's complicated." Looking at him, she tried to keep her expression blank and knew she failed miserably. Definitely not the first time her willpower had failed with a mate. Apparently, she'd begun with Quill what she meant to go on with Kienan.

"Everything is complicated. That doesn't mean you can run away from it."

"Leave it alone," she snapped back.

"No, this affects me, too. You may be too gutless to claim him, but don't think I won't. I want what's mine." His gaze made it clear that he also considered *her* his.

How long would she be able to hold him off? If he told Quill about being mates, how long would it take him to figure out the whole truth? Moments. Quill was too smart not to deduce what would be pretty obvious—that Kienan wouldn't have slept with her if she wasn't also involved in this twisted little mating triangle.

Deus help her.

Terror streaked through her, icy and hot at the same time. It felt as if her entire world were melting around her. The careful balancing act she'd managed with Quill for the last year was about to topple.

"What are you so afraid of?" He drew even closer to her, and his scent swamped her. So intoxicating. So titillating. "What would make a woman want to avoid mating?"

She gripped the edge of her desk to keep from reaching for him. "So all women have to want to mate? We want some big, strong man to save us from real life? Spare me."

"I didn't make this about sexism. You did." He snorted, coming around to lean against the side of her desk. Near enough to touch. "The kind of women I've worked with or worked against have made sure there's no way I could ever doubt how capable women are of every evil thing."

"But not good things?"

"I don't deal in good things." His brows arched. "I can't speak to that kind of behavior."

"Ouch."

He shrugged. "That's my life. Was. Was my life."

"And what's your life now?"

"Whatever I decide to make of it." His gaze sharpened on her. "And what have you decided to make of yours?"

"I've already made something of my life. Unlike you, I'm not exactly at loose ends here—I'm good at what I do." She gave a pointed glance around her office.

"I don't doubt it. Quill seems to think you're good at ferreting out information. I've spent the week with him, and he likes you a lot more than he wants to admit to himself. Could it be he's drawn to his mate?" He let that knowledge sink in. She'd suspected they'd been together without her, but now she knew and the fox within her *hated* it, hated that she'd let herself be left out. Kienan ran his tongue down a canine tooth. "Why choose to spend your life alone when you don't have to?"

She crossed her arms, refusing to give in to him or to her animalistic nature. She knew which way that road went, and she wasn't having it. "There's nothing wrong with being alone. It's safer that way."

"Safer for you."

"Maybe." She tossed her head. "What's wrong with that?"

"Everything. And nothing." His gaze narrowed, his words measured and cool. "If that's how you want to live your life, scared of what gifts fate does give you."

"Mates are not a *gift.*" She slapped her hand on her desk for emphasis.

"You've had a mate before?" His expression showed how likely it was that she had three. It was possible. She'd known someone who did, but she had to admit he was right. It wasn't very probable.

She ground her teeth together and gritted out, "No."

Straightening from where he stood, he towered over her. "Then what do you have against mating? Why are you so afraid?"

"I'm not afraid." No, the utter terror she felt went far, far beyond anything that could be labeled as merely *afraid*. She growled up at him. "Everything was fine until you showed up!"

He rocked back on his heels, paling as if she'd struck him. There was pain and anger in his voice when he spoke. "It wasn't fine. It was a lie. You're lying to Quill, and he doesn't seem the kind of man who forgives lightly." A harsh laugh spilled out. "But that *is* perfect for you, isn't it, Gea? You can't make yourself walk away, so if he ever did find out, he'd make it easy for you and do the walking himself. That's brilliant. And cowardly."

Those words stung like acid. He was right, and a tiny part of her hated him for saying it. "You don't know me. You have no fucking right to judge me."

"You won't let me know you. You won't let Quill know you either."

She didn't respond to that, because they were far too close for her comfort already. Under her skin and in her head. "Everyone tells lies."

"Not to their mates." His expression flattened and he sliced a hand through the air.

"Oh, hell yes to their mates." She huffed out a laugh. Deus, how many times had she found her mother sobbing over some half-truth her father had told her? "Trust me on this."

He growled, the wolf's hackles rising. "Why should I trust you when you won't answer one simple question about yourself? Why should I trust you when I know you've been lying to my mate—to *our* mate—for an entire year?"

"Only a week and you're feeling awfully possessive, aren't you?" She kept her tone light and mocking, but it pained her that the two of them had obviously bonded without her.

Leaning into her space, he asked, "Are you hoping I get possessive enough that I don't want to share him with you, that I'm willing to let you bow out?"

She clenched her teeth but forced herself to say the words. "It might be best for all concerned if that's what happens."

"No," he snapped.

Tilting her chin up, she glared at him, wishing he'd go away and stop tempting her with what she could never have. "You can't force me to mate with you. Or Quill."

His nose was no more than a hairsbreadth from hers, his gaze a burning silver. "And you can't force yourself to walk away, can you? If you could, you would have done it with Quill long before now."

"So, I'm weak." She tried to make her shrug nonchalant, but it was a stiff jerk of her shoulder instead. "Thanks for pointing it out. You can go now."

"No. It takes a strength most people couldn't imagine to fight your instinct to mate. It's got to be a powerful motivation for you. No one suffers this way without a reason." He searched her face, probably seeing far more than she was comfortable with. "Just tell me why."

"No." Her body warmed at his closeness, the fox within her writhing in mating heat. She clenched her thighs together, trying to still the rising passion. It was no use. Helpless anger fought with her lust. "Leave me alone."

His sigh brushed across her cheek. "I can't do that. I won't."

"Yes, you can." She hated how desperate she sounded, but she couldn't stop it. Her chest tightened and she balled her hands into fists. The fox within her wanted its mates, pushing her to reach out and take instead of pushing away what it craved the most. Her voice cracked when she spoke. "You can have Quill all to yourself. Just leave me out of it."

Something close to sympathy shone in his gaze and he shook his head slowly. "You're forgetting something."

She swallowed. "Oh yeah? What's that?"

"You're my mate, too." Lifting his hand, he brushed his fingertips down her cheek in a gesture that made humiliating tears back up in her eyes. "I don't want just him, and whether he knows it yet or not, he doesn't want just me or just you. All three of us are in this together."

It sounded perfect. Too perfect. Like every fantasy she'd never allowed herself to have. She turned her face away from his touch and forced herself to her feet, then reached out to gather her knapsack. The cheating wife holopics would hold until she got back. Now was the time to get the hell away from Kienan and chase down this Meier guy. "I have to go now. I have work to do."

"Running away again." The disappointment in his tone made her flinch, but she made herself keep moving.

"Discretion is the better part of valor." Her father had said that a lot. She hadn't cared for his definition of *discretion,* but that didn't mean he was wrong in every instance. Like this one. "Running *is* sometimes the best option."

"Yes, but it's always a temporary option. In the end, you do have to come up with a permanent solution to your problems. You can't retreat forever."

Yes, she could. She didn't bother to say that to him. "I'm leaving now."

He growled, grabbed her arm, and made her face him. His hands bracketed her shoulders to keep her in place. "There's only so long I'm willing to wait before I tell Quill the truth. I'm not going to live a lie for you, mate or not."

"No one told you to lie in the first place. Or not to tell the truth. That was *your* choice." Her belly knotted tight as she said it. She'd thought having a mate—Quill—was bad. But Kienan was worse because he was her mate *and he knew it.* Her very worst nightmare, in the flesh.

His silver eyes glinted dangerously, a predator barely leashed. "It was pretty clear you wanted the truth kept quiet when Quill didn't know what you were to him, and when you ran off with your tail tucked between your legs after our night together. At first, I was concerned, but it seems this is your standard operating procedure with mates. Just fuck them and run."

It was the longest speech she'd heard from the man so far, and it was to chastise her. Nice. She swallowed and wished she were somewhere else. Anywhere else. She'd take a stroll through the Vermilion buck ass naked over this.

"You're going to tell Quill eventually anyway, so you might as well get the inevitable over with. Don't worry about me. I can take care of myself."

His hands tightened on her arms as if he wanted to shake her, and she tensed, bracing for the violence. Instead, he hauled her flush against his chest and kissed her. She went rigid, expecting a rough claiming, a show of dominance from a male animal.

It didn't happen.

The contact was almost gentle, so sweet it made her heart ache and wetness stung her eyes. The shock of what he did versus what she'd anticipated sent a quiver through her. Treacherous heat wound through her body and she throbbed. Her sex went slick in nanoseconds, her nipples drawing to tight peaks. She moaned, and he took the opportunity to sweep his tongue into her mouth.

The taste of him was as intoxicating as it had been the first time their lips had touched. It went to her head faster than a dozen synthbrews, sending her thoughts spinning. Her instincts clamored the same message, the same mating urge. She ignored it, stuffed it into the deepest, darkest corner of her soul.

His hands slid down from her shoulders, one wrapping around her waist, the other wedging between them to cup her breast. Gooseflesh broke over her skin when his thumb stroked back and forth over her nipple, circling the beaded crest. She wanted his clever mouth on them, too. Just the thought made her thighs clench on the explosion of need. She tangled her tongue with his, unable to resist. When had she ever been able to with her mate—either of them? Her heart turned over in her chest, cinching tight, but there was no saving her now.

The slow movements of his lips were worshipful, savoring. She hated herself for loving it so much, but she knew her time with him, with Quill, could be measured in nanoseconds. The moment Kienan had shown up, a countdown had started, ticking away with the relentless precision of a chrono. Then it would blow up in her face like a cluster of biobombs. Quill was going to find out. And when he did, he would hate her because she'd lied, taken away his choices, denied him his vaunted control. And that, she knew he'd never tolerate. Not for a nanosecond. Not even from a mate. When he shoved her out of his life the way she'd always assumed, that was it. Over. Done.

Just the way it should be.

For now, for as long as this lasted, she'd let herself have it. If only because she knew, she *knew* it was going to end. Kienan wouldn't keep her secret for long, he'd been honest about that, and so her nightmare would explode in her face. And she would be alone. For the rest of her life. Even if she managed to take on sexual partners again, it would never be like this. They would never be her mates.

She could only hope she was stronger than her mother when it all ended. At least she hadn't claimed them. That might be the only thing that saved her sanity. She could only pray that was true.

Kienan nipped at her bottom lip, sending a jolt through her. Reaching up, she threaded her fingers through his soft hair. Her tongue dueled with his, and she arched her body into his hard planes. Deus, it felt good. Too good, but she pushed that notion away and focused on this, on him, and nothing more. She twined one leg around him, rubbing her sex against the hardness of his thigh through their clothing. He flexed the muscle, wedging his leg against her clit. Excitement fizzed through her, ratcheting up her heart rate and speeding her breath to ragged puffs of air. Grinding herself down on his leg, she rode him until her pussy began to clench with each movement. She was so hot for him, so wet and wanton. But she wanted more.

As if he'd sensed her thought, he eased away from her just enough to unseal her pants, slipping his fingers in to brush over the tight curls between her thighs. She shivered, her body tensing as she waited for his touch. A ragged cry broke from her throat when he dipped into her sex. He circled his fingertips over her clit and her hips heaved in response.

She gasped. "Deus."

"Touch me." His words were half-command and half-plea. So different from Quill, who would have simply demanded. He controlled their pleasure, while Kienan shared it. She couldn't decide which she liked better.

Tugging at the bottom of his shirt, she pulled it over his head and tossed it aside. Then her palms were coasting across his broad chest, a pure tactile pleasure. He was all crisp hair and warm skin over hard musculature.

His fingers slipped from her sex, but before she could protest, he'd bent to work her pants down her legs. She stepped out of the garment and her boots, then stripped her top off while he straightened. Arching a brow, she trailed a nail across his pec to his nipple. It beaded for her. Nice.

"You're overdressed, Vaughn."

She brushed her thumb over his flat, brown nipple, circled it, pinched it, and rolled it between her fingers. As she teased him, she watched his eyes burn to molten silver. His fangs slid down and she could see his body begin to shake with the struggle not to let his feral side take over. It was a heady rush of power for her, and she loved it.

"Take your clothes off, Kienan."

"Yes." He ripped open the seal to his pants, shoving them down and off along with his heavy boots. They thudded when they hit the floor. And then he was nude, his cock a hard arc against his belly, and she remembered the taste of him in her mouth. A throb went through her, her sex growing damper.

Snaking an arm around her waist, he hauled her flush against him, making them both moan. He dipped down to suck her nipple into his mouth, and a shock of heat went through her. The feel of his fangs scraping her sensitive flesh made her gasp, sent wildness careening through her. Talons slid from her fingertips, scoring his shoulders when he offered the same treatment to her other breast, flicking the tight crest with his tongue, suckling and biting. Her pussy flexed, her hips beginning to undulate without any direction from her mind.

His hands curved over her ass, and he lifted her to sit on the edge of her desk, pushing his way between her thighs. She arched herself for his penetration, wanting him inside her. Needing it. The fox in her craved the ecstasy of being with its mate, and she struggled to restrain the beast within. The head of Kienan's cock slid over her wet slit, seeking her opening. Sinking into her micrometer by micrometer, the thickness of his dick stretched her. Perfect. She squeezed her thighs around his hips, drawing him as close as possible. Deeper. She wanted him deeper.

"Deus, it's even better than I imagined."

She struggled to draw enough breath to speak, barely managing to gather enough wits. "What is?"

"Being inside you." His gaze was focused on her face, the intensity making her shiver. "Hot, wet, tight."

Her pussy clenched in response to his words, fisting around his cock. They both groaned at the sensation. "I like you inside me, too."

The rough sound he made was one of pure feral need. He shoved into her again, hard, and she cried out when he filled her. Deus, she'd forgotten how thick he was. The stretch was agony and ecstasy all rolled into one, just as everything with her mates was for her. She craved it so much, despite the pain she knew was inevitable.

If his thrusts were swift and deep, his kiss was a shocking, arousing contrast. He brushed his lips over hers, tender and sweet enough that tears stung her eyes. She blinked them back, refusing to give in. Sex was one thing, but she offered nothing more to either of her mates. She couldn't. Down that road lay madness and death, an end to everything that made her who and what she was.

Shoving her tongue into his mouth, she turned the kiss into something animalistic, purely carnal. They nipped at each other with their fangs, and she tasted blood. His or hers, she didn't know, but it made the wildness within her claw for freedom. Kienan plunged into her pussy, his hips picking up a faster pace that had her moaning with each powerful thrust. She squeezed the walls of her sex around his dick, and he choked on a groan, his fingers biting into her hips as they moved together in perfect sync, racing each other for orgasm.

She cinched her legs around his waist, holding him close and reveling in the feel of his big body sliding against hers. The light hair on his chest chafed nipples his mouth had already sensitized, and it was exquisite pleasured-pain. The discomfort only revved her up more. Climax beckoned, her muscles tightening with every movement they made.

His breath rushed against her cheek, his lungs bellowing. "You could have this forever, Gea, if you'd just let us in."

No, she couldn't. Everything in her wanted it, but she *could not* do that. She shook her head, opened her mouth to deny him. But he plunged inside her, ground his pelvis against her clit, and orgasm hit her in a tsunami wave, dragged her under, and she had no choice but to *feel* everything. Her pussy clenched around his cock, milking the length of him.

An animalistic scream wrenched up from within her, her body bowing as pleasure rocketed through her, frying her systems. He fucked her hard, pounding inside her, dragging out her climax until she couldn't stand it any longer. Aftershocks pulsed through her, and she dropped her forehead to his chest, gasping for breath, her heart galloping.

Reality returned by degrees, and she realized Kienan was still thick and hard inside of her. She blinked her eyes open, saw his features were taut with unspent lust, his claws digging into her hips.

"You didn't come?" It was a stupid question, but it was the best her scattered wits could come up with.

"Not yet. If this is all I get, I want to make it last as long as I can." He nipped at the sensitive spot at the base of her throat, sending a shiver through her. "And I want to make you come again."

5

Deus, she was beautiful.

Flushed with satisfaction, her lips swollen from his kisses, her sex hot and slick around his. Kienan held on to his control by the thinnest thread of mercurite.

Trailing kisses down her neck, he pressed her backward until she was spread out like a feast before him on her desk. He liked that thought and couldn't stop the wicked grin that formed on his lips. He leaned back a bit, wanting to see all of her, every naked centimeter. Yes, beautiful. Her pale hair fanned around her, a sharp contrast to the dark wood. He palmed the roundness of her hips, moved to her waist, slid his fingers up her soft, soft skin, and cupped her breasts in his hands.

She moaned, arched her torso, and forced his cock deeper inside of her. Lust pounded through him and he shuddered. It took every ounce of his restraint not to fuck her hard and fast until he came inside her. He wanted more from her, wanted to wring another orgasm or two out of her before he let her up. He squeezed her breasts, rubbing his thumbs over her nipples.

They tightened for him, stabbing into his hands. He pinched them, flicking his talons over the beaded crests, and he watched her lust reawaken. The scent of her desire filled his nostrils, made his dick throb.

She writhed against the desktop, her tight sheath slick around his cock. "Kienan."

He shuddered. "I like it when you say my name."

"Why's that?" A little grin curled her full lips, but her breath caught when he surged inside her. "Kienan."

Deus, he loved the way she moaned his name. His hips rocked, and he reached between them to stroke a fingertip over her clit. "I haven't told anyone my real name in a long time. Only my bosses knew it. I never used it when I was working."

Her brows drew together as she struggled to focus, and he liked that she had to struggle, that he could make a woman as focused as she was lose it. "Really?"

"Yes, I got tired of the lies." He teased her wet flesh, the lips of her pussy, stretched around his cock. "Got tired of never knowing anyone or having them know me. I want to know you, Gea. You and Quill."

The words spilled from his mouth, stupid, weak words that were like speaking a foreign language to him, but he didn't care. There was some part deep inside him that *hated* the thought of losing either of them now. He wanted this, wanted to see where it went with both his mates. Doubts shadowed her gaze, and she opened her mouth to speak, but he pinched her clit hard before she could protest. He rolled it under his thumb, flicking it with the tip of one talon. Hard.

Her back arched and she cried out. He felt the squeeze of her inner muscles around his cock as she came. And his control broke. He bracketed her hips in his hands and hammered inside of her sweet pussy. Grabbing for his arms, she held on for the ride, there with him the whole way. Her fangs bared and the feral display only made him drive his cock into her harder, forging their bodies together until he couldn't tell where he ended and she began.

Just the way he wanted it.

"Kienan, Kienan, *Kienan*," she chanted, and he groaned, thrusting deeper into her pussy. She screamed his name, her sheath locking tight around his cock again as she came for him.

It was more than he could resist. He exploded inside of her, shuddering and groaning as he jetted come deep into her pussy. The feel of her fisting around him while he came made him choke and sink his softening dick into her, craving the connection that he knew would end the second she came down from the climactic high. Collapsing forward, he rested his head between the mounds of her breasts, her scent dragging into his lungs while he sucked in oxygen. His muscles shook and burned from the workout, but it felt damn good anyway. He had no regrets about hunting her down today.

She stirred beneath him and he reluctantly straightened. "You all right?"

A sigh slid out of her. "Yeah. You?"

"Me?" He lifted an eyebrow. "I'm prime right now, thanks to you."

Chuckling, she pushed herself upright, winced a bit, and rubbed a hand over her back. She felt around the desk behind her and came up with her palmtop computer. "That explains the backache."

"Sorry, I was more focused on you than what you were lying on."

She set the palmtop aside and slipped off the desk to stand before him. "I'm really not trying to rush you out, but I got a message before you arrived and I have a contact to meet. It might be the break in the case I'm working on."

"Looking for Felicia Tamryn. Quill mentioned it, in case I heard anything at Tail." Surprise flickered across her expression, but he could see the barriers sliding back into place. He sighed but knew he couldn't let her walk away from him now. She was still flush with passion and wet with his seed. His cock jerked at the thought, and a shudder ran through him. "Let's shower before you go. We smell like sex."

"Probably not the most professional perfume." She flashed a smile and led the way through her main space to a wash closet with a small shower. "Unless you're a jade and it is your profession."

They kept it quick, and he waited until they were back in her office and sorting their clothes out before he spoke again. He hoped this was a gamble that would pay off. "I understand the case is important to you and you have to go now, but I want to come with you to watch your back."

"I'm working." She stuffed herself into her pants and boots, sealing both. "That means I'm dealing with sensitive information for my client and going places you probably don't want to be."

He snorted, pulling his shirt on. "I worked covert ops for a national intelligence agency. Do you think I can't keep a secret? Do you think I can't handle myself anytime, anywhere?"

Her jaw clenched. "That isn't the point."

"I can follow you. Do you really want me tailing you while you try to do your work?" Everything in him said if he let her shut him out now, he might never get her to talk about why she had such a deep aversion to mating. He needed to press his advantage now. "Wouldn't it be easier to just let me come this one time?"

She growled, the fox in her ready to snap at him. "This one time, you swear it?"

"You trust me to keep my promise?"

"Yes," she barked.

"You don't know me." He bent down until they were eye to

eye, until he was close enough to see the gold flecks in her irises. "Could it be that pesky mating instinct telling you that you can trust me?"

"Go fuck yourself."

Putting on his boots, he shot back at her. "Fucking you is so much better, but your suggestion is noted."

She threw a few things into her ever-present bag, spun on a heel, and walked away. He sealed his pants and followed her out. The silence was chilly, and she refused to even glance at him as she jogged down the street to catch a public transport.

"Was it your parents who were mates?"

She stumbled, catching herself against the side of a building to keep from falling. She shrugged away from his touch when he tried to help her and pushed herself to a standing position. Not looking at him, she kept walking. "Leave it alone, Vaughn."

"You know I can't do that. I'm your—"

"*Stop saying it.* Deus!" She hurried to clamor onto a transport headed toward the Vermilion. No one else was on board, but he sat close enough that their thighs brushed anyway.

"So it was your parents." He drew in a breath, pushing her and hoping it didn't push her away. "Was it your mother who lied to your father or your father who lied to your mother?"

"My parents were never married." She stared out the window at the passing scenery.

He narrowed his gaze, noting the way she held herself, the inflection of her tone. It didn't ring true. She was lying about something. "They weren't married. Were they mates?"

She sighed, closing her eyes briefly. "Yes."

"And who was the liar?" He kept his voice low and undemanding, knowing he could only press her for information so much before it backfired on him.

"My father."

He bumped her leg with his. "What did he lie about?"

"Everything. And nothing." Her shoulder twitched in a

shrug, and she eased away from him subtly. "It doesn't matter now. He's dead. They both are."

"Why didn't they marry?" Some people didn't, but she'd been the one to point out a lack of matrimony, and he suspected it meant something deeper.

Her mouth worked for a moment before she spoke. "Because he was already married when he met my mother."

That surprised him. "He didn't divorce to be with his mate?"

"No, his wife was a wealthy, influential woman. If he'd left her, she would have ruined him." There was an inflection to her words, as if reciting something she'd been told by someone else. Often.

"So, you were the result of an affair between them?"

She snorted but still didn't meet his gaze. "Something like that."

"Tell me. Please. Give me this, if nothing else." He covered her hand with his, and she balled her fingers under his touch. He brought her fist to his lips and kissed it. "Let me understand why you don't want us to be together."

Her defiance crumpled, her head bowing. She tugged her hand away from him. "He kept her as his mistress until he died."

Deus, the man had turned his *mate* into a whore. The very idea was outlandish to Kienan. "How did she deal with that?"

"She didn't." She folded her arms over her chest and hunched her shoulders. "She spent her life waiting for him. We both did. Everything revolved around him and whether or not he was coming to visit. She was the happiest person alive, joyful when he was around. But then he left again. He always left. There was always something more important than his family. Like his wife, his business associates. We were always last place. That's what mating means to me."

Mated to one woman, married to another for power and

prestige. What a fucking prick. He wanted to go back and punch the bastard in the face, if for no other reason than the man had hurt Gea. Protectiveness bristled through Kienan. "That's not mating, that was just him. He sounds like a selfish person. I'm not."

"Maybe, but what if I come to depend on you like she did on him?" She turned to look at him squarely, her gaze troubled. "What if I buy into this whole whacked-out mating thing and invest myself in it heart and soul?"

Deus, he wanted that. He wanted this woman's heart and soul. He wanted everything she had to offer and more.

She shook her head, pressing shaking lips together. "And then what happens when you die and I'm alone again? Only I don't have a life without you. I'm just a weak shadow of a person, and I'll wither up without you."

That didn't sound like her at all, this fearsome female. What he knew of her so far was that she was tough and redefined obstinate. Talking to Quill this past week had only confirmed his suspicions about her. "Is that what your mother did?"

"Yes." She dashed away a tear as if it shamed her to have shed it. "I decided as a kid that that would *never* be me. I would never be in so deep with someone that there was no me without him. That's what mating is, that's what it means, and I am *not* going there. Not for you or Quill or anyone else. I can't, Kienan. I just can't. I hope the two of you are happy together, I really do, but I can't be part of it."

"You already are." His gut clenched at the sight of her tears, and he reached over to squeeze her leg.

"No." Her gaze was stormy, her face paling. "I may not have any say in whether or not a mate or two exists out there in the world for me, but I *can* decide whether or not to do anything about it. I've made my choice."

"You can't blame me for wanting to change your mind. I'm

nothing like your father, Gea. Neither is Quill. We both protect what's ours; we value what we have." He pitched his voice low as a ragged-looking woman boarded the transport and shuffled to the opposite end. As far away as possible, but still within earshot. However, the noise of the moving transport should cover his quiet words. "If we had you as a mate, openly and honestly, then that would apply to you, too. Neither of us is like your father."

She sniffed, ignoring the personal comments to focus on her parent. Her stubbornness was intact. "He valued his wealth and comfort more than he valued his mate."

"Or his daughter." And she valued her independence more than her mates. He didn't say it aloud. He doubted it would win him any favors from her to compare her with her father. Even less if he said anything about her mother. What kind of woman stood by and allowed her mate to treat her that way? Why hadn't she come out fighting, claws bared, at the mere mention that he'd remain with his wife and treat her like a cheap jade he'd picked up on a street corner? Hell, why hadn't she walked away rather than take that shit from anyone? It showed a lack of respect. She hadn't had any kind of self-respect, and her mate hadn't respected her as a person or a mate. Neither of them had respected what a mate was. Kienan shook his head.

The line of his thoughts was appallingly idealistic, which wasn't like him at all. He knew the world was a mean, dirty place. He'd spent enough years in the gutter cleaning up the trash in the world to know. The one person he knew he could trust was himself and his instincts. His instincts said his mates were *his,* and he took care of what was his. That was what mating meant to him.

"After my father died, I watched my mother just...fade away. She lost touch with reality, stopped caring about anything, especially me. All I became was a painful reminder of what she'd lost." Her shoulder brushed against his when she shrugged. "His death ate at her until there was nothing left. And then she went, too. Gratefully, I think."

The pain in her tone made him ache. It had been such a long time since he'd bothered with sympathy for another person that he shied away from it, asking another question instead. "How old were you when they died?"

"Fifteen when my father kicked, and sixteen when my mother followed him." She leaned her head against the seatback, looking tired.

He rubbed a hand up and down her thigh, hoping it was comforting, but what the hell did he know about comforting anyone? Genuine comfort and not some manipulation he was using for the sake of a mission? Not a damn thing. "So you were still a minor. How did you get by? Did someone take you in? A relative?"

"No relatives." She rolled her head on the seat to look at him. "Any family they had died before I was even born. And his wife certainly wasn't going to help me."

He arched an eyebrow. "Did she know about you?"

"Yes, but acknowledging that wouldn't be keeping up appearances for their friends." She assumed a haughty expression, staring down her nose at him.

"How did you get by?" he repeated, ignoring her attempt at humor. Another person he'd like to hunt down for being a selfish ass and abandoning a young girl in the name of their own interests. Irresponsible. There were a lot of people like that in the world, but he hated to see the scars it had left on a woman who was coming to mean far too much to him, far too quickly. He couldn't help it. He wasn't even sure he wanted to.

She rolled her eyes at him. "I got a job working in the office at Prime Investigations. My boss taught me everything I know about PI work."

"So someone did look after you." The statement was aimed

at Gea, but he kept an eye on the old woman as she stumped off the transport at the next stop.

"Don't make it prettier than it was. Mickey was nobody's role model." Gea huffed out a short laugh. "He wasn't a good man, let alone a kind or loving one. He needed someone to look after the office work, and he could tell I was desperate and would do anything he wanted while he paid me next to nothing and worked me like a slave. But I paid attention and I learned the ropes, so when he got too old to do the fieldwork, I took over and he handled the office. After he died, I kept his clients."

Kienan angled a glance at her, let his incredulity seep into his tone. "He left his business to you?"

"More like he had no heirs to care that I just took it over and made it mine." She gave him a little salute. "Prime Investigations, at your service."

He gestured as they pulled into the last stop. "This is where we get off?"

This was as close to the Vermilion as most normal people ever wanted to get, which wasn't all that close. They had quite a walk ahead of them.

She nodded and rose to disembark. "So, we talked about me. What's your story, Vaughn? You owe me."

As they walked, he told her. Anything she wanted to know that wasn't classified intel. A week ago, it would have been inconceivable to him to reveal anything real or personal, but he'd told her the truth—he was tired of the lies. It was a risk, exposing himself to her and to Quill, but he figured if he was going to take the chance with anyone, it should be his mates. All he could do was hope they didn't use the information to damage him later.

Hope. Not an emotion he had any experience with, but the last week had been so far outside his comfort zone that he was in foreign territory. He'd have to play it by ear and brace himself for the worst, knowing it was always an option. With as skittish as his mates were, it wasn't even an unlikely option. Still, he had to try.

The demarcation to the Vermilion was a subtle decay into filth and poverty. Skyrises gave way to multiplexes, which degraded in cleanliness and quality until they hit the shanty towns that marked the east side of the crime-ridden district. The deeper into the quagmire they went, the more eyes he felt on them, watching for weakness, debating whether to attack.

His battle instincts sharpened the way they always did on an assignment, his awareness expanding, every detail of his surroundings seeping into his consciousness. But this was different. Then, he'd been a tool, a weapon to be aimed and fired. This time, the mission was of his choosing. He answered to no one except himself. And Gea. He doubted she'd appreciate being left out of that equation.

No one told him to do this. He did it because he wanted to, because he'd decided it was the best course of action. It was liberating. He'd chosen to follow orders before, but that wasn't the same as being the master of his own fate. He wasn't sure he agreed with Quill's need to control everything, but there was something to having a bit more say in where he went and when.

He liked it.

Tucking those thoughts away as something to consider later, he focused on the task at hand—helping his mate dig up information. He'd done this before, just under different circumstances. An ironic smile touched his lips. It had been decades since he'd needed to prove himself to anyone, but he felt the need to impress her, to make her believe there was one part of her life where she could trust him, where there was nothing to fear.

Perhaps that one area would bleed over into other areas.

She nodded to a derelict building across the road from where they stood. "This is the place. You can wait out here, if you want."

"And spend the time being propositioned because people think only jades hang out on street corners in this district?" Or maybe he'd be attacked by friendly locals like Niso and his thugs. It was a toss-up which sounded less appealing.

"You'd be worth every cred." She slapped his ass before she darted to the other side of the street.

Chuckling, he followed a step behind her, but his longer stride caught up to her before they reached the entryway. She tapped a vidpad with a wavy screen by the door. He smoothed his face to impassivity, waiting for her cues to see if she needed him to play good cop or bad cop.

"Who's that?" A man's voice growled from the vidpad, though no image appeared. The accent was thick—German, Kienan thought—but there was too much static crackling to tell which country the man hailed from.

"Ison sent me," Gea replied cryptically. "He said you'd have what I'm looking for."

The door creaked open, rust making the ancient iron squeal. Kienan scanned the area to see if anyone was taking too much interest in their actions. No.

A large man appeared on the threshold, his dark hair slicked back, his eyebrows growing into a single line across his forehead. Beyond him, the interior of the building was far too plush for this area of town. Whatever the man dealt in was lucrative.

"What you want to buy?" The man's face was flushed, as if he'd had a few too many synthbrews, his heavy jowls weighing down his heavier features.

"Are you Meier?" Gea's nostrils flared at that same time the stench of alcohol hit Kienan.

The big guy arched his unibrow at her. "Depends on who wants to know."

"Your new best friends, Meier." Kienan figured this might go faster if he made their recalcitrant German think Gea was the reasonable one. He lounged against the entry as if he hadn't a care in the world, offering up his most charming smile. "How are you this fine evening? Mind if we come in and chat awhile, friend?"

"No." Annoyance crossed Meier's features. "Crazy fool. Who are you and what do you want?"

"I'm Gea Crevan. I'm not looking for your normal merchandise." Gea rushed into speech. "I want to buy information."

Suspicion flashed in his gaze. "What information?"

"I'm looking for a woman named Tam." She held up her palmtop to show an image of the dark-haired female. "Do you know her?"

"*Ja*, I know her," Meier barked. "Why? She owe you money?"

"Maybe she does. Maybe she doesn't." Kienan made his smile more ingratiating, which seemed to irritate Meier further. Distract and confuse, then hopefully Gea gets her answers.

She cast him a disbelieving glance but focused on the German. "When was the last time you saw her?"

He grunted, his gaze narrowing. "Why do you care?"

"Please, it's not like the brigade is going to come breaking down your door for making time with a grifter. We're just looking for the lady." Kienan waggled his eyebrows but gave a quick glance over his shoulder to check the street. Empty. He met Meier's gaze and winked. "She's a prime piece. Wouldn't mind bending her over."

The German looked between Gea and Kienan, confusion contorting his face.

Gea jumped in. "Look, I don't care why you were talking to her, or how legal or not legal your business with her was. I just need to know where she went after. Do you know?"

The hinges on the door squeaked as Meier started to swing it shut, but Kienan held up a mercurite chip that gleamed in the fading sunlight. He winked at the German when he froze, staring at the chip. "There's enough creds on here to make it worth your while. Try to remember, friend."

He licked his lips, considering. "*Ja,* I know. She went wiz a man."

"Do you know him?" Gea pressed. "Can you describe him?"

"English, like her. Dark hair, like her. But older. Skinny. Smelled like a rodent." His chin jutted. "Don't know her man's name. Don't want to know it."

Kienan flipped the chip at him and he caught it, moving faster than a man of his bulk should be able to. Gea pushed a holopic into his hand as well. "My card. Call me if you hear any more about where Tam might be."

"You leave me to my bizness now." He grunted, slamming the door in their faces.

Kienan straightened from his nonchalant slouch. "Nice guy."

"He was somewhat helpful at least." Gea shrugged and turned to face him. "But what was that, *friend*? You just feeling sassy and a little chatty today?"

He *had* talked more in the last week than he had in years, but how else was he supposed to make this mating thing happen? Not that he knew shit about what a good mating was like, but he'd give it his best shot. Shrugging, he lifted his hands. "Just making sure Meier wanted us gone, and that he wasn't thinking too long or too deeply about whether or not he really *wanted* to answer your questions."

She chuckled, shook her head. "I figured you'd just stand back and be a silent, scary enforcer type."

"I can do that, too. I didn't think it was the best approach here."

"Apparently." Her eyes glinted with amusement. "But thanks, that went about as well as it was going to. I'll repay you the creds you gave him."

He was going to protest that, but something wavered at the edges of his senses. Danger lurked. Not unusual in this district, but this was aimed at them. He glanced around and saw a group of four people at the end of the street coming toward them a little too casually. "We have company."

Gea's nostrils flared; then her expression tightened. "Aw, shit."

"Friends of yours?" He glanced between her and the approaching trouble.

"Not exactly." She pulled in another breath. "But by the reptilian stench of him, the one on the left is the Komodo dragon-shifter who jacked up my leg the other day."

"Want me to kill him?" He was only partially joking, his muscles tensing with the need to defend his mate.

She hummed in her throat, shook her head, and started down the cracked and crumbling sidewalk in the opposite direction. "Broken bones can be explained to the police. Concussions. Bruises. Dead bodies? Not so much. And I'd rather stay on their good side."

"You like the police?" He kept pace with her but didn't touch her, keeping his hands free in case of attack.

She shrugged and picked up speed until she was not-quite-jogging. "I scratch their back, they scratch mine. It's business."

"Ah." Then he sighed. "Ah, shit."

A trio of men turned the corner, blocking their exit. Men he recognized.

She glanced back at him, pulling to a stop. "Friends of *yours?*"

Adrenaline flooded his veins as he realized they wouldn't get out of here without a fight. He sensed the two groups weren't working together, but that made the situation even more dangerous. Every group for itself, all fighting each other over the prey. "The short one is called Niso. I didn't catch the names of the other two, but they were hoping to be close, *personal* friends. I declined, and they took the rejection badly."

"I see." Her gaze darted around as if looking for an exit strategy, and the fox-shifter snarled in frustration. "I had my vidcam earlier, so no room for the grappler gun. I don't have it with me. Up isn't an option."

Whatever that meant. "We may not escape the need for dead bodies."

She blew out a frustrated breath, watching the two gangs close in on them. "Do you have a weapon on you?"

"No, you?"

"Yeah."

"Use it."

Reaching behind her, she slipped a nasty-looking blade out of some hidden pocket on the underside of her bag. "What about you?"

"I don't need it." Not with the training and experience he'd had. His talons slid out of his fingertips as he watched a cruel smile twist up the corners of Niso's lips. Bruises stood in dark contrast against his skin, a reminder of their first meeting.

Kienan should have ended the bastard when he had the chance.

Gea and Kienan backed up into a building, each facing one of the gangs, making their position as defensible as possible. He had no idea how good his mate was in a fight, and he didn't care for being in a situation where he had to find out, but such was life. No one gave a shit what he wanted.

A hiss came out of Niso's throat as he looked at the competition. "We claim them. Our pretties."

A growl was the reply to that. "Girlie there's been ours for days now. Just needed to catch up with her. You can't have her."

Kienan felt Gea vibrate against his back, and he reached over to hold her in place. With any luck the two gangs would start fighting with each other, giving them a chance to bolt. Or a better chance at fighting their way out if the gangs were more occupied with besting each other than claiming Gea and Kienan.

A deep roar sounded through the street, silencing the arguing thugs. A leopard leaped toward them, stretching into a full sprint. Quill. He was on them in seconds, fangs bared, claws slashing.

All hell broke loose; the gangs didn't know which direction to turn.

Kienan grabbed one of Niso's henchmen and shoved him into one of the other gang members. The two went down howling, shifting into their animal forms, clawing and tearing at each other. Quill sliced his claws through another gangster's calf and he squealed, swinging a fist to slam into the leopard's skull. Niso's other thug drew a gun, aiming it at Quill's head, and Gea screamed, her knife winging through the air with deadly accuracy. Her blade embedded in the man's throat and he gurgled, slumping to the ground, his gun trapped underneath him.

Niso took down Gea's dragon-shifter just in time for her to put a boot in his chest, knocking him backward. Kienan jammed the tips of his fingers into Niso's temple and the man crumpled. Dead. There was no way Kienan would risk the bastard coming after his mates or him again. It ended now.

A gorilla-shifter came at him, screaming, huge fangs bared. Adrenaline exploded through Kienan's system, and he welcomed the rush, channeled it. Ducking a massive fist, he brought his knee up to connect with the gorilla's stomach. Air whooshed out of the gangster's lungs, and Kienan wrapped an arm around the gorilla's neck from behind. He used his other arm to lock it into place. Bucking and twisting, the gorilla clawed at Kienan's arms, trying to dislodge them. The stench of his own blood singed Kienan's nose, but he gritted his teeth and held fast. The gorilla slammed them backward into a building, and the breath was forced from Kienan's lungs. He gagged, dark spots swimming in front of his vision. Agony ricocheted up and down his body each time he was battered against the wall. He blinked, tried to hang on, tried to keep from blacking out. Just a little longer. The gorilla began to sag from the lack of oxygen, dropping to his knees so Kienan's feet hit the floor, giving him the leverage he needed. With a swift wrench, he heard the neck bones crack and the fight was over. The gorilla hit the ground with a heavy thud.

When Kienan looked around, he saw only his mates standing. Thank Deus. One gang member shifted into a bird and took flight, but Quill launched himself upward with feline precision and the bird was dragged from the sky in a hail of feathers and squawking. One sickening *crunch* and the bird was no more.

"Okay, these two gangs clearly killed each other. If anyone asks, we were just in the wrong place at the wrong time. Self-defense, etcetera. But I'd rather not stand around long enough for anyone to ask." Gea grabbed her knife from where it protruded from the thug's neck, then wiped it off on his shirt. The blade disappeared into her hidden pocket, and her chin lifted in the defiant gesture Kienan was coming to associate with her. "Time to go. Now."

Quill dipped his head, turning to pad down the street in the direction he'd come. Gea hopped over a couple of bodies and hurried after him, and Kienan followed behind, watching his mates' backs.

A painfully skinny man stood at the intersection at the end of the road, clutching an armload of clothes. "I kept your stuff, Mr. North."

The leopard twisted into the shape of a tall man and Quill stood there naked, his skin missing the black slashing nanotats that Kienan had grown used to. Had he had them reconfigured to look like regular skin? "Where are your tats?"

Quill grunted, shoving himself into his clothing as quickly

as possible. "I have a program on my palmtop that can turn them on and off if I need to be more respectable for certain partners. I had a meeting in the Lakeshore District this morning."

Interesting. Kienan's superiors would have preferred he had a program like that as well. They hadn't approved of the tats he'd collected over the years, but he'd reconfigured them often enough that he hadn't had the same distinguishing marks from one job to the next. It had placated them. Of course, they hadn't seemed to mind the distinguishing marks he'd gotten working for them. Multiple knife wounds, a few bullet holes, an acid burn from a spitting cobra-shifter. Figures.

Now that he was out of that line of work, maybe he should have the nanotat on his back configured to its original form: two wolves baying at the moon. One red for his mother, the other gray for his father.

Quill glanced at the skinny man. "Thanks for making sure my things weren't stolen, Janus."

"No problem." He flashed a gap-toothed smile, his face congenial, but his gaze was assessing as he looked over Gea and Kienan. There was a keen intelligence there that Kienan wasn't willing to overlook.

"We can finish our discussion at a later date, Janus. I'm sure you're very busy." The dismissal was clear, but Quill covered any rudeness with a charming grin. "I apologize for keeping you so long."

"Later." Janus nodded and split down a winding side street that curved sharply out of sight.

"Let's get out of here. As Gea said, law enforcement might get curious." Kienan sighed, checking his mates over for injuries. Nothing major, that he could sense anyway. Gea fished around in her pack for a moment and then handed him a large nanopatch to put over the gorilla claw gouges on his arms. He nodded his thanks and slapped the patch in place. It could have been a lot worse. He didn't care for how close they'd come to disaster, but death was only a misstep away around here.

It probably wasn't a good sign that he enjoyed how it kept him on his toes, but he still couldn't say that he craved his old lifestyle. His mates had kept him more than occupied during his short retirement.

Quill made a face as he finished sealing his clothes. "Law enforcement doesn't spend much time here unless they're collecting kickbacks, but you never know when they might feel the sudden need to be dutiful."

6

Quill shoved his hand through his hair. Why had he thrown himself into someone else's fight? It wasn't like him at all. He kept to himself and his own business. Meddling in the affairs of others came back to bite you in the Vermilion, but he'd fought and killed to protect these two people. He hadn't even thought about it, hadn't stopped to consider the consequences. He'd simply reacted; something inside him refused to be impartial. His lovers were being attacked, outnumbered at least three to one, and he *could not* stand back and do nothing. It was nothing like him, and that worried him. He sighed and looked at them. "Come back to my place."

"Tail is closer," Gea countered, glancing at Kienan.

Had they spent a lot of time there without Quill? He hated to admit that he hated that thought. He couldn't be jealous—he'd had both of them before. Why would he care if they shagged each other's minds out anytime they wanted? He wouldn't. He didn't.

"So? I'd rather not be inside the Vermilion right now. This is better." He arched his eyebrow, turning to lead the way back to his building.

Why he was so insistent about this, he didn't know. He normally didn't care for people in his private space. The occasional business dinner and a few sex partners, but even then, he preferred not to use his flat for that. Other than this week with Kienan, Quill couldn't remember the last time he'd had anyone there besides Gea, and she never stayed for anything other than fucking. So, why now? Why these two? He wasn't sure, and he didn't like that either.

The three of them together discouraged anyone from messing with them—a person alone made a much easier target—and they made it out of the Vermilion in short order. Quill went through the rear entrance of his building, then swiped his ident card to engage his private lift to the penthouse. They reeked of adrenaline and sweat, their clothes torn from the fight, and each of them sported a few cuts and bruises, which didn't need to be advertised to his associates.

"How's your arm, Kienan?" Gea asked as the lift doors slid open. She stepped out into the foyer, glancing back at the wolf.

"It's good. The nanopatch is helping." He followed her out into the main space. "Built-in painkillers?"

"Yeah." Gea drifted over to a large window in his main space. Unlike the view from his bedroom, this window faced away from the Vermilion and overlooked the vast stretch of the city and Lake Michigan in the distance. The cluster of glittering mercurite and polyglass skyrises demarcated the Downtown District.

Her head bowed, and her reflection showed a pensive expression. Quill didn't know what to make of it. He'd expected her to try to bolt before now. It was the first time he hadn't had to argue, cajole, or seduce her into staying for more than five minutes. She wasn't trying to get laid now, so . . . what was different?

He glanced at Kienan, his eyebrows arching in question, but the other man just shrugged. Quill turned away from the wolf and walked into his kitchen. "Fighting always makes me hungry, and I'm not eating alone with the two of you standing here. So, what would you like to eat?"

"Protein." Kienan sat on the kleather couch and winced a little—probably bruised from the battle. "Lots of it."

Gea's stomach rumbled loudly enough that Quill could hear it. She sighed and nodded an agreement. "I'm not picky, but something substantial sounds good."

Engaging the vidpad on his food storage unit, he browsed through the options his catering company had stocked. "I have bison steaks."

"Mmm, bisteak." She slapped a hand over her belly as it grumbled again, glancing over her shoulder with a self-effacing grin on her face. "I could *maybe* be convinced to eat that, sure."

Quill watched her turn back to press her nose to the window. "I can see my building from here. I never noticed before."

She'd never looked before, too busy ripping Quill's clothes off. Ignoring the twinge of irritation that thought brought, he keyed the unit to dispense three plates of bisteak, sweet potatoes, and greens. The information uplinked into the system; then the door clicked as it opened.

"I'll take them," Kienan said softly, right behind Quill.

He froze, wariness sliding through him. He hadn't heard the wolf move, and his senses hadn't warned him of another predator approaching. It had happened a couple of times over the last few days, and he didn't know what to make of it. Was it some skill the wolf had cultivated in his work as an operative? It made Quill uneasy. Things slipping past his notice was an unpleasant development. People died when they got sloppy, and he'd always prided himself on never losing his edge. His jaw clenched. He'd never had anyone sneak up on him before, but no feeling of danger slid through him when the other man was near. Only sexual awareness. It crawled through him now, the hot scent of the wolf curling into Quill's nostril, and his loins tightened, his cock beginning to lengthen and stiffen.

Kienan reached past him into the unit and pulled the food out. He balanced two steaming plates on one arm and carried the third in his other hand. Shaking himself, Quill keyed in a code for a bottle of chilled ginger wine, then retrieved glasses from a cabinet.

"Utensils?" Gea walked into the kitchen, her gaze a bit wary, a bit uncertain, as if anything outside their normal sex-on-arrival worried her.

The novelty of Gea-the-mystery was wearing off. He'd contented himself with nothing more than sex until now, but he wanted to know more about her. No more mystery. Perhaps it was having Kienan the last week that completed the change, perhaps it was just time. The attraction was as powerful as always, having her a few steps away brought his stiffening cock to full arousal. Deus, the two of them would kill him.

He nodded to the cutlery drawer and walked past her to join Kienan in the main space. He was aware of every movement his lovers made, knew when Gea came up behind him, her scent ripening. He sat beside the wolf while the fox curled onto the couch next to Quill, putting him in the middle. He set the glasses on the low table in front of his couch and poured wine for everyone. Kienan slid the plates down the table until there was one in front of each of them, and Gea dispensed the utensils. There was little conversation as they settled in to eat, but the silence was comfortable. Kienan's shoulder brushed against Quill's as they ate, and Gea leaned into him, for once content to simply remain with him. With them.

The scene was so domestic it made some emotion Quill couldn't name tangle inside his chest. Some kind of longing that he couldn't put his finger on. Hardly nostalgia—there'd been no domesticity in his childhood with an absent father and drug addict mother. He'd never had a home or family to call his own, was never even exposed to such a thing. His friends had lived in a nightmare much like his own, a cage with no way out but violence, death, or sinking into the same bliss-addled avoidance his mother had enjoyed so much.

He shook his head, focusing on his food. So he liked having them here, so what? They weren't staying, and he had work to do. Gea might not be ready to bolt at the moment, but she would. She always did. Nothing had changed, and he wasn't even sure it should. Kienan wouldn't be in New Chicago forever, and what would Quill do if Gea ever did decide to stick around? Hell, he had no idea what a real relationship would be like. He didn't even want one. He controlled his affairs like everything else, and he severed them like a business deal gone bad when they got too deep. He'd gone around and around with this in his mind the last week, and he could come up with no better explanation now than he had before. It didn't make sense.

He growled, letting his empty plate clatter onto the table.

Gea tensed beside him. "What's wrong?"

"Nothing." There shouldn't *be* anything wrong with him.

She twitched as if she sensed how deep that lie was. Setting her plate on the table beside his, she moved to rise. "Maybe I should go."

"Of course." He hissed the words, the leopard inside of him bristling. "You need to run. As usual."

Upset flickered across her expression, but she stayed seated. "You've never had a problem with it before. I thought we both preferred not to get too close."

So had he. But he was finding he *did* have a problem with it. Damn it, what was wrong with him? How had things gotten so jumbled up in a few short days? He'd missed her since the night they'd spent in Kienan's room, and as much as he'd enjoyed the wolf, it had been better with all three of them. When had he ever cared enough to *miss* anyone? Never. Not once in his entire life had anyone mattered to him that much, and he'd never mattered to anyone else enough for them to miss him. It was simpler that way.

And yet, here he was. Missing them when they were away. Doubting they missed him. They'd been together when he'd found them, and he could smell the lingering odor of sex on them. They'd fucked without him. Why should he care? He had fucked Kienan when Gea wasn't there. How was this any different? If they wanted each other, they should take advantage of the opportunity. He always had.

The kleather creaked when Gea twisted to kneel beside him. Her eyes were wide, churning with emotion. "You know... I can't be involved with anyone."

"Are you married?" A question he'd never let himself ask. Even with his taunting questions about her, he'd never put to words what might push her away.

"No!" Her face went pale, hurt molding her features. "I would never, *could never* do that to someone. Deus, I'm not that kind of person. If you believe nothing else, believe that. I just don't want to be involved with anyone. What's so wrong about that?"

"You were *involved* with Kienan earlier." He hated the jealousy in his voice, hated himself for saying anything.

She reared back as if he'd slapped her. "Just sex, the same as what I offer you. I don't play favorites with my lovers."

Arching an eyebrow, he crossed his arms. "How many other men do you fuck and drop, like me?"

"Just the two of you." Her throat moved when she swallowed, something like resignation entering her gaze.

He didn't understand that, didn't understand anything about her, just that he wanted to. "At the moment."

"Since we started—"

"You haven't been with anyone else in a year?" Disbelief

dripped from his words. He couldn't help it. A woman as beautiful and sexual as her had limited herself to a night here or there with him? It was difficult to believe, though he despised the idea of her fucking anyone else except him. And Kienan. That didn't bother him, and he didn't know why. What a fucked-up mess.

Her chin lifted and she stared down her nose at him. "I'm a busy woman. If I have an itch to scratch, I have a dildo . . . or you."

"Note that I come second on that list," he retorted. Kienan vibrated beside him, but remained silent to let them have their argument. Smart wolf.

"Shut up, Quill," she snapped, her cheeks flushing. "You've fucked other people in the last year, so don't act like the scorned lover now. Until this very nanosecond, you haven't behaved as if you wanted more than a quick shag either. We were convenient to each other, and that was the end of it."

The cold truth took the wind out of Quill's temper. He sighed and reached out to run a knuckle down her silky jaw. There was no good answer he could give her. He didn't have a good answer to give himself. Hell, he didn't have a *bad* answer for either of them. "Do you want me right now?"

"Yes." She glanced away, took a deep breath, and then met his gaze again. "I always want you. I don't know how to stop."

"Why would you want to?"

Instead of answering him, she leaned in and kissed him. There was a bittersweetness to it that he didn't like, but the heat spiraling through him distracted him. She pushed her tongue into his mouth, and his cock went hard in moments, chafing against his fly. He wanted inside her with a fierceness that should have shocked him, but didn't. Thrusting his fingers into her hair, he took over the contact, twining his tongue with hers, nipping at her lower lip.

A moan bubbled out of her and into his mouth. She set her

hand on his shoulder and straddled his lap, the motion breaking their kiss. She leaned over and reached out to drag Kienan forward, sealing her mouth to his while her hips ground down on Quill's cock. Deus, yes. This was exactly how he wanted it. All three of them.

One of his hands cupped her breast, pinched and twisted her tight nipple. His other hand slid down Kienan's torso until he could reach the other man's dick. Both of his lovers moaned, arching into his touch, and he liked that power. It was heady, how they reacted for him. Gea's sex moved on his, and he could feel the heat of her through their clothes, could smell the scent of her desire. She was hot and creamy for him, for Kienan. Hell, he was hot for both of them. He couldn't decide which one he wanted to slide his cock inside first. His hips surged upward at the thought, and Gea's fingers turned into claws on his shoulder.

He sucked in a breath, trying to speak in more than an animalistic growl. "This will be more comfortable in my bed."

Tearing herself out of his arms, Gea stood and jerked her shirt over her head. She dropped it in his lap. "Last one who's naked gets to come last."

He laughed up at her, glanced at Kienan, but the wolf was already on his feet, pulling off his clothes. Quill laughed harder as he stood, reaching back to grab a handful of his shirt and jerk it over his head. The race was on, each of them stripping on their way to the bedroom. Gea giggled, Kienan chuckling as he watched her dive for the bed, her pale body bared.

"Oh, Quill." Gea lay on her side and grinned at him, propping her head on her hand. "Looks like you're waiting for us to come."

He snorted, shaking his head at her, but he couldn't deny she was right. His pants were unsealed but still on. Kienan stood beside the bed nude, his silver gaze burning into Quill. The wolf-shifter's cock was hard, his expression even hotter.

Lust pulsed through Quill with every beat of his heart. He pushed his pants down, shuddering as both his lovers took in the motion, hunger in their gazes as they looked him over.

He nodded to Kienan, flicking his fingers toward the bed. "Stretch out."

The wolf moved to do just that, settling his body against the mattress, stuffing a pillow under his head. "Since you like to be the boss . . . now what?"

Chuckling, Quill scooped Gea up from where she lay and swung her over to straddle the wolf's thighs. "I think you can figure out what comes next."

"I can figure out *who* comes next, and it isn't you." Her brown eyes sparkled when she looked at him, a wicked grin on her lips.

He laughed, and it felt good. He liked being with them. Just eating dinner with them had been good. It didn't mean he needed them or was coming to depend on their presence in his life. He could do without them as easily as he could anyone else, but he was able to admit he enjoyed his time with them. And he was about to enjoy it a great deal more.

Gea lifted herself, and Kienan grasped her hips to bring her down on his cock. Her head fell back on a moan, and the muscles clenched in Kienan's jaw, his fangs bared as he panted for breath. They moved together, slowly, her body rising and falling on the wolf's thick cock. The sight made Quill's dick jerk.

"Are you just going to watch?" Gea rolled her head on her shoulder to look at him, her gaze glinting with humor and passion. "Come join us."

The invitation was more than he could resist, but there was one more thing he needed before he gave in to temptation. He stepped over to open the drawer in the bedside table, pulling a canister of lubricant out. They were going to need this.

He unsealed the container and poured the liquid onto his

fingers. Bending forward, he kissed the nanotat on her back and slipped his hand down between the soft globes of her ass. She sucked in a breath when he pierced her anus, a shudder running through her.

A groan wrenched out of him when the wolf reached out and caught his cock in one hand, rolling a thumb over the crest. Quill hissed, rocking his hips into the other man's touch to the same rhythm he finger-fucked Gea's ass. He had to grit his teeth to hold on to his self-restraint. He'd never had to fight so hard for control in his life. Only with the two of them. Maybe that was part of the fascination, but he was too far gone to care about that now.

Each time Gea sank down on Kienan's cock, she took Quill's slick fingers deep inside of her. He added a third digit, widening her. He wanted inside her ass. Soon. Very soon. He stretched her, adding more lubricant so the slide was all pleasure for her. Her cries grew frantic, her hips moving faster and faster until she froze, her inner muscles rippling in climax.

Kienan's grip on Quill's cock grew painful as Gea came, her pussy milking the wolf's dick. Quill caught the wolf's hand, pulling it away before he lost his tenuous hold on self-discipline. He set a knee on the edge of the bed, pushing Kienan's legs apart so he could kneel between them. Slipping a hand up to Gea's shoulder, he held her in place as he used his other hand to guide his cock to her anus. He pressed the head in, hissing at how good it felt.

And it would only get better.

"Oh, Deus," Gea moaned, arching her back as he filled her.

It was tight, with Kienan still long and hard in her pussy. That only heightened the already intense sensations. The feel of Kienan's cock through the thin layer of flesh that separated them was enough to drive him wild. Both of them at the same time, taking the sexiest woman in the galaxy. He loved it. He couldn't remember anything being this hot before.

Her rear channel flexed around his cock, squeezing him until it was almost painful. The lubricant made the glide nothing short of erotic. Kienan and Quill plunged into her, again and again, and Quill lost himself in the moment. There was nothing in the world except her and Kienan and what they were doing together. He stroked his hands over her shoulders, pulling her ass tight to the base of his shaft with each stroke, loving the sound of her round buttocks slapping against his stomach.

Kienan moved in counterpoint to him, sliding out of her pussy as Quill pushed in to her anus. Every few strokes, they filled Gea together. She screamed at the double penetration, and both men groaned at the tight fit. So good.

"I'm going to come," Kienan gasped. His big body shuddered, and he arched his hips, slamming deep into Gea. Quill entered her a nanosecond later, and that was enough to set her off again. She sobbed on a breath, and he felt the clench and release of her internal muscles.

Quill hissed, the leopard breaking free as he threw his head back and a feline shriek ripped from his throat. Orgasm crashed over him, dragged him under as he pumped his come into Gea. His fingers had turned to claws on her shoulders, holding her in place. His muscles shook when it was over, a climax that drained everything from him. The best of his life. A tired chuckle rolled out and he dropped his forehead between her shoulder blades, trying to catch his breath. He brushed a kiss over the hummingbird zooming wildly around on her back as it did when she was excited, her heart racing.

Kienan shifted a bit beneath them, so Quill pulled Gea to the side, rolling them onto the wide mattress. They lay there for long moments that were . . . sweet. Peace wound through Quill, insidious and weakening. He closed his eyes for a moment, shaking his head.

With a groan, Gea wriggled out from between them, crawling over Quill. She heaved herself to her feet, wavering as she stood. No. Not again. She couldn't walk away like this on him—on them—again.

He reached out and caught her hand.

"Stay the night. Don't leave." It was the neediest utterance that had ever come out of his mouth. He released his hold, clamped his jaw shut, turning his face away from her. Kienan was there, the wolf's gaze as steady as ever. There was understanding in that silver gaze, sympathy. Some enormous, snaking emotion that Quill refused to name filled his chest. He swallowed, closed his eyes again, and blocked them both out.

His heart squeezed when he felt the bed dip and Gea's slim body settle beside him. She threw her leg over his and set her hand on his stomach. None of them said a word to acknowledge the huge shift in their relationship with those simple actions. Kienan rolled onto his side, wrapping his arm around Quill's chest and twining his fingers with Gea's.

Nothing had ever felt this good, this right in Quill's entire life. The thought should scare the shit out of him, but he was too content, too exhausted to pay heed to the warning alarm going off in his head. Unconsciousness rolled over him in a wave, dragging him into dreams that were filled with Gea and Kienan.

They'd spent the night screwing like minks in heat. By some unspoken understanding, Quill and Kienan had kept Gea between them, made sure she couldn't escape them while they buried their cocks inside her every possible way there was. Quill's muscles sang with the strain, but it was a good kind of pain. One he wouldn't mind having more of, and more often. A grin curved his lips, but it was ruined when he yawned.

"I need to shower." Gea sighed. "Really, really need to shower."

After everything they'd done the night before, he didn't

doubt it. That brought his grin back. He watched the hummingbird nanotat flutter around on her shoulder as she dragged herself to her feet. She stretched her arms over her head, bowing her body hard enough to raise her to her tiptoes.

Kienan issued a low growl at the sight, and Quill couldn't help but agree with the sentiment. Deus, all that bare, silky skin was lovely.

"Shall we join you?" He arched an eyebrow in question.

Her laugh was breathy, nearly smothered by a yawn. "No, I actually want to make it out of there while I can still walk upright."

Both men chuckled, and Quill reached out an arm to swat her ass as she turned for the wash closet. She squeaked and stumbled forward, looking back to stick her tongue out at him. She had to walk around to Kienan's side of the bed to get to the wash closet, and she shut the door on Quill's laughter. A moment later, he heard the spray of water.

Kienan turned on his side, propping his jaw in his hand. "Do you have plans for the day?"

With most people, Quill wouldn't answer the question. His business was no one else's. With Kienan, he didn't hesitate. "I always have plans. Nothing urgent this morning, but I have a meeting later with a start-up firm I might want to invest in. Underwater salvage. They've been finding a few interesting pre-war relics."

"Huh." Kienan's mouth compressed into a line as he considered that. "If there's money to be made, I'm sure you'll find it."

"There's money to be made." Quill nodded, but his interest wasn't really on the topic. "Think we can talk Gea into one more round before she goes?"

A chuckle rumbled in the wolf's broad chest. "You're the one who specializes in talking people into giving you what you want. I'm in if the two of you are. And that's a standing offer."

That same hot, sweet emotion expanded in Quill chest, but

he squelched it. His eyebrows arched and he let a wicked grin form on his lips. "The three of us have the combustibility of a biobomb."

Nodding, Kienan leaned in to lick Quill's nipple. "Two of us do just fine together, but all three? Explosive."

Quill shuddered at the feel of the wolf's fangs scraping at his nipple. He watched over Kienan's shoulder as Gea appeared in the doorway of the wash closet. She flashed a sassy grin at him, propping herself against the door frame with her hand on her hip.

"Yes, she really is the perfect third for us. It all just fits together." In every erotic way. Quill grinned, desire twining with the contentment humming through him.

Kienan flicked his tongue against the tight nipple, making Quill jerk. "It was meant to be."

"*Yesss,*" he hissed. But his smile faded as he watched the blood drain out of Gea's face, leaving her creamy skin ashen. He sat up, pulling away from Kienan's lips. In the year he'd known her, he'd never seen such a haunted, agonized look on her face.

"Kienan, you *told* him?" Her voice was a mere ragged rasp of air.

The wolf twisted on the mattress until he too faced her. Quill shifted so he could see both their expressions. His skin prickled, his gut clenching as he sensed something was very, very wrong. His mind scrambled to understand what, but he had no idea.

"Told me what?" The two of them went silent, and unease slid down his spine. "Told. Me. *What?* Someone had better start talking."

Cold sweat gathered on his forehead, and he felt a tremor run down his limbs. His gaze met Gea's and he saw the usual shadows dancing in her eyes. Secrets. Lies. This was it, the mystery was about to unravel, and somehow he knew it would be far worse than he'd ever imagined. He tried to brace himself as he looked to Kienan.

"Tell me."

"No!" Gea burst out, but Quill didn't look at her. Couldn't. He focused on Kienan.

"We're mates."

The words were flat, with no intonation to give them any meaning, and it took Quill a moment to process what the wolf had said. He shook his head. "The two of you are mates?"

Somehow that thought made the ground shake beneath his feet. It felt as if his world were crumbling. If the two of them mated, that would be it. He'd be cut out. Done. Dismissed from their happy lives. He thought he might need to vomit.

But Kienan shook his head, his gaze going from Gea to Quill and back again, as if he weren't sure which way to turn, and that uncertainty was so unlike the steady wolf that it made the situation even more unreal. "No, not just the two of us. The *three* of us. You, me, and her."

The universe spun around Quill, shaken and tossed about like pieces on one of Lorelei's gaming tables.

"Wh-what?" He looked to Gea, saw her face grow even paler, watched resignation fill her eyes, and her shoulders slumped as if something broke inside of her. "This is why you never let me know you. This is what you've been keeping from me."

Her chin tilted up. "Yes."

"You've known all along, sensed it all along?" He jerked to his feet, unable to take this lying down like some helpless fool.

She wrapped her arms protectively around her waist. "Yes."

"You too?" He looked down at Kienan, who remained where he was. Quill couldn't help the horrible disbelief that crept into his voice, the echo of pain. "Since we met?"

"I knew the moment we shook hands. We touched and *bam.* I knew." The wolf's chin dipped in a sharp nod, but he didn't meet either Gea's or Quill's gazes. "Yes."

It felt as if deadly claws were ripping him open. He'd been a fool. Lied to, jerked around, played like a puppet in some game of theirs. They'd held all the cards, and he'd been the pathetic idiot who just wanted them near. His voice went cold, as cold as he felt inside. "And neither of you felt the need to let me in on this little secret?"

"We just did," Gea said, her tone almost pleading.

"Not because you wanted to!" Red swam before his vision, and he had to reach for that icy numbness, for a modicum of his usual control. He wanted to hit them both, to hurt them the way he hurt. "I had a right to know. I'm not some child or jade you can toss aside when you're done playing with me."

"I know." Tears glutted her eyes, and any other day but today that would have moved him to bring the world to its knees for her. "I'm sorry."

Kienan sat forward, his normal lupine grace turning to rough movements. "She had her reasons, Quill, if you'll calm down and listen."

But he didn't want to listen. He didn't want to hear any more. He went to the clothing refresher built into the wall of his bedroom, pain stabbing into him when he saw their clothes hanging beside his. They'd put them in there to cleanse overnight, but he wrenched out one of his suits and jerked it on, stuffing his feet into prime kleather shoes. It felt familiar, this microsilk and wool uniform that meant power when he wore it in a boardroom. He was never supposed to feel like that helpless child he'd once been, but that was what his *mates* had reduced him to, and he hated them for it. Anger at them and self-loathing squeezed like a giant fist inside him until he wanted to scream.

"Don't do this, Quill." Kienan came around to stand in front of him, blocking his exit. "Don't walk away from something this good."

Quill's laugh was an ugly, horrible sound. "This isn't good for me."

"Look, I don't believe in much." The wolf-shifter's smile was a bitter twist of his lips. "Hell, a week ago, I would have said I didn't believe in anything. With the things I've seen? With the things I've *done* in the name of honor and country? But I believe in this. I believe in us."

"Why, because we're *mates?*" Quill sneered the word as if it were a foul curse. It felt like one. Deus help him, it felt like one.

Kienan didn't so much as flinch. "Yes. Because we're mates. Because not everyone *gets* a mate. Because this is a fucking gift that I refuse to squander. In my entire life, I've never wanted anything as much as I want this. You can kick us out now, but you won't be able to stay away. You won't be able to resist this any more than we can."

The ice inside of Quill began to solidify, to give him some cold distance between him and his devastating pain. "Watch me."

"You think I was a tenacious son of a bitch for the government? You haven't seen anything yet." Kienan shot back. "I don't give up that easily. I'm going to haunt you."

Quill cocked an eyebrow, his voice disinterested. "So you're threatening to stalk me?"

"I won't need to. You won't be able to get this out of your head. You're going to be thinking about it all the time, and if I do happen to drop into your life every now and then, just as a physical reminder, it's going to stay there in the back of your mind." Kienan's words rang with desperation, and Quill could smell the cold sweat on the other man's body. "You could have a mate. Two of them. If you weren't so determined to be in control every fucking nanosecond of every fucking day. When you finally get your head out of your feline ass, I'll be here. Waiting."

"Two mates." He glanced at the silent, pale woman who stood in his wash closet doorway, so still she could have been a statue. "Is that what you think, Gea? That mates are a gift?"

She dragged in a breath, a tear sliding down one cheek. "No."

Kienan snorted. "Of course. When the *two* of you get your heads out of your respective asses, come find me."

"You're going to be waiting the rest of your life." Quill couldn't stand around and watch them leave. He refused to be the one abandoned. Not again. He decided when this ended, and it ended now. Stepping around the wolf, he all but dared him to try and stop him. The wolf shook his head but didn't move. Quill stalked out the door.

"Then that's how long I'll wait. I'm a patient man." The wolf's gaze bored into Quill's back as he left. "I'm sure I'll find ways to keep myself occupied in the meantime."

"Occupy yourself somewhere else." Quill boarded his private lift, turning to look at them as the door closed behind him. Both of them stood in his bedroom doorway, watching him. "I expect both of you out of here within twenty minutes or I'm sending security to throw you out. I'm done with you."

A week had ground by with no contact from either of his mates.

Kienan stared out the window of his new flat and tried not to think about Gea or Quill. It was an exercise in futility. Pierce and his two mates had assured Kienan he was welcome to remain at Tail as long as he liked, but as much as he'd once wanted *any* connection, it was a knife to the heart to see how content the three of them were. He had to sort out his own life, figure out what he wanted to do with himself. A few discreet inquiries had come in from local branches of federal and city law enforcement agencies, but he hadn't accepted meetings with any of them. Not yet.

He should, he knew. Finding his footing professionally might help him feel less in limbo, but he couldn't help but think he'd be exchanging one master for another. He'd be living the same life, just answering to someone else.

It was far too tempting, to slip back into the familiar darkness. Let it consume him, rip whatever was left of his soul away. He could focus on the mission and put the last couple of weeks behind him, sever the tender connections that now felt like hot brands set to his skin. Maybe if he did that, this pain would stop eating him alive.

But he couldn't.

Even with the agony of it, he couldn't walk away yet. He didn't know *what* he wanted to do with the rest of his life yet, but falling back into his old life wasn't it. He'd had reasons for leaving, even if it felt like those reasons were evaporating. His finances were healthy enough that he could take his time deciding what to do next. It was what came from drawing a paycheck while having no home or living expenses for several decades. Creds went into the bank, and he'd rarely spent any of them. When had he had time to slow down and do so?

Not until now. His new flat was halfway between downtown and the Vermilion. Halfway between his mates, but not really with either of them. It was a perfect metaphor for where he was in life.

"This is nice." Lorelei strode out of the kitchen and around the main space, and Kienan turned to watch her. "Not large, but clean, and without any of the vermin issues we have in my part of town."

"She means the human vermin," Nolan, the third in his cousin's triad mating, quipped from where he stood by another of the windows.

He was without a doubt the most gorgeous man Kienan had ever seen. But Kienan couldn't muster an ounce of sexual interest. Probably for the best, considering he was mated to Pierce. Something about Nolan's nanotats and wicked, knowing smile reminded Kienan too much of Quill. It hurt to look at him.

Nolan's dark gaze roamed the flat. "Good escape routes, but easily defensible, if needed. Good choice."

Of course a government assassin would look at it from a security standpoint. Then again, so had Kienan when he'd gone searching for somewhere to live.

Pierce walked over and clapped a hand on Kienan's shoulder, something that might almost have been called sympathy flashing across the older man's face. "They'll come around."

It didn't surprise Kienan that his cousin knew what was going on. Maybe it should have, but it didn't.

"Come have dinner with us later this week. You can meet my younger sister and her husband." Lorelei flashed her lovely smile, still the most beautiful female ever born, but she wasn't half as attractive to Kienan as Gea. No woman ever would be.

"I will. Thanks." He tried to smile back and knew it looked more like a grimace, but he leaned forward so she could hug him. The men shook hands and then they were gone, leaving Kienan alone to lick his wounds in solitude. He could only be grateful for the courtesy.

He glanced around at the empty flat and knew it would never be home. Nowhere he'd been in all the many years he'd roamed had ever been home. His insides twisted as the truth of his situation sank its claws even deeper. Home was wherever his mates were. Home was Quill and Gea.

They were the connection he'd been lacking for so long, what he'd been unconsciously seeking when he arrived. He'd come to New Chicago for no logical reason other than a long-lost and barely remembered cousin, and within hours he'd had both his mates in his bed. It wasn't a coincidence. His instincts had led him to this.

His mates made him feel alive as nothing else ever had or would. He understood with painful clarity that he could never go back to his old life, no matter how tempting it might seem. He wasn't the man he'd been before he met them. There was no locking himself down with them, no withdrawing. With them, he *felt*. Everything. He was connected to other people in a way he'd never known he could be. It was terrifying, but he couldn't back away, couldn't divorce himself from this. They were his mates. They were his. And he was theirs. It was done. Game over.

He loved them with every fiber of his blackened, battered, lonely soul.

He couldn't give them up. He'd allow them a few weeks to cool off and think, but he wasn't going to walk away from this. He couldn't. It was easy to resist something that wasn't right in your face. Out of sight, out of mind. But if he were standing in front of them, he doubted they'd be able to restrain themselves. That was how it was supposed to be with mates. Better sex, better relationships. *If* you worked on it. And running away and denying it wasn't working on it, which was what his mates were currently doing.

Letting out a breath, he tried to ignore the emptiness inside him that seemed to grow by the nanosecond. It felt as if he had a slow-leaking, mortal wound where his heart used to be.

Deus, it fucking hurt.

7

Gea ached, inside and out. Thank Deus for the investigation. It gave her something to focus on besides the pain that threatened to consume her. It gave her life some purpose, forced her to drag her ass out of bed when all she wanted to do was sleep until it all just went away.

She really was as pitiable as her mother.

Shaking her head, she skirted both Quill's and Kienan's places on her way into the Vermilion. She knew Kienan had moved, but she still had to pass him to get where she needed to go. She could smell them, and it was the hardest thing she'd ever done to stay away from getting her fix.

They'd done the right thing walking away from each other, saved them all from a great deal of suffering. The words rang hollowly in her mind, mocking her. As if she weren't suffering now. But it would get better. It *had* to get better. Just put one foot in front of the other, and eventually she'd feel normal again.

Tightening the strap on her pack, she wove through the narrow streets, keeping a wary eye on those who watched her, but trying not to draw attention to herself. She'd gotten a call from Meier an hour before, saying he had information for her, for a price. And he'd only deliver it in person.

It was worth the trip to see if he had anything useful, and it got her out of her flat, where she'd spent far more time than she'd want to admit staring at the walls and remembering the feel of her mates' hands upon her, the way they laughed when they were together, the way they made her feel so damn good. The contrast to her current misery just made her want to crawl out of her own skin to escape herself.

So she'd grabbed her bag and run from her office as if the fires of hell were licking at her heels.

The wind ripped through her hair, the city earning its nickname this evening. Dark had settled around her, and only her enhanced fox sight kept the world in focus. Bits of trash swirled around the streets in little tornadoes, and she glanced around to get her bearings. She was close to where Meier had wanted to meet, deep in the district. He was nearby, she could smell him, though the wind made it difficult to pinpoint where.

A block later, his hulking form separated itself from the shadows. He nodded to her but didn't bother with pleasantries. "I know where Tam is."

"Oh, really?" She searched his face, looking for lies, but she sensed no dishonesty. He knew where Tam was, or truly believed he did. "Where?"

"Not far." The German smiled, and it wasn't a pleasant sight. Deus hadn't done this man any favors in the looks department. "There's a finder's fee, of course."

"Of course." She handed over a chip with enough creds to make anyone happy. She should be excited, elated that there might be a break in this case, but she didn't give a shit. Probably not the best frame of mind to be in, but she doubted her clients would care if she was in a fragile emotional state. They

wanted results, not excuses. Especially Constantine Breckenridge. The man didn't suffer fools.

"Let us go." Meier rolled his shoulders in a way that reminded her of the bear-shifter he was. Lumbering, but still dangerous. She motioned him ahead of her and stayed a step
behind him, ostensibly so she could follow him, but mostly so
she could keep an eye on him. He hadn't done anything wrong
so far, but she still didn't trust him.

For a moment, she wished she had Kienan there to watch
her back again. It had been easier to deal with the big bear when
she had her mate nearby. Quill had proved he could hold his
own in a fight, too, but her heart seized as she remembered the
look on his face when he'd found out the truth, when her worst
nightmare had come to pass and he'd walked away from her.
His parting words had rung in her mind for days: *I'm done
with you.* Even now, her stomach heaved at the thought.

Meier stopped abruptly, and she was so distracted she stumbled, trying not to careen into his back. He twisted around and
caught her arm, jerking her upright.

"Thanks," she said, but when she tried to pull away, he
tightened his grip.

He wasn't looking at her, so she followed his gaze and met
the coldest eyes she'd ever seen. Fuck. She'd let herself be preoccupied by her mating woes and she'd missed the oncoming
danger.

Too late. Far too late.

She froze, prey before a far deadlier predator than she would
ever be. Suppressing all fear that might show on her face, she
gave Meier's beefy hand a pointed stare. "You can let me go
now."

He grunted and pushed her toward the other man. "Got
your girl for you. There's a finder's fee."

"Of course." The man smiled pleasantly, his English accent
crisp. "Why don't you come with me, Ms. Crevan?"

Tilting her head as if she were actually considering it, she pursed her lips. "Why would I want to do that, exactly? I don't know you."

"My name is Stefan." His eyes were like shards of ice, but his smile remained benevolent. It sent a chill down her spine. "You've been looking for Felicia, is that right?"

She nodded, curling her hands into fists and hoping he didn't smell the cold sweat that coated her palms. "I have, yes. Do you know where she is?"

"She's here." He waved a hand into the house. Despite being in the Vermilion, it looked tidy. The porch didn't sag; there were no rotting boards or rusty nails that threatened to pierce feet. That in itself was unusual. Everything about this was off, and would have made her hackles rise had she been in fox form. But for the first time since she'd taken this case, she could smell the other woman. Her heart rate bumped up. Breck had given her a few items that had belonged to Tam so Gea could get the cheetah-shifter's scent. And coming out of that house was Tam's very distinct essence.

Whether or not she was alive was another thing. A fresh dead body didn't smell much different from a live one, depending on how the killing was done.

"May I speak to her?"

"Of course." Stefan gestured inside, but his gaze flickered to something behind her. Two armed men closed in, and the disquiet that hummed along Gea's senses intensified. It was like ants crawling over her skin. Fire ants that bit and stung.

Tam might be inside, but Gea had little doubt that the cheetah was as unwilling as Gea to be anywhere near this cold-blooded predator.

There was a sadistic glint in Stefan's chill gaze as his guards urged her past him, and she knew he'd enjoy killing her. He'd probably play with his prey first. Rape, torture, both. Bile burned at the back of her throat, her stomach turning. She didn't want this man's hands on her, or any other man's except Quill's or Kienan's. Her heart cinched tight, and she wished for one last moment with her mates, one last chance to tell them the truth about how she felt.

But this was the Vermilion, and it wasn't a place where wishes were even possible. Only cold, harsh reality existed here.

She lifted her chin and stepped forward, hoping she'd find a way out of this mess she'd let herself be led into like a lamb to slaughter. More than anything, she wished she had one of her mates at her back. Or both of them. But she was alone, the way she'd decided she should be, and that was how she had to face this. She'd made her choices, and now she got to deal with them.

Alone.

Quill's eyes were gritty with exhaustion, and he'd worked himself into the ground every day, all day. Most of the night, too. Even then, he was lucky if he got a few hours of sleep before his demons began haunting him. He set his elbows on his desk, dropped his face into his hands, and rubbed the heels of his palms over burning eyes.

"Deus."

Would there ever be a time when he closed his eyes and *didn't* see the looks on his mates' faces when he stormed away from them? It was difficult to hold on to his rage when night settled around him and he was alone. He could go out. There were any number of parties he could attend, from the posh to the prurient. A snap of his fingers and he could fill his bed with any man or woman he wanted. Several of each, if that was what he felt like.

He didn't.

That was the damnable problem, wasn't it? He didn't want anyone but his mates. Deus, *mates*. The concept still boggled his mind. He was a leopard. His species couldn't sense mates, so he'd never even considered it as an option. A person fated just for him. A perfect match. And he had two of them.

The thought made his gut clench. Most people would be happy at the idea, overjoyed even, but not him. Especially when he considered who his mates were. Those two wouldn't allow him to have power over them. They wouldn't do what he said, when he said it. They *might* talk to him before doing whatever the hell they wanted.

He couldn't control them.

He wasn't even sure he wanted to. Deus, he'd lost his mind. He'd spent his entire life arranging things to suit himself, so that he never had to worry about anything being outside his command, and here he was thinking he'd found something he didn't want to control. He blew a breath out through his nose. Better that he'd walked away than spend his life wallowing in that kind of lunacy.

A ping sounded from his palmtop and he jerked. Scrambling to pick it up, he was almost grateful for something else to think about. His thoughts had been chasing themselves in the same circles for days.

Janus's gaunt face appeared on the screen and Quill frowned, but accepted the call. There was no reason he could think of that Janus would be calling now. "North, thought you'd like to know I saw that bit of pretty you were with the other day going into the den of a man named Stefan. Nasty guy. People go in and don't come out again, if you catch my meaning." It was difficult not to, and Quill felt all the blood leech from his face. Janus rubbed his nose, coughed. "She didn't look all that willing to go in. Big, ugly guy took her there, had a hold of her so she couldn't get away. Two other guys with guns made sure she went in."

Quill's expression froze in place, his heart seizing in his

chest. He didn't trust many people, but he trusted their greed. Janus wouldn't bother telling him anything if he wasn't sure it would get him some creds. And Quill didn't pay if information wasn't legitimate. So this was for real.

"When?"

"Few minutes ago, no longer."

Which didn't mean she'd lasted the first few moments after she'd gotten in that door. Nanoseconds counted when dealing with villains in the district. "Thanks."

"Always happy to keep a buyer satisfied." Janus's face was grave, and that made the situation more horrifying.

Quill cleared his throat. "I appreciate that, and you know I'm always generous with my appreciation."

"I do know." The man nodded, gave Quill the address for Stefan's den, and signed off the call.

Quill swallowed hard, his mind scrambling for what to do. He could walk into any establishment in the Vermilion, could claim he had a business proposition for this Stefan, but from there it would be tricky getting both of them out of the place. He needed help, and he cursed himself for admitting the weakness, hated himself for not being able to control all of the situation without begging for handouts. He could use his own security, but Gea wouldn't trust them.

There was only one person he could call.

His heart leapt, and he hated that, too.

Keying in a code on his palmtop, he waited for the other end to pick up. And there he was, those gray eyes haunted. He looked tired, as tired as Quill felt, as if he hadn't slept well since the last time they'd all been together.

"Kienan, I need you."

"You heard about Gea, too?" The screen wobbled as if the wolf were running while he talked. "I'm on my way there now."

Somehow it didn't surprise Quill that Kienan already knew what was going on, already planned to deal with it in his quiet, efficient way. That was just Kienan. He always knew more than he should, always seemed to be one step ahead of Quill. He should hate it, but in this case, he was just grateful. Gea's life was on the line. He could let Kienan handle it, then. He didn't have to involve himself any further. But he couldn't. "I'll meet you there."

He cut the call and bolted up the single flight of stairs to his flat. Changing into clothes that wouldn't get him mugged in the Vermilion, he pulled on a thin nanoarmor vest and grabbed his gun from the safe in his bedroom wall. He was on his way in record time. Even then, he pushed his body to the limits sprinting toward the address Janus had given him, used every ounce of the speed his leopard side granted him.

If he'd thought seeing his mates outnumbered in a fight had pulled at emotions in him he didn't like, it was nothing to this. He was a fool. A fool who'd lied to himself. He couldn't imagine a world without them in it. The very thought made his stomach heave. Never see Gea give him that sly, mischievous grin again. Never have Kienan reach for him in the middle of the night again, with a need that wouldn't quit.

He loved them. Both of them.

It was the most gut-wrenching, horrifying realization of his life. Nothing would ever be the same without them. Something besides his cold, hard logic controlled his actions.

A month ago, it would have been inconceivable. Now, it felt inevitable. They were his mates. Kienan was the sealant that kept them together, the one who believed in nothing except the sanctity of mating. Gea was as wary as he was, but just as unable to resist.

Somehow, he could learn to live with the lack of control over that one part of his life, but he was far less certain he could learn to live without them. The last week apart had been bad enough, but he'd known they were out there, living their lives.

Now he just hoped he wasn't about to lose everything that had become so precious to him in such a short amount of time. Deus, please let her be all right. Please let them all make it out of this alive.

Please.

8

Stefan moved with an elegance that Gea would wager disguised more musculature than he cared for people to know he had. He wanted his thugs to be seen as the threat, but Gea wasn't buying it. Stefan was the real danger.

His thugs patted her down, took her pack away, but didn't harm her. Yet. The promise of violence hung in the air, heavy and noxious as smoke. It coated her tongue, made her muscles tense until they cramped. Her instincts screamed at her to run, to get out of this place and never come back.

She bit back a snarl when Stefan set his hand on her back and urged her down a flight of steps into a basement. "This way, my dear."

Skipping forward a step to get away from his touch, she ignored the mockery in his chuckle. There was a short hallway with several doors opening off of it. "Which one?"

"The second on the right."

The knob turned easily in her hand. Not locked. Was Tam so incapacitated that she couldn't get out, or was she already dead? Gea wasn't sure which was the better option. Neither would help her get out of here unscathed. Her heartbeat rabbited when Stefan slid his fingers down her back, and she stumbled forward, away from him, just as he'd intended.

The door closed behind her with a distinct click. She didn't bother testing to see if it was locked. Instead, she glanced around the room. A small, empty bed. One table, two chairs. In one of them sat a still, slender woman who watched her with dark eyes.

"Tam."

Her chin tipped down in a nod. "And you must be Gea Crevan."

"I am." Stepping closer, Gea looked the cheetah over to see if she was harmed. Didn't look like it, but looks could deceive.

Tam folded her hands on the tabletop, her long fingers graceful. "You need to leave here. Now."

"I will." The sooner, the better. "Come with me."

"I'm afraid I can't do that." A small smile formed on her lips, made her breathtakingly beautiful. No wonder she had a rep for making every man she met fall in love with her. Was Stefan included in that number? He was old enough to be her father, but that meant little. Tam's shoulder dipped in a shrug. "I'm needed here."

Gea sat in the chair opposite the other woman. "My client needs you, too."

"No, he doesn't." Tam snorted, derision in the sound, but the expression in her eyes gave away a flash of pain, longing. "He's just upset his toy ran away. It's best for him that he moves on."

"He's not going to do that." Not with his mate in the hands of a man who scared the piss out of Gea with a single look.

"He will." Now the smile turned sad, resigned. "They all do, in the end."

"You're wrong about this one."

"Leave now, Ms. Crevan." Tam's gaze hardened, flicking for just a moment to one corner of the room. Gea let her hair fall forward into her face, glanced in the same direction, and saw a tiny vidmonitor. This conversation was being watched. How much of what Tam said was the truth and how much was just what she wanted Stefan to hear? "Tell your client to stop looking, stop poking his nose in my business, and stop being a stubborn, birdbrained ass."

The look in Tam's eyes warned her not to argue, and realization sparked in Gea's mind. Tam was trying to get her out of there alive, trying to give Stefan a good reason to let her go. Perhaps that had been his aim all along, but Gea doubted it. Letting her see Tam felt like a game he was playing with her, a cat taunting his prey before he pounced. Gea folded her hands, mirroring Tam's pose. She needed to start giving the other woman what she wanted, but not too easily. "I'll tell him. He won't listen, though."

Her chin jerked to the side in a dismissive gesture. "Fool."

"Maybe, but he's a fool who loves you." That much was true, and Gea thought the other woman deserved to know. In her place, she'd want someone to tell her that about her mates. But she'd thrown them away, hadn't she? She'd been too gutless to even try to claim them. As much as she'd pitied her mother, at least she'd had the courage to reach out and take what she wanted. She should have demanded more, *all* of her mate, but she hadn't run from love. Gea had.

Shame washed through her, and she hated herself for having discarded two good men out of fear. Her mother had been too scared that she'd get nothing if she demanded more, and Gea had been too scared of depending on men like her father. But her mates had both thrown themselves into danger for her before—something her father would never have done for anyone—and she'd rejected them anyway. She drew in a deep breath, wiping her clammy palms on her pant legs. There'd be no rectifying her mating situation if she didn't get out of the Stefan situation.

One thing at a time.

Tam laid her hands flat on the table, recapturing Gea's attention. "He's a fool if he loves me."

The lady protested a little too much, Gea thought. She narrowed her gaze. "You love him back."

Tam didn't bother denying it. "And that makes me an even bigger fool."

"Don't run. Trust me, it won't save you from love." Deus, didn't she know that? Didn't she burn with it every nanosecond of every damn day?

Tam's laugh was a painful, heartbreaking rasp of air. "Nothing can save me now. It's far too late for me."

"You're wrong." But Gea studied the other woman's face, the coldly determined resignation in her eyes. "Stefan has something on you, doesn't he? That's why you're here. That's why you don't want to be followed."

"Of course." Tam inclined her head, her long, inky hair falling around her shoulders.

"He's going to kill you," Gea said flatly. She wanted to get out of there alive, but she needed to be certain Tam knew what would happen when she left. Nothing had ever indicated Tam wasn't the kind of woman who always knew the score, but desperation could blind a person.

"Or worse, make me do something that will get me locked in jail for the rest of my life. He'd probably alert the authorities himself to make certain of it." The cheetah-shifter shrugged, her voice just a little too light. "Yes, I know."

And if Gea didn't walk away from this, and convince Breck to do the same, Stefan was going to kill her, too. If Breck kept coming after Tam, Gea had the feeling her client wasn't going to fare much better than his mate. "What does he have on you?"

Whatever it was had to be powerful to make a woman leave a man who loved her and she loved in return, give up her freedom, and possibly her life.

"He's taken something from me that I would do anything to get back." The cheetah's gaze was clear and steady. "Yes, it really is worth dying for to keep it safe."

"What is it? Is he holding it here?"

She shook her head. "No, it's being held in Europe, and that's all I know right now. Other than that, it's better for all concerned if your client and you put this—put *me*—behind you. Walk away . . . while you still can. Not everyone gets that opportunity." Her gaze was sharp, assessing. "You're in love, I can see it. Heartsick. Don't you want the chance to mend those ties? You won't get it if you don't leave now."

Gea nodded. "All right. I'll tell my client what you've told me, try to get him to back off."

"That's for the best." Tam swallowed and stared down at the table in front of her. "Tell him . . . tell him I'm done with him. I got what I wanted, and he's of no further use to me. Chasing after me like a lovesick puppy just makes him pathetic. It's over between us. Tell him I said that."

Done with him. The echo of Quill's words sent pain shafting through Gea. She almost doubled over and groaned with the piercing agony, barely managing to keep herself upright. Her voice came out choked and stifled. "I'll make sure he gets the message."

"Thank you." A single tear slid down Tam's cheek, the one farthest from the vidmonitor, so Stefan wouldn't see it, but Gea did. She reached over and squeezed Tam's hand, a silent message of support and sympathy. There was nothing more that she could do to help than make sure Breck understood the kind of danger his mate was in. She'd let him know Tam didn't want him following her, but she already knew he wouldn't listen.

In his place, if her mates were in peril, she wouldn't listen either.

"Good luck." Pushing to her feet, Gea walked away from Tam with a quiet prayer that the cheetah came through this all right.

Now, if she could only get herself through this in one piece, she might be in business. She opened the door but wasn't surprised when one of Stefan's goons was there. She nodded to him and turned for the stairs as if she wasn't at all intimidated by the gun he had pointed at her. "I assume your boss would like to speak with me before I leave."

If they let her leave. She didn't mention that part, just offered up a bright smile and walked by. He didn't stop her, and she let a breath ease out of her lungs as she took the steps two at a time.

"Ah, Ms. Crevan. I take it your chat with Felicia went well?" Stefan stepped through a doorway, his other guard close behind, meeting her in the house's main space. She could see the front door, could almost taste freedom, which was no doubt why Stefan had allowed her to come back up from the basement. Another game he was playing with her.

She smiled at him, just to throw him off a little. "It went really well, actually. It was kind of you to arrange our visit. I can let my client know she's fine and doesn't want to see him again."

Closing the space between them, Stefan examined her face with those icy eyes of his. His henchmen arranged themselves around her. Surrounded. Trapped. The fox in her bristled. She swallowed, raised her chin, and fixed her smile in place as Stefan spoke.

"I will be very . . . displeased if your client keeps sending people looking for her. What I have in mind requires discretion. It's difficult to be discreet when being hounded by little investigators." He ran a finger down her jaw, the tip suddenly curling into a talon that threatened to pierce her jugular.

"I understand."

"Do you?" His sweet breath brushed her skin as he leaned too close for her comfort. "You seem a stubborn woman. Perhaps you need a taste of what displeasing me would entail, so you know just how serious I am."

One of the goons chuckled, and it wasn't a nice sound. It was pure evil. Stefan certainly recruited like-minded men. Men who wanted to hurt, who enjoyed it. Fuck.

She arched her eyebrows, letting her incredulity show instead of her terror. "My client isn't an idiot. Do you think he'll believe anything I say about Tam being safe and willing to go with you if I show up injured in any way? The only way you're going to get exactly what you want from him *and me* is if I walk out of here untouched."

The argument was working. He was starting to relent, she could see it in his eyes. Her heart leaped, but she let no excitement cross her expression. She might just get to walk out of here. She'd get her second chance with Kienan and Quill.

Thank Deus.

As if her thought had conjured him, she saw a flash of Kienan's face through one of the windows. He met her gaze, nodded once he knew she'd seen him, and then disappeared again. Her heart seized, her mind scrambling for what to do next, how to make the best of the situation.

Kienan caught Quill's scent before he saw him. It was heady, the battle fever mixing with the punch of lust that had become familiar in so short a time. His pulse sped, and he clenched his fists, letting his claws score his palms to ground him back in reality. Gea was in danger. One of his old contacts had been watching this Stefan for a while. They knew he was up to his eyeballs in shit but hadn't caught him in the act. Yet.

Of course, Kienan's old contacts had also been watching Kienan to see what he'd do next. It wasn't often someone like him dropped out of that world, and none of them was certain what to make of it. Most would expect him to take one of the offers with another law enforcement agency. It had been pretty obvious his contact had gotten in touch with him in an attempt to sway him in that agency's direction.

The motive didn't matter here. That he'd gotten to Gea while she was still breathing was what was important. He'd done some quick recon of the place, made sure she'd seen him through a window, and counted three men on the main level. All armed. All carried themselves in a way that said they knew how to use the weapons they carried. The smallest one was obviously in charge.

Kienan wasn't sure if there were others inside or how many, but he hadn't found any security systems in place. Looked like they were relying on firepower. Hopefully, that worked to Kienan's advantage. He'd guess this was a temporary den for them, which could also be an advantage for him.

Quill whipped around the corner of the street, moving so fast he was almost a blur. Kienan stepped out of the shadow of the building beside Stefan's house. "Quilliam."

Deus, it was good to see him, even under such thoroughly fucked circumstances. The leopard-shifter's tanned skin was flushed and he was sweating despite the chill wind that blew off Lake Michigan. Kienan quickly explained the situation to him while he caught his breath.

The leopard's expression turned grim. "What's our next move?"

"How good are you at breaking and entering?" Kienan countered. That the other man was here said a lot, made Kienan's chest go tight with emotion that he had to ruthlessly suppress. Focus on the job, on getting Gea to safety, then deal with emotion. Now wasn't the time.

A wicked grin formed on Quill's face. "I've never been caught yet, does that answer the question?"

Kienan snorted. "Fine. The three of them have weapons, though only two of them have drawn them. They're pointed at her, so let's not give anyone time to get twitchy."

"Agreed."

"There's a door in the back with a lock that looks pretty flimsy. I'll take that, come up behind their leader." He gestured to the window closest to them. "That opens into a small office that will put you between them and the front door."

"Pincher them in. Got it. Let's do it." Quill reached out and squeezed Kienan's shoulder. "When this is over, we need to talk."

He just nodded, not sure if wanting to talk was a good thing or a bad thing. He pushed it out of his mind. Something else to deal with later. Spinning away, he slipped around the building and checked again for vidmonitors. Just one, which he'd already disabled. No wires or traps around the door, but on closer inspection, the hinges looked rusted shut. Shit. No one had used this door in years.

Rising voices sounded from inside, and he didn't have time to wait. Panic gripped his gut, and he swung toward the window beside the door. It fed into the kitchen but was so small it would be one hell of a tight squeeze. Good enough.

Using his lock-picking kit, he finessed the old latch on the window, easing it up with only a single squeak. Grabbing the sides of the frame, he hoisted himself in feetfirst, wriggling like a hooked fish to get through. If one of the two guards came looking, he was fucked.

They didn't. He landed on the cracked tile floor silently, then crept forward to the doorway off a short hall. He could hear them speaking, Gea talking fast. She sounded controlled, not panicked or terrified. Good.

A loud creak came from the front of the house. Quill must

have stepped on a loose floorboard. All conversation stopped. A cold voice said, "Check it out."

Kienan winced, a bead of sweat sliding down his temple. Deus, when was the last time a job had made him break out in a cold sweat? Then again, when had his mates been involved? He peeked out the doorway, saw a guard walking into the room he knew Quill was in. That separated one from the group. Not bad.

"Who do you have with you, Ms. Crevan?" that same chilly voice asked.

"No one, unless Meier decided to become a hero." Her tone said how likely she thought that was. "Have you made any enemies lately who might be stopping in for a visit?"

No one bothered to answer that question.

A short scuffle sounded from the room Quill was in, a shout, a gunshot, then the kind of sudden silence that raised the hairs on the back of Kienan's neck. He clenched his jaw and stepped out into the open, coming up behind the second guard. A quick jab of his fingers and the man's arm was useless, his gun clattering to the floor.

The man was shorter than Kienan, making it easier to reach around and wrap a hand around his throat. He squeezed just enough so the man froze, knowing that death could come for him at any moment. Kienan's heart thundered in his ears, drowning out any sound that might be coming from Quill. He strained to hear, needed to know what was happening with his other mate. Deus help him if that shot had claimed Quill's life.

Icy fear spread through him, and he tightened his grip, making the guard he held gurgle. If his partner had killed Quill, Kienan would rip this henchman's throat out without a second thought or a single regret. Gea's brown eyes were wide and a little wild as they bounced from him to the doorway of Quill's room.

Stefan smoothly drew his weapon, grabbing for Gea, but she

scrambled back out of his reach. He leveled the weapon at her head. "Now, gentlemen, really. Are these heroics necessary?"

"We thought so, yes." Quill stepped out of the room, his weapon leading the way. The leopard-shifter had blood on his face, but it wasn't his. His gun was steady as he aimed it at Stefan.

Impasse.

Thick tension filled the main space, humming like static along Kienan's nerves. His gaze shot around the room. Two windows, sealed but breakable. The front door was the easiest escape route, and they needed out of here. Now. He began to crabwalk the guard in that direction.

"Keep moving and she dies," Stefan bit out.

"Hurt her and you die." Quill held out his free hand for Gea, who took it. "We outnumber you, and I'm betting your life is more important to you than hers."

Rage mottled Stefan's face, his jaw twitching. Kienan saw his finger tighten on the trigger, and he positioned himself to dive for the other man, his muscles coiling to spring. He might die in the process, but he *would not* fail to protect his mates.

Gea pitched her voice low. "Remember that you have a message you want me to deliver. Hurt any of us and I guarantee it won't get to my client."

That trigger finger eased just slightly, but Kienan stayed ready.

"We're going to leave with our woman, nice and slow." Quill shoved Gea behind him, the two of them backing toward the front door. "Your other man's got a nasty hole in him, but he'll live if you get him to a medic soon. You have enough to deal with, so you're not going to bother coming after us."

Stefan growled at him but didn't bother denying it. "Leave now."

Kienan waited until his mates were safely out, then dragged the henchman over to the door, using him as a human shield.

Stefan took a step forward and Kienan met his gaze, shaking his head slowly. "You don't want to play that game with us, Stefan. I will kill you if you come after any of us, if I ever even see your face again, I promise you that."

Perhaps it was the bald honesty in his voice; perhaps it was that Stefan knew a killer when he saw one, but he nodded slowly. Kienan shoved the guard forward so he stumbled into his boss. Kienan used the resulting confusion to disappear out the door and join his mates down the street, motioning for them to keep running.

Turning back as they reached the corner, Gea pushed her wind-whipped hair out of her face so she could see. "They'll be gone before the police or brigade could get here."

"Yeah." Kienan caught her arm, drew her farther from the place. Shadows moved in the windows, and he didn't want to catch their attention. Let them deal with their own issues. He was still trying to wrap his head around the fact that they were all safe. Luck had been on their side. This time. Adrenaline still pumped through his veins, made his muscles tremble. "The best you can do is tell your client who has Tam and let him decide what to do from there."

She sighed and nodded, allowing herself to be led away. "It'll have to wait until I get home. Stefan took my bag, with my palmtop inside it. And my knife, damn him."

Quill stared at them both with an inscrutable expression. He swallowed, glanced away, then suggested, "You can call him from my place."

Tensing, Kienan waited for Gea's response. So much hung on what she'd do next. Would they take a step forward or another step back?

"Okay." Her hand made a graceful arc in the air. "Lead on, North. It's freezing out here."

Kienan stripped off his kleather jacket and wrapped it around her. Surprise flickered across her face, but her gaze warmed with an expression that made his heart jam into his ribs. She slipped her arm through his, her slim body pressing to his side. He let a breath ease out of his lungs. Hope—pure, sweet, and terrifying—filled him. Deus, please. He could handle anything else, but he didn't think he could stand to have them turn away from him again. Not again.

He loved them too much to lose them now, and he didn't know if he could resist sliding back into that familiar soul-stealing world of shadows and lies to escape the shattering agony of it. Putting one foot in front of the other, he gritted his teeth to ride out the uncertainty that threatened to drive him mad, questions and hope and fear chasing themselves through his mind.

Would this night give him everything he'd never known he wanted . . . or would he lose it all? His heart, his soul, the only connections that kept him tethered to his humanity. Or would he become that killing machine, that government tool he'd been for so long, without a chance to know a life of anything more than serving a cause?

9

And there they were again. All three of them in his flat. Quill hadn't realized how empty it had been without them. Filled with expensive furnishing, but cold and empty without the human warmth of his mates. He ignored the warning in his head that that was a weak thought. He was too fucking glad they were all here and alive to care right now about what made him weak or strong, in control or out of it.

The moment they stepped out of the lift and into his flat, Kienan reached out and wrapped an arm around his neck, hauling him forward. The wolf used his other hand to drag Gea in until they were all tangled in a hug. Quill didn't remember the last time he'd had anyone offer him a simple hug, a gesture of support and comfort, and salty moisture burned his eyes. He cleared his throat, embarrassed, and tried to step back, but his mates wouldn't let him. They each had an arm around him and held on tight. For some reason, that made his eyes sting more. He swallowed, his fist balling in Kienan's shirt while he slid his other hand up to thread through Gea's silky hair.

The scent of them, their nearness, made some tightness relax deep inside him. They were here, they were alive. It was enough. A breath shuddered out of him. "Let's not do that again."

Ragged chuckles broke from Gea and Kienan, and she squeezed them both tighter. "Thanks for coming. I'd pretty much talked Stefan into letting me walk out of there, but... I'm glad you guys showed up."

Her voice was clogged with tears, and that made emotion cinch in Quill's chest. "Anytime."

And he meant it. Deus, what would he have done if anything had happened to her? To either of them? What if he could have done something about it and hadn't? The guilt would have eaten him alive. He was a man who didn't bother with guilt about any of his actions, but this? This would have been more than he could handle. He hated admitting it, even to himself, but there it was.

She stirred against his side, pulling back a little to look up at him. Her beautiful eyes were glassy with unshed moisture. "I am so sorry I lied to you, Quill. I know it's inexcusable. I've been pretty messed up about mates my whole life because my parents' mating was such a joke. A terrible, twisted joke."

"I know." He ran his thumb across her cheek, wiping away the single tear that escaped. "I hired someone to look into you—both of you—this past week. After I found out about the mate thing, I had to know what I was dealing with."

The dossier his investigator had pulled together showed him that they were exactly who he thought they were. He had more details, more specifics, but there was nothing that surprised him. At the time, he hadn't known if that was a blessing or a curse.

And it showed him that he *knew* them. What he'd gathered this week were merely details. But he already knew the fundamental, important parts of them. Gea's fierce independence, her lively curiosity, her stubbornness, her passion. The painful past that had put shadows in her eyes. Kienan's determination, his protectiveness, his willingness to walk away from everything he'd ever known because he knew it was the right thing to do. That took courage. It wasn't easy to cut ties with what was comfortable and step into the unknown. A lot of men wouldn't have had the fortitude. But Kienan did.

What he'd discovered shouldn't have shocked him, but it did. Two people who fit him perfectly, who could understand why he'd done the things he'd done, and not judge him harshly for it or worship the wealth he'd acquired in the process.

"I love you. Both of you." Another tear slipped from the corner of Gea's eye. Her arms tightened around them convulsively. "I promised myself I'd tell you that if I got out of Stefan's alive. So . . . I love you. I'm sorry I pushed you both away and hurt you."

A shudder passed through Kienan. "I love you both, too. I don't care how we make this work out, but I want us to be together. I'm tired of never having people or a place to call mine. I want you both in my life."

"I want that, too." A sob tangled with a laugh as it escaped from Gea's throat.

Pressure built in Quill's chest, a feeling that seared his very soul. He'd never experienced anything like it. He opened his mouth to speak, but nothing came out. For perhaps the first time in his life, he didn't know what to say, what to do. They *loved* him. Deus, it was as horrifying as it was wonderful. "I never expected . . . I . . ."

No, he'd never expected any of this, didn't have a plan in place for how to deal with it. He hadn't anticipated a mate, let alone two. He hadn't imagined they might have the ability to twist him into knots.

Gea rose on tiptoes, brushing her lips over his throat, his jaw, his mouth. "I love you, Quill. I love you, Kienan. I don't know what happens next—I'm scared of what might come next. But I'm here, I'm not going anywhere if you want me, too, and I love you. Believe that, if nothing else."

"I believe it," Kienan said. He curved a hand under Gea's chin and pulled her up for a kiss. Quill could feel the heat of it, and the sight made his cock harden. It had been days since he'd had them. Far too long. Kienan's hand slipped down from Quill's shoulder to curl over his ass. His cock went stiffer than mercurite and he clenched his teeth. He wanted them more than he'd ever wanted anything in his life, more than he'd even wanted to escape the grinding poverty of his youth. Gea's fingers curled around his dick through his pants and he hissed, his fangs erupting from his gum. Damn, how they got to him.

Their kiss broke, and they turned to Quill. Kienan pushed Quill's protective vest off, then yanked his shirt off. Gea fumbled for his fly, unsealing it to reach in and stroke his cock. His hips jerked, lust setting its hooks deep inside him. The tension that had been building up for the last week eased. This he understood, this carnal craving. He pulled at their garments, and it was a race to be naked.

Clothing was discarded, and they left a path of boots, pants, and shirts on their way to the bedroom. Right where he wanted them. A place that had been so barren he couldn't face it for the last week, choosing to get what little sleep he could on the couch instead. Stopping beside the bed, Kienan slammed his mouth over Quill's, and the kiss was wild, exactly what Quill needed. It was lips, fangs, and tongues. He tasted blood, his and Kienan's, and the mingling was far more erotic than it should be. His heart pounded, his cock throbbing with pleasured-pain as their nude bodies rubbed against each other. Gea's breasts pressed to his back, her teeth nipping his shoulder blade. More. He wanted more. Everything. It was terrifying and he couldn't stop it. He didn't even want to. Deus save him.

Kienan broke their kiss, and Gea slid around to his front. She brushed her lips over his before she slipped down to kneel before him, rubbing her tight little nipples against his torso on the way. He groaned, loving the way she stared at his cock, licked her lips, and then offered him a grin that was as wicked as it was tender. It was the tenderness that made his heart stop. He'd never seen such an expression from her, never even imagined it.

"I love you, Quill. *We* love you."

She closed her mouth over his cock and sucked. He groaned, then gritted his teeth when Kienan parted his buttocks, eased lubricant into his anus, and spread his fingers to widen Quill for penetration. Deus, when was the last time he'd allowed himself to be fucked by another man? Years. It had felt too out of control. But now the excitement made his heart hammer in his chest. That it was Kienan made the difference. That Gea was here, watching them, sucking him, made the difference.

"We want you right here between us. For the rest of our lives, if I have my way." The wolf growled, pulling his hand away to replace it with his cock. He eased the head in and Quill groaned, pushing his hips back to take more. Kienan worked his cock deep, his hot breath rushing against Quill's skin as he panted. He realized they were both panting. He'd never been so turned on in his life.

"More." Yes. Please. Closing his eyes, he arched his hips back and forth between them in mindless abandon. His thoughts were scattered incoherency as they sucked and fucked him.

Gea let his cock slide from her mouth, her tongue flicking out to tease the head. "You can't control us, you know."

Choking on a broken groan, he slid his fingers into her hair, flexed them, wanting to force her to take him back into her hot mouth, but knowing she wouldn't let him get away with that. "I know."

"Do you really want to?" Her fingers circled his shaft, squeezed and stroked him. "Is that what love means to you?"

"No." He tightened his hand in her hair, trying to make a

few of his brain cells work while Kienan continued to fuck his ass. "It means being totally out of control. Being at someone else's mercy."

The wolf growled in his ear, then bit the back of his neck. Hard. "Why is that a bad thing, if they love you back, if they're just as much at your mercy?"

He'd . . . never thought of it that way. Love had always been something that weakened him, never something that made him stronger. The idea made his head spin.

But then there was no more thinking, only feeling. Gea took him so deep he felt the back of her throat contract around the head of his cock. Sweat slipped down his temples as he watched his dick slide in and out of her mouth. "Touch yourself, Gea. I want you to come with us."

She peeked up at him, her pupils dilated with passion, but he saw her knees spread and one of her hands moved between her thighs. He had to clench his jaw when her moans vibrated along his shaft. Deus, he could smell how hot she was, how wet.

Kienan sank deeper into Quill's ass, grinding his pelvis upward until a ragged shout burst from Quill's throat. The way the wolf-shifter's broad cock stretched his anus was agony and ecstasy at the same time. The dichotomy had him on the edge of orgasm, so close he could taste it. In and out, the drag of flesh had him groaning, ready to beg for the surcease only they could grant him. The other man reached around and caught Quill's nipples, squeezing them, twisting them. It was too much. Deus, it was far too much for him to take. And he loved it. Gea's mouth on him, her tongue working down the underside of his cock while she rolled his balls between her slim fingers. Kienan fucking his ass with the swift, urgent rhythm that would send him over the edge. Soon.

The sound of Gea's moans increased, and he could hear how slick she was every time she thrust her fingers into her pussy.

Her body undulated before him, her suckling growing harder, faster.

"Come for me, Gea." He groaned. The way she responded, the heat of her passion, making him burn even hotter. As it had always done. Because she was his mate.

Her back bowed and she screamed around his cock as she shattered, just as he'd wanted. Her teeth scraped his dick, and prickles broke down his skin. He shuddered, choked when Kienan shoved into his ass again, thick and hard and so fucking erotic, Quill thought he might die. And go out a happy man.

"Say it, Quilliam. You know you want to. You know you feel it, too. How good this is, how right." Kienan's voice was so guttural it was barely human, and he ground Quill's nipples between his fingers. "Tell me you really want to lose this."

He didn't want to. Deus, no. Quill wanted to hold on to this forever. He was a man who had everything but had never had any*one*. Now he did. Now he had them, if he had the guts to let go of control and hold on to them.

"I love you." He rocked his hips back and felt how his words shredded Kienan. The wolf growled, jutting his cock into Quill's ass as he came. The hot spurt of his fluids was Quill's undoing. The leopard within him clawed for freedom, and he let the animal win, giving in. His fangs slid forward and he hovered right on the edge of shifting, danced on a razor's edge that sharpened the experience. He'd never felt so good in his entire life. "I love you." He gripped Gea's hair, shoved his cock into her mouth and came hard, groaning as she sucked him dry. The orgasm lasted longer than any he'd ever had before, and his body moved between them, his muscles shuddering, his knees threatening to buckle. "Gea, Kienan. Deus, I fucking love you."

A leopard's scream ripped from him, and he threw his head back against Kienan's shoulder. A last pulse of come jetted from Quill, the scent of sex and his mates the most arousing aroma he'd ever smelled. Perfection. Everything was exactly as it should be. Peace unlike any he'd ever known unfurled inside him. A deep sigh slid out of him.

Groaning, Kienan slipped out of him and staggered over to collapse on the bed. Quill offered Gea a hand up and stroked her hair back from her flushed face. He pressed a kiss to her forehead. "Are you all right?"

She nodded, her gaze searching his. "Are you?"

"I love you." It felt good to say, to let it out. "We'll figure the rest out later."

"Good." A lopsided smile formed on her lips. "You forgive me for not telling you we were mates?"

Stooping forward, he swept her into his arms and carried her over to lay her on the mattress beside Kienan. Offering her a wicked grin, Quill bent down to bite the lower curve of her belly. "I can think of ways for you to make it up to me."

He slipped to the mattress beside them, glad his bed was big enough to hold them all. Silence enveloped the room, and Quill figured they were trying to sort through the huge changes that this night had wrought. Life would never be the same again, no matter where they went from here.

Kienan curled an arm under his head, looking at Gea. His brow furrowed for a long time; then he nodded as if he'd made a decision, smiling.

She lifted an eyebrow. "What?"

"You get into too much trouble left to your own devices." The wolf's voice was rusty, but the smile stayed in place.

"I can get myself out of trouble, so don't worry about me." She folded her arms over her chest.

"Too late," the men retorted together. Never in his life would Quill forget the utter terror of racing through the night, praying he got there in time, hoping she wasn't being tortured or raped or murdered. Or all of the above.

Kienan sighed, and there was contentment in the sound.

"I've been thinking a lot about what to do with the rest of my career, and I've figured it out. I think you need a partner. Me, specifically."

Sounded like a good idea to Quill. He knew Gea was a capable, competent investigator, but he wouldn't mind knowing Kienan was working alongside her. And he'd rather that the wolf-shifter not go back to the covert ops that had put so many shadows in his gaze and scars on his body. It might be selfish, but if Quill was going to be mated, he wanted them with him. He wanted to know where they were, not wonder if they were still alive after weeks of no contact while they were on a job. Private investigation might take them out of town for a day or two, but it was nowhere near as deadly as black ops.

A derisive snort came out of the fox-shifter. "You want fifty percent of my business, just like that?"

"I have enough to buy in, and you know I can do the work." Kienan reached out with his free hand and ran a fingertip down her arm. "Or I can start my own PI firm if you're really not comfortable with it."

Her eyes narrowed to slits. "So I either share with you or compete with you?"

"Yes." He gave that decisive nod again. "This is what I want to do, and I want to do it with you."

Her lips pressed together, but Quill could see her stubbornness beginning to waver. "Let me think about it. I've been hanging on to my independence so long that ... this is enough for today." She waved a hand to indicate the three of them, the commitments they'd just made to each other.

"There's time. We have the rest of our lives."

She grinned. "Yeah, we do, don't we?"

"Sounds good to me," Quill said. And it did. The band around his chest tightened, but he'd gotten used to the feeling, the way love gripped him, forced him to feel. It wasn't bad at all. Everything had fallen into place far better than he could have anticipated. Things could still fall apart, but he'd survived before, and he'd survive again. He could only take one day at a time. But for every one of those days, they were his. His for the rest of his life. In bed, out of bed, whenever he wanted them. Just as they could have him. Whenever, wherever. With them at his side, he didn't feel weak. He loved them, they loved him. That was a strength he hadn't even known existed until them. Somehow, with Gea and Kienan, giving up a little control didn't seem like such a bad thing. He couldn't imagine relaxing his iron-fisted grip on any other aspect of his life, but for them?

It was worth it.

Gea stared at the pale face of Constantine Breckenridge as she explained the situation his mate was in. His eyes had gone glassy with pain when she'd related Tam's parting words to him—that she was done with him. A bit of Gea's heart had broken being the one to relay a message that caused the kind of agony that seared into a person's soul. But she'd promised Tam, and Breck paid Gea to be upfront with him.

"I'm sorry we couldn't get her out. The best we could do was get out alive in order to let you know what was going on."

"I appreciate that." He didn't look happy, but he didn't look angry either. That was a relief, but there was little she could do about it. What happened had happened.

She was just grateful Quill, Kienan, and she were all right. She hoped for the best for Tam and Breck, but she was selfish enough to be glad she wasn't in their shoes.

"According to one of our contacts, Stefan, Tam, and his one remaining guard boarded a transport to London an hour ago." According to one of Kienan's many mysterious contacts, in fact. She pushed aside a flash of guilt that she'd seen to her own relationship before she'd seen to her work. Tam was willing to go with Stefan, more or less, and stopping them before they'd left town wouldn't have helped her reclaim whatever Stefan had stolen. "From what I could glean from her, she's on her way to England for a job. He has something he's threatening her with to make her do it for him."

"Then it appears I have some business to take care of in London." Breck's chair squeaked as he shifted, downed a glass of amber liquid, and set it on his desk.

Gea hesitated for a moment before she offered, "Do you want help? I have an . . . associate who might be available to assist. He's apprised of the situation."

The blond man lifted a brow, running the tip of his finger around the rim of his empty snifter. "Is he?"

"Yes, I'm taking him on as a partner. And a mate." Her heart fluttered at the thought, but her voice was remarkably steady. She'd committed to the relationship, and she was an all-or-nothing kind of woman. So, she was all in.

The man's eyebrow arched higher. "I thought your mate was Quilliam North."

Figures Breck would have had her background checked out. He was too careful not to. She shrugged. "He is, too."

"Interesting." He steepled his fingers and pressed them to his lips. "This other mate, what's his name?"

"Kienan Vaughn. You might know his cousin, Pierce."

"Indeed." He grunted. "I'll keep Mr. Vaughn in mind, contact you if I need extra manpower. For the moment, I think I need to take care of this on my own."

She nodded. "If you're certain."

"Yes. Thank you for all your work. I'll transfer your commission to your account immediately."

"Thank you. Good luck."

His laugh held little humor. "I'll need it. Good-bye, Ms. Crevan."

The screen went blank and she sighed, shaking her head. What a mess. Stefan wasn't a man she'd cross lightly, and she couldn't even imagine what he'd taken from Tam that she would be so willing to die for. She shivered, glad she was away from him. She could have gotten out on her own, she was sure of that. Stefan wanted Breck warned off, and he was calculating enough to realize Gea was the best person to do it.

But it had felt damn good to have her mates come for her. It had proved to her, once and for all, that they were nothing like her father. And she was stronger than her mother. She didn't *have* to rely on them—she was capable of taking care of herself. She'd been doing just that for years. Why that hadn't gotten through her head before now, she didn't know. Pure terror.

She drew in a breath, felt old resentments and fears crack and give way. No more letting them rule her life, make her decisions for her. Time to move forward. She and her mates would make mistakes, hurt each other. They already had. But they'd get through it. In their own way, each of them were survivors. Neither of her parents had been. They'd been dependent on others. That wasn't her, and it certainly wasn't Quill or Kienan.

The scents of her mates came to her, and Kienan ran a broad palm down her arm, nuzzled the nape of her neck. "He didn't want help?"

She sighed and leaned back into him. "Not yet."

"I might not be able to get there in time if I'm not in-country."

Rolling her head on his shoulder, she tilted her head to meet his beautiful silver eyes. "I know, but we can't force him."

"True enough." He brushed his lips over hers, tender and reverent as always. "I have some contacts in England that I can tap if it becomes an emergency."

"Why am I not surprised?"

Quill chuckled, moving into his office to join them. "Because you're a very smart woman."

She turned to him, allowed them both to embrace her, and she embraced her very fine fate. Whatever happened, she had them at her side. They'd thrown themselves into danger for her more than once, and she knew they'd do it again without hesitating. How could she walk away from men like them? The bottom line was, only a fool would do so. Only a fool wouldn't love them with all her heart. In a world like theirs, something could always go wrong, she could always end up alone, but while she had the chance at love, she was going to take it. Unlike her mother, she could and would still stand on her own two feet, supporting her mates as much as they supported her. It would be a bond of *equals*—she wouldn't give her whole self up to it. She was who she was; they knew it, and they loved her for it.

"I love you," Kienan whispered. "Both."

"I love you, too," Quill and Gea echoed. She tightened her arms around them, and they held her closer. A grin curved her lips, joy unfurling within her.

What more could she ask for than this?

Not one damn thing.

Reclaiming Temptation

I

His hands moved down Tam's naked back, his lips brushing a kiss over her shoulder. The sweet touch was in sharp contrast with the way his cock thrust inside her. He sat against the headboard, and she straddled his lap, her hips rising and falling as she rode him.

Deus, she was so wet. So hot. So greedy and needy.

"Tam," he groaned. "My beloved."

A pang went through her at those words. Breck would never call her *beloved* again. He would never even see her again. This was just a dream. She knew that, but she reached for it anyway, held it close, grateful for any escape from reality. Even if it was an empty, pointless fantasy. She'd take what little she could get.

Her dream lover cupped her hips, pulling her tight to the base of his cock while he ground his pelvis upward. A gasp strangled from her, and she didn't care if it was a fantasy. It felt good. Sex with Breck had always been good. The best of her life. In the privacy of her own mind, she could admit that. Nowhere else.

Pain mingled with her pleasure, but even in dreams, Breck

wouldn't be swayed. He wanted her attention. All of it. All of her. His mouth opened over the sensitive tendon that connected shoulder to neck, and he bit down. A shudder went through her and her hips arched, forcing him deep inside of her. The stretch was divine, and her sex spasmed. Tingles broke down her skin in a wave of sensation that bordered on perfection.

Grasping the edge of the headboard behind his wide shoulders, she used it for leverage to pump herself on his cock, faster and faster. More. She wanted to come. Her breathing was little more than gasps of air, but it drew his scent to her. Masculine musk mixed with expensive cologne. Pure Breck. She drew in a deep drag of that smell, like a blisshead taking a hit. She loved that aroma.

He rocked his pelvis upward, meeting each of her movements. She ground her clit down on him, felt the rasp of the hair at his groin against her sensitive flesh. His fingers bit into her hips, and she watched his jaw flex, knew he fought an orgasm. She purred, loving that she could push him as much as he could return the favor.

"You're so beautiful, beloved." His eyes were so blue she could drown in them. "I love you."

Boom. She exploded, her body seizing as she catapulted over the edge into ecstasy. Her sex clenched around his thrusting cock, and she threw back her head, arching into him. He drew her nipple into his mouth, biting down on the tight tip. Mouth falling open in a silent scream, she felt another wave of climax wash over her, and her pussy milked his cock. His body went rigid; then she felt his seed pump into her, filling her. The moment stretched on, so lovely and perfect that she wished it would never end.

But it always did. Nothing this good could ever be real, or hers to keep.

Tam startled awake, jerking upright in her seat. Sucking in a breath, she tried to calm her rabbiting heartbeat. Just a dream. Nothing more. Reality returned with a hard crash. Pushing locks of hair out of her face, she glanced around. It appeared they'd just arrived in London.

"Have a nice catnap, Felicia?" Stefan's silky voice all but purred. His hand closed over her shoulder, the gesture affectionate to anyone who looked.

Affection, hell. She clenched her jaw, fighting the urge to shrug away from his touch. He would only tighten his grip to the point of excruciating pain, enjoying the twisted little mind games he could play. He had her right where he wanted her and he knew it. Anything he asked, she would do. Everyone had their weakness, and he'd found hers.

Damn it. Damn *him*.

Arching an eyebrow at him, she smiled. "Yes, it was a lovely bit of rest. Shall we?"

When she rose, he had no choice but to release her or let the others on the transport know he was an abusive bastard. His bodyguard-cum-assassin Leland pushed into the aisle in front of her, making sure she couldn't run once she got off the transport. As if she would. If she'd wanted to escape, she would have done it by now. The trouble was, until she got back what he'd stolen, she couldn't leave. She just had to bide her time.

Stepping out into the open air, she dragged in a breath of London. Home. Or the place she'd been born and raised until she was ten. When she'd started down the road to perdition she was now on. Sighing, she followed along behind Leland, swallowing her gorge when Stefan brushed too close and his overly sweet scent filled her nose.

It took little time to get to the luxurious flat Stefan kept in town. The Royale was an interesting establishment that allowed exclusive clientele to stay short-term as hotel guests or buy the suites outright as condominiums with a concierge service always on staff. This place was one of Stefan's many properties scattered across the globe. Always good to have some-where to hide if one needed to hole up and lie low for a while. She pushed back the curtains in the main space, watching the stream of people flood by on the walkways below. All scurrying about on their way to work, to school, to pick up their children, or meet with a lover. So normal. So far away from anything she'd ever experienced. That was the life she'd always wanted for Sophie. Normalcy. And Stefan was trying to ruin that for her.

He stood behind her, watching her. Assessing, as he always did. Looking for how to get the upper hand. He'd taught her that trick long ago. She didn't bother turning to face him when she spoke. "When will I see Sophie?"

"Soon, Felicia. Soon." The platitude in his voice made her hackles rise.

She glanced back, keeping her expression neutral. She arched an eyebrow. "Now, Stefan. Or I'm going to become a great deal less cooperative."

His eyes narrowed. "You have no room to threaten me."

"Your power over me extends only so long as I know she's alive and unharmed. If you want me to do what you want, when you want, I suggest you provide some proof of life. And I don't mean a holopic or a vid. We both know those can be forged." She turned back to the window, though now she looked at his reflection rather than the people outside. "I want to see her, speak to her, *touch* her."

Hug her. Sweet Deus, she wanted to hold that child in her arms so badly, she burned with the need.

She brushed her hands down her hips, smoothing her skirt. "I'm not going even one more step until that happens."

Rage tightened his face, the expression clear even in the wavy image on the glass. He wanted to hit her, hurt her, and she watched him wrestle with himself for control. Whatever he wanted her to do required skills only she had, which meant he needed her.

And he knew there was only so far he could push anyone before the game spun out of his control. His nostrils flared. "Fine."

Two days later, she walked along the Thames, observing a member of the House of Lords who happened to be out for an evening stroll with his latest mistress. For reasons yet unknown to her, Stefan wanted her to get to know Lord Abernathy. Thus far, he was deadly boring, with a deep affection for German synthbrew and English thoroughbreds. He was attending the races at Ascot that weekend and a polo match at the end of the month. His mistress had tried several times to divert his monologue with sexual advances and, thus far, she'd been entirely unsuccessful. Tam had a feeling if the other woman had been a horse, she'd have had more luck getting him excited.

Deus, what was she doing here? How was she supposed to formulate a plan for doing whatever it was Stefan wanted if she had no idea what his endgame was? His *other* endgame, besides making sure she wound up dead or behind bars for the rest of her life? She gritted her teeth and willed her fangs not to slide down. Relief flooded her when Abernathy finally got the message from his mistress and they went upstairs to the flat he rented for her.

Tam had already been inside the flat, searched the place and found nothing she wouldn't expect in a kept woman's flat. The only interesting thing was that it appeared the mistress was also sleeping with Abernathy's wife. She wondered if His Lordship knew.

But now what? She could go back to the Royale and watch Sophie sleep, her little face so peaceful and innocent. Tam's heart squeezed at the thought. It was so good to have the girl near. But it also made it easier for Stefan to manipulate Tam. She knew that, and so she resisted returning.

Sighing, she leaned up against the railing that overlooked the river. The water rushed by, inky black in the night. The sound should have been soothing, but it wasn't. Wind rushed at her face, sweeping her hair back. She dropped her head forward, and not for the first time wondered what she was doing, and how she was ever going to find a way out of this mess. No matter what, Sophie had to get out of this alive. Tam would take the risk with her own fate.

"Hello, Tam."

The words were smooth and so cold they froze her in place. Her head came up and she cast a wary glance over her shoulder. Deus, no. It couldn't be him. It just couldn't be. How had he found her?

"You're wondering how I tracked you down."

She remained silent, refused to turn and face him. Instead, she watched the river, the ripples of water. Her mind scrambled, her body tensing. She shot a glance to her right, away from him. She could be gone before he could ever catch her. She was a cheetah-shifter, faster than any other animal out there.

"Don't. Don't run from me. Not again." The ice in his voice cracked, just for a moment, and she heard the pain.

Pain she knew only too well. She'd felt it every moment since the last time she was in his arms. She swallowed, her hands biting into the railing as she gripped tight. "Why are you here, Breck?"

"Because I can't be anywhere else."

She shook her head, a pang shooting through her. "Please leave me alone."

"I can't do that." The words were quiet, almost lost in the wind.

"*Why?* Why won't you just walk away?" The metal dug into her flesh, and frustration flashed through her. "I told Gea to tell you I was done—"

"Done with me, I know." His tone dropped from chilly to subarctic. "She relayed the message, just the way she said she would. I paid her well to find any information about your whereabouts. She's good at her job, clearly."

"Clearly." Tam pried her hands free of the railing, pivoting to face him and look into those deep blue eyes. Her heart clenched. Deus, but she had fallen hard for him. He'd been the worst mistake of her entire career. "If you got the message, then why are you here?"

"I told you—I can't be anywhere else." His hand lifted and he caught her chin. His gaze searched her face. For what, she didn't know, but she kept her expression carefully blank. This man had already played her as much as she'd hoped to play him. She almost smiled. Breck and then Stefan. She was slipping.

"You can't be here either." She didn't bother wrestling with him to get away. Speed was her forte, not brute strength. He could overpower her easily if he wanted to. "If you're near me, you'll get hurt. I'll get hurt."

Sophie would get hurt, and that was the worst prospect of all. She loved that child more than anything in the world. She'd sworn to protect her, sworn to herself that Sophie would have a better life than she'd had—safe, secure, never worrying where the next meal would come from or whom she'd have to con just to get by.

"Stefan will hurt us both, is that it?"

She tilted her head. "That's what he does best, so it's a safe assumption."

"And he has you working on something for him." His gaze drifted to the building Abernathy had just entered. "Gea said he's stolen something from you, and you're working with him until you can find a way to get it back."

"More or less, yes."

"What's worth that much to you, Tam?" He shook his head, brushing his thumb along her jaw. "No . . . object or amount of money is worth this game you're playing."

Of course he'd think that of her. All a person like her could care about was money, possessions. Because she was so beneath his contempt, wasn't she? She sighed. Perhaps she *was* beneath his contempt, thief and con artist that she was. But she knew what love was, knew what her priorities were. She wanted the people she cared about to be safe, and Deus help her, that included the stubborn male in front of her.

She straightened her shoulders and met his gaze squarely. "I've said it before and I'll say it again. I want you gone from my life. I never want to see you again. I'm done with you, Breck."

Pain flashed through his gaze a moment before temper took over, and anger tightened his features. The eagle's feathers were more than a little ruffled. "That's too bad, because I'm *not* done with you."

His grip tightened on her jaw, his fingers biting into her flesh. He slammed his mouth down over hers. The kiss was an act of possession and dominance, but that didn't stop her body from reacting. He shoved his tongue into her mouth, filled her, forced her to taste him. She kept back the moan that wanted to escape but couldn't prevent the way her body bowed toward his, pressing to the hard planes of his muscular form. Her eyes fluttered closed.

Her core melted, the lips of her sex going slick and soft in moments. Whether she liked it or not, her tongue met his, twined with his. She slipped her hands into his thick, silken hair, loved the texture of it against her palms. Every micrometer of her flesh tingled from the contact with him; her nipples went hard, thrusting against her shirt.

His hands slid down her back, cupping her ass to bring her closer. The hard thrust of his cock prodded her belly and she squirmed against him. His groan was a harsh sound that made her shiver. Her pussy throbbed, clenched on an emptiness she wanted him to fill. She wanted his cock thrusting into her sex the way his tongue thrust into her mouth.

Just like it used to be.

But it would never be like that again. The truth always made it impossible to repair the bridges she'd burned. They'd played each other, fallen in love despite it, and ripped each other's hearts out in the process.

It was madness. Insanity. She couldn't do this again. Not to him, not to herself. *No.*

She tore herself from his arms, spun and darted away with the speed her cheetah side had blessed her with. But no matter how fast she ran, she could never escape herself.

2

Her taste lingered on his tongue.

Breck spread his wings wide, let the breeze carry him as he soared above a city so different from his own. The air was different here, the way the wind blew. He could see the old buildings that had survived the Third Great War; some still majestic, but some pockets of the city were no better than the slums of the Vermilion District back in New Chicago. Skyrises dominated, mercurite and polyglass towers that he winged around on his aerial tour of London.

The Royale had been very accommodating in providing him the location of Stefan's flat and making sure Breck got a penthouse suite that took up half of the top floor—on the same side of the building as Stefan's flat. Breck was three floors above where Stefan was keeping Tam.

Closer than he'd been in months, and still not close enough.

That single taste of her hadn't been enough. He craved her. Both the man who loved her and the golden eagle who wanted its mate. Every part of him needed her by his side.

He'd intended to tell her the truth the night they'd spent at Tail. Who she was to him, what they were to each other. Her kind couldn't sense it, and he'd used that to his advantage at first. She wouldn't know *why* she was so drawn to him, why they connected so deeply, so fast. But when he'd awoken the next morning, he'd been in bed alone. As alone as he'd been during the long days—and nights—without her since.

He'd hoped to bind her to him before he'd had to reveal anything. She'd wanted a rich mark for her next scheme; he'd wanted to make her love him. They'd both been overly confident in their ability to get what they wanted from the other.

It remained to be seen who'd won their game of hearts.

Knowing he should back off for the night after he'd told her he was in town didn't stop him from swooping down to land on the railing to her balcony. There were lights on inside, and the sheer curtains revealed people moving around in the room. His stomach contracted as he realized he was looking at Stefan himself. And the man was in his mate's bedroom.

It was a question Breck hadn't allowed himself to ask until now. Was Stefan her lover? She'd made her living seducing men out of things they possessed. Now Stefan possessed something she wanted desperately. Would she try to seduce him to get it back? Breck tensed, his talons digging into the railing. He should fly away, shouldn't stay to watch this. Only *he* was bound by the mating, only he felt the need for fidelity. She was free to do whatever she wanted, and the thought of his mate with another man turned his stomach.

Tam's voice carried clearly through the window. "Constantine Breckenridge followed us to London."

Breck cocked his head, suddenly intent on what they were saying, not just what they might be doing. Why would she tell Stefan about him? What game was she playing now?

* * *

Tam hated having Stefan in her room. Hated having him near her. She tightened the belt on her microsilk robe, wishing it were made of a thicker fabric.

His gaze slid down her body, but thankfully showed no sexual interest. "How was your evening? Discover anything interesting?"

The hairs rose on the back of her neck. He knew. He knew about Breck. Lying would get her nowhere. She shrugged. "Constantine Breckenridge followed us to London. He got the message we sent through Ms. Crevan and he decided to ignore it, for reasons I have yet to fathom."

"He's a problem."

"Perhaps." Her brows drew together, her heart thumping hard as she scrambled to come up with a way to turn Stefan against his normal inclination toward violence. He kept it leashed for his work, but he wasn't trying to con Breck, which made him fair game. "But doing something to a person that high profile is bound to be noticed. I've always found it's better to use the situation to one's advantage rather than try to force a more permanent solution."

That caught his attention. "What do you suggest?"

"We use him." She dipped one shoulder in a shrug. "You want me to watch Lord Abernathy, for whatever reason. He's not the type to let me seduce him. He's not truly interested in the women he already has. He has them because a man like him *should* have women like them. If you want me to get close to him, it won't be through my usual methods."

Stefan's eyes narrowed. "And Breckenridge comes into the equation how?"

"He's a man like Abernathy. Rich and well-bred. Unlike us." So true. Breck was so far removed from the type of people Stefan and she were, they might as well be from different galaxies. She spread her hands in an expressive gesture. "He can get in to the kinds of functions where Abernathy will be. Clubhouses, charity events and the like. Abernathy is attending the races this weekend. Breck can take me with him, and I can circulate with the people who know your mark best. His friends. I can speak to him directly. But I'll need an in. Breck can be that in."

"Why would he do that for you?"

She snorted. "Because, like all my marks, he's madly in love with me."

"Yet he knows you betrayed him." He crossed his arms over his chest, his gaze calculating as he searched her face.

"The perversity of men is what makes them so malleable, Stefan." She arched her eyebrows, widening her eyes innocently. "You're the one who taught me that."

"So I did." He slid his hands in his pockets; then he nodded. "We'll play it your way. For now. If Breckenridge continues to be a problem ..."

He didn't bother finishing the sentence, just closed her bedroom door behind him as he left.

A breath whooshed out of her. One small hurdle overcome, but so many more in her path to trip her up. She pushed away the despair that threatened to overwhelm her.

"He seems like such a nice man. I can see why you'd want to spend time with him."

The words were muffled, but clear. All the blood fled her face and she strode forward to wrench open the door to her balcony. Breck stood there naked, obviously having just shifted from his eagle form.

"What are you doing here?" she hissed.

He arched an incredulous brow and pushed past her into the room. "Eavesdropping."

"You shouldn't be here." Deus, if Stefan caught him here, they'd both be dead. She scurried over to her door and flicked the lock shut. It wouldn't keep Stefan out, but he wouldn't be able to just walk right in either.

"Really, Tam. You're starting to sound like a vid on the fritz. Repeating yourself endlessly." Breck walked around the room, touching her hairbrush, the back of her desk chair, the microsilk cover on her bed. "So, you're going to use me. Again. That's your plan?"

She gave him the sweetest smile in her arsenal, stepping away from the door and into the middle of the room. "The other option was to have him kill you for being a birdbrained idiot who doesn't know how to take no for an answer. Which would you prefer?"

His other eyebrow rose to join its twin, a grin curving his lips. "You're protecting me, are you?"

"Someone has to," she muttered, annoyed that a simple smile from him could make her insides quiver. Really, she hadn't had such a schoolgirl crush even when she'd been a schoolgirl. "Your self-preservation is somewhat lacking at the moment. Stefan is not a man to be toyed with. He will hurt you. And me. And anyone who gets in his way."

"Has he hurt you before?" Breck's expression went murderous.

"Yes." Many times. So many times, she'd lost count. She still had a scar or two to remind her of his brand of affection.

The eagle-shifter's hands fisted and unfisted at his sides. "How do you know him?"

Such a simple question, with such a complicated answer. She gave him the shortest response possible, one that was only half-truth. "He got me into the game, many years ago. Taught me most of what I know about getting people to do what I want."

"*He* was your mentor?" His nostrils flared in disgust. "You have terrible taste."

"He chose me. I didn't choose him." More honest words had never left her mouth.

He moved toward her and she backed away, her heart skipping a beat as the scent of him hit her. Drugging. The sight of his naked body made her insides clench with need. She wanted her hands on his skin again, wanted to feel that blissful abandon that she always experienced with him. He was the only man she'd ever lost herself in, lost control with. It was forbidden for someone like her, which had made it so exhilarating.

"But you did choose *me*, didn't you, Tam? You want me with you now, while you try to outmaneuver Stefan. You *want* me." Breck's voice was a deep rumble that did nothing to ease her needs. He used that tone on her in bed, when he whispered wicked nothings in her ear and made her pant and moan and scream his name.

His gaze searched her face, demanded an answer. Her back hit the wall, and she couldn't escape him. When had she ever been able to? "Yes, I want you. With me. But that doesn't mean you should be here. You can still leave, Breck. You can still save yourself from this mess and walk away."

"No, I really can't." His heavy weight pinned her to the wall, all those delicious muscles plastered against her softer curves. He jerked at the tie on her robe, parting the microsilk. She shivered as it slithered against her flesh. Her pussy went hot and wet, her channel clenching with the unstoppable craving that never seemed to ease its hold on her.

This. This was what her dreams couldn't capture. The overwhelming feeling of him. His presence, the way he seemed to draw all the oxygen out of the room and leave her gasping for breath. She loved it and hated it all at once. And she couldn't resist it.

Then he kissed her.

Her tongue twined with his, the taste of him heady and masculine and exactly what a man should be. He was hot against her, his cock pressed to her lower belly. Their kiss earlier had only primed her for this; she was all but ready to explode from her skin. His hands coasted down her sides to curve over her hips, pulling her tighter to him. Gooseflesh rippled in the wake of his touch, and her nipples jutted against his hard, unyielding chest.

He groaned, and she pulled her mouth from his. "Be quiet. We can't get caught."

"Talking less is a good idea, then." He lifted her and she wrapped her thighs around him, arching herself in offering. He didn't hesitate, thrusting into her. The thickness of him was a shock after all these weeks without him, would have been painful if she hadn't been so wet.

As it was, it just excited her more.

He dipped his head and sipped kisses up the side of her neck, then sucked her earlobe into his mouth. She purred, writhing against him, which only increased her agony as she rubbed every micrometer of their bodies together. His cock seemed to expand, growing longer and harder inside of her. Deus, it felt good. He bit down on her earlobe, sending a shock of pleasured-pain streaking through her. A gasp ripped out of her and she clutched at his shoulders, barely holding back a scream.

His chuckle was a rich sound of satisfaction, knowing exactly how he affected her. For revenge, she squeezed her inner muscles around him, clamping down tight on his dick. His breathing stopped and a shudder went through him. His hands curled under her thighs, hitching her higher against the wall. Then he slid his cock out until the head caught on the edge of her channel, only to shove back into her. Hard.

Closing her eyes, she held on tight for the amazing ride. The blood rushed hot and wild through her veins, pounding loudly in her ears. The feel of him filling her pussy was exquisite—so full, so good. The fit was perfection. Gravity made certain he sank deep with each thrust, and she arched her body to meet his upward movements. The rough wall abraded her back, but she was beyond caring about anything as trivial as comfort. The drive for orgasm was all that mattered now.

No one had ever been able to get to her this fast, make her struggle for control. A smile curved her lips, and she let the sensations rush over her. The rasp of his chest hair against her nipples, the scent of him and her and sex mingling in the air, the sound of their ragged breathing. Lust coiled tightly within her, and her sex clenched, a precursor to the orgasm that gathered deep inside her.

"Look at me, Tam," he breathed. "I want to watch you come for me."

She couldn't resist him, didn't bother trying. Her eyes opened and she met his intense blue gaze. His face was flushed, beads of sweat slipping down his temples. A muscle ticked in his jaw and she knew he struggled to suppress his groans. He pistoned in and out of her, pressing her hard into the wall. His swift movements pushed her onward, made her sex clench. So close. So very close. He slammed deep, rolling his hips to grind himself against her clit.

It was more than enough to send her over the edge.

She gritted her teeth to hold back her scream, her claws digging into his shoulders. Every muscle in her body locked tight as orgasm throbbed through her. He continued to power into her pussy, his hips slapping against hers. Another wave crashed over her, and her sex fisted on his cock. Again and again, dragging sensations out of her until she couldn't breathe, couldn't think, until there was nothing else in the world but him.

Talons bit into her hips as he buried his dick within her. The low sound he made as he came inside her sent a shiver racing through her. His breath rushed against her shoulder, and she could hear the way his heart raced. So did hers.

It took her long moments to gather her scattered wits enough to speak again. She didn't want to say the words, but she had to. "You need to go before Stefan or Leland come to check on me."

And they would. Even knowing she'd never leave without Sophie, they didn't trust her to stay.

"Leland?"

"Stefan's right-hand man and general troubleshooter." Literally. As in, if anyone was trouble, he shot them. She shuddered for entirely unpleasant reasons. Another of Stefan's goons had come to replace the one they'd left behind in New Chicago, so that they easily outnumbered her and could always have someone watching. "There's Nichols, too. He just got here."

Sighing, Breck slipped his softening cock out of her body, leaving damp emptiness behind him. She hated sending him away, had missed him so damn much, but that was her reality. Locking her knees, she forced herself to remain upright when he pulled away from her.

"I'll see you soon." He brushed a kiss over her mouth. "Whether you believe it or not, I'm on your side. I want to help you out of this . . . situation with Stefan."

She shook her head, unable to find words to say to him. Her throat closed. Deus, when was the last time anyone had offered her support without demanding something in return? She couldn't trust it. There was no man who gave without some benefit for himself. She just didn't know what Breck's help would cost her, or if the price was higher than she could afford to pay.

3

Can you meet me in the lobby in 10 minutes?

Breck frowned at the message that popped up on his palmtop. Tam wanted to meet him.... Was this something Stefan was orchestrating, or was she doing something behind the man's back? Did it matter? He was going to meet her regardless. Keying an affirmative response into his palmtop, he sent the reply and went to pull clothes out of his 'fresher.

His mind dwelled on the Tam problem as he dressed. Then again, where else had his mind been in the last couple of months? He needed to figure out what it was Stefan had stolen from Tam and why the hell it was so valuable to her that she'd risk her life to try to get it back. What could she want that Breck couldn't buy her? Hell, that she couldn't convince someone to give her? A rare artifact of some kind? Something with personal meaning to her?

The damnable problem was, he had very little information to go on. Of course he'd looked into Tam's background the moment he'd realized she was his mate, which was why he'd known she was a grifter who seduced men out of their money.

But outside of that? He had no idea. She'd been playing him the entire time, so the particulars she'd given about her life were probably lies, and the details the investigators could dig up about her were thin.

He'd had Gea put together a file on Stefan, but other than the crimes he'd committed—or was *suspected* of committing—there wasn't much information there either. The list of criminal activity was impressive, though. The man had had a long and sordid career. He liked the finer things in life—expensive clothes, food, and hotels—thought he was smarter than anyone else, and people who got close to him had a tendency to end up dead. That Tam was anywhere near him sent a chill down Breck's spine. He wanted her away from him. Now, if not sooner; but unless she came with him willingly, he knew he'd never be able to keep her.

He had to bide his time, get her to trust him, to admit she wanted to spend her life with him. Forcing her to do anything would put him in the same league as Stefan in her mind. Breck had to figure out how to outwit them both. No small task.

Shrugging into a jacket, he slipped his slim palmtop into the inside pocket before he walked out the door and took the lift down to the ground level.

Tam stood near the exit, staring out a wide window that overlooked the street. As he walked up behind her, he scanned the lobby of the hotel, checking for signs of Stefan. He was so focused on finding his enemy that he almost overlooked Hunter Avery.

"Shit," he breathed.

He was a scant meter away from Tam, so she heard him. Her shoulders went rigid and she turned to look at him, worry pinching her lovely face. "What?"

Then her eyes went round as she followed his nod and saw what Breck had seen. Hunter Avery was from New Chicago, like Breck, a friendly rival in business whom he'd always respected. The man had recently mated with Delilah Chase, a woman who used to be a thief and also happened to be the sister of a notorious technobrothel owner. The newsvids had had a field day when that naughty Cinderella story had gone public. Breck would be forever grateful that his family was nowhere near as wealthy as the Averys. Last time anyone checked, the Averys were the most moneyed people on the planet. Breck was rich enough, but not so rich his life ended up entertaining the masses on the newsvids.

"Tam, Breck. What a surprise." Avery's sharp gaze took them in, while his wife appeared at his side.

"Tam." Delilah grinned, her short blond hair a stark contrast to Tam's darkness as the two women embraced.

Breck startled when Avery hauled him in for a hug. The other man was known for his reclusive ways, and while the two had always gotten along well enough in business, they were hardly friends.

Avery's words were a mere breath in his ear. "Are the two of you in trouble? Do you need help?"

Ah. He was...touched by the concern. Surprised, but touched. He wouldn't have expected it from Avery, but the man had changed quite a bit since he'd found his mate. Then again, so had Breck. A year before, he'd never have imagined abandoning his work to chase after a woman. He whispered back to Avery, "Only the help a psychologist would be qualified to give. The rest I can work out on my own."

He hoped.

The other man dropped his arms, chuckling. "Good to see you again."

"And you." He slid his hands in his pockets. Of all the times to run into each other, this seemed a little too coincidental. There was a tug of suspicion that Gea might have mentioned Breck would be here and was in over his head. Gea and Delilah's sister had each mated to gray wolf cousins, and that family connection meant it wasn't unfeasible that Gea might have talked to Delilah and Hunter. "What brings the two of you to London?"

"I'm breaking into the palace," Delilah replied with a saucy grin, "to steal the personal jewel collection of the royal family."

Tam's eyes widened. "You're going after the Queen's Jewels?"

Chortling, Delilah held up a staying hand. "Don't worry, they're paying me to do it."

That was right. Avery's mate had gone from thief to hired security consultant who could be called upon to test a system's ability to keep out thieves. Or former thieves, in her case. Breck arched an eyebrow at her. "So, good old Vicky the Third wants you to pretend to rob her?"

"Deus save the queen," Tam drawled, her English accent thickening.

"Indeed." Avery quirked a brow.

"Although I imagine she's hoping for a show with a pretty thief in her house." Tam's tone went tart. "She does tend to enjoy the ladies."

"The newsvids think Victoria III is going to be the end of her line." Delilah rocked back on her heels, an irreverent grin on her face. "She's got that German woman scientist they call her 'special friend and confidante.' I'm guessing those two are bumping clits."

Breck choked at the expression, trying not to laugh.

Tam shrugged. "She can always marry some appropriate male and keep her scientist on the side. It wouldn't be the first time in the royal family. One does what one must."

"I doubt it." The blond woman lifted her hands. "Golden eagles mate for life. It's unfortunate for the monarchy that the queen happened to be born a mating species of shifter."

A golden eagle. Just like Breck. He watched suspicion flash through Tam's gaze, and he knew the moment denial kicked in.

He sighed. "*If* that's what the German woman is. A mate is a mate, so that would be all there is to it. Unless we're talking artificial insemination, but I'm not sure the Brits would go for an heir that came out of a Petri dish."

"Should be interesting." Delilah's green eyes twinkled and she rubbed her hands together. "Maybe I'll catch the two of them going at it like rabbits when I break in. I'll let you know."

Avery shook his head at his mate. "I doubt they'd risk keeping the queen in the palace when you have your break-in scheduled. She'll be off on a diplomatic visit or vacationing up north."

"But if I'm going to test the real strength of the system, it has to be on a day they don't expect to be robbed. I'm going in a day early." She grinned. "Come on, I need to scout the place out, so you get to play tourist with me and take lots of holopics."

"Wonderful," Avery grumbled, but he followed along behind her gamely enough.

Tam looked stricken as they walked away. Breck set his hand on her shoulder. "What is it?"

"She seems . . . happy."

"I'm sure she is." He shrugged. "What's more impressive is that *he* seems happy. It's not a word I would have associated with Avery a year ago. Or ever."

Her lips twisted. "I don't think I've ever looked that happy."

Bringing her fingers to his lips, he brushed a kiss over her knuckles. "I could make you that happy if you let me."

"If you knew half the things I've done, you wouldn't be that interested. You know I'm a villain, Breck." She shook her head, tugging her hand away from him. "You shouldn't even be here. You should go, and never look back."

"We've been over this. I'm not leaving." Frustration flared to life within him, and he tamped it down. Today he was already much closer to his goals than he had been even a week ago. He was here, with Tam, and she needed his help for the foreseeable future. She wanted him with her.

Wrapping her arms protectively around herself, she turned back to face the window. Her voice pitched low. "I don't understand you at all, Breck. I conned you, and even if you knew and were playing me from the start, I'm still a thief, a con artist, a grifter. I'm a terrible person for—"

"You're my mate."

"No!"

He laughed, but there was no humor in the sound. "My reaction exactly. But it's the truth, nonetheless." He hadn't been opposed to mating, but realizing the woman he was destined to mate with was a criminal hadn't been pleasant. How did he know what was truth and what was lie? He loved her and he thought she loved him in return, but she made her living getting rich men to love her, shower her in jewels, clothes, anything she wanted. Her running away to hook up with Stefan had opened the gulf between them even wider. Breck didn't know how to bridge that gap, only that he had to try. He sighed again, rubbing at the tight muscles at the nape of his neck, weary frustration and anger weighing down on him. "So, you see. I have no choice. I'm here because I have to be."

"I'm sorry," she whispered. "I wouldn't wish a mate like me on anyone, let alone an upstanding citizen like you."

"Ah, Tam. Don't." The backs of his knuckles slid up and down the side of her arm, and gooseflesh erupted in the wake of that simple touch.

He loved how she reacted to him. When she went wild for him it was the only time he knew he had the real Tam in his arms, and not whatever act she was putting on. Pretending to be the woman she thought he wanted instead of the real one. He stepped up behind her, running his hands up her arms to cup her shoulders. It went beyond any kind of physical craving, this need to touch her. It satisfied something deep and primal within him.

Perhaps because they were mates.

The feel of her soft skin against his was sweet. How he'd missed her, craved her, longed for her. A part of him had hated how dependent he'd become on this bond between them, but the long hours alone had burned away the anger and just left him with cold, hard determination to get her back and keep her. He'd do whatever it took.

And he was a man used to getting what he wanted.

Tam didn't know whether to laugh or be appalled as that revelation sank in. Mates. She had a mate.

What a time to find this out, right when she expected Stefan to make sure her life of freedom came to a rather permanent end. Panic closed her throat, threatened to bring her to her knees. She couldn't handle this, not on top of everything else. Stefan. Sophie. And now Breck.

She dragged a slow breath into her lungs, focusing on the view of the small courtyard that made up the front of the hotel. Sophie played out there, running in gleeful circles around a small fountain, a wide smile on her face. Tears smarted Tam's eyes. No matter what happened to her, she couldn't let harm come to one of the tiny patches of joy still left in this ugly world.

Breck rested his chin on top of her head. "Where's Stefan and his goons?"

"Stefan is out. Where, I'm not sure. He hardly confides in me." She shrugged. "Leland is outside with Stefan's other man, Nichols, watching us through the window."

And watching Sophie, but Tam didn't say that. As long as Leland and Nichols could see both Tam and Sophie, and be certain they weren't going anywhere, the goons didn't care about much else. Stefan left instructions that they were to be watched, and that was what would happen. Leland preferred that Sophie never be in a position where Tam could grab the girl and run, which was the only reason he'd agreed to let her stay inside to speak with Breck.

They were right to worry about that. If they let their guard down for even a moment, Tam would disappear with Sophie so fast they wouldn't even have time to blink. She watched for such an opportunity as closely as they watched her to make sure it didn't happen.

Breck's hands ran up her arms. "Everyone has a weakness. What's Stefan's? How can we use it to get back what he took from you?"

The unspoken question there was that he wanted to know *what* Stefan had taken from her. She had to tell him. If he was going to be helping her and planned to stay near her, he was bound to see the girl and wonder about her. "Stefan has a daughter. Sophie."

An irritated growl issued from the eagle-shifter. "What does he have on *you*? Is it blackmail, proof that you did something illegal? How is he making you do what he wants? Why haven't you escaped yet?"

She drew in a deep breath, about to tell him, when she saw Sophie skipping toward the hotel, Leland and Nichols close behind her. Perhaps it was better to show Breck than it was to tell him. She stepped out of his arms and turned to face the entrance.

"Tam!" Sophie's smile eclipsed her face and she ran to wrap her arms around Tam's waist.

She hugged the child back, glad she was safe and whole and unaware of the situation she was in. At least for now. "Hello, Sophie. Did you have fun running around like a wild child?"

"I did." The girl giggled and squeezed tighter.

Tam glanced up to see the men eyeing each other. Leland

gave Breck an emotionless stare, and Nichols took a deep drag on his ever-present cigartine and kept a suspicious gaze pinned on Sophie.

Breck's smile was closer to a baring of teeth. "Which of you is Leland and which is Nichols?"

"I'm Nichols." The beefy man blew out a cloud of smoke and twitched a shoulder, his gaze never leaving Tam and Sophie. Neither of the men offered a hand to shake. Leland just grunted and continued to stare at Breck.

It took a moment for Breck's gaze to drop to the child who'd thrown herself against Tam's legs. She watched his big body go rigid when Sophie looked at him. He'd noted the name, knew this was Stefan's daughter, but now he'd understand so much more.

The girl was a miniature of Tam.

Breck all but staggered as the small girl turned wide dark eyes on him. Questions and confusion ricocheted through his mind. *This* was the Sophie Tam had mentioned? *This* was Stefan's daughter?

She grinned up at him, leaning back against Tam, who had her arms around the girl. "Hello."

It took him a moment to gather his wits and do more than stare, gape-mouthed. "Hello, how are you?"

"Good." She bounced on her toes. "I'm Sophie. What's your name?"

He offered up a smile, not allowing himself to look at Tam or else all his questions would come flying out of his mouth. Best not to ask them in front of the girl. Or the goons. "My friends call me Breck."

She tilted her head as if considering that from all angles. "What do people who aren't your friends call you?"

"Constantine," he whispered conspiratorially, winking. "Or Mr. Breckenridge."

"I'll call you Breck." She stepped forward and tucked her hand into his. "We're going to be friends."

Charming and disarming, just like Tam. Such a pretty child, with her urchin's grin. She looked like a younger version of Tam, with the potential to be every bit as beautiful. But without the shadows and cynicism in her dark gaze.

She looked up at him. "Leland said we could have ices from across the street." She pointed to a tiny bistro with striped awnings. "Would you like to come, too?"

Leland growled and stepped forward, but Breck let his smile widen. "Of course. I can't imagine anything I'd love more."

The girl laughed. "You're funny. Your accent is funny, too."

"That's because I'm from New Chicago. We speak differently there."

She nodded sagely, tugging him toward the door. "There are girls in my school who talk like you. We have girls from all over the world."

"How exciting for you to know so many exotic people." Letting her pull away from him to lead the way, Breck shook his head at her enthusiasm. Leland shouldered past him to keep the girl close, while Nichols closed in behind Tam and Breck, making sure Tam didn't escape or run off with Sophie. Of course, since the girl was apparently Stefan's key to getting Tam's compliance. Things clicked into place, and Breck at least understood why Tam was so set on going through with whatever Stefan wanted of her. It wasn't a *thing* that had been stolen, but a child.

A child who would be at Stefan's mercy if Tam balked.

That seriously complicated matters, and he still had many questions left unanswered. He paused, waiting for Tam to come up beside him as they followed Sophie across the lane.

He set his hand at the small of her back, refusing to worry about Nichols overhearing them. "Is she your daughter?"

"Would you care if she was?" She glanced at him from the corner of her eye, reading him and his reactions.

"Of course. She's your family, then, and what matters to you matters to me." Though he knew she was asking a far more important question. Would he be jealous that his mate had had a child before he'd met her? He searched within himself, past the shock of seeing the girl and realizing Stefan and Tam had a deeper, more complex connection than he'd have ever imagined. He... wasn't jealous. It wasn't her past that interested him, but her present and future. They'd both had prior relationships. If she'd slept with Stefan and had a child in the past, Breck could live with that. What he couldn't live with was her sleeping with another man now . . . or ever again.

A soft sigh slipped out of Tam. "She's not my daughter. She's my sister. My half-sister, technically. A child from my mother's second marriage."

"Which explains the large gap between your births." Relief swept through him. Everything he'd found out about Stefan went from bad to worse. He was glad that Tam hadn't chosen to be in a relationship with someone like that. It was unfortunate that her mother hadn't had the same discretion.

"Yes, my mother was only sixteen when I was born, and thirty-eight when Sophie came along." Her shoulder dipped in an eloquent shrug. "I was twenty-two and long out of the house by then, but I've been looking after Sophie as much as possible since Mother passed."

"When was that?"

Her brow contracted. "Sophie was four—no, five—at the time, so five years ago."

More questions buzzed through his mind, but they were on the edge of the street, about to cross and join an impatient Sophie, who was bouncing on her toes, waving for them to hurry. "She's a lovely child."

Tam paused beside him, turning to look at him fully. There was pleading in her dark eyes, but her tone was calm and even. "She doesn't...she doesn't know about what I do. Or what her father does. The kind of people we are. I'd prefer that she never know."

The entreaty in her gaze was more than Breck could resist. He slid his hand up her back to squeeze her shoulder. "I'm not going to tell her anything about your...interesting occupations."

A breath eased out of her. "Thank you."

"Of course, beloved."

She stiffened but said nothing in response. It surprised him how easily it had fallen from his lips. He hadn't used the endearment since the last time she'd been in his house, before he'd tracked her to Tail.

"Let's go," Nichols grumbled behind them, the stink of his cigartine smoke wafting through the air.

Clearing his throat, Breck urged her forward to join Leland and Sophie. "We'll continue this discussion later."

4

Breck knocked on the door to Stefan's suite later that evening. He'd decided showing up unannounced was his best bet at catching everyone off guard. He wanted to meet the man himself, take Stefan's measure. There was only so much that files could tell him. Breck had found in his business dealings that it helped to look an opponent in the eyes. Body language, expression, little tells that could help him get the upper hand.

He looked into the old-fashioned peephole in the door, knowing it hid a tiny, high-tech vidmonitor. There was a thump, the sound of locks disengaging, and then the hulking bulk of Nichols filled the space. "What do you want?"

"I'm here to surprise Tam and take her to dinner." Breck made his smile guileless. "She wants to go to Ascot this weekend, and we'll need to make a few plans. Why not combine business and pleasure?"

Nichols's gaze narrowed, and he opened his mouth to retort when a light male voice sounded behind him. "Don't leave Mr. Breckenridge standing on the doorstep, Nichols. Let him come in and meet the family."

There was a chilly bite to the words, and Breck didn't like associating *family* with what he'd heard of Stefan. However, if the man was Tam's stepfather and Sophie's father, there was no escaping the connection. If—*when*—Breck mated with Tam, Stefan would be his father-in-law for all intents and purposes. The thought made bitterness coat his tongue, but he pushed past Nichols into the main space.

At first, Stefan appeared slight, almost slender, but then Breck could see it was an illusion. Wiry strength ran through the ropy muscles in the older man's whipcord lean body. But it was the eyes that gave him away. As cold and dangerous as black ice. Probably just as slippery, too. Keeping his smile in place, Breck offered his hand to Stefan to shake.

"Hello, Stefan."

"Constantine," he replied.

Breck fought a wince. He hated his first name. Mostly because his father had named him after *his* father, and the old man had been a complete bastard. Breck had hated every minute he'd been forced to spend in his grandfather's company, and he knew his father had hated it more. Why he'd named his only child after a man he despised, Breck had never surmised. It had been a relief for everyone when the elder Constantine passed.

"Call me Breck. As you said, we're practically family." How he managed the words without choking on them, he wasn't sure, but it made Stefan's gaze sharpen with an emotion Breck couldn't read. "I understand that Tam and I are being sent to the country for the weekend. I'm hoping to hammer out a few details over dinner. Is she free?"

Free wasn't a term he'd use to describe what Tam was right now, and he placed a little too much emphasis on that word. Enough to make Stefan's hand tighten on his. Breck didn't bother with a wrestling match, but he also didn't succumb to the pain of the older man's grip. Such a petty show of dominance that meant nothing in the end. He arched an eyebrow and allowed his amusement to show. After a moment, Stefan snorted and let his hand drop.

"She's putting Sophie to bed." The older man led the way to a beautifully appointed bedroom, complete with a child-sized castle in one corner, a personal gaming console embedded in one wall, and moving nanotoys littering every available surface. Most of them looked brand new. Something Stefan had bought the girl when he'd stolen her from wherever Tam had had her stashed? Bribes to keep Sophie compliant?

The girl was tucked into bed, while Tam sat against the headboard, reading her a story where each page was a series of colorful holopics. Sophie struggled valiantly to stay awake, but it was a losing battle, and her eyes drifted closed. Tam's smile was soft and loving as she bent to kiss her sister's forehead, tucking the covers around her. The scene sent a pang through Breck. He'd rarely seen such an unguarded expression on Tam's face, except when she let loose during sex.

"Lovely, aren't they? I'd hate to see anything happen to either of them." The soft threat in Stefan's voice was unmistakable.

"As would I." Breck met the other man's gaze squarely.

"Then you have a vested interest in making sure that my plans are followed exactly." Stefan's smile was a terrifying thing to witness. "Remember, Tam will never leave without Sophie, and I am Sophie's father. She belongs to me. Therefore, for the time being, Tam also belongs to me."

"For the time being," Breck agreed, working to keep his voice light, to prevent his muscles from tensing, to stop himself from ripping the other man's throat out. Leland and Nichols were nearby. Such a move wouldn't end well, and Breck needed to think, not just react the way he wanted to.

Stefan's gaze was cool and flat, every bit as ruthless as

190 / *Crystal Jordan*

Breck's private investigator had speculated in the files. There was no exaggeration there. This was a man who would use whatever means were at his disposal to get what he wanted. Including his own daughter. "What exactly do you want from her? From us?"

"For his wife's birthday, Lord Abernathy is hosting a ball at his house in Surrey. Next Friday. I want you to gain his confidences. Be invited to the ball and to the private events he's holding throughout that weekend." Stefan shrugged one shoulder. "That shouldn't be too difficult for someone as skilled as Tam."

"And then what?" Tam closed the bedroom door behind her, a pleasant mask firmly in place again.

"When you need to know, I will tell you." Stefan's lip lifted in a small sneer. "You'll forgive me if I don't trust you with any real confidences. A woman who's whored herself on so many men simply can't be trusted." He flicked a glance at Breck. "Even now, you've got one gagging for it."

Tam's face went blank at the insult, her chin lifting. "Breck, I wasn't expecting to see you tonight."

"I'm taking you to dinner. We need to plan this weekend." Breck slid his hands into his pockets, hiding his clenched fists and keeping him from breaking Stefan's nose.

She nodded, not sparing a glance for her stepfather. "Do I need to change clothes or will these do?"

"You look fine. Let's go."

"I'll be back in a few hours." The glare she gave Stefan was sulfuric. "I trust that Sophie will still be here sleeping when I return."

The man widened his eyes, exuding innocence. "So long as you return on time, there's no reason to assume otherwise. Enjoy your dinner."

"We'll show ourselves out." Breck grasped Tam's elbow,

drawing her away from Stefan. He'd like to keep going and never come back, but Sophie's existence made that impossible. They'd have to ride it out the way Tam had planned. Something would break their way, and they'd be able to get the girl from her father. They had to be patient and watchful.

Breck let a breath ease from his lungs as Leland shut the door behind them. He pressed the button to call the lift, ignoring Tam's subtle attempts to pull away from him. No doubt Stefan, Nichols, and Leland were watching their interactions through the peephole.

They stepped onto the lift and Breck punched the button to take them down to the lobby. When they reached the ground floor, he held on to Tam's arm to keep her inside. A few other passengers got on, and he pressed the button to take them back up to his penthouse. They made three stops along the way for the others to get off, and Tam and he remained silent the entire ride. Her scent teased his nose, exotic spices mixed with sensual female. Irresistible. She brushed against him as she moved aside to let another woman out, and he barely resisted pulling her into his arms. He wanted her. Always. There were so many things he needed to speak to her about, but he wanted to throw that aside and bury his cock in her tight, welcoming sheath.

Deus, she really was going to drive him insane someday. She didn't even have to try.

The lift slid to a stop on the top floor, and he drew her out into the circular entryway. There were two sets of double doors—one to the right of the elevator and one to the left. Straight ahead was a round polyglass window that overlooked the London skyline. Swirling around the window was a mercurite sculpture that seemed to grow out of the floor and twine toward the ceiling.

"Impressive." Tam's mouth formed a little moue.

"Yes, it is. This way." He tugged her to the right, but

pointed left. "I found out the Averys are staying in the other penthouse."

"Of course they are."

A tiny smile touched his lips. "They were practically shagging against the wall this afternoon, with Hunter fumbling for the vidpad while Delilah had both hands down his pants."

"Ah." Tam brought her fist to her mouth, coughing to cover a laugh. "Newlyweds."

He tapped his entry code into the vidpad beside his doors and they disarmed with a quiet *snick*. Pulling one open, he ushered Tam inside. "I had the concierge send up dinner from Le Monde."

The dining table was long enough to seat thirty and could also be used as a conference table for business meetings. The huge main space opened to an even more massive balcony, and several bedrooms and wash closets opened off of the long hallway. At the end was a private lift he could use whenever he wanted. It was an exquisitely appointed home away from home, and it had been boring until Tam stepped inside.

She moved to the dinner set at one end of the table and slid into a chair. "What did you order for us?"

"The concierge recommended the duck." He removed the sealed lids that kept the dishes as fresh as the moment they were covered, and rich aromas filled the room.

"It looks lovely." Tam leaned forward and drew in the scent. "And smells even better. I do love the food at Le Monde."

"So I was informed." He poured them both a glass of wine. "The staff here said you preferred the Madeira."

"I do." She accepted the glass he offered, startling a bit when he bent down to brush a kiss over her lips. Sweet. Headier than the wine could ever be.

Walking around the table, he took his own seat and set his napkin on his lap. He watched her pick up her utensils and begin to eat. Her body seemed relaxed, but there was a tension around her eyes and mouth that gave her away. She was worried, scared. It made fury spurt through him, protectiveness following on its heels. He hated how helpless he was to fix this problem for her, but they were dancing to Stefan's tune.

They chatted lightly through the meal, touching on nothing important, and some of the tautness eased from both of them. It was good to be alone with her again, where no one was watching and neither of them was in imminent danger.

He'd missed her. Missed talking to her, being around her, looking at her. Everything.

Sighing, she sat back when she was done, a wan smile crossing her face. "All right, you didn't just bring me here to feed me."

He nodded, wishing that the tranquil moment didn't have to fade so quickly, but time was not a luxury they had. "So, Stefan doesn't have evidence against you or some precious object you owned. He has your only family held hostage. Is that all, or is there more you haven't told me yet?"

"No, that sums it up nicely. He has my sister." She shrugged, her smile growing sharper. "I'm not quite as materialistic as you imagined, despite my professional proclivities."

He settled back in his chair, unwilling to let her get away with so quick an assumption of his judgment. "I didn't know what to think. Mostly because you ran off and didn't tell me anything. Or lied to me."

She took a sip of her wine. "Both."

"I know." He blew out a breath. "My willing assistance comes with one condition."

"What's that?" Resignation settled over her lovely features, as if she'd expected him to demand something from her. Well, too bad. Nothing in life was free, not really. Not even love. It demanded everything from you, turned you inside out. No, nothing was free, *especially* not love.

"Don't ever lie to me again."

Her expression wavered, emotions flitting across her face so fast he couldn't read them. "I won't. You have my word."

Could he trust her to be honest, even if she promised? He didn't know, but they couldn't be mates if they didn't trust each other, and that had to start somewhere. So he was going to start here, now. "I want to help you keep your sister safe, but to do that, I need to know you're not keeping secrets from me, or telling me what you think I want to hear. Just be honest. I can take it."

"I never thought you couldn't." She shifted her shoulders against her chair. "If I thought you were so weak that making you my mark would break you, I wouldn't have done it. There is *some* honor among thieves. Some of us anyway. Not Stefan."

"It's a shame your mother married him." So, she thought he could handle her using him and stealing from him? He didn't know if he should be flattered or insulted.

"Yes, but Sophie is all I have left of my mother. It's not her fault Stefan is her father." She refused to meet his gaze. "My mother was beautiful and he wanted her. He made sure my father died in order to get her."

"Deus." The man had murdered to steal someone else's wife? For some reason, that reached a new level of bottom-feeding in Breck's estimation and made his stomach turn. "What did your mother think about that?"

"Denial was her dearest friend." Tam snorted, resignation and sadness mixing in her expression. "We lived on the London docks. She wanted out, like everyone else, and Stefan offered her that. She didn't look a gift horse in the mouth."

He shook his head, unable to wrap his mind around such an easy acquiesce. "Even though he killed her husband?"

"Denial."

"What about him forcing her daughter into a life of crime?"

He didn't buy the *mentoring* bullshit. Tam was too wary of Stefan to have been willing to be his protégé. Perhaps it had started that way—though he had his doubts—but she'd have been no freer to leave then than she was now. That she didn't deny it made it that much more obvious.

"Denial, Breck. Always denial." She toasted him and then took a gulp of her wine. "She didn't see what was going on because she didn't *want* to see it."

"How old were you when he married her?"

"Ten."

So young. The same age as little Sophie was now. "And how old were you when he forced you to commit a crime?"

"Still ten," she said, confirming his suspicion. She shrugged, the movement lithe and elegant. "I was a cheetah, so I was faster than anyone else on his payroll. That made me useful. Looking back, I think that was the only reason he didn't have me killed along with my father."

If she had died then, Breck would never have known her. The thought made his heart stop. He couldn't even imagine a world without her now. "How did he convince you to do it?"

He didn't want to know. Deus, he didn't, but the shadows that lurked in her eyes told him he'd hit on a sore point, an ugly memory for his mate. His fists balled on his thighs. He ached to reach for her, but the rigid way she held herself made it clear she wouldn't accept comfort from him now.

"When I told him no, he had one of his men break my arm and then lock me in a room for a week. They fed me only bread and water. When I finally broke, he let me out and told me the next time I defied him it would be worse for me. He'd lock me in with Kessler—one of his men then. Dead now, thank Deus." She shuddered, her fingers going white-knuckled on her glass. Her gaze was faraway, looking at a horror only she could see. "I knew what that meant. Kessler had had that look in his eyes when he stared at me. He'd have raped me and enjoyed every second of it. Hurting me would have been part of the fun." She ran her fingertip along a thin old scar on her forearm. "Stefan gave me this as a reminder of the occasion. After that, I did whatever he wanted."

Breck swallowed the bile that burned its way up the back of his throat. More than ever, he wanted to make sure that not only Tam and her sister came through this safely, but that Stefan got what was coming to him. "How did you get away from him?"

"There's always someone higher on every food chain." Her smile was wry, her eyes dark and sad as she met his gaze. "There was a man name Alissander who liked my work, liked my face. He paid Stefan a substantial amount to give me to him. Once Alissander died, I was a free agent."

The man had *sold* her, like she was nothing. A possession, a toy to be discarded after he was done playing with it. After he was done breaking it. Yes, Stefan would pay. Breck didn't know how or when, but the son of a bitch would pay. Rage curdled in his gut, and he struggled to unlock his jaw, to say something more intelligible than a string of curses. "I'm glad you escaped him."

"For a while, anyway." Her chin firmed. "Don't pity me, Breck."

"I don't." How could he? He felt rage for what Stefan had done, and respect for all she had survived and come out the woman he loved. She wasn't perfect, but she was his. Since she would never listen to him if he told her that simple truth, he changed the subject. "What about Sophie? How does she play into all of this? If he stole her, then she didn't live with her father after your mother died."

"No, I put her in an isolated, secure Swiss boarding school." She spread her hands. "My lifestyle is hardly conducive to child rearing, but what sane person would leave a little girl alone with a man like Stefan?" Her gaze went hard and flat. "Stefan doesn't give a damn about her. She's an inconvenience at best. She helped keep my mother tied to him, and that was all he cared about. When my mother died, I took Sophie away on vacation and just never brought her back. Stefan never even noticed, until now."

"Until she was useful to him." That seemed to be the only pattern with Stefan—people who were useful got to live. People who got in his way ended up dead. Probably far more of them than Gea had been able to find information on.

"Yes, he's using her to bring me back into the family fold and keep me in line." She drew in a breath that raised her lush breasts, and Breck had to force his gaze away.

"Why leave her alone? Why not go legit so you could keep her with you?"

Her laugh was brittle, nothing like her usual husky tones. "Who in their right mind would hire me? I can put together a fake ident with the best of them, but the real me wouldn't stand up to a simple background check. And I didn't want to make Sophie live a lie, pretending to be someone she's not." She shook her head. "Maybe I should have, but this is all I know how to do. Sad that the only job skills I have are from Stefan. I just . . . wanted better for Sophie."

"What will he do to her if you don't do what he wants?"

"At worst? Give her to one of his many disreputable associates for a little playtime. And make me watch. At best?" She closed her eyes for a moment. "Hell, I don't know. Turn her into me?"

A muscle flexed in his jaw. "He'd let a man rape his own daughter just to get to you?"

"She's a means to an end, Breck. We *all* are in Stefan's eyes. Never forget that." Her gaze was clear and calm. "No matter how nice he is to you, there's always an angle in it for him. He always has an agenda, an ulterior motive."

"Even when it came to your mother?"

She sighed, rubbing a hand over her forehead. "No, she was his only exception that I know of, but she would never have gainsaid him, so it didn't matter. As long as no one tried to use her against him, then he was immune to everyone and everything else."

Snorting, Breck forced his fingers to relax. "So, he loved her, but not his daughter or his stepdaughter."

"He was obsessed with her. I suppose that's as close to love as Stefan could get." Pushing back from the table, Tam took her plate and glass into the kitchen.

He rose to follow suit, still trying to quell the rage boiling through him. He wasn't naïve—far from it. He knew there were monsters in the world, and only some of them were professional criminals. There were quite a few in his world of high-stakes business who got away with as much or more than Stefan had. But the people they'd hurt weren't Tam. She hid it well, but he could see the pain in her eyes, the way she'd suffered, the way she still suffered for what her stepfather had done to her and her family.

It made Breck forget he was a rational, reasonable man. Calculating, even. He always assessed before he acted. He liked taking risks, but he wanted to know the score first. Except when it came to his mate. He'd been flying blind most of the time he'd been with her. No matter how deep he tried to dig so he knew what to anticipate, she seemed to have a knack for jerking the rug out from under him.

He blew out a breath and turned to join her in the kitchen. He found her with her hands braced on the counter, her head down. She looked defeated, hopeless.

Setting his plate aside, he pulled her into his arms and tangled a hand in her long hair. "Keep your chin up, Tam."

"You don't know what he's like, what he's capable of. Not really." Her fingers balled in the back of his shirt, holding on tight.

A quiver ran through her slender body, and he dropped his forehead to hers, looking into her dark eyes. "No, but I know what you're like. You can take him. I've got your back, beloved. He won't win. He won't hurt your sister. *We* won't let him."

"Breck—"

For a moment, he thought she might burst into tears. Her lips shook and her eyes brightened, but then she buried her hands in his hair and dragged his mouth down to hers. He went rigid for a moment. Deus, he'd pulled her close to offer her comfort, but there was no way his body wouldn't react to her. The animal within him craved her, demanded he touch and take. Claim her as his.

A groan spilled out of him, and she thrust her tongue between his lips, her fingers turning into claws that sliced through his shirt. Her flavor burst into his mouth, and the experience was visceral. He'd gone so long without tasting her, taking her. The agony of it had knifed into his soul every second of every day they'd been apart. The one time he'd had the night before hadn't been enough. Once was never enough with her.

His hands roamed her body, relearning her shape, her every soft curve.

Fire pulsed through his veins, flowing like lava. His cock went hard, and every little movement she made rubbed her against his swollen shaft. It was maddening, made him shudder. He cupped her ass, pulling her tight against him, pressing into the notch between her thighs. Exactly where he wanted to be. Her low whimper filled his mouth, drove him wild.

Trailing kisses down her throat, he bit the tendon that connected neck to shoulder lightly. She moaned, letting her head drop back. "Take me to bed, Breck. I want you on top of me, inside of me."

He didn't think it was possible, but his cock grew even stiffer. The sound of his own heartbeat rushed in his ears, and he bent to scoop Tam off her feet. She looped her arms around his neck, holding tight. The sight of her lips swollen with his kisses, her dark eyes glazed with passion, her lush breasts rising and falling as she panted was enough to shove him over the edge into feral. He wanted to slide inside her tight pussy and feel how her inner muscles gripped his shaft. A shudder ran through him, and he thought his skull might explode.

Kicking the bedroom door open, he strode in to set her on her feet beside the bed. "I think we're both wearing far too many clothes. Strip."

"Yes." Her fingers were already busy unfastening her top, her gaze gleaming with amusement.

Jerking his shirt over his head, he tossed it across the room. He had his pants and boots unsealed in moments and pushed them down, kicking them aside. He watched her slip off the last of her clothing, loving her smooth curves bared for him. "So beautiful."

He reached out and slid his fingertip across her collarbone and down to the valley of her cleavage. Her breath caught when he trailed his finger up the slope of one breast and circled her nipple. It went taut, beading tight and jutting toward him. He chuckled and dipped forward to suck the peak into his mouth.

Slim fingers speared into his hair, and he felt the drag of her claws against his scalp. Goose bumps broke down his limbs at the sensation, and he batted her nipple with his tongue, scraped her flesh with his teeth, and bit down ever so lightly. A cry broke from her and she fisted her hands in his hair. The slight pain served to sharpen his pleasure.

Deus, he didn't think he could wait much longer. He had to

be inside her again. The eagle within him demanded he take his mate, link their bodies until there was no question that they could ever be parted again. The man knew how many obstacles lay in their path, but the beast didn't care. All it wanted was its mate. Always. Backing her toward the bed, he let her tumble onto the mattress while he came down on top of her. A rough sound burst from his throat at the feel of all her soft, silky skin against his. So good. So amazing.

Wrapping her legs around him, she arched into his body, rubbing against his straining cock. He slid his hands up her arms, capturing her wrists. She stilled, her breath going shallow. When she tugged at her bound wrists, he held fast, knowing how much she loved it when she couldn't escape during sex. Her whimper tangled with a purr as she writhed against him. "Please, Breck. Please."

"If I had time, I'd tie you up and make you scream and beg while I went down on you."

"Oh, Deus." A shiver rippled through her body, and her legs tightened around his waist. "Please."

There was no resisting her. He transferred her wrists to one hand and reached the other between them to grasp his dick, guiding it to her wet slit. He eased the head in, felt her inner muscles clamp around him.

"Breck!" Desperation laced that one word, and her fangs bared, the feline just below the surface.

He felt his own talons slide forth, knew she felt the bite of them where his fingers gripped her arms, holding her down while he penetrated her. Shoving deep, he hilted his cock within her in a single thrust. She screamed his name, her body undulating beneath him, already moving in the carnal rhythm of sex. Any chance of finesse or control rushed away faster than an eagle diving from the sky. He withdrew, thrust, filled her and reveled in the sensation of her wet heat closing around his cock.

Picking up speed each time he entered her, he pushed them both to the end of their endurance, but he couldn't stop, couldn't slow down. He needed this connection, craved it, man and beast united in the unadulterated lust for this one woman. The sound of their skin slapping together echoed in the wide room, and the mattress creaked beneath them.

"I'm going to come." She moaned, jerking at her caged wrists. Her legs tightened around his hips, angling herself so that he sank even deeper on the next thrust.

"*Deus.*" His muscles burned as he moved. Faster. Harder. He reached between them, flicking the tip of one talon against her clit.

"Breck, Breck, *Breck!*" Her sex fisted around his cock as she went over into orgasm.

The feel of her channel clenching on his dick was more than enough to make him explode. He jetted come into her pussy, and kept pumping his cock inside her until she sobbed and pulled at her arms, another climax shuddering through her. A smug grin curled his lips. Deus, he loved how he could make her react. In bed, there were no pretenses.

Her dark eyes unfocused, her breasts heaving as she panted for breath. Which wouldn't be any easier with him weighing down on her. He heaved himself to the side, letting her loose as he rolled to his back. Contentment unfurled inside of him. If he could have this for the rest of his life, he'd die a happy man. Then again, if Stefan did him in, Breck might just get his wish far sooner than he'd care for.

He sighed, pushing thoughts of their problems away, and closed his eyes. The scent of sex and Tam filled the air, and he groped blindly for her hand, lifting it to his lips for a kiss. "I think we get better every time."

She chuckled, the sound sleepy and fulfilled. "You might be right."

"Only *might*?" He smiled, but bit the base of her thumb as retribution.

"Well, I wouldn't want you to stop *trying* to improve and just assume it will." She laid her cheek on his shoulder. "It does a man good to make him work a little. Makes him appreciate what he's got."

There was a moment of awkward silence. She tensed, and he could all but feel her regret in having said those words. Considering he'd been chasing her for months and had left his business in order to come to London, he'd say he'd worked more than a little for her. And it wasn't over yet. He sighed, leaning over to kiss her forehead. "Then consider yourself the most appreciated woman in the galaxy."

"Only this galaxy?" She injected teasing into her voice, using a bit of banter they'd said to each other before.

So he gave her his usual reply. "All of them, beloved. All of them."

Tilting her head back, she met his lips in a sweet kiss. Her tongue tangled with his, her fingers stroking his jaw. The eagle within him preened at the feel of its mate's touch. Such a primal effect on both beast and man. His cock began to stir again. He'd never get enough of her. He didn't want to.

A disgruntled groan sounded from her and she fell back, breaking the kiss. "I have to get back."

"I know."

She pushed herself off the bed, staggered as she looked around the room for her clothes. "Stefan will be waiting and my time is almost up."

"I'll see you tomorrow." He watched her gather her things into a pile on the end of the bed, then use her cheetah speed to put everything back on. "I've secured a hired transit to take us to Ascot. We leave just before dawn. I'll wait in the lobby for you."

She nodded, fastening her skirt as she stepped into her shoes. "Will you need any help finding somewhere for us to stay overnight?"

"No, one of my secretaries handled it. I left a message in their cache." Hating to let her go, but knowing he had no choice, he caught her arm and pulled her close, then brushed a tender kiss across her lips. "Be safe."

The smell of horses, hay, and churned earth tickled Tam's nose. So unlike the stink of city that she was used to. The open air was so foreign, no gleaming mercurite skyrises overhead, no crush of people to wade through. A light patter of rain drizzled from the sky, mist winding over the hills in the distance.

The Ascot Raceplex spread out before her, and the box she was in overlooked the huge crowd gathered to watch the race. Vidscreens levitated above the grassy midfield, broadcasting every moment of the action. Horses reared in excitement, eyes rolling. Of course, that could be the scent of thousands of predator-shifters crowding around them. Poor beasties.

This weekend was for the ponies, but the raceplex was also used for dog racing and even shifter-beast racing where humans in their animal forms would compete in speed and endurance competitions. Some of those were somewhat less than legally sanctioned by the crown, but such was the way of the world.

Breck stepped up beside her, running his palm down to the small of her back. He had a glass of champagne in his other hand, delivered to their box along with a few choice hors d'oeuvres. "Any sign of him?"

"Not yet." But he was here. She could smell him, some-where in the throng of people. But they'd track him down eventually. Breck had made certain they were in a prime loca-tion, and after the race they were attending an exclusive party that Abernathy had also been invited to. She'd had to work every charming bit of manipulation she had to secure that invitation for them. With any luck, she and Breck would make a new friend.

With any luck, they could all get out of this alive.

As glad as she was to be away from Stefan for the weekend, she hated that she'd had to leave her little sister with him. She hated every second that Sophie spent in his company. Or near Leland and Nichols. Or anywhere within a hundred kilometers of anyone Stefan had any influence over. It made her skin crawl, knowing what could happen to her baby sister.

Which was why this was such an effective weapon to use against her, the son of a bitch. And there was no legal way to get Sophie away from him. He was her father. He had legal custody. He could bring every illegal, immoral thing Tam had ever done against her if she tried to sue for any kind of rights. No, they had to settle this the way their kind did—quietly and without any law involved.

What made her stomach turn was how she was ever going to keep Sophie safe once this was over. Stefan had to be dead or in jail for life. Preferably dead. But Tam had never killed anyone. She manipulated, she stole, but she didn't physically hurt people. Could she coldly kill a man? To keep her sister safe, she hoped so. But how and when? His two guard dogs were always nearby, and Stefan might be twice her age, but he was also stronger than he looked.

And she was afraid of him.

So many years of him beating her down, threatening her, terrifying her. The psychological effect was something she couldn't deny and shouldn't underestimate.

"There," Breck said, jolting her back into the here and now. He nodded toward the ring the trainers and handlers walked the horses in.

She had to focus on using her feline vision to see the man

where he stood by the rail inspecting a tall black stallion. "Good eye."

Breck grunted. "I'm an eagle. And I'm motivated."

So was she. They had to play this game until they found a way out. "If he sticks to pattern, we'll see him at the Duke of Gemini's winner's celebration."

"Gemini?" Breck blinked down at her, his eyebrows lifting. "That's not an English title."

"No, he's not English." She shrugged. "I believe it's a self-bestowed title."

His lips twitched in a grin, his brows rising higher. "They allow that?"

"When you own your own island in the middle of the Atlantic, you can call yourself whatever you want." She smiled back, amusement darting through her. His Grace was nothing if not eccentric, given to flamboyant displays and colorfully covered in nanotats he liked to reconfigure every other day. The buzz was he had his own personal nanotat artist on staff to service him whenever a new whim struck. "Most believe he was quite restrained in leaving it at duke and not trying for king or emperor."

"Very restrained. What kind of shifter is he?"

She frowned. "Some kind of reptile, I believe. I'm not certain which species, though."

"What kind of shifter is Stefan?" There was a hint of disgust in his voice when he said the other man's name. "It wasn't listed in any of the files I have on him."

"A weasel." Her smile wasn't nice. Neither was Breck's answering snort. She met his gaze. "Appropriate, but being a lesser predator species doesn't help him in a fight. He doesn't often shift unless he's using his small size to escape someone. Or hide in some dark hole until the coast is clear."

"And his men?"

"Nichols is a dingo. Nasty little mongrel, very dangerous. Leland, you don't have to worry about shifting on you. Unless you're near water, in which case, you're sunk."

"He's a fish-shifter?"

"A great white shark."

"Of course he is," Breck muttered, huffing on a laugh and shaking his head. The breeze tossed around his blond hair, and the sun made the strands shine like gold. He was so handsome. His white teeth flashed in a little smile that was warm and just for her. Her heart turned over, even as she tried to harden it against him.

No matter which way this situation flipped, she couldn't see how someone like her could ever end up with someone like him, mates or not. The thought made her ache inside, but she couldn't lie to herself. She was a criminal, and he was a golden eagle—the golden boy from a golden family that had been wealthy and influential since before the Third Great War, when most people had lost everything. Circumstances might have brought them together for a little while, but in the end he'd have to fly away. A woman like her would be toxic to him, dragging him down into the gutter with her.

Reaching up, she brushed back a lock of hair from his forehead. He caught her hand, kissed her fingers. "That's a very serious look you're wearing, beloved."

Beloved. She loved it when he called her that, though she knew she shouldn't. She wished it could last, this thing between them. Nothing had ever felt as good. Not even the rush of pulling off a heist. But she had to focus on getting Sophie free of Stefan, even if it cost Tam's life to do it. A future wasn't a luxury she had anymore.

Instead of responding to him verbally, she rose up on tiptoe and kissed him, telling him with actions what she'd never said outright. He hummed, his hands settling on her hips to pull her close. She could feel his rising erection against her stomach, and her body responded with alarming enthusiasm. They both jolted when a loud horn blared out across the raceplex.

"And they're off!" The announcer's voice echoed across the grandstands, calling out the actions of the current race. A deafening cheer went up when the horses swept past.

The rest of the day went the same, the tension before a race building up, the horses parading by, the horn blaring, and then a few minutes of controlled chaos before it started all over again.

Breck rolled his shoulders beside her, stepping back to throw himself into one of the kleather chairs in their private box. "Deus, how many more of these are there?"

She glanced at the nanosheet she'd been given when they arrived. "We've done six, so . . . three more, according to the program."

A groan was his only answer. He pinched the bridge of his nose.

Tossing the nanosheet onto a low, hammered mercurite table, she reached out to press a button embedded in the wall. A privacy screen engaged, so they could see and hear everything going on around them, but no one could see or hear them. Then she walked over to Breck and crouched beside him. "You don't have to be involved in—"

"Don't. Just don't." His hand dropped to the arm of the chair and his eyes met hers. "I'm just impatient to do this thing. It's how I get before closing any big deal. Now is the time I'd usually shift and go for a long flight to burn off some energy." He shrugged, tapping his fingers restlessly against the kleather. "I'm fine."

She could definitely understand that. The tension had been winding tighter and tighter inside of her since she'd kissed a sleeping Sophie's forehead this morning before leaving her in the dubious care of Stefan, Leland, and Nichols.

A little distraction before they went after Abernathy would be a good thing for both of them. She ran the tip of her nail up the inseam of his pants, grinning when the muscles in his leg went taut and his cock began to swell against his fly.

His throat worked when he swallowed, his Adam's apple bobbing. "What are you doing?"

"No one can see us." Glancing at the privacy screen that made the air waver ever so slightly, she tugged at the seal on his fly. "I know you've tried exhibitionism before. I remember the night we spent in the Peep Show at Tail. Pressed up against the glass for everyone in the technobrothel to watch."

The look in his eyes was hot enough to burn. A little smile quirked up one side of his lips. "I remember. I remember every nanosecond we've ever spent together. Every word, every sigh, every moan. I'm not the one who's been running away from what we have."

Now it was her turn to swallow, her hands stilling. "It was for your own good."

"Was it?" His finger crooked under her chin, forcing her to meet his gaze. "Or was it because you're scared to be with a man you're not trying to scam?"

"It's more complicated than that and you know it. My life is . . ." She rolled a shoulder forward, unable to find the right words. The convincing words. But who was she trying to convince? Him or herself? She didn't know anymore, and that disturbed her more than she liked.

Breck shook his head. "Your life is what it's always been, Tamryn. This specific situation is especially personal for you, but . . . this is your life. Playing the game. On the grift."

Never safe. Never trusting anyone. Never knowing if or when her cover might be blown. Never letting anyone in. She'd been lying to everyone so long, it threw her off balance that he knew the truth, that he was seeing the sordid ugliness of her reality. She might have learned to pass for someone wealthy and worthy of a man like Breck, but she knew what was fiction and what wasn't. She didn't lie to herself.

He leaned forward, his lips a micrometer from hers. They stayed that way for a protracted moment, gazes locked. The scent of him filled her nose, and her muscles loosened, heated. His breath brushed against her skin when he spoke. "Maybe if you stay around me long enough, it won't be so scary to have something real with someone who knows you."

Butterflies winged through her stomach and she wanted to pull back, wanted to hide behind a convenient mask, a charming smile, but there were no masks with this man. He'd seen behind them. But he was wrong. It wasn't just scary to consider having something real with someone who wasn't just another grifter like her.

It was terrifying.

Gut-wrenching. Utterly horrifying.

It couldn't happen. This wasn't her reality. There were no fairy-tale endings for people like her. She was no one's sweet, innocent little Cinderella. She was more akin to the wicked witch. And she didn't have time for fantasies. She had bigger problems to deal with—like keeping her sister alive and well. *That* was no game to her.

Pushing to her feet, she twisted away from Breck. "Let's watch the—"

His hands snapped around her waist, jerking her backward into his lap. She squealed, her claws unsheathing on instinct as she grabbed the arms of the chair for balance. Struggling against his grip, she hissed. "I can slice you open, birdbrain. Don't forget that."

He controlled her movements, and she could feel his rigid

cock rubbing against her backside as she wriggled. His voice was a low growl in her ear. "Ah, but you know I like it when you use your claws on me, kitty cat. Just like I know that you like it when I make sure you can't."

Meaning when he tied her down and did whatever he wanted with her. Wicked, carnal things that made her moan and beg for him to make her come. Over and over again. And he did. He always did.

His arms locked tight around her waist, holding her still. One hand gathered up the front of her dress until he could reach under it and slide his palm up her thigh to cup her sex.

Excitement whipped through her, made her breath rush in little pants and her heart pound in her ears. It almost drowned out the sound of the horn that announced the next race. His talons shredded her panties, left her hot, slick sex exposed. He jerked the scrap of microsilk away and threw it to the floor. The brush of cool air against her heated skin made her shudder and writhe. He ran the tip of one talon along the lips of her pussy, and her hands clenched on the arms of the chair.

"Breck," she hissed through gritted teeth, feeling her fangs rub against her bottom lip.

Not bothering to answer, he flicked his talon across her hardened clit, and the muscles in her thighs jerked in response. She moaned, opened her legs to hook over his, and let her head fall back on his broad shoulder. The fabric of his shirt rustled, and there was something undeniably erotic about the fact that the only parts of them that were unclothed were their sexes. His cock prodded her backside, making her burn for the surcease that only he could give her.

"Slide my cock into your pussy, Tam." His voice was a rough, intimate growl that sent shivers racing down her skin.

Releasing her hold on the arm of the chair, she had to concentrate on retracting her claws before she could do as he bid.

She reached between her spread thighs to grasp his straining dick. Pressing the head to her entrance, she rocked her hips backward to take him into her while he thrust up. They both moaned as he filled her.

"Breck!"

"Tam," he groaned in return. "Ride me, beloved."

As if there was any other choice now. She had to finish this, her body screeched for fulfillment, the cheetah within her little more than a cat in heat. She lifted and lowered her hips, and his rocked to the same quick rhythm she set for them. Now. She wanted to come now. He slipped one hand up to fondle her breasts through her dress, roughly pinching and twisting each tight nipple in turn. Pinpricks of sensation radiated out from where he touched her. It was exquisite torment.

Using her grip on the chair for leverage to move ever faster, she took advantage of her cheetah speed. The cat and woman wrestled for control, and she wasn't sure who won. They both got what they wanted.

Sweeping the finger on his other hand back and forth across her clit in time with her movements, Breck pushed her to the edge of her endurance. The way his cock filled her, stretched her to the limit, made her clench her teeth. It was too much, each deep penetration sent tingles skipping down her limbs. She could feel orgasm building inside her, her muscles tightening until she knew she'd snap. Up, down, up, down, she rode him hard and fast, sweat slipping down her temples and her lungs heaving as she chased after that inevitable conclusion.

"Come for me, Tam," he ordered, pinching her clit.

She imploded, her channel fisting around his cock in hard pulses that left her gasping. His hands bracketed her hips, holding tight enough to leave bruises. He took over the motion, forcing her to move on his cock as he kept thrusting into her pussy, dragging her orgasm out while low cries burst from her throat. Her inner muscles flexed on his cock again and again until she thought she might die from the overwhelming sensation, but then he froze beneath her, jerked her down to seal her sex to his, and ground his pelvis upward into her pussy. She screamed as another climax streaked through her, and his come pumped inside of her while he groaned, long and loud.

Relaxing bonelessly against him when it was over, she felt quivers of aftershock running through her limbs. It was headier than a hit of bliss. She sighed and pried her claws out of the kleather. "I ruined the chair."

"Worth every cred they're going to charge me for it," he replied, stroking his fingers in lazy circles on the inside of her thigh. A satiated sigh heaved from his broad chest. "We need to get ready for the party."

But he made no move to rise, just stayed right where he was. Which made it that much harder for her to do the right thing, but a flash of Sophie's face went through her mind and she had to act.

She rose on shaky legs, his cock sliding free as she stood. Her thighs were damp with her wetness and his seed. Keeping her dress bunched in her hands, she turned for the wash closet. "I'll be right back."

"I can clean up out here." Grabbing for a napkin that had arrived with the champagne and appetizers, he groaned. "Hurry, I think the last race is about to start."

As if to prove his point, the blast of the horn echoed over the raceplex. She put a bit of cheetah speed behind her clean up, using water, sanitizer, and a hand towel to take care of as much of the mess they'd made as possible. It would have to do. They didn't have time to go back to the inn where they were staying to change clothing. She smoothed her dress down her legs and tidied her hair, then stepped out in time to see him sealing his pants.

"Time to go."

Stooping down, he picked something up off the floor. He

dangled what was left of her panties from one finger, bringing them up to his nose to sniff. "Ah, the scent of a woman who's wet." His grin was wicked. "I don't think you'll be wearing these to the party. Let's hope there's no breeze to lift that skirt up."

"The party is indoors."

The sound of his rich laughter followed her out of the box.

5

Two steps forward and three steps back. It was the endless dance between Breck and Tam. He tried to pull her toward him, and she pushed back. There was a hollow fear in the pit of his stomach every time he thought about what happened once this was over. Assuming they came through this in one piece—and he could only hope that was even possible—he still had no idea if she would want anything permanent with him. The cheetah-shifter was a moving target. A very fast one, at that.

She knew they were mates now, but what did that really mean to her? She didn't feel this connection, this compulsion to stay with one person forever. That was the albatross around his neck, not hers. For all he knew, she didn't even give a shit. She might want him, might care about him, might even love him, but that hadn't kept her with him before. What chance did he have that it would keep her with him now?

How long could he keep chasing her? How many times did she have to shove him away before giving up was better than trying again?

He sighed. Now wasn't the time. Her mind was on the situation with her sister, as it should be. He couldn't hold that against her. If he had any family left, he'd do whatever it took to help, too. Just as he was willing to do whatever it took to help his mate. But in the back of his mind, the nagging worry was constantly there.

What if she disappeared again?

Slipping his arm around her trim waist, he led her into the Duke of Gemini's party. He blinked. The place was . . . *gaudy* was the best word he could come up with. It was festooned with microsilk rosettes in every imaginable shade. Most of them ugly. There were ice sculptures, gyrating belly dancers, a fountain burbling liquid that looked remarkably like blood, and a banal few vidscreens replaying the racing highlights of the day. Somehow, he'd expected something a bit more tasteful. Polished and refined.

This was none of those things.

Glancing up at him, Tam snorted. "You really hadn't heard of His Grace's tastes?"

"What taste?" He whispered from the corner of his mouth, smoothing his expression into the polite lines his mother had always insisted on when the Breckenridges were in public.

A giggle spilled from her, and she covered her mouth with her fingertips. She was so beautiful. Her black microsilk dress managed to be sexy, chic, and sophisticated at the same time. Her hair had been up this morning, but their session in the raceplex box had left it trailing down her back in soft waves. He wanted to get his hands into it again, loved that he knew she wore nothing under the dress. He wanted his hands under that again, too.

She poked his arm. "Here he comes."

He didn't have to ask which of the many men milling in the huge room was the duke. No, there was only one who fit right in to this tacky monstrosity. He was as round as he was tall and rolled toward them, loud laughter bursting from his throat at something the painfully skinny man beside him said.

Tam bent her head and curtsied deeply when the duke stopped in front of them. Breck managed to incline his head respectfully, but he wasn't going to bow. He'd probably fall over laughing. The man was the most ridiculous thing he'd ever seen. A brilliant green snake nanotat wound up from under his shirt, wrapped around his neck and up his face. It writhed under his skin, blinking and flicking out its forked tongue. Another nanotat was a single blue tear that rolled down his cheek from the corner of one eye, rolled back up again, and then trailed down once more.

"Your Grace," Tam purred as she rose from her curtsy. "It's a pleasure to meet you."

"Ah, who's this?" The man's puffy cheeks made his eyes disappear when he smiled.

"I'm Constantine Breckenridge, and this lovely lady is Felicia Tamryn." Summoning up his most winning grin, Breck introduced them with a flourish of his hand. A man like this would appreciate a bit of ostentation. "By odd coincidence, we both prefer our last names to our first, so please call us Breck and Tam, Your Grace."

The rotund man's laugh boomed out. "It is quite the coincidence, no?"

Tam's hand tucked into the crook of Breck's elbow. The look she gave him was nothing short of adoring. "I've always liked to think it's part of what makes us perfect for each other. We have so much in common."

"You are a beautiful couple." His Grace favored them with a little wave that would have made the queen proud. "Enjoy my party. Have a drink to celebrate all the winners today, and another to commiserate with those who weren't as lucky."

He and his entourage rolled by, leaving Breck and Tam to circulate with the other guests. She poured on the charm whenever they spoke to anyone, and he was reminded why she was so good at getting people to do whatever she wanted. She was beautiful, smart, witty, and she had enough charisma to draw even the most resistant out of their shells. Some of it was real, he knew, but some was an act for the benefit of those watching. He doubted anyone except him could tell the difference. She was damn good at what she did. If only she used her abilities for something slightly less nefarious.

An hour and a half passed before they got their first glimpse of Abernathy. Finally. Breck took a step in his direction, but Tam's hand restrained him. She murmured, "Let him come to us."

"Why?"

Her eyes sparkled with laughter when she met his gaze. "Who does this for a living, again?"

Snorting, he pinched her backside, making her jolt forward a bit. "I wasn't arguing with your expertise, just trying to learn something."

"Considering a new career?" She arched an eyebrow.

"Your tactics would work in my line of work, beloved." Something he'd thought more than once before. Would that be a way to keep her? Give her a legitimate outlet for her skills and the opportunity to keep Sophie with her? She'd said this was the only thing she could do once she'd become a criminal, because no one would hire her. Perhaps he could change that for her. Then again, he wasn't certain being her boss was a direction he wanted to take their relationship. Something to consider at a later date.

Another member of the House of Lords drifted near, and Tam drew her and her husband into a conversation. Catherine and Kenneth Fordythe seemed to like to hear themselves speak expansively on everything. The topics went from horse racing to laws regulating betting on human races. It was then that Abernathy and his wife came to say hello to the other couple, and Breck realized that somehow Tam had known this would happen, that the two members of the House of Lords were friends and talking to one would bring over the other.

Impressive.

He engaged lightly in the discussion. Most of it was about English politics, which was something he knew little about. He did participate in conversations about business. Mostly, he just watched Tam do her thing, making both the other couples fall in love with her.

Abernathy's wife sighed, glancing at a troupe of gyrating belly dancers with a small smile. She had a face that could rival any of the horses at the raceplex today. "This is a very . . . exotic party. We don't get anything like this in London."

"Is that really a bad thing, Drusilla?" Breck arched his eyebrows in mock surprise, making the politicians try to hide a snicker.

"I like it. It adds a bit of . . . something to the occasion." Mrs. Fordythe waved her champagne flute, indicating the ice sculptures shaped like famous racehorses and lit in eye-searing phosphorescent colors. Her husband hummed in agreement with her, but he didn't seem to disagree with her about anything. She had him well trained.

Lord Abernathy huffed, his thick mustache ruffling. "I do like things a bit more dignified, but this is the place to be after the Classic."

It took Breck a moment to remember the final race today had been a big annual event called the Ascot Classic.

"Well, perhaps we can accommodate your tastes." His smile included both couples. "Tam and I are hosting a party back in town at my penthouse. The Royale. You'll all be sure to come, won't you?"

Abernathy's eyebrows rose at the mention of the exclusive establishment. If Breck had the penthouse there, it said something about his affluence as well as his influence. He let his smile widen. "I'm in town on business for a few weeks. Always good to meet new people, make new connections. You never know what might come of it."

"What business is that, if you don't mind my boldness?" Mr. Fordythe asked.

Breck took a sip of his scotch. "I own the Breckenridge Group, among other enterprises."

And that was when his last name connected with what the newsvids said about New Chicago corporations. He watched their eyes light as comprehension dawned, and a bit of calculated greed came from both politicians.

"Good friends of ours, Hunter Avery and his mate, will also be there." Tam rested her head against Breck's shoulder, the very image of innocent curiosity. "Have you met the Averys before?"

Few had. Before his mating, Hunter had been a well-known recluse, shying away from the public because he was guaranteed to end up on the newsvids. Now, however, if his wife had a job in London or Beijing or any other city on the planet, he was likely to be close behind.

Tam offered a sweet smile. "They're a charming couple. Really, you must meet them, mustn't they, darling?"

"Of course." Breck grinned back, trying to look as adoring as she did, but doubting he pulled it off.

"I'll be certain to send details around to your secretaries." When they came up with those details, she meant.

There wasn't a reciprocal offer to attend the Abernathy's ball, but at least they had an additional opportunity to wrangle that out of them. Breck was willing to bet if the Averys showed at the party, he and Tam could command any audience they wanted. People would use any angle to get a piece of Hunter Avery.

Tam ran a hand down Breck's arm. "Darling, I seem to have run out of champagne."

"We can't have that. Let's see if we can find a waiter." After they stepped away, he bent and whispered in her ear, "How are you going to guarantee the Averys are there? Darling."

She grinned at him. "I thought I'd try asking them."

"You think that will work?" His tone was dubious, he couldn't help it. "Hunter hates society parties."

Her shoulder dipped in a nonchalant shrug. "Delilah would come for me."

"She's a friend?"

"*Friend* is perhaps too strong a word, but we've developed a respect for each other's work over the years." Tam's eyes crinkled at the corners, but she didn't quite smile. "We're both very good at what we do, and that can occasionally be ... mutually beneficial."

He frowned down at her. "You've worked together before?"

"I can't say." She winked. "Discretion."

"Honor among thieves." He chuckled as they reached a table filled with miniaturized dishes from all imaginable food groups. He picked up one that looked like it might have been a tiny chicken.

"Yes, as a matter of fact," she retorted a little too sharply. "There *are* certain codes of conduct that people adhere to. It keeps us all safe. Or safer, as the case may be."

"Stop assuming that every word I say about your profession is a criticism." He shot her a look.

"I'm not." But the protest was weak; she tried to hide a wince and didn't quite succeed.

"You are. Stop it." He held up the chicken. "What kind of gene-junking do you think made this possible?"

"More importantly, is it safe to consume?" Her lips twisted into a funny shape, though he thought he saw a flash of relief that he wasn't going to pursue the disagreement.

"I don't think I'll risk it." He set the dish back down and got

222 / *Crystal Jordan*

back to their original discussion. "I like the Averys. I'm sure they'll be delightful additions to our party. I assume you know someone who can plan it for us."

"Yes. Me. I may have grown up on the London docks, but I can throw a party that won't shame you." She hurried on when he gave her a pointed look. "I'll speak to the Royale catering staff when we return to town tomorrow."

It was moments like this that showed the cracks in the veneer she'd applied so carefully. When she was manipulating people, she was the most confident woman he'd ever met. When it came to the woman beneath the act, she had flashes of vulnerability that caught him off guard. Sometimes it even seemed to border on self-loathing, and that worried him. "Well, then. Better you than me."

"I assume you have an assistant who handles these things for you." She gingerly bit into what looked like a mutated strawberry. It was fluorescent blue. Her eyes widened in horror and she snatched up a flute of champagne, gulping it down.

"Glad I didn't risk it." He laughed at the expression on her face. "But I have three assistants, at last count. They handle everything. Terrifyingly efficient women. You remember them."

She frowned. "You only had two."

Shrugging, he slid a hand into his pocket. "I had to add another when some of my focus was taken up by tracking down a certain cheetah."

"Ah."

He pressed his free hand to the middle of her back and urged her away from the questionable delicacies the Duke of Gemini was offering. "They're making sure my board of directors doesn't stage a coup while I'm on . . . vacation."

"Some vacation." Her glance was dubious.

He met her gaze squarely. "I'm exactly where I'd like to be, with who I want to be with, and I'm not working. That's a vacation."

Clearing her throat, she made her tone light and teasing. "You should really try somewhere warmer next time. Get a little sun."

"Only if you plan to join me." He drew her fingers to his lips, kissing them. "I'm sure Sophie would love a trip to the beach."

Her dark gaze softened. "My sister is invited, hm?"

"She's family, isn't she?" He pressed his lips to the middle of her palm. "My family always vacationed together, even after I reached adulthood. Before my parents passed, that is."

"I'm sorry." Her fingers tightened around his, sympathy in her gaze.

"It was a long time ago, but thank you." He cleared his throat and glanced away. It was probably one of the reasons he wanted her with him so badly. He wanted the connections he'd lost when his parents died. Their transport had collided with another and no one had survived the accident. Most of the people in his life now were there because of his work, but not Tam. He wanted that closeness, people who mattered to him. In his life, in his home. Sophie was part of that image now, too; because she was someone Tam loved, he automatically widened his circle of family to include the girl.

The belly dancers came near, pulling his thoughts back to the present. He realized that they were naked except for the huge albino pythons wrapped around their bodies. The pythons shifted into naked women and the two original dancers quickly shifted into massive black anaconda snakes, twining themselves around the paler dancers.

Breck's eyebrows arched. "Maybe there's something to be said for Gemini's parties. Should we have them perform at—"

His breath whooshed out when Tam elbowed him in the ribs.

* * *

Tam slept fitfully in the transport back the next day. She hadn't slept much at all since leaving London. Breck had been insatiable, reaching for her again and again during the night. She hadn't complained. She wanted him every bit as much as he wanted her. It would scare her less if it was just the sex she wanted, but she stuffed that thought down to the deepest, darkest corner of her soul. She was just using him. That was what she did with men. And that was what men did with her. It was a lesson Stefan had taught her well.

It stung her to think of Breck in those terms, but she was brutally honest with herself. If she didn't expect this to last, then she was using him to help get Sophie away from Stefan. Forcing Breck into the same category with all the other men she'd ever known felt wrong, but she couldn't deny it was true.

She just hated that it was true. There was nothing she could do about it, but that was her life.

Turning her thoughts away from her pathetic excuse for a love life, she reviewed the weekend. Stefan probably wasn't going to be pleased they hadn't secured the invitation to the Abernathys' ball, but Tam thought this might be even better. It would give her the opportunity to study them more and perhaps uncover what it was about them that interested Stefan. Anything to get some kind of advantage. Did they have something valuable to steal? An ancient artifact, encrypted information, a vault filled with cred chips? None of the research she, Breck, or his hired investigators had done had turned up anything that was particularly unusual about Lord Abernathy or his wife.

Tam and Breck had left for London after another mind-numbing day of horse races, but they'd again managed to mingle with the Abernathys. Good, but best not to press too fast. She sensed the couple was used to people trying to leech from them. Drusilla had casually mentioned that Abernathy was the queen's cousin—a by-blow of some affair her uncle had had with his interior designer. Hardly the first royal bastard, but it seemed Abernathy was quite close to the queen, which meant he had influence. It was the most interesting thing about the man, which wasn't very. He was probably used to pandering sycophants who hoped he'd drop a word to his cousin for them.

The Averys were as close to royalty as Americans claimed, so having them at the party was imperative. In the Abernathys' minds, it would put Breck and Tam into the same category as they were in—able to bend the ear of one of the most powerful people on the planet. Of course, the English would never consider upstart Americans in quite the same class, but Hunter Avery was the wealthiest man alive. Money talked.

"We're here." When they rocked to a stop in front of the Royale, Breck exited their private transport and helped her out. "I'll have them send our bags up."

"Good." She brushed a kiss over his cheek. "I'm going to speak to the concierge and catering staff about our little soiree."

When she turned to do just that, he caught her arm and spun her around, jerking her into his arms. His lips covered hers, and he licked his way into her mouth. Molding herself against him, she wrapped her arms around his neck and rose on tiptoe. His teeth scraped her lower lip, making her shudder. Her tongue twined with his, and his flavor burst over her taste buds. Her body reacted as it always did whenever he was near. Her nipples tightened, her pussy dampened, and the cheetah within her writhed in feral need.

He groaned, his hands coasting down her sides to cup her hips. The tips of his fingers almost brushed her ass, but not quite. They managed to keep it mostly civilized in public.

This time.

When he lifted his head, they were both panting for breath. She could see the sharp look of the eagle in his eyes, saw how he wrestled with control as much as she did. A wry smile curled her lips. She let herself drop back down, enjoying the slide of their bodies together, the feel of his erection prodding her. Laying her cheek on his shoulder, she let herself lean on him for just a moment. His solid, steady strength was such a balm right now. She shouldn't let herself rely on it, but for just a few more seconds she let herself cling.

His palm cupped the back of her head. "It's going to be all right."

"You can't know that." She swallowed hard, battling back the emotion that threatened to drag her under.

"No, you're right. I can't know it." He kissed her forehead, then released her to step back. His blue eyes met hers. "But I can believe it. Someone has to."

"Such an optimist." She tsked. "Who'd have ever thought it of Constantine Breckenridge?"

He winked, turned to speak to the bellman, and she took the opportunity to slip away to speak to the Royale staff as she'd promised.

It took an hour of persuading, but she got her way. The party would be in two days. Three days before the Abernathy ball. Perfect. The menu, the waitstaff, and all the other major details had been negotiated. She was certain they'd come up with more that needed deciding, but the important arrangements were finalized. Good.

She would have heaved a sigh of relief, but that was only the first step of many to make sure everything went according to Stefan's master plan.

Pulling out her palmtop, she stepped into a private alcove outside the staff offices and called Delilah. Almost immediately, the woman's face appeared on the vidscreen, her spiky blond hair a bit mussed on one side. No doubt Hunter was to blame there. Curiosity sparkled in Delilah's green eyes. "What did you need, Tam?"

Of course Tam wouldn't be calling unless she wanted something. She would have assumed the same if Delilah ever called her. "A very small thing, actually."

The blonde smirked. "You can't have my kidneys."

Tam snorted. "I haven't taken to human organ trafficking, but I wouldn't start with Hunter Avery's mate if I were getting into that business."

Delilah tilted her head. "Well, since you know I'm not into shady business anymore, then I'm guessing this *does* have to do with being Hunter Avery's mate."

"You always were a smart one."

"Thank you," she demurred. "What did you need?"

"Breck and I are hosting a small event in his penthouse the day after tomorrow." Tam flashed her most charming smile. "I'd like you to attend."

Delilah's nose wrinkled. "And bring my mate, right?"

"Right."

"He'd hate that. He hates nobbing with the rich and pretentious. What makes you think we'd go for something like that?"

Trepidation flooded Tam, and she tried to keep the desperation out of her expression and voice. She widened her smile. "Because I asked you?"

Delilah's brows contracted. "Do I owe you a favor I'm forgetting about?"

"No, but I have a feeling I'm about to owe you one," Tam returned wryly.

The blond woman's grin made her look every millimeter the lynx she was. "I'm not in the business of needing favors anymore, Tam."

"I know." Tam took a breath. "You have a sister you love. What would you be willing to do if she were in danger?"

The lynx-shifter's eyes narrowed to dangerous slits. "Is that a threat? Is my sister in danger?"

228 / *Crystal Jordan*

"No, *your* sister isn't in danger."

She blinked, her eyebrows rising until they almost met her hairline. "I didn't know you had any family."

"In this business, it's safer that way if they aren't in the game." Tam let her shoulder dip into a shrug. It was as true as possible. Sophie wasn't in the game, and Stefan wasn't someone she really considered family.

"Yeah, I could see that." Delilah snorted. "My sister's reputation is far more notorious than mine. Legalized, but still." She shrugged. "I'm glad this wasn't a threat, Tam. That's never been your style. I'd like to think you wouldn't stoop so low."

"I'd like to think so, too. We all have the lines we won't cross, no matter what profession we're in." And they all had things that would break them, make them cross every line they'd ever had. Tam had once told herself she would *never* work with Stefan again. She knew the smile she offered Delilah was crooked. "I'm not asking your mate or you to get involved in anything south of legal, but your presence would certainly make my mark more willing to attend." She swallowed, let her tone go soft and pleading. "I don't want to bring anyone I don't have to in on this, but for my family . . ."

"Breck seemed pretty involved when we saw you together the other day."

She huffed out a breath. "His choice and his stubborn persistence. I tried to keep him out of it."

"Men."

"Rich, powerful men used to getting everything they want," she agreed.

"Exactly when they want it, yeah." Delilah sighed. "We'll be there. I can't promise how long I can get Hunter to stay, but we'll be there."

"Make a fashionably late entrance, then." She let her relief and gratitude show. "I appreciate it."

"You owe me one."

"I understand." And she did. If Delilah ever needed any-thing, Tam would pay up. She might be a despicable human being in a lot of respects, but she honored her obligations, and if this got her one step closer to getting Sophie out of her fa-ther's clutches, then there weren't a lot of limits Tam would place on repaying such a favor. "I'll send you details in the morning."

She ended the call and closed her eyes, dragging in a deep breath that almost turned into a sob. The strain was getting to her, ruffling her normal calm when she was on a job. But this wasn't a *job*, this was her sister's life they were talking about. The job usually came with the thrill of the chase, the anticipa-tion of her mark's next move, outwitting everyone and over-coming obstacles. There was none of that this time. She hadn't even felt that thrill for the job in a long time, if she were honest with herself. She was exhausted, she was spent, and she just wanted out. She wanted her sister out of this and wanted to make sure she was never threatened again.

More and more, it looked like the only way to do that was to take Stefan out of her sister's life permanently, and that might mean taking herself out of Sophie's life, too. Tam had an exit plan for Sophie, had set it in place years ago. In a worst-case scenario, there were people who'd agreed to take her sister, raise her, and keep her far, far away from people like Tam and Stefan.

She'd just hoped she'd never have to use it; but unless Stefan was dead and gone, there didn't seem to be another option. She could not—*would not*—allow Sophie to be used as a pawn again.

Tears burned the backs of her eyes, and she desperately wished this would all go away, but there were no easy answers, no simple solutions. Dragging in a deep breath, she caught Breck's scent, and that sent a whole new wave of emotions washing through her. She wished things were simpler, that she had the chance to figure out if anything might develop between them. She wished she were someone else, someone who was worthy of a man like him. But she wasn't and she never would be. She forced herself to straighten and keep going. That was the only thing she could do. Put one foot in front of the other. Smoothing her hands down her skirt and flipping her hair back over her shoulder, she curved her mouth into a smile that was bright enough to fool anyone.

Breck stepped out from behind one of the many pillars that graced the lobby, and that tsunami wave hit her again. He was so handsome, like some prince in an ancient fairy tale. His gaze sharpened with concern and she knew there was at least one person her smile hadn't fooled. A part of her loved how well he could read her, anticipate her, and another part hated it, feared it.

His hand came up to stroke down her cheek. "Have you finished up?"

Leaning into his touch, she closed her eyes. There were too many thoughts and feelings ricocheting around inside of her. She just needed his strength and stillness for a moment, long enough to make the world stop spinning. His lips brushed over her forehead, his arm circling her waist.

She opened her eyes when he propelled her forward, but steered her away from the bank of lifts. "Where are we going? Stefan surely knows we're back by now. I have to go upstairs and check on my sister."

"I know," he replied. "There's a private lift for each of the penthouse suites. For when the über-rich don't care to socialize with the merely well-off."

"How convenient."

"Yes." He slanted her a look. "We can stop on your floor, but I thought you could use a little more . . . distraction . . . before you had to deal with daddy dearest again."

She could definitely use some distracting, that was certain. And as long as they were going in the right direction, there was no reason not to multitask. He was so very good at *distracting* her. Warmth spread through her at the thought. The man could make her wet with a single glance. She probably shouldn't enjoy it quite so much, but she did. "You want to shag in the lift, don't you?"

She said it out loud because it made it so much more real, more solid and right in front of her than her situation with Sophie.

His expression was wicked, giving her what she needed. A reason to think about something else. Just for a few minutes.

"I never have before. It might be fun to try. Take the edge off before you have to deal with Stefan."

Her throat closed. Dread curdled inside of her. She wanted to see Sophie, not just on her palmtop as she had the last two days, but in person. But seeing Sophie meant seeing Stefan. She quelled the familiar rush of rage and terror.

"Sounds like fun," she whispered, pressing her cheek to Breck's shoulder as they stopped in front of an ornate door of etched mercurite.

"Yes, everything with Stefan is so much—"

He cut himself off, his movements rough as he swiped his ident card over the tiny vidpad that would call the lift. Looked like she wasn't the only one who could use something else to think about. She didn't want to consider why Breck was so tense about Stefan. Factoring in Breck's feelings for her made things even more complicated. She tried not to think about that either.

The door swished open, silent except for a rush of displaced air. If the normal lift was lovely with polyglass panes that overlooked the lobby, this screamed luxury. The wood paneling looked pre-war era, smooth and polished to a high gleam. As blasé as she'd learned to act when faced with this kind of elegance, it never failed to impress her and make her remember the

232 / *Crystal Jordan*

crumbling hovel she'd grown up in. Breck urged her inside the lift and used the vidpad to key in the floors they wanted to stop on. The door closed and they began to slide upward.

"You realize the Royale staff is probably gathered around a vidscreen watching this. An establishment like this has to have vidmonitors in their lifts." She glanced around the lift but didn't see an obvious vidmonitor. That didn't mean it wasn't there, just well hidden.

He shrugged. "Being watched never bothered either of us before. Remember the Peep Show at Tail?"

A shiver went through her remembering that night. "Oh, yes."

"We should do it again some time." He gave her a sinful little grin.

She opened her mouth to agree, then snapped it shut again. There was no way she could realistically make a promise like that, and she'd told him she'd never lie to him again. Instead of answering, she tapped the vidpad to stop the lift mid-glide and pressed herself against his muscular form.

His pupils dilated and he drew in a sharp breath. "Tam."

"Hm?" She rubbed her breasts back and forth across his chest, loving the feel of her nipples tightening. The microsilk of her dress abraded her sensitive flesh. Lovely. The heat in his eyes was even lovelier.

Rising on her toes to torment them both a little more, she brushed her lips over his. He backed her up against the wall, sliding his tongue into her mouth. She purred, the feline in her reveling in the layers of sensation stroking over every heightened sense. His hands clamped on her hips, holding her in place while he kissed her. He gathered her skirt in his hands, and she shuddered as the microsilk slid against her flesh. Cool air circulated around her thighs, and gooseflesh rose on her skin. She panted into his mouth, her tongue mated with his, her fangs scraped his lips, and she grew wetter, more excited.

She couldn't wait to have him inside of her. She writhed against his hard length; her hands streaked over him, caressing his muscles through his clothes. Heat bellowed through her, spreading to every centimeter of her body, and tingles followed in its wake.

A low whimper spilled out of her when he abandoned her lips and dropped to his knees before her. Excitement screamed through her when he lifted her leg and hooked it over his shoulder, opening her to his gaze, his mouth. Her claws curled into the fabric of her skirt, pulling it even higher for him. Yes. She wanted this, him. Pleasure. Any way he wanted to give it to her.

The heat of his breath rushed over her bare flesh. He chuckled. "No underwear."

"No." She rolled her head against the wooden panel, arching her hips in offering.

"You're ready for me," he growled.

"Yes." She could feel his gaze on her, knew he saw how wet she was for him. His fingers stroked the insides of her thighs, and her need built to a fever pitch that made the impatient cheetah within her want to scream with frustration. Deus, it was delicious. She grinned, felt her lips pull against her fangs.

His mouth closed over her clit and she did scream. "Breck!"

He chuckled and the sound vibrated against her sensitive flesh. She shuddered, her sex contracting once. The tips of his fingers skimmed up her thighs to stroke across her slit. He parted the lips of her pussy, pressing two big fingers into her channel. Yes. Sweet heat billowed through her, making her shake with desire. Her pulse sped, hot blood racing through her veins.

His tongue batted at her clit while his fingers drove her crazy. Her hips moved to the rhythm his hand and mouth set. Only her feline reflexes and balance kept her from toppling, with one leg draped over his broad shoulder. Sweat gathered in beads at her temples, slipping down her skin. She shivered at the sensation.

Moving his hand, he drew his fingers back to swirl her own wetness around the pucker of her anus. Her muscles jerked and her breath stopped in her lungs. Circling his hand back and forth from her pussy and her anus, he eased his digits into her ass, stretching her rear channel. She heard her claws shred holes through her skirt as he worked three long fingers into her.

His tongue curled around her clit, his mouth working her as relentlessly as his hand did. Panting, she felt climax building within her. It was all she could do to stay on her feet. He finger-fucked her ass, harder and faster, and her hips bucked to meet his thrusts. So close. She was so close.

"Breck! I'm going to . . . I'm going to . . ."

Orgasm crashed through her, and the scream that ripped from her was more cheetah than woman. Her inner muscles fisted around his thrusting digits while he sucked and bit at her clit. He continued to stroke into her ass, driving deep, stretching her wider with each pass. Heat sparked back to life within her, made her hips undulate with renewed need, and she moved with those talented fingers that pushed into her anus.

"I'm going to fuck you here. Now." His voice was guttural, barely human. The beast and man struggled for control and she loved that she could push him so far.

"Deus, yes." Her breath sobbed out, and she could barely suck in enough oxygen.

He dragged her down to the floor so she was on her hands and knees in front of him. The position was so feral, it called to the animal in her, and she purred with rough anticipation. Arching her back, she offered herself for penetration.

A groan wrenched from him. His talons scraped over her flesh as he held her in place. The head of his cock probed her anus and she panted, shivers running through her muscles. Deus, *Deus*. He pressed in, stretching her as he eased one micrometer in at a time. Moans spilled from her throat, and her claws dug into the expensive carpeting on the floor of the lift. The feel of him inside her was so good, just as it had been from the first time he'd touched her. She feared nothing would ever be as good again with anyone else. Who else had ever turned her inside out this way?

But her thoughts scattered when he withdrew from her ass as slowly as he'd entered her. He reached beneath her and rubbed the tip of one finger over her clit. It made the glide of him inside of her even better, sent tingles skittering down her limbs. Her sex clenched on emptiness, but they both groaned as the involuntary action squeezed her inner muscles around his cock.

"Faster, Breck. Make me come."

His free hand slapped her buttock. Hard. She squealed and jolted, her pussy burning even hotter at the stinging contact. A bead of her wetness trailed down the inside of her thigh.

"I can smell how much that turned you on, Tam." He swatted her ass again, driving his dick into her anus at the same time.

Shock robbed her of breath, and there was no time to get it back as he began pounding inside her at a swift, demanding pace. Every few thrusts, he'd smack her backside. The rhythm was unpredictable, peppering over her buttocks and upper thighs. It only increased her pleasure, twisting it with a bite of pain.

He stretched her ass with every hard penetration, and his fingers played over her clit. It was too much. She danced on the edge of her control within moments. He dragged his talons over the swollen cheek of her ass, and she knew her punished flesh was red from his spanking. Her pussy fisted once, twice. Digging her claws into the carpet, she tried to hold out, tried to keep this from ending for a while longer. She didn't want it to end. Never, ever wanted it to end.

Sinking deep into her anus, deeper than he'd been before, he shoved her over that edge. She closed her eyes as orgasm sent her flying. Groans echoed in the small lift as they both came, shuddering, harsh cries breaking from them. His fluids filled her ass, and her pussy clenched in rhythmic waves that made stars burst behind her eyelids. He flicked his finger over her clit, working her through her climax, and those hot pulses of release kept sweeping through her body until her muscles shook. Sweat slipped down her skin, and she could hear the thundering of her heartbeat in her ears.

Long moments passed before she came down off the incredible high. Amazing. It had been rough and wild and a little desperate. Exactly suiting her mood.

He always gave her exactly what she needed.

How was she going to live without him? Deus, how was she even going to live through this? She didn't know, and tears burned the backs of her eyes. A few days before, she'd had a clear understanding of who she was, what she wanted, and what she needed to sacrifice in order to get it. All of that seemed to have jumbled up and shaken loose so quickly.

6

The next day, Tam was pacing in a circle around her room. Sophie was working through some educational programming in her room, so Tam couldn't use her as a distraction. Which meant she was cooling her heels, trapped in her own head, her thoughts chasing each other around. She was ready to crawl the walls. She needed to *run*. The cheetah in her all but screamed with the need. So many conflicting emotions collided inside her that she simply didn't know how to deal with any of them anymore. Sophie, Breck, Stefan, her past, her present, her future. Sophie's future. Breck's future. What she should do, what she shouldn't do.

Deus, she didn't even know who she was anymore.

Spinning on a heel, she strode out into the main space, sparing Leland a mere glance on her way to the door. He didn't try to stop her, smart man. "Tell Stefan I'll be back later."

"Going to *meet* with Breckenridge again? You're like an alley cat in heat with him." Leland smirked. "Doesn't matter what he or you think up, you're still going to do exactly what the boss wants, or the kid gets it."

"I know." Weariness reflected in her voice, and she didn't bother to correct his assumption about where she was going. Let him think what he would.

Her thoughts churned as she stepped onto the lift and had it shoot her down to the lobby. Before she'd reached the ground level, she'd shifted into her animal form, her body twisting and remolding itself into a cheetah. She left her clothes in the lift. The ever-efficient staff of the Royale would have them cleaned, pressed, and sent back upstairs.

Darting out of the lift, she stretched her spotted forelegs into a dead sprint. Her muscles sang from the sudden use, but it felt good to have a few moments of freedom away from everyone so she could *think*.

She had resigned herself to death or imprisonment since the moment Stefan called her and told her he had her sister. For Sophie, she'd willingly make the sacrifice. Among all the lies she'd told in her life, all the cons she'd pulled off, she'd always known that her one true thing was her family. Her mother and sister, and now just her sister. She could and would do anything, go anywhere to make sure they were happy and safe. It was a shame that her mother had been happy with Stefan, but the man had kept her safe, and that was all Tam had required of him. After that, Tam had done what was necessary to ensure security for Sophie. She was still doing that, and she always would.

But then Breck had shown back up in her life and announced they were mates.

It had shaken her far more than she'd like to admit, and having him near, having him in her arms, having him support and protect her was doing nothing to help her maintain her resolve.

She loved him as much as she ever had. More. This time, there was no hiding the real Felicia Tamryn from him. This time, she couldn't lie and tell herself that he only wanted the woman she was pretending to be. Everything was laid bare for him to see, to judge. To condemn, if he wanted. It had been horrifying enough to realize the first time that she'd fallen for one of her marks, but this time, it could lead to sheer devastation. This time, there was so much more on the line. Her life. *Sophie's* life.

She might be able to lie to anyone else, but she'd always been brutally honest with herself. Wasn't her love for Breck every bit as strong as the love for her family? Wasn't that just as true and pure and real? If she let it, wouldn't it be just as much a guiding force in her life? She could have it. Breck was there, tempting her, offering her everything she could dream of— safety and a home for Sophie, a permanent escape from the poverty that had shaped Tam's childhood, and love. A mate. A person fashioned just for her, who would never abandon her or turn on her.

Deus, it was such a fantasy come to life. The prince come to take her away to his castle. But she wasn't a heroine in some story; she was the villain. Because the reality was, she was as likely to get him killed as she was to have any part of that fairy tale come true.

No!

The thought of Breck dying, of living with that guilt, spurred her onward, made her want to outrun herself and her own life, no matter how impossible that might be. Because she hated who and what she was, and there was no making herself someone she wasn't. She was a bad person who'd done bad things. That was the life she'd led. Stefan had forced her into it as a child, but she'd certainly excelled at it, hadn't she? Oh, yes. She was very, very good at being bad. Her breathing hitched in a sob, and she ran faster.

The world went by in a blur as her strides ate up the distance. It felt good to cut loose and run, racing the wind. Pedestrians leaped out of her way as she ran, weaving in and out of traffic. She didn't even care where she went, just as long as she could keep moving.

When she looked up, she was in the middle of a crumbling wasteland. The London docks—a disgusting cesspool that was an assault on the senses. People screamed, haggled over spoiled food, children shrieked and ran wild in packs. And there, in the middle of it, Tam saw that her mad flight had taken her to the last place she'd ever had even a scrap of innocence to her name. This kind of place didn't leave a lot of room for naiveté, but here she'd had a father and a mother, a place where someone looked out for her best interests.

Before Stefan had come into her life and shattered it. The first time, anyway. The man had a knack for setting biobombs under her life and letting them detonate, leaving nothing but a ragged mutating mess in his wake. Nothing had ever been the same again.

And it all started right here.

Breck had been standing on his balcony when he saw Tam streak out of the Royale's lobby. The cheetah had almost been a blur, she'd moved so fast, but he'd know her anywhere, in any form. He'd debated flying after her for a split second, but decided against it. She didn't look as if she were running toward something, but just...running for the sake of running. He'd seen her do it before, when they were together in New Chicago. It was her way of escaping for a while to think. When she ran out of steam, she was going to need a ride home, and he couldn't carry a cheetah in his eagle form.

How he could read her mood from so far away, he wasn't sure. The eagle knew what it knew about its mate. He didn't stop to analyze it. There was no time, not with her pelting down the street at top speed.

Shooting into the penthouse, he ran for his private lift, his palmtop already out as he keyed in the number for the driver he'd hired while he was in town. The man's face appeared almost immediately, and Breck asked, "Did you see the cheetah go past just now? Do you think you can keep up with her?"

"Yes, sir. Ms. Tamryn is headed west at the moment. Even if we lose her, I can track her." He touched the side of his nose. "Iberian wolf-shifter."

The lift slid straight to the lobby in moments. "Excellent. I'll join you. Now."

Fifteen minutes later, he watched the driver lean his head out of the transport's open window and drag in a deep breath. He made a few switchback turns in traffic, and Breck tried not to grow impatient. Perhaps he should have flown when he had the chance. Too late to change his mind now.

He scanned the windows, hoping for a glimpse of Tam again. They passed the reconstructed business neighborhoods and from there the buildings grew older and closer together, degrading in repair from shabby to shanty. But he caught sight of a spotted coat, and his heart leapt. Tam. "There. *Stop.*"

He saw her through a stack of pallets that blocked off an alley. She just sat in the middle of a road on the far side, staring at something. Or someone. From this angle, he couldn't see what. The transport rocked to a halt, and Breck's hand was already on the door, pushing it open.

The driver craned his head around. "I'll need to go around the block to get through to her, sir."

"Do that." Breck stepped out. "I'll walk from here."

"Are you sure? The docks ain't the nicest area of town."

"No, it's not." He glanced back before he shut the door. "And she's out there alone."

"Yes, sir." The driver's voice was muffled, but clear, and the transport sped away.

Breck braced himself against the alley wall while he hopped up onto the pallets, praying the wood wasn't so rotted through that it would give under his weight. He leaped down as quickly as possible and sped through the narrow passage to the street beyond. She sat there, her gaze glued to a building. The place was all but collapsing in on itself; the brick had crumbled so badly in some areas that he could see the people moving around inside their flats. The surrounding buildings were no better. This was a slum, the stink of it singeing his nose.

What the driver had said clicked in his mind with what he knew of Tam's upbringing. The London docks. "This is where you grew up, isn't it? In this flathouse?"

She slanted a glance up at him, her chin dipping in a sharp nod. Something close to shame shone in the cheetah's eyes.

He sighed. Again, she was so quick to assume that he'd judge her. "And you believe I'll think worse of you because I know this?"

Her shoulder rolled in a shrug as if it made no difference to her, but she dropped her gaze to the ground.

"I don't think you're a terrible person, Tam." How could he say this to her and not make it sound condescending or foolish? "Yes, you lie. You cheat. You steal. How many people haven't done those things before? I certainly have when it would get me ahead in a negotiation. The right bluff, played at the right time, can be priceless. Snatching a deal out from someone else's nose is a rush, especially if you know they want it badly, and you're better, smarter, more devious and clever. It's the nature of the beast." He sighed. Perhaps he was justifying things too much, but Deus knew he'd had plenty of long, miserable hours without her to think about this.

She bumped his leg with her shoulder, and he reached down, stroking his hand through her soft spotted fur.

"Living an honest life would have kept you here, slaving all your days in abject poverty, freezing to death in winter because the roof has holes in it." He nodded toward the building. "I don't blame you for doing *whatever* it took to get away from here. I would have done the same."

A low purr rumbled from her, so quiet he wouldn't have noticed it if he hadn't had his hand on her back.

"Even then, it wasn't that simple, was it? You didn't *choose* the life you've led, did you? Stefan got you into it, didn't he? And then you were too deep in to ever get out. That's what you said, right?"

She tensed under his palm, her purr dying as if it had never been.

Dropping to his haunches beside her, he rubbed his fingers over her silken ear. "I know I'm right, Tam. Maybe you enjoyed the perks that came from this life, but what choice did you have? You couldn't get out. So, the only thing you could do was protect your sister and keep her away from crime or poverty. The only lifestyles you've ever known."

A small choking sound came from her, and she buried her muzzle in his shoulder. Her whiskers tickled his throat. He rested his chin on the top of her head and ran a hand down her back. She hadn't been able to say anything in her animal form, and somehow it felt like one of the most honest exchanges they'd ever had.

No room for lies, for word games, when only one of them could speak.

His private transport pulled up beside them, the door opening with a soft displacement of air. He gestured for Tam to get in, and she stepped onto one of the plush kleather seats. She shifted as he climbed in and shut the door behind him. The driver handed a folded blanket over the seat to her and she wrapped it around herself, easing away from Breck as she tucked it around her tight.

244 / Crystal Jordan

He quirked an eyebrow. "I've seen everything you have to offer, Tam. It's too late to hide from me."

Reaching out to engage the privacy screen between them and the driver, she sighed. "I'm not hiding."

"Then come here." He opened his arms and she scooted over to sit beside him, letting him fold her into his embrace. A breath slipped out of his lungs, and some of the tightness eased around his chest. He swallowed hard. "I worried about you when I saw you go running out of the hotel."

"I'm sorry." Her head nestled against his shoulder, her hair smelling of something sweet and feminine. "I just needed some privacy to think. I like to run when I do that."

"I know." He kissed her forehead, savoring the contact. He loved having her in his arms. He just wished he knew how to keep her there.

"I wasn't really thinking about anyone else, or anyone bothering to follow me." She shifted against him restlessly, as if the thought of anyone caring enough to worry and come after her made her uncomfortable. Perhaps it did. "I didn't mean to worry you. I apologize."

"Thank you." He shook his head. After everything that had happened, he'd have hoped that she understood how much he cared, how far he was willing to go for her, but she didn't seem to see it. Hell, at this point, he didn't know what more he could do to prove it to her.

"You're right. About this being the only lifestyle I've ever known. Crime. Poverty. You're right. I want better for Sophie. I want her to be a better person than I could ever be." He heard her swallow. "I want to protect her the way no one protected me."

"The way your mother should have protected you and didn't." Anger and pain on her behalf burned through him and he squeezed her closer, wishing more than ever that he could have spared her all that she'd survived.

"Yes." She cleared her throat. "I want Sophie to have the life I never had a chance at. I would have been buried in poverty if I hadn't turned to crime, and I want the best for her on every score. I have the means to make her life what mine could never be, and I want that for her."

He crooked a finger under her chin, forcing her to meet his gaze. "If you have the means, why didn't you quit to take care of her?"

"Because this is what I do." She shrugged. "This is who I am now. I put all the money I steal into accounts that will pay for Sophie's schooling no matter what happens to me. I want to make sure she's as secure as possible financially. And while I'm free and breathing, I want to make sure I'm as financially secure as possible, too." She pressed her lips together for a moment. "I remember very clearly what it was like to have nothing, to *be* nothing. There was never enough food, nothing was ever clean, let alone new. What little we had could always be taken away by crooked police or stolen by our neighbors. Because when you're that desperate, you'll slit your best friend's throat to survive. It's every man for himself. Or woman. Or child."

What she described was so far outside the realm of his experience, he didn't know what to say to her. He could give her sympathy, but he couldn't really understand. He was glad, too. That life was one nobody should have to live. He knew that was reality, but it was still horrible. He tried to offer her a smile, but failed.

"What would you do with your life if you didn't do this?"

Her smile was much more genuine, almost gentle and a little sad. "I'm good at this. Good at conning people into trusting me with things they value."

"You'd be good in business." He ran a fingertip down her soft cheek.

"Legitimate business?" She snorted, leaning away from him a little. "I've been caught a time or two. I've managed to charm the right people in order to escape a prison sentence, but no reputable company would hire me."

According to the dossier his investigator had put together for him, Tam had been caught three times, to be precise. The charges had been dropped in the first two cases, and she'd spent ten days in jail awaiting trial for the third. She'd been given "time served" and released. Charmed the right people, indeed. Seduced, more likely. It hadn't escaped his notice that the judge in all three cases had been male.

He gave her a lopsided grin. "Does that mean you wouldn't mind honest employment, beloved? I might have a position or two you could try."

"New positions to try, huh?" Shaking her head, she huffed a laugh. "You're impossible."

It took effort to fix an innocent expression on his face. "What? I own several companies. I'm certain there might be a job for you in one of them."

She hummed in her throat, giving him a skeptical glance. "I'm sure that's all you meant."

"What else do you think I meant?" But the smile slid off his face and he sobered, staring her straight in the eye. "I would trust you in my business. Come work for me."

He'd considered this before but still hadn't decided if it was the best course of action. Too late now, he'd just have to go with his gut.

"Ha." The look she gave him questioned his sanity. "Very funny."

"I'm not joking." He continued to hold her gaze, let her see how serious he was. "Don't you want the chance to make sure Sophie grows up well? What if you put her back in school, or in another school, and Stefan takes her again? You'd be back in this nightmare." A chill went down his spine at the idea of either female in that bastard's clutches. No. Never again. This was already bad enough. "What if you could get legal custody of her? I could help you with that. Pay the right people and they won't notice any shadiness in your past. You'd have a lot more legal recourse if you had custody."

She snorted again, louder and more derisive. "Men like Stefan don't care about legalities. Pay the right people and he can get what he wants, too."

"How is it going to help her if you're in jail, too? He wants you in prison or dead—that's what you told Gea."

Tam glanced away, not answering.

"Exactly." He pressed. "How are you going to get her away from him now?"

"I don't know, all right? I don't bloody well *know!* Do you think this is helping?" She struggled against his hold, but he refused to let her go. Wedging her hands between them, she glared at him. "Do you think I don't stay up at night trying to find a way around him? Do you think I'm not terrified of what he'll do to her? Do you think I wouldn't do anything to save her, to make him go away?" Tears stood out in her eyes and she used one hand to dash them away. "I don't know what to do, but I know I can't abandon her."

Breck tangled his fingers in her hair, shaking his head. His chest squeezed tight at the sight of her tears. "I'm sorry."

"So am I." Her laugh was bitter, and she turned her face away to stare out the tinted transport window. "Just leave me alone, Breck. I have enough to handle right now without you poking at me for not being some paragon of virtue."

That made him growl in frustration. "I don't expect you to be a paragon of virtue."

"Don't you?"

"I just want you to be safe, and your career isn't a safe one." He stroked her hair back, then cupped her cheek until she met his gaze again.

"I'm good at what I do." Her dark eyes were sad, resigned, but she stopped resisting his hold and leaned against his chest.

"You could be good at other things, too, things that didn't keep you away from Sophie." He pressed a finger to her lips when she tried to interrupt him. "If, by some miracle, we get out of this and Stefan is the one who ends up jailed or buried, I want you to at least think about my offer."

She shook her head slowly, regret in her voice. "An offer that comes with many, many strings to tie me down, since you claim we're mates."

"We *are* mates. It's a simple fact. And the job offer didn't come with any strings about being in a relationship with me. Do I want that? Yes. Would I force you? No." He blew out a breath. "I know you too well to think I could force you to stay. But you say you didn't choose this career, that you don't have any other options. I'm giving you an option. I'm giving you the chance to raise Sophie yourself, to have her close by and *know* she's well cared for. *If* we get out of this in one piece, I hope you'll consider it."

Her mouth opened and closed. Emotion he couldn't read flickered across her expression. "I ... I don't know what to say."

"Don't say anything. Just think about it." He brushed his lips over hers, and she pressed forward into the contact, letting it linger. Desire unfurled inside of him, but he didn't push, just savored the small intimacy, the tart flavor of her.

When he tried to pull back, she clutched his lapels, holding him close as she shoved her tongue into his mouth. He groaned, startling in surprise. But just that quickly, the moment exploded into something far more intense than he'd intended. The fire between them was always there, waiting to consume them both. She scooted around until she could straddle his lap, aligning their sexes so she could grind her clit down on his erection.

His hands cupped her hips, pulled her to him, and he arched himself into her. The friction of her moving against him made his cock chafe in his pants, exquisite pleasured-pain. She hissed into his mouth and he could smell her moisture. The scent of her passion was headier than a shot of fine whiskey.

Wrapping her arms around his neck, she kissed him harder, held him closer. Yes, that was what he wanted, too. More. All of her, all of him. Together. He fisted his hand in the blanket around her and ripped it away, thanking Deus for the privacy screen that blocked the rest of the world out. He threw the blanket to the floor of the transport. Then she was bared for him, creamy curves and ebony hair spilling around her shoulders. He bent forward and sucked a rosy nipple into his mouth.

A purr vibrated her chest, and she speared her fingers into his hair. He batted at the tight tip with his tongue, biting down just hard enough to sting. He switched to the other breast and offered it the same treatment. She hissed, and the scent of her wetness increased. Lust punched through him, and he wanted to feel how damp she was for him. Only for him. Sliding one palm down her back, he dipped between her buttocks and eased forward until he reached the hot core of her. Soaking wet. Deus, she was so responsive. He groaned, clamping down on her nipple.

"Breck!" Her claws scored his scalp, and she sobbed when he speared two fingers inside of her slick pussy.

Lava flowed through his veins, burning away his control, and his cock throbbed with the need to be inside of her. Every time she squirmed, he thought his skull might explode from the cravings pounding through him. The eagle inside of him screeched with the need to claim its mate. Mate, mate, *mate*. The word ricocheted within him, so powerful it made him shake. Sweat broke on his forehead, and he thrust his fingers in and out of her sex. More. Now. He released her breast and dropped his head back against the transport seat. "Ride me, Tam. I want to feel you all wet and tight around my cock."

Her cheeks were flushed with desire, and her chin bobbed down in a nod. A slight tremor shook her hands when she reached between them to unseal his fly. The first touch of her slim fingers on his cock made him clench his jaw. Deus, it was fucking good. *Mate.*

They swayed together as the transport rounded a corner. Her free hand clutched his shoulder to try to maintain her balance. He pulled his fingers from her pussy to grasp her hips and keep her in place over him. She shivered, her eyelids dropping to half-mast as she stroked up and down his cock.

"Put my cock inside of you, Tam."

"Deus, Breck." She moaned, rubbing the head of his dick over her hard clit and the soft wet lips of her sex. "I want you."

"I want you more. Hurry." He watched her face as she filled herself with his cock. Any subterfuge had been burned away, and all that was left was wanton woman. Her eyes lost focus, her lips parting as she sank down to take all of him. Her slick walls closed on his dick, and a groan ripped from his throat.

She lifted and lowered herself on him, rolling her hips to meet his. They moved together in perfect sync, and gooseflesh broke down his flesh. He caught her mouth in a swift kiss, tangling his tongue with hers. Every sense grew more intense. Taste, scent, feel . . . even the sound of their pounding hearts reached his ears, her low purring, the smack of their skin meeting.

Breaking the kiss, she fell back on her hands, bracing them on his knees. She offered him a wicked smile with a hint of fangs. She used the leverage to thrust herself harder onto his cock. "Deus, this does get better every time."

Her tongue darted out to lick her lips, and her eyes slid

closed as she moved faster. He reached down to rub his fingers over her clitoris and she whimpered. His muscles burned as he rocked his pelvis up again and again, trying to meld their bodies together. He wanted no distance between them. The eagle inside of him demanded he claim her. Mate. The instinct that never quit, that always craved more. The human fought for control over the animal, focusing on the pure carnality of their joining.

"Look at me," he growled. He wanted to see her come, wanted to watch her lose every scrap of her self-restraint until there was nothing left but the naked truth of her desire for him.

He flicked the pad of his thumb over her clit hard enough to make her body jolt, and her breath caught as she went over the edge into climax. The walls of her sex clenched around his cock and it was too much, far too much. He slammed into his own orgasm. His hips rose from the seat, grinding against her clit. The rush of it broke over him in a giant wave. His heart pounded and he clamped his hands down on her waist to pull her tight to the base of his cock. They both groaned, and his come exploded from his dick in hard jets, pumping into her slick pussy. He worked himself inside of her until every sensation had been wrung from the experience, until he was left shaking in the aftermath.

A last wave of orgasm hit her, and her internal muscles continued to milk his spent cock, making him groan. She threw her head back, her body arching as she leaned back on her hands. Her mouth opened in a silent scream, her bared fangs glistening. In that moment, she was the most beautiful thing he'd ever seen. Strong and vulnerable, sweet and passionate, feral woman. Everything he'd ever wanted. All he'd ever need.

I love you. The words filled his mind, but he didn't give them voice. As with everything else between them, he didn't think she'd really hear him.

He honestly wasn't sure if she ever would. Helpless pain and frustration washed over him. He tried to battle it back, but he wasn't sure how much longer he could keep this up—putting himself out there for her and getting nothing but doubt and rejection in return.

7

Tam ignored the knowing smirk from Leland when she returned to the suite wrapped in a blanket and reeking of Breck and sex. She made a beeline for her room, showered, and put on clothes quickly. Fifteen minutes later, she emerged and went looking for Sophie. It was unusual for her not to come bouncing over to meet Tam anytime she came home. She tapped her knuckles against her sister's bedroom door. "Sophie, love, are you there?"

Her feline hearing picked up a flurry of movements, the rapid patter of footsteps, and then a door closing.

"I'm in the wash closet taking a bath," the little girl's voice called back. The sound of water running reached Tam. "I'll be out later."

Pinpricks tingled down Tam's skin, and the hair rose on the back of her neck. "Are you feeling all right?"

There was no response.

She pushed her way into Sophie's room and went straight to the wash closet door. She tried the knob and found it locked. "Sophia Melissande, you open this door right this instant."

"I don't w-want to." Sophie's voice caught in the middle as if she suppressed a sob.

Alarm streaked through Tam. This wasn't normal behavior for her sister. Something was very wrong here. Tam jerked a pin out of her hair and was able to pick the lock in moments. What she saw when she pushed into the wash closet confirmed her fears.

Sophie stood beside the small whirlpool, her right eye puffy and swollen, already blackening. Bruises in the distinct shape of hard-gripping fingers laced across her forearms. Her lip was split and still oozing blood.

Rage unlike anything she'd ever known exploded inside of Tam. Her hands balled into fists, and her voice lowered to a guttural hiss. "Who did this to you?"

Sophie's lips pressed together, tears slipping from her dark eyes to trail down her cheeks.

"Tell me who did this."

She shook her head, her hair flying around her pale face. "If you do something to them, they'll do bad things back to both of us. They might take you away from me."

"No one is taking me away." Over her dead body, which was what it might take to get out of this. "Tell me who hurt you. Was it Leland, Nichols, or your father?"

Stefan wasn't here now and hadn't been when she'd left, but Tam had been gone for several hours. Plenty of time to return and abuse a child.

"Leland. I—I was playing too loudly and made him mad. He shook me and slapped me."

"I see." Red hazed the corners of Tam's vision. "Stay right here, Sophie."

"But—"

"Stay here." She spun on a heel and went hunting for the son of a bitch.

Leland rounded the corner from the kitchen, a bottle of synth-brew tucked under one arm while he pried open a hardened plastin container. No one used plastin anymore, so likely whatever was in the canister was illegally made. She offered him a charming smile and he blinked. She was on him in a nanosecond, claws bared. He dropped his goodies to try and fend her off, but it was too late. The tips of her claws pressed to his jugular, and she backed him up against the wall.

"What the fuck?" His lips curled back to reveal a shark's razor-sharp teeth. "If this is about the brat—"

"Say anything else and you die right here, right now. Call Nichols to help you and it's the last sound you'll make," she snarled, feeling the feral side of her nature ripping free of restraint. She smiled, showing fangs. "I might just kill you anyway."

For the very first time, she saw real fear in his eyes. A comprehension that he was seconds away from watching his life get snuffed out. Good.

"Let me make this clear to you. You touch her in *any* way and I will kill you. I don't give a damn what Stefan says you can do to my sister. This is an understanding between the two of us. Hurt her again and I *will* end you. Let Nichols hurt her and I will end you. I will rip off your balls and force you to eat them." She dug her claws into his neck, enough to have thin trickles of blood trail down his flesh. "Then I'll slit your throat and do a happy little dance through the puddles of your blood. Is this in any way unclear to you?"

"Clear," he gasped, his eyes rolling back as he tried to stand on tiptoes to escape her.

She just dug in harder. "This is your one warning, Leland. Take it seriously."

"I do. I do, I swear." His voice rose, his breathing growing rapid as beads of sweat formed at his temples.

Letting him go, she stepped back.

The breath wheezed out of his lungs. He coughed, touching his neck and coming away with crimson coating his beefy fingers. Hate flashed in his gaze. "You try to leave here and I will kill you."

"I understand." She backed away from him slowly, shaking with the adrenaline overload. "I'll be with my sister. Don't disturb us."

She turned and found Nichols watching them silently from the balcony doorway, a cigartine dangling between his fingers. She lifted her chin and gave him a chilling, bared-fangs smile. Nichols blanched and glanced away as she strode toward Sophie's bedroom.

She had to get her sister away from these men. The lack of any harm to either her or her sister had lulled her into a false sense of security. If she just stayed the course, she'd get them out of this before anything bad happened. If she just did what they wanted, no one would get hurt. An illusion. One she should have been old enough not to fall prey to. Getting pulled into Stefan's web *was* the bad thing that had happened.

Sophie hovered just inside her bedroom door, gulping back sobs. She threw herself into Tam's arms the moment she returned. "I don't want to stay here anymore."

"I know. Neither do I." Hot and cold tingles raced through Tam as her adrenaline crashed. She picked up her sister and walked her into the wash closet. Sitting on the edge of the whirlpool, she held the little girl while she cried, and Tam's heart broke with every sob. She'd tried to protect Sophie from this, and she'd failed. Utterly and completely failed.

Sophie hiccupped and looked up at Tam. "You promise you won't leave me alone with them again?"

"Not for a moment longer than I have to, darling. I'm going to get you away from them."

A fat tear slid down her cheek. "Why can't we go now?"

Tam brushed her sister's hair back from her face. "Because they won't let us, and they're watching us too closely now, but I'll find a way. Just be brave for me for a little while longer."

Dragging in a deep breath, Sophie gave her a nod. "I can be brave. I love you."

"I love you too, sweets."

"They're bad men, Tam." Sophie's eyes were wide and far too mature when she looked at Tam. "One of the girls at school told me about what Father is, and about what you both do to make money."

The bottom dropped out of Tam's stomach, chill dread prickling over her skin. "And how did this girl know anything about either of us?"

Her sister swallowed. "Her father is the minister of defense, so he knows all about people like . . . people who've committed crimes."

People like Stefan, Leland, Nichols . . . and Tam. Hot shame washed over her, churning inside her until she wanted to sob. She'd never, *ever* wanted her sister to know about her profession. About the kind of person she really was. "I'm sorry you had to hear about that."

"Her father said she wasn't to speak to me anymore because I'm from bad stock." Sophie's voice dropped to a whisper. "So she's not my friend anymore."

Deus, could it get any worse? This was the very thing Tam had hoped to avoid. She didn't want Sophie to be tarred by the same brush that had smeared Tam's entire existence. She'd thought she could protect her, but she'd failed at that, too. "I'm so sorry, Sophie."

"Father doesn't love me, does he? He doesn't want me. He never did. He's bad." Sophie's fingers clutched Tam's. "He's

258 / Crystal Jordan

making you do something bad or else he's going to hurt me. That's why we're not allowed to leave, isn't it?"

Those words shredded Tam inside, gutting her. "Yes, my darling. That's why we're not allowed to leave."

Sophie wrapped her arms tight around Tam's waist. "I love you. You'll find a way to get us away from the bad men. I know it."

She'd find a way to get Sophie away from them, that was for certain. She wasn't as certain about herself. Holding the small, warm body to her chest, she rocked Sophie in her lap. Blinking fast, Tam held back her tears, needing to be strong for a little girl who'd had her life ripped apart. She forced herself to give her sister a bath, washing away the blood, and then applying multiple nanopatches to the girl's cuts and bruises. By tomorrow, they'd be gone, but the psychological marks would still be there.

Through it all, a sense of finality filled Tam, a white-hot agony to cauterize a wound that would leave Tam with ugly emotional scars. No matter what, Sophie was going to be safe from Stefan forever. Even if that meant Tam had to cut ties with her sister, too. It was best for Sophie.

Tam had arranged a worst-case scenario escape for Sophie years ago, but it wasn't until today that she understood that this *was* the worst case. Just being who she was made Tam a danger to Sophie. It was a horrible thing to face, to admit, but it was the truth. In the end, Tam would end up getting her sister hurt or killed. If it wasn't Stefan who did it, then some other enemy she'd made over the years. Tam was a poison for the people she loved, and she had to save them from herself.

Deus help her, she wanted to crawl out of her own skin to escape that fact, but she couldn't deny it. She tucked her sister into bed, curled up beside her, closed her eyes, and held Sophie tight, knowing it was one of the last times she'd ever have the chance.

* * *

"A birthday ball? How fun." Delilah leaned her head against her mate's shoulder. "Hunter threw the *best* party for me on my last birthday. I loved it."

The Averys stood with Tam, Breck, and the Abernathys at the soiree at Breck's penthouse. Could Delilah have offered a better opening for them? Satisfaction curled through Breck when Lady Abernathy gave that all-important invitation.

"You must come, then. All of you. It will be the party of the century. Anyone who's anyone will be there." Drusilla's top-knot wobbled just a bit as she gestured expansively with her champagne flute. "It lasts all weekend, none of this one-day nonsense for me. I deserve more than that. If I'm turning sixty, I want to celebrate."

"You deserve whatever you want." Lord Abernathy's smile was indulgent. He'd enjoyed more than his fair share of the bubbly, but whatever got them in the mood to give Breck what he wanted was worth the cost.

The penthouse party had gone off without a hitch—he couldn't have asked for better. The food was delicious, the string quartet elegant, the guests strictly prime-list. Tam had pulled everything together beautifully. He'd been surprised when she'd arrived early with her entire entourage in tow. Sophie had been charming to the first few guests, showing off her fancy dress, and then she'd entertained herself quietly in a corner with Leland and Nichols silently guarding her. Tam kept a sharp eye on her sister, and Breck understood without being told that something had happened to make Tam unwilling to leave the girl alone. He wanted to ask, but now wasn't the time.

Stefan was clearly there to watch them and make certain they got the invitation to Lady Abernathy's birthday party. He mingled with other guests, but Breck felt the older man's gaze boring into his back throughout the evening.

He set his hand on Tam's back and smiled at Drusilla. "We'd love to attend, of course. My Tam does love a party."

"I like meeting interesting new people." Tam gave a dimpled grin, bumping Breck with her shoulder. "Plus, it gives me the opportunity to pry this man away from his work and get him to pay attention to me."

Breck managed not to choke on a laugh and was saved from digging up an appropriate response by Hunter. "I'm afraid we'll have to pass. My wife and I both have separate business matters to attend to."

"Ah, yes." Lord Abernathy peered at Delilah. "You've meetings with my cousin's security staff. Final debriefings and what have you."

The lynx-shifter nodded. "Yes, exactly. Palace security is prime. The queen should be very satisfied with my report."

"Excellent, excellent." Abernathy beamed as though he'd had a hand in the matter, and Breck noted that Delilah didn't mention whether or not she'd actually breached the palace's security systems, just that they were prime. Interesting.

Drusilla tilted her head, a smile curving her face that only accentuated her horsey features. "It's unfortunate you can't make it to my party, but if anything should change in your schedule, I'd adore having you."

More likely, she'd adore having the Averys at an event in her honor, where people could see what a coup she'd pulled off by getting them there. Breck could sympathize since the Averys were what had clinched having the Abernathys at *his* party, but he'd gotten what he needed, so he let a relieved sigh ease out. This job Stefan had Tam on was going to drive Breck crazy. The tension was getting to him. He drained his champagne flute and signaled a waiter for another. He couldn't afford to have too much, just enough to take the edge off.

Even securing the invitation to the birthday party didn't do a thing to help him figure out what the hell Stefan wanted them to do for this job. Neither he nor Tam—nor any of their considerable contacts—had been able to uncover what made Lord Abernathy so interesting to Stefan. Breck felt as if he'd spent the last week flying blind in that famous London fog. Dangerous for an eagle like him. He had no idea where he was or what direction he was supposed to be going. Not with Tam and not with this kamikaze mission she was on.

Her hand slid into his and squeezed hard. She glanced up at him, a radiant smile on her face. Her dark eyes crinkled at the corners, dancing with secrets, drawing him in. *Mate.* He lifted her fingers to his lips and kissed them. Deus, but he loved her. He would do anything to make her happy, keep her smiling at him just like that for the rest of their lives.

"What business brought you to London, Breckenridge?" Lord Abernathy dabbed a few drops of wine from his mustache. "If it's not too prying of me to inquire."

"Not at all." Breck shifted his attention away from Tam and back to the conversation with his guests. "I'm looking into investing in some of the commodities traded in the London Metal Exchange. I want to get a feel for the market, so I thought a visit was in order." Not a complete lie. One of his subsidiaries *was* considering such an investment. He just wasn't directly involved. Turning his head, he grinned at Tam. "And Tam wanted to tour her hometown again. Or, rather, the many shopping opportunities found here. She hasn't been back in a while."

She played along, shrugging with a self-deprecating grin. "Guilty as charged. Breck is so good to indulge me." She laid a hand on his chest, giving him a look that was so openly adoring, it made his heart stop, even though he reminded himself it was just an act for their audience. "I do love Harrods. Plus, there's a new designer I just adore, and her showroom is here."

"Peta Burton?" Lady Abernathy asked, her eyes lighting with interest.

"One and the same." Tam brushed a hand down her hip. "This is one of her creations."

Drusilla waved her hand, indicating she wanted Tam to spin around and show off the dress. It was a short, lacy affair that was *almost* see-through but managed to be classy at the same time. More than one man at the party had gone slack-jawed and stared at Tam in it. It clung to her every curve and made her legs look a kilometer long. Breck would have liked to send everyone home and peel her out of it.

"Ooh. I love her work." Lady Abernathy winced. "I haven't the figure to pull off her designs, though. I've commissioned her to make a hat for me for one of the birthday events this weekend, though."

"I can't wait to see it." Tam toasted the other woman with a glass.

Drusilla laughed. "I can't wait to show it off."

One of the other guests came up, bowing slightly. "My lord, I wonder if I might have a word?"

The group broke apart, and Tam and Breck mingled with the crème de la crème of London society. She'd managed to get them all to attend, probably with a whisper about Hunter Avery being in attendance. Breck still had no idea how she'd pulled off that feat, and she wasn't telling.

"Stefan wants to speak to me. Keep an eye on Sophie for me, please." Tam rose up on tiptoe and breathed the words in his ear. "I'll be right back."

"I'll come looking for you if you aren't." He brushed a kiss over her cheek, letting go of her when he wanted to hold her tight and protect her.

He watched her walk away, feeling that same worry and tension he always experienced when she was out of his sight now.

He couldn't help it. Every time he saw her might be the last, and he knew it. He had no guarantee that she wouldn't disappear on him again, given the slightest opportunity. The moments were slipping away. He could feel them sifting through his fingers like sand, and the harder he tried to hold on to them, the faster they escaped him. Like Tam.

8

Stefan cupped his hand under Tam's elbow, squeezing tight enough to be painful, but not so tight that others could tell he was hurting her. Bastard. His grip dug deeper into her elbow, making agony shoot through the joint. She struggled not to wince, fought through the pain, and offered a brilliant smile to Delilah as they passed the lynx-shifter. The other woman's green gaze sharpened on Stefan, but she did nothing to interfere as he steered Tam through the small crowd of guests, down a short hall, and shoved her into a wash closet.

She caught herself against the marble counter that stretched across one side of the small room. Flecks of gold in the marble sparkled in the light. She dragged in a breath while Stefan closed the door, shutting them in together. His sweet scent made her nauseous, and she swallowed down her gorge. Deus, she hated being this close to him. Which he knew, and used to his advantage. Straightening her shoulders, she looked at her reflection in the mirror. She looked cool, calm, and in control, just the way she wanted to appear tonight. But it was a sham.

Putting her in a pretty dress didn't change who she was or how she felt. It was all an act, a lie, just like the rest of her life.

"Did you get the invitation?" Stefan demanded, crowding her even further until she could feel his breath on the back of her neck.

She ignored her discomfort, fussing with her hair in the mirror instead. "Of course I did. I told you I would. I always deliver."

"Good." His smug grin made her want to scratch his eyes out, and she had to concentrate to keep her claws retracted.

"I think it's time you tell me what I'll be looking for when I'm at Abernathy's house, don't you?" She arched an eyebrow at his reflection.

He pursed his lips, calculating shrewdness flashing in his cold gaze.

Huffing out a breath, she let her impatience show. "Stefan, this is ridiculous. What the hell do you want me to steal? I can't bloody well get it for you if you don't tell me what it is."

His nostrils flared in annoyance, but he didn't attempt to contradict her. "In his office, there's a safe. I'm sure you won't have any trouble ferreting it out."

Ferreting, ha. She refrained from firing back a comment about his weasel-shifter nature, the cheetah in her wanting to pounce on the little rodent. "What kind of safe?"

"A Helax 1600." His benevolent smile was anything but. "You'll have a day or so to look up the specs for that model."

The Helax brand was one of the most difficult to crack, and the number indicated a newer model than she'd ever dealt with. Shit. She narrowed her eyes at him. "What's inside the safe?"

"Many things, I'm certain." He waved a dismissive hand. "When you get in the safe, you'll know what to take. Trust me."

"I don't trust you. Why would I?" She flicked her fingers.

"What if I do what you say and what I leave with isn't what you wanted? Your vagueness could bite you in the ass."

"Jewels, dearest. Sparkly, pretty, and priceless." He leaned in to whisper in her ear, and revulsion made her stomach clench. "You'll know which ones are most valuable."

Yes, she would. A hazard of the trade, knowing how much antiquities and hard currencies were worth. Jewelry, precious metals, paintings, sculptures . . . she knew which were valuable, which were not, and how to tell a fake from the real thing. She sighed. "Has anyone ever cracked the 1600 model?"

"No." He chortled, clearly enjoying himself.

She curled her fingers into her palms to hide the claws that slid forward. "And it's well guarded?"

"I'm sure those are obstacles you can charm your way through." He curled his hands over her shoulders.

She startled and jerked away, sidestepping his touch. "I'll see what I can do."

"See that you do. I want those jewels. And you want me to have them, or Sophie will be the one who pays."

Jewels. Jewels precious enough for Stefan to stage an elaborate kidnapping scheme. All those pieces of information she'd been collecting finally clicked into place. "Delilah."

Abernathy was the queen's cousin. Delilah had been hired to steal the Queen's Jewels. But would they risk having the real jewels in the palace during a staged robbery? She didn't think so.

"What about her?" Stefan lifted an eyebrow.

"*She's* the reason you were in New Chicago. You were confirming that she was the one hired to steal the Queen's Jewels. That's why we stayed in New Chicago so long after you roped me in." Tam let a breath out. "They're holding the Queen's Jewels at Abernathy's Surrey house, aren't they? Until Delilah's work is done, they took the real pieces out of the palace and put them in his Helax 1600. Those are the jewels you want me to steal."

A muscle ticked in Stefan's jaw. His hand snapped out to grip her jaw, sharp, weasel-like claws digging into her flesh. The pain was enough to force tears to her eyes, and he got right in her face, the evil showing so clearly in his gaze that she flinched. "You think you're so smart, don't you, Felicia? Well, I'm still going to win in the end. Don't doubt it for a moment."

"Why do you hate me so much, Stefan?" The words were muffled by his hand, but she knew he heard her.

"Because you dare to look like her, always reminding me of her." His eyes glazed with madness for a moment, before they became as clear and cold as ever. His fingers bit deeper into her skin. "Because you're alive and she's not. A little whore like you should be the one who's dead. Not her."

Her mother. He hated her for outliving her mother. The only thing he'd ever loved. "You want me dead."

"Yes. I want that," he whispered. "I get my jewels while they hunt down the thief who stole them. If you're lucky, they'll just arrest you instead of shoot you on sight. But luck hasn't really been with you, has it? I hear the queen can be quite vicious when provoked. How do you think she'll react when she finds out someone stole priceless family heirlooms?" His smile sent a chill down Tam's spine. "Either way, I never have to see your face again."

"And what becomes of Sophie when you get what you want?" She forced herself not to struggle, not to pull away from his hold. "She's your only child, the only thing you have left of my mother. Doesn't that mean anything to you?"

"But she's not your mother, is she? She's just another reminder." He shook his head. "Nothing will bring my wife back to me. Not you, not Sophie."

He released his grip on her, shoving her backward so her hip hit the corner of the vanity. She grabbed for the counter to keep her balance and stay on her feet.

"Get my jewels and the brat lives to see that Swiss boarding school again. Don't get them and she dies with you. Is that clear?"

"Clear." She swallowed, forcing a breath into her lungs. But she had no guarantee he'd keep his word, did she? She had to get Sophie away from him before then. Somehow.

"And you'd best keep loverboy on a leash, or he's going the same way you are. He'd better not interfere with my plans for the jewels. Do you understand me, Felicia?"

"Yes." Forcing her mind to something other than the Sword of Damocles hanging over her head, she tried to dig for more information. "How are you going to move them? The Queen's Jewels are distinctive. Not many would risk having them."

He straightened his bowtie, smoothing down his tuxedo jacket. "I have a buyer willing to pay prime creds for them. The embarrassment to the queen is an added bonus. Don't worry, Felicia. I'll come out of this just fine."

Unlike her. And Sophie. And maybe even Breck.

He turned on his heel and exited the wash closet. Tam sank down on the commode, her thoughts whirling. She'd been right. Being anywhere near her now would get Sophie and Breck killed. She had to get them away from her; that was the only way to make sure they were safe. She had more enemies than just Stefan, which made her a constant danger to them. Even if they managed to outwit her stepfather, it wouldn't change the simple facts. She'd been bad most of her life, and now she would pay the price—giving up the people she loved. Forever. Dragging in one slow, steadying breath after another, she found the strength to climb to her feet. When she glanced in the mirror, she saw a composed woman, not one who'd had her life ripped to pieces. Fraud. Liar. Sham.

"Tam?" Breck appeared in the doorway. "Stefan came back to the party, but you didn't."

"Where's Sophie?" she asked, her voice sharper than she'd intended.

He stepped closer to her. "She's fine. Hunter is watching her until we get back. I'm more concerned about you."

Worry pinched his features, drew his blond brows together in a deep frown. Worry for her. It broke something deep inside her to see that caring. He shouldn't be here. He should never have been dragged into this. And he was at risk now, because of her. Because he was her mate. A sob caught in her throat, and she stepped toward him, burying her face in his chest, knowing this would be the last time she allowed herself to touch him. This had to stop; it had to end before he got killed. She would never forgive herself if he died because of her. She'd go into the afterlife hating herself for it.

His arms came around her, secure and protective, and she just breathed in the clean, masculine scent of him. Nothing like Stefan's cloying smell.

"Are you all right?" Breck's deep voice rumbled in her ear, and he ran his warm palms up and down her back.

She'd promised not to lie to him, so she chose not to answer at all. Instead, she leaned to the side and closed the door to the wash closet, engaging the lock. She didn't want to take the chance of anyone overhearing what she had to say.

Tilting her head back, she let herself take in Breck's handsome features. She wanted to lock in the memory forever. She tried to smile, but knew she failed. "Kiss me, please."

Yes, she wanted the taste of him on her lips. She'd never craved anything so much in her entire life.

He cupped her shoulders, his gaze searching her face. "Only if you promise to tell me what happened with Stefan."

"I swear it." Not a difficult promise to make, considering the plan she had in mind required his cooperation. She was going to have to tell him everything. But not just yet. She wanted just a few more minutes before she broke something that felt so good.

He gathered her closer, pressing a kiss to her forehead, her cheek, the tip of her nose. So sweet. Kinder than she could ever deserve. She swallowed hard, slipping her fingers into the rough silk of his hair to pull him down for the proper kiss she craved. Her tongue tangled with his, letting his flavor, his scent, the feel of him pressed against her seep into her senses. Slipping her hands up his hard chest, she twined her arms around his neck, holding him closer. He felt perfect, like the closest to heaven a woman like her could ever get.

Slow desire wound through her, that unstoppable reaction that she experienced whenever Breck was anywhere nearby. His hands slid down her back, cupped her hips, and pulled her even closer. They both groaned when she came into full contact with his rising erection. Her sex clenched with utter want, her core going damp. She twisted against him, loving the feel of her nipples beading as her sensitive flesh moved against his musculature. The lace of her dress only intensified the sensation. A shiver ran through her, tingles of heat that sparked into fire within her.

His hands dropped to her ass, kneading the curve of her buttocks and drawing her dress slowly upward. She felt cool air brush over her thighs, and the fire inside her turned into a blazing inferno. She wanted his cock to thrust within her, hard and fast, obliterating everything else. She wanted to enjoy that rush with him, one last time.

She let her head fall back. "More. Give me more."

Sucking and biting his way down her neck, he grazed his teeth over the tender spot right at the base of her throat. "Don't think this gets you out of telling me what happened."

She chuckled, the sound throaty. "I won't."

"Good." His hands slid inside her panties to grip her naked backside. He pushed that scrap of fabric down, and she let it slip along her legs until she could step out of her underwear.

"I want you, Breck. Inside me." She trailed her tongue up

the column of his neck, nipping at his earlobe to make him shudder. "Now, please."

"Yes." His grip tightened on her backside, turning her to face the vanity. "I want you from behind. And stay in this pretty little dress. I like it."

She grinned at him in the mirror, the expression wicked. Her face was flushed with desire, her lips swollen from his kiss. "I was hoping you would. I wore it for you."

Heat whipped through her when she heard the distinct sound of him unsealing his fly. She shivered, some muscles loosening as others clenched within her, her body readying itself for sex. Bracing her palms on the vanity, she bent forward to give him all the access he could want.

His hands covered hers, pinning them to the vanity. With his big body surrounding her, she was trapped. It made her heart pound harder, her breath rush faster. For a cheetah-shifter who specialized in a speedy escape, there was something intoxicatingly erotic about being trapped by a man as sexually skilled as Breck, a man she knew would never harm her and would always make her scream with pleasure.

The head of his dick nudged the lips of her sex, sliding down her slit until he reached her center. Then he entered her. She shoved her hips back to take him in one quick thrust. Her fangs erupted from her gums as his thick cock stretched her. It was pleasure and pain all rolled into one, the line between the two blurring. A purr spilled from her. This was exactly what she needed now. She bowed her head forward, arching her body to meet the swift pace he set for them.

The impact of skin meeting skin echoed through the marble-tiled wash closet. He bent forward and bit her shoulder, making the lace rasp against her skin. A low snarl wrenched from her, the cheetah not far from the surface now. Wild and free, that was how she felt with Breck. Even if it wasn't true, if it could *never* be true, she let herself feel it, just for this one moment.

He sank deep into her pussy, her body rocking with the force of each thrust. The angle was amazing, and she leaned even farther forward to intensify the sensation. Oh, Deus. Her pussy spasmed, a precursor of what was to come. She could feel climax rising inside her already, though she tried to hold it off and cling to this feeling for as long as possible. It was a futile effort, but she tried.

"Don't fight it, beloved." Breck bit her shoulder again, harder this time, calling to the feral side of her nature.

A hiss rattled her throat, her claws scraping against the marble vanity. "Breck!"

Picking up speed, he fucked her hard and fast and exactly the way she'd wanted him to. It was too much for her to resist. Orgasm rushed over her in a huge wave that threatened to drown her, and she reveled in it, let herself be whipped into the carnal storm. Her pussy fisted tight around his cock, contracting again and again on the thick length of his shaft. Pinpricks of light burst behind her eyes, gooseflesh breaking down her limbs. She shuddered every time her pussy clenched on his dick. The way he filled her was sublime, and her climax went on forever as he continued to drive inside her.

His thrusts grew rougher, less even, and she knew he was close to that edge. A ragged groan burst from him, and his big body locked behind her. He gripped her hands painfully against the vanity as he came within her. His hot come filled her sex, pumping deep inside her. There was no holding back her moan, or the aftershocks of orgasm that shook her. Her sex spasmed again, squeezing his cock.

"Deus, Tam." He dropped his forehead between her shoulder blades, and she felt the bellowing of his breath through the thin lace of her dress. "That was . . ."

"Hotter than a cluster of biobombs detonating," she finished.

He chuckled, kissing her nape before he straightened away from her slowly. She sighed when his cock slipped from her body, already missing the connection.

But reality crashed down around her, killing the high of her climax. To keep busy, she grabbed a hand towel and used some sanitizer to clean herself up. Anything to hold off this conversation for just a few more moments.

"Tam."

She froze in place, then set the towel down and turned to face him. "Yes, I did promise, didn't I?"

He leaned back against the closed door and crossed his arms. "You did. What did stepdaddy have to say?"

"He wants me to crack the safe in Abernathy's office." She met his gaze. "They're holding the Queen's Jewels there while Delilah is doing her security checks at the palace."

The Adam's apple in his throat bobbed when he swallowed. "What's our next move?"

"I'm going to Drusilla's birthday ball and stealing those jewels." She drew in a slow breath. "You're going to stay at the Royale, and I'll make your apologies for you when I get to the gala."

His expression darkened. "We're in this together, Tam. How many times do I have to say that? I can help."

"No, you can't." She quickly outlined the information that Stefan had given her, and Breck's face settled into a glower. She squared her shoulders, readying herself for the oncoming battle. "I won't have you sully your hands with this. It's bad enough that you're being seen with me. They're bound to question you when this is all said and done. I want you to be able to honestly say you had nothing to do with any crimes I committed."

He shook his head, his jaw tightening. "Tam, just trust me to—"

"This isn't about trust." She held up a hand to still his words. "I *do* trust you. But I need you to do something else for me while I'm pulling this job."

That got his attention. His eyebrows arched. "What's more important than being there with you?"

"Sophie." She dragged in a breath, forcing herself to say the words that would sever the most important connections of her life. "Stefan is going to want to be nearby for this. I wouldn't be surprised if he's managed to finagle an invitation to the gala as well. He won't trust me not to try something to deprive him of his prize, and he's right not to trust me. He'll be preoccupied with his treasure, not with keeping Sophie on lockdown."

Breck tensed, straightening away from the door. "So, you want me to snatch her?"

If only it were that simple. "I want you to call the police and have them go in and get her. Leland and Nichols both have outstanding warrants for their arrest, I'm sure. You said you could pay the right people to legally get Sophie, and that's what I want you to do."

He scrubbed a hand down his face, every movement broadcasting his frustration. "You think I can't handle Leland and Nichols?"

Setting a hand on his arm, she squeezed gently. "I think you don't want to get involved in anything illegal. This way we get what we want without you breaking any laws."

"Why do you have to steal the jewels?" He spread his hands. "Why wait? Why can't we just do this tonight after the party, or tomorrow?"

The very thought made her blood freeze, and her voice rose with the urgency of trying to convince him to do this her way. "You think Stefan wouldn't kill Sophie right then and there just to spite me? His men aren't authorized to kill her without his permission, because *as things stand* she's only of value to him alive. If we change how things stand while he's around . . ." She shook her head. "No, we have to do this when we know he'll be out of the suite. And while I'm at the Abernathys' is a time I can guarantee it."

"How can you be so sure?"

She gave him a lopsided grin. "Because I know him. I know how he operates. He'll be at the Abernathys' that night."

His frown didn't ease. "You could be risking your life, Tam."

"She's more important than my life, don't you understand that? I want her to have the chances I never had. I want her to be able to meet a man like you and be worthy of him. I want her to be able to have him tell her they're mates and not feel the need to apologize to him for it." Tears rose in her eyes and she blinked fast to get rid of them.

He closed his hands over her shoulders, pain and sympathy in his gaze. "Tam . . ."

"There's more." The worst was yet to come. Deus, nothing had ever been so difficult in her entire life. "When . . . when you pay off whoever you have to in order to get Sophie free of the system, I want you to send her to some friends of mine."

His brows contracted, confusion filling his expression. "To guard her until you can come get her?"

"No." She stepped away from him, knowing she wouldn't be able to say this with him touching her, offering her comfort she didn't deserve. Coldness spread through her, making her feel frozen. "No, they're going to take her forever. They'll adopt her."

A flash of pure incredulous rage crossed his handsome face. "What the fuck are you talking about?"

That ice spread through her, making her feel as if she could crack into a trillion tiny pieces. "Stefan isn't my only enemy, Breck. I've conned a lot of people in my life. Many of them would be happy to see me rot in prison for the rest of my days. Some of them wouldn't hesitate to use Sophie against me if it got them what they wanted. As long as I'm part of her life, she's in danger." She was so cold, shivers began to run through her, and she hugged herself tight. *Breathe, Tam. Just breathe.* "As long as I'm in her life, she'll be tarred with the same brush that I am. Criminal. Degenerate. She's only ten and it's already happened to her at school. She's been scorned because of who her relatives are, had a friend tell her exactly what Stefan and I do to make money."

Not an ounce of empathy showed in Breck's expression now, just anger, rejection of what she was saying. "So you're just going to get rid of her?"

She clenched her teeth together for a moment to keep them from clattering. "I'm going to protect her the only way I can."

Crossing his arms again, he gave her a disbelieving glance. "Won't these enemies of yours be able to track down the friends you're leaving her with?"

"Not really." She snorted, holding herself tighter. She might shake apart at any moment. "They're missionaries. Good, honest, upstanding people. People unlikely to associate with someone like me."

"Yet you know them."

She nodded, the movement jerky. "They helped me once. In Asia."

"How?" He tilted his head, as if he had no idea how she might have gotten tangled up with missionaries.

Did she really have to tell him this? Strip herself bare again? The man knew all her sordid ugliness. She'd never wanted that. "I was doing a job, charming a very wealthy gentleman, and his wife poisoned me."

"She didn't like her husband cheating?"

"No, she was fine with him having mistresses." Her nails bit into her arms as she tightened her hold. Please, please let this be over with soon. She couldn't take much more. "As long as she didn't think they were prettier than her. I found that out the

hard way. She poisoned me and dumped me in a river to die."
She glanced away from him, but there was no escaping. She
could see his expression in the mirror. "These very kind missionaries fished me out and nursed me back to health. They
know about Sophie and understand that someday she might ar-
rive unannounced on their doorstep. They've agreed to adopt
her should such a moment ever come, change her name, and ba-
sically erase any connection between her and me."

"You don't need to do this," he snapped, his tone implacable.

"Yes, I do. As long as she's in my life, she's at risk," she repeated. They both needed to hear it out loud again, because the
truth was a harsh thing. "I've been denying that fact by staying
away from her, but Stefan has made it painfully clear to me.
Even tucked away in a boarding school, she's not safe."

He threw up his hands in exasperation. "She's only in danger as long as you're associating with criminal elements. Go
clean."

As if it was that simple. No. She shoved that idea away, no
matter how tempting it was. And, Deus, it was tempting. But
she was too far gone to go straight now. Her past would never
be erased, it would come back to haunt her. There were too
many people who knew her face, who had seen how corrupt
she was inside. Sophie knew what she was. Breck knew. They
might say they loved her now, but someday it would matter to
them. Someday they'd understand that she wasn't good enough
to be around people like them. She'd only get them hurt, one
way or another. If not now, then in the future.

This had to end. There was no more pretending she was
something she wasn't.

Dread was a lead weight in his stomach, and a band of emotion tightened painfully around his chest. Anger and agony
twisted inside him. She was actually going to do this. Throw
away everything that meant anything to her. Fuck. He wanted

to shake her, shout at her, demand that she not use that cheetah speed to run for once in her life, that she stand and *fight*. It wasn't about cowardice, not this time. No, he knew this was probably the hardest thing she'd ever done, but it was so unnecessary.

"Go clean?" She huffed out a breath. "It's too late for that."

He fisted his hands at his sides to keep from reaching out to shake her the way he wanted to. Maybe then she'd come to her senses. "*Why?* Why is it too late?"

Her shoulders hunched, and she curled into herself. But her eyes sparked with determination. "Because I promised myself that I would protect her and give her a good life. This is the best way."

"That's not true. She should be with the people who love her the most. And that's you. She loves you. You love her. You should be together. It doesn't matter what you've done in your life. You can change." Why was he still arguing? She wouldn't listen. It was as effective as bashing his head into a solid mercurite wall.

"Of course it matters what I've done. I'm a thief. I'm a terrible person. How many times and in how many ways can you have it pointed out to you before you understand, Breck?" Her jaw jutted stubbornly. "I lie, I cheat, I manipulate. I do whatever is necessary to make people do what I want. Mostly men."

"What other choice did you have? Become a jade? Stay on those docks, marry too young to a man who beat you, spend the rest of your life popping out babies, and then dope yourself up on bliss to forget the hellhole of your existence? Does that sound so much fucking better?" He stepped forward until he was in her space, urging her to hear him. Just this once, really hear him. "You did what you had to to survive. To thrive. Don't you *ever* apologize for that."

Tears sheened her dark eyes, but she blinked fast to keep them from falling. Her chin notched higher. "So I shouldn't have to live with the consequences of my actions? Because my other options were worse? No. That's not how it works. I broke the law, and one way or another I'm going to pay for it. I just don't want Sophie to pay for it. Or you."

"You're not a bad person, Tam. Everyone's success comes at the expense of someone else. Rich people's fortunes are built on the backs of poor people. It's a fact of life." He reached out to grab her shoulders, squeezing tight. "I try not to abuse that system too much, but the bottom line is, my lowest paid employee in my smallest company makes just enough to get by. I've destroyed people in some of my business deals. That's how it works. I'm not better than you are just because I was born rich."

"But what you did was *legal*. That's the difference between you and me." Resignation reflected in her dark eyes, and he hated that.

"Don't do this, Tam. Please. It's not too late." The words were desperate, a plea ripped straight from his soul. "I can help you change your life, I can help you keep Sophie. Be with me, my mate."

She tried to jerk from his grasp, but he held fast, too afraid to let her go lest she disappear again. Giving up her struggle, she glared at him. "And what are you going to do when what happened to Sophie happens to you? When some rich business associate of yours comes up to me, says I stole a priceless Picasso from him, and calls me Dayna or Kate or Lori or one of the many other aliases I've used?"

"Why *did* you use your real name with me?" It was something he'd always wanted to know. And hell, he'd rather talk about anything other than her leaving. Again.

"I don't know. I've asked myself the same thing, but I don't have a good reason. I hadn't planned to." She shrugged, her gaze hitting his chest. "That's beside the point."

"Okay, fine." He sighed. "If and when that happens, it'll be a little embarrassing, but we'll work it out."

Shame flooded her gaze, her face flushing. "I don't want to be an *embarrassment* to you, Breck."

"You wouldn't be." He shook her again, harder this time. "Deus, Tam. Quit twisting things around."

"I'm not the one with a warped idea of reality here. It's a fantasy, Breck. I don't belong in your world. I'll never belong in your world. You deserve better than me. Sophie deserves better than me." She shoved herself backward, so he'd have to hurt her to keep her close, and he let her go.

He had no choice.

It hit him then, the final, ugly truth. He couldn't win this one. He couldn't fight her demons for her. Even if he beat Stefan, even if he saved Sophie, even if he threw every cred he had at solving all of Tam's problems, he'd still lose her. Because she thought he deserved better than her.

He laughed, the crack of sound echoing in the wash closet. Pressure built behind his eyes, and the band of emotion around his chest cinched so tight he wasn't sure how he was still breathing. "You know what the real difference between us is, Tam?"

Her lips pressed together. "What's that?"

"*I* don't judge you," he stated flatly, knowing it wouldn't matter, but he had to say it while he had the chance. "You keep acting as if I'm going to look at you and tell you what a morally bankrupt individual you are. That you're trash because of where you grew up and what you did to make your life better. But that's what you think about you. That's not what I think. I don't judge you, *you do.*"

"That's not—"

"Yes, it is. Why won't you fight to keep Sophie? Why send her away? Because you don't think you're worthy of happiness." He grasped her chin and forced her to look him in the eyes. He wanted that connection in these final moments. "Deep down, you think you deserve whatever Stefan has in store for you. All you can see is what he made you. A criminal. You don't see all the other things you are. A sister. A friend. A lover. My mate."

"I know what I am." But her lips shook, and he could see the lie in her eyes, could see the denial and rejection of what he said. Of him. It hurt as nothing in his life ever had before.

"I love you."

She flinched away from his words, but he saw the desperate hunger in her gaze. She wanted his love, she just didn't want to believe she'd earned it. "No, you don't. Not really. It's just the mating instinct."

"Maybe at first, but not anymore. I know you now. I've seen the shithole you grew up in; I've met your warped asshole of a stepfather. I've seen behind the mask, Tam, and I *know* you. I know you're a stronger, better person than you give yourself credit for. I love you. But I want you to love you, too. I want *you* to think you're worthy of happiness." Pain spread like a bruise inside of him, and he didn't even know why he kept talking. It was useless. Pointless. "What would make you happy is being close to Sophie, making sure she's safe and growing up well. But you don't think you're worthy of the life you want for her, do you? That's why you're sending her away, and that's why you're determined to push me away. You could have *everything* you really want, and instead you're running scared. You're not fighting to keep it. You love me, Tam. I know it. You love Sophie. You want us near so bad you can taste it, but you're so certain you'll ruin us by being yourself that you're not even willing to try."

Her breathing hitched in a sob, and a tear slid down her cheek. "You don't know what you're talking about."

He stepped toward the door and opened it, knowing when he closed it behind him, he'd be walking away from his mate forever. "I give up, Tam. It doesn't matter what I say or do, I can't convince you to believe in yourself enough to make any relationship work. Not with your sister, and not with me."

Love and relationships took work. And he couldn't do it alone. Both of them had to believe enough to show up, and she didn't. She never would. He had to accept that. Finally. He loved her too much to stand aside and watch her destroy herself.

"Does this mean you won't help me with Sophie?" Her question stopped him before he slipped through the door.

He closed his eyes. It felt like she'd shredded his heart with her claws, left him bleeding and broken. "I'll save Sophie. She deserves better than what Stefan has planned for her. She deserves someone who'll love her enough to stick around. Which, apparently, isn't her sister."

9

"Your driver is about to drop me off at the Abernathy manor. I'll go inside and make sure Stefan really is here, then leave a message in your cache to let you know to call the police." Though Tam could see Breck's face clearly on the screen of her palmtop, she glanced away often. It hurt to look at him now. They hadn't spoken in the days since the party at his penthouse. She'd uplinked the encrypted information he would need about the couple who'd take Sophie.

"If you insist." The look he gave her was blank and removed, not at all the warm, animated lover she'd known.

She swallowed, squeezing words past her suddenly tight throat. "Thank you for doing this, Breck. I know it wouldn't be what you'd choose."

A muscle twitched in his jaw, and he reached toward his screen to cut the call. "Good-bye, Tam."

Agony seared her chest, but a broken heart would do that, wouldn't it? She'd lost Breck, and she was soon to lose Sophie, too. That was for the best. But what was best sometimes hurt. She pressed together lips that quivered, tucking her palmtop into her handbag. Breck's words rang through her mind on an endless loop, and they had for days. *You want us near so bad you can taste it, but you're so certain you'll ruin us by being yourself that you're not even willing to try.*

Staying in their lives would ruin them, but he'd made it sound so ugly. She was trying to do the right thing, to be *good* for the first time since she was ten years old, and he'd slapped her in the face with it. Righteous anger flooded her, and she welcomed it. Better than the depression that had swamped her since she'd last seen him. She'd done her best to hide it from Sophie, but losing them was a wound that would never heal.

The transport rocked to a gentle stop, and the door swished open. An Abernathy footman gave her a hand out, and she smoothed her long gown, lifted her chin, and walked into the manor as if she belonged there. The place was posh, the decorations tasteful, but clearly priceless. While standing in the receiving line, she greeted a few people who'd been at Breck's party or the Duke's post-race celebration. She made her curtsy to the Abernathys, wished Drusilla a happy birthday, and gave them Breck's excuses for not coming with her. A holo chandelier floated above the ballroom, casting light on the polyglass ceiling that lit the enormous room in an amber glow. That had set the Abernathys back a load of creds.

She smelled him as soon as she entered the room. Stefan. Her stomach clenched, but she kept her expression pleasant as she smiled at passing guests. She plucked out her palmtop and keyed in the message to Breck that would be the beginning of the end of this thing.

Stefan is here.

And there he was, standing across the room, decked out in the kind of fancy tuxedo that disguised the villain he really was. She snorted. Not long ago, she'd thought the same thing about her fancy dresses disguising what she really was underneath.

That hit her right between the eyes. Deus, is that what she

really thought? That she was the same as someone like Stefan? Someone who'd murdered people for fun, kidnapped and threatened his own child, abused Tam when *she* was a child. Someone who wanted Sophie and Tam dead because they happened to look like their mother. That was how she saw herself, deep down?

She rocked back on her heels, felt the blood rush out of her face. Deus, Breck was right. About her. About everything. All these years, this picture she had of herself in her mind had been building, insidious and ugly. She was what Stefan had made her. No better than him. Criminal. Immoral. Degenerate. A pathetic excuse for a human being.

Not worth anything. Not worthy of raising a child she loved. Certainly not worthy of a good man for a mate.

The realization slammed into her with the subtle force of a biobomb. Deus, what was she doing? Did she really hate herself so much that she was willing to let Stefan kill her or get her thrown in jail for the rest of her life? She'd told herself she was being noble, sacrificing herself so Sophie and Breck could have good lives without her, but who was she fooling? This was a suicide mission. She couldn't beat Stefan alone.

Glancing in his direction again, she saw him staring at her. His lips twisted up in a cruel smile and he toasted her with his whiskey glass. He knew she was here, and he wasn't going to let her get out of here unharmed. But Breck was saving Sophie, so he wasn't going to rescue Tam. She was on her own.

Hoisted by her own petard.

No. She would not let the weasel win. She wouldn't let him hurt Sophie, but now she realized that *she* deserved better than that, too. She didn't deserve how he'd treated her. It wasn't her fault he'd become obsessed with her mother and killed her father, and it wasn't her fault that he'd thought her cheetah speed was useful. *It wasn't her fault.* And she would not lie down and take it from him anymore. She would *not* let her fear of him steal her life. Damn it, *no.* She would not be his victim anymore.

She stepped behind a large potted plant and lifted her palmtop, keying in the code to make a call she'd never have thought she'd make.

The connection picked up on the other end, and Tam made herself breathe normally when she wanted to hyperventilate. "How would you like to steal the Queen's Jewels? The real ones this time? That *is* what they paid you for, isn't it?"

On the small screen, Delilah's eyebrows arched, and a perfectly wicked grin curled her lips. "When and where?"

"Right now." She smiled back, though the muscles in her face felt unnatural and stiff. "You'll want to accept that invitation to Lady Abernathy's birthday ball. And bring the fake jewels with you."

The lynx-shifter tilted her head, her green eyes going narrow. "Why are *you* doing this?"

For once, Tam could answer in perfect honesty. "I want to make sure they end up exactly where they're supposed to."

Delilah nodded slowly. "Is this the problem your sister got tangled up in? She's a little young, but . . . I started young, too."

"So did I." Understatement of the millennium, but since the lynx had grown up in the Vermilion, Tam figured Delilah would understand. Her circumstances would have been no better. Tam sighed. "She's not involved. Her safe return is my payment for services rendered on this job."

Delilah leaned closer to the screen. "Who's holding her?"

"Her father," Tam ground the words out. "A slimy little weasel of a man. My mother had terrible taste in men."

"My mother was a whore. My sister and I can't even be certain who our fathers were." The lynx snorted. "I can relate."

"So you can." Tam dipped her chin in a nod. "Breck is taking care of my sister. With your help, I can make certain her father doesn't get the Queen's Jewels."

Delilah hummed, her eyes crinkling at the corners. "And if anyone asks, I'll say you were working with me and not with him. Since I have a legitimate reason to be stealing them."

"Exactly. I want my sister, Breck, and me to get out of this alive and *not* end up in jail." More than anything else in the world, she wanted that. She didn't know how things would go with Breck, but if she had the chance to find out, she wouldn't waste it.

Delilah nodded. "All right, I'll help you. If for no other reason than I don't like it when men hurt little girls, and I don't like to see assholes win."

"Thank you."

"Thank *you*." Delilah's grin was back in full force. "I have to admit it chapped my ass that they didn't let me swipe the real jewels. Getting my hands on them anyway is going to be fun. They're shiny and pretty and I want to try them all on before I give them back." She rubbed her hands together. "I'll be there as soon as I throw on a ball gown and find my biggest handbag to carry my usual equipment."

"Hurry." Faster was better. She could do some mingling in the meantime, make sure she was seen as a regular guest before she disappeared into the bowels of the manor.

The view bobbled as if the lynx-shifter carried her palmtop as she was moving around. "You have a plan in place?"

"Of course." She'd spent day and night trying to get a plan together since Stefan had let her know what the real job was. Something like this should have been months in the works, but it was one more obstacle Stefan had thrown in her path.

By now she knew the exact layout of the manor, the guard rotation, the type of security system they had in place, where each vidmonitor was located, and the backgrounds of every employee they had working for them. Every waking hour she'd had in the last couple of days had been spent preparing for the job. She'd downlinked every piece of information she could get her hands on about the Helax 1600 model of safe. She knew the specs, she knew when it had been installed in the Abernathy manor, she knew who'd done the installing. A few discreet inquiries to colleagues had turned up some valuable information on cracking it, but there were no guarantees there. Getting caught during a failed attempt was yet another reason to bring in Delilah, who'd be able to excuse herself as doing the job she'd been paid for.

Relief swam through Tam. There was a chance she might actually see the other side of this. Of course, she might not. It could still all go terribly wrong, and she could still wind up dead.

But for the first time in as long as she could remember, she had hope that there might be something better for her in life. She might actually have a chance at one of those fairy-tale endings. If she managed that, she'd spend the rest of her days proving that she'd gotten what she deserved.

A life that was of her own choosing.

Breck sat staring at his palmtop for a long time after Tam messaged him. He was supposed to call the police and involve them in this mess. He was supposed to stand aside while they rescued Sophie; then he'd use his money to get her out of the system and ship her to the middle of nowhere with some missionaries who'd raise her to be "good." He knew the plan, knew his role in it, and how that role would cut him out of Tam's and Sophie's lives forever.

But even if Tam managed to survive Stefan and avoid becoming a suspect in the Queen's Jewels theft, calling the police now meant they'd be investigating Sophie's family and why she was being held by two wanted criminals. A chat with the Royale's staff would implicate Tam, and they'd dig into her past. Which meant she was going to end up getting arrested, one way or the other.

Fuck. He hated this. He couldn't save her from herself. He knew that. Deus, how he knew that. But making this call now really would screw her over. Even if she didn't want to keep him in her life, and even if she wanted to cut ties with her sister, he couldn't bring himself to do something that might hurt her.

But how else could he get the little girl away from two men who made their living as hired guns? He'd need help. Tam wanted him to call the police to get that help, but there was someone else he could call. He tapped the code into his palm-top and waited for it to connect. Please, let the man be in the mood to chat.

Hunter's face filled the screen, tanned except for the thin white scar that ran down one side. "Breck."

"Avery." Breck nodded a greeting. "When you got here, you asked if I needed help. Is that offer still good?"

The other man blinked. "Yes."

"Good." Breck let a breath ease out. This was probably among the most reckless ideas he'd ever had, and that was saying something. "It'll be dangerous."

A small smile touched Hunter's lips. "I'll wear my nano-armor vest."

"You have it with you?" Really? Breck's eyebrow rose, and he couldn't stop his answering smile.

Hunter shrugged. "I bring it any time Delilah's working. She's needed a hand a few times, and her work carries certain risk."

There was a thought. The feisty lynx-shifter would definitely be an asset. She was ferocious and occasionally unpredictable. "I wouldn't mind Delilah's help, too. I've heard she can handle herself in a fight."

A chuckle spilled out of Hunter. "She can, but she's out right now. You just get me."

"That'll do. Thank you."

What the hell was he doing? He was out of his mind. Certifiable.

Ten minutes later, he perched on the edge of his balcony in his eagle form, and Hunter clutched the railing beside him in his hawk form. They had to take advantage of the only real advantages they had—the element of surprise and the fact that they could fly. If Nichols and Leland stuck to their usual schedule, Nichols would walk out onto the main balcony of Stefan's suite in the next few minutes to smoke. Easy pickings for a diving bird of prey.

Breck launched himself upward, then circled back to pick up a bag of clothing that he'd left on his balcony. He'd figured they might scare the shit out of Sophie if two large, stark ass naked men showed up to rescue her. Hunter followed suit, only his bag included his nanoarmor vest, which he'd use as a weapon to drop on Nichols's head. They winged through the night, silent and watchful.

There.

Nichols stepped outside, his cigartine a red spot of light in the darkness. Hunter swooped forward, and the hawk let his bag fall. It slammed into Nichols's shoulder and he cried out as he fell to his knees. Shit. Breck had been hoping for a knockout, but that shout was going to bring Leland running.

Tucking his wings in for a straight dive, Breck shifted just before he hit the balcony floor. His bag rolled away, and he swung his fist at Nichols's face. The man snarled, his eyes glowing yellow in the dark. His nose crunched under Breck's fist, but he jabbed his fingers upward into Breck's ribs. There was desperate power in that hit, and all the breath whooshed out of Breck's lungs. He stumbled back, and Nichols came after him, growling like the dingo that he was. Wild and vicious.

Fuck.

A shrieking cry rent the air as Hunter dove down, his talons aimed straight for Nichols's face. The dingo-shifter ducked, and the hawk raked his claws down the man's arm. Breck took the opportunity to jump Nichols, and the two of them tumbled across the balcony to hit the railing. Pain shot straight to Breck's skull when his back hit the hard metal. The dingo tried to punch him, and Breck blocked it. Nichols shoved them into a roll, trying to get another hit in.

"*Shit.*" That was from Hunter, and when Breck and Nichols rolled again, he saw Leland tangling with the hawk-shifter. He'd managed to get his nanoarmor on, and he seemed to be holding his own in the fight, but that was all the attention Breck could pay the other men.

Shoving the dingo-shifter backward, Breck staggered to his feet. Sweat slid down his face to burn his eyes, and adrenaline burned through his veins. Talons sprang from his fingertips, and he sliced at the dingo-shifter when he came at him, catching him across the chest. Blood splattered the ground, and Breck took another swipe. Nichols ducked in close and landed another punch, slamming his fist right into the same ribs he'd struck before. Breck gagged, pain darkening his vision, and it was all he could do to remain conscious. So he let himself go limp, and Nichols stumbled under the sudden deadweight. Before he went all the way down, Breck powered upward with his legs, swung his elbow around, and used the momentum to drive it into Nichols's face.

The dingo-shifter went down, finally. Breck bent forward and braced his hands on his knees, sucking in breaths. It felt as if a white-hot brand had been pressed against his ribs, and the pain radiated up his side. He gingerly pressed a hand to them and winced. Bruised, but not broken. He'd broken a rib before and it had been worse than this.

This was bad enough.

Grunts and the sound of flesh hitting flesh filled the air, and Breck straightened to see Leland slam his foot into Hunter's knee. Hunter's leg crumpled under him, and he rolled with the fall. Leland spun toward Breck, razored shark's teeth bared. Dangerous if he tried to bite, but they both knew he wouldn't be shifting. Not if he wanted to breathe. He came at Breck, but Breck dropped down, shooting a foot out to kick. Leland jumped back, and Breck only grazed his calf. Not enough to do real damage. Damn it. They stood, circling each other to look for an opening to strike.

Breck's breath came in ragged pants, but he watched Hunter weave to his feet behind Leland. "Hey, fuckwit."

Leland spun to face the new threat. Hunter lifted his hand and the shark-shifter dropped.

"You didn't even touch him." Breck felt his jaw sag in shock. "What the hell?"

Holding up a small canister, Hunter shrugged. "It's Delilah's trademark. I had some in my bag. A little spray of this stuff and a guy is out cold with nothing but a headache to remember her by."

"Nice." Breck found his bag and pulled on a pair of pants. "Let's get Sophie and get out of here."

He led the way into the suite, heading straight for the child's room. Hunter hobbled after him, favoring the knee Leland had hit.

"Sophie?" Breck called when he didn't see her. Was she hiding somewhere? His blood ran cold. Had they already done something terrible to the girl? Were they too late? "Sophie!"

"Get me out of here!" A muffled little voice shouted, and it sounded like fists pounded against wood.

"There," Hunter said, nodding toward a closet.

Breck was across the room in three strides. He disengaged the lock and jerked the door open. Sophie tumbled out into his arms. "Breck! Where are the bad men?"

"We knocked them out on the balcony." He quickly checked the girl for injuries and found none.

Sophie pulled away and ran to see the scene on the balcony. "How long will they be that way?"

"Not very long. We need to go." Breck held out a hand for her to take, but she trotted past him.

She returned a moment later and handed him two long

pieces of black cloth. "The belts from Father's robes. Microsilk makes very tight knots."

Hunter snorted in amusement, leaning against a wall for support. "Nice."

"We should put them in the closet in my bedroom." Her little mouth set in a firm line. "See if they like being locked in there."

Sounded like a decent plan to Breck. "Then that's where they're going."

"I'll help you tie them up."

He shook his head, but quickly trussed up the other men, tying the knots far tighter than he should. If they woke up, they'd have a hard time shifting in the tight space, and Breck was going to make them as uncomfortable as possible in the meantime. Any little thing that might slow them down once they came to.

Hunter stood out of the way as Breck hoisted the men over his shoulder one at a time and carted them into Sophie's bedroom to dump in the closet.

"Wait! I just thought of something." Sophie grabbed his hand, desperation in her grip. "*You* know where Tam went tonight, don't you?"

"Of course." How could he forget?

"Good!" Her eyes lit with relief and hope. "You can go save *her* now. They put me in the closet when I got mad because they were talking about the bad things Father was going to do to Tam tonight. You have to go save her." Tears brightened her eyes and her small hand clutched his. "*Please*, Breck. He's not a nice man. He'll *do* those bad things they said."

How could he explain to a ten-year-old that her sister didn't want to be saved? That her sister intended to dump her on some good little missionaries at the earliest opportunity? There was no kind way to deliver that message. He might have to anyway, but not now. Besides, could he really live with himself if he let Stefan get his hands on Tam? No. She might have a death wish, but Breck would be damned if he'd let the weasel win.

"My mate is with Tam." Hunter's words jarred Breck back to reality.

"What?"

"She left just before you called. Something about stealing the real jewels instead of the fakes. I'm going after her." He turned toward the door, stumbling as his injured leg tried to buckle underneath him.

"No, you're injured. I'll go." Breck transferred Sophie's hand into Hunter's. "Take Sophie somewhere else. I don't care where. Any other hotel in the city, just not here, then call a medic to see to your leg."

The man's face had gone pale. "If anything happens to Delilah . . ."

"Nothing will, I promise. I have to go now." He shifted to eagle form, flew out the balcony doors and up to his penthouse. Another quick shift and he'd stuffed his tux and shoes into a bag and winged his way out again. Toward Surrey. And Tam. And Stefan.

What would have taken almost forty-five minutes in London traffic took him less than twenty flying. He landed on the Abernathy grounds, changed into his tux, and tried to appear calm and composed when he entered the manor.

No more than three steps into the ballroom, Stefan was at his side, hissing in his ear. "You're late, loverboy, which tells me you're up to something."

Breck cast the older man a disdainful glance. "I had a meeting. I *do* have business to attend to outside of playing your lackey, and that business has been sorely neglected while I chased after Tam."

"You're lying," Stefan replied, his voice silken and chilly at the same time. "Now, Constantine, my men haven't answered my calls, which tells me something is wrong. You did something to them."

A shiver of danger went up Breck's spine, but he held that chilling gaze and continued to lie. "I have no idea what you're talking about."

The weasel-shifter jabbed a gun into Breck's ribs, right where Nichols had nailed him. He winced, hunching forward a bit, beads of cold sweat breaking out on his forehead.

"No idea, huh?" Stefan's smile turned smug. "Business meetings don't usually leave wounds."

The lights overhead flickered for just a moment, then went completely black for thirty full seconds before they flared back to life. Stefan grabbed Breck's arm, keeping his gun pressed to Breck's side. There were a few exclamations from around the ballroom, but the musicians quickly resumed playing and the party was back under way.

"What was that?" Stefan snapped. He ground his weapon into Breck's injured ribs with bruising force, and it was all he could do not to vomit.

"I don't know." Sweat slipped down Breck's face, and his limbs began to shake. He fisted his hands and rode out the agony, refusing to give the older man the satisfaction of making him cry out.

"Right. Assuming that you've managed to remove Sophie from my men's guardianship, I'm going to need something to make sure Tam does as she's told. Specifically you, Constantine." Stefan jerked his chin toward a doorway that opened off the ballroom. "Move or I will kill you. Don't doubt it."

As if there was any room for doubt. Breck walked in the direction of the door, and presumably the office and safe that held the Queen's Jewels beyond. "You're assuming pointing a gun at me will make Tam do anything."

Now, there was a sad truth that burned straight down to Breck's soul. On the one hand, he didn't want to be a pawn Stefan could use to manipulate her. On the other hand, did he *want* more evidence that his mate didn't care for him as much as he cared for her? Not really. He *knew* she loved Sophie, but him? Not really. Not enough to stay.

The blue light of a freeze torch illuminated the sharp angles of Delilah's face. A triumphant grin curled her lips. "We cracked the Helax 1600. We're going to be fucking legendary."

Tam checked the chrono hanging on the office wall. Fifteen seconds left. "We unlocked the door, we haven't stolen anything from it yet."

"What's your plan for that?" Delilah shut down her freeze torch and stowed it in her bag.

Tam kept her gaze fixed on the chrono but set one hand on the handle of the safe. "You'll see. Get ready to open it in . . . three . . . two . . . one . . ."

The lights flashed, then darkened. All sounds of electronic devices cut off. People called out in the distance, and she could hear running feet outside the window. Not a moment to lose.

Delilah threw her weight behind opening the door, which no longer had electricity to help it swing. The two women grunted and the door gave, its hinges squeaking.

"Stand guard, Dee." Tam grabbed a bag and used her cheetah speed to dart through the opening. Her feline sight gave her the ability to see what she wanted and she shoved the necklaces, tiaras, diadems, earrings, brooches, and parures into the bag. *Hurry.* She counted down the seconds she had left before the power would come back on. *Faster, Tam, faster.* She pushed her speed to the absolute limit. If so much as a toe was still in the safe when that happened, she was dead.

Snatching up the last silver coronet, she spun and threw it to Delilah, sprinting for the door and diving through it headfirst. The lights flickered back to life.

"Fuck me." Delilah stared into the safe, as the laser beams

laced back and forth across the interior. "Those are the ones that'll slice your legs off. They aren't just motion detectors."

"They're both." Tam gasped for breath on the floor, rolling to her back and pushing the bag of jewels to the side. "And if you set off the detectors, they trigger a gas that'll kill your nervous system."

"Upgrades from the last Helax model." The lynx-shifter shuddered but shoved the door closed. "How long before they know it's been breached?"

"If we're lucky? An hour. I had the power knocked out across all of Surrey, not just this house, so they won't automatically know they were targeted." Pushing herself upright, Tam tried to stiffen her shaking legs. She helped Delilah slide the armoire that hid the safe back into place, then heaved a sighed. "Deus, we did it."

"Cracked a Helax 1600 *and* stole the Queen's Jewels," Delilah crowed. "When that bit of buzz gets around, we are going to be *notorious.*"

Tam chuckled and handed the lynx-shifter the bulging bag. "Enjoy your dress-up session before you give them back."

"You know I will. I might do a naked show for Hunter in them. He'd love that."

Tam dabbed the sweat from her forehead, trying to come to grips with the fact that she'd made it out of that safe alive when no one else who'd tried to break into it ever had. "Rumor has it you met him trying to steal the famed Avery ruby."

"I like shiny things. And I like when people pay me to steal them." The lynx-shifter hummed in her throat as she peered into the bag. "Now those are some prime bits of pretty right there."

"You have to hand it to them, the royals really know their expensive baubles." Tam swept back a lock of hair that had come loose in her tumble out of the safe. "Give me the fakes. They're going to Stefan."

She'd already looked at them, and they were good. They'd pass anything but a close inspection. That might throw the little weasel off just long enough. She had to try. There was no way she'd risk him touching the real things. They'd be gone and Tam would be to blame. Tam *and* Delilah, and she wouldn't do that to someone who'd helped her more than once.

Delilah cocked her head to the side, her body going still. "Someone's coming."

"Shit." Tam heard it, too, the sound of footsteps approaching. "Stash the goods."

They each stuffed their bags behind different pieces of furniture. Tam grabbed Delilah's arm and shoved her onto the long kleather sofa that dominated one wall. Delilah landed in a sprawl on her back, and Tam knelt between her legs. She shoved the other woman's skirt up her thighs, then tugged her own dress down to her waist, baring her breasts.

"Wha—"

The door swung open and Tam giggled drunkenly, leaning over Delilah's prone form. A large man stood in the doorway, his mouth sagging open when he took in the scene before him. His gaze went straight to Tam's breasts and glazed a bit. Just as she'd intended. She giggled harder. "Oops, Dee, we got caught."

Delilah pouted and glared at their intruder. "Why did you have to ruin our fun?"

He cleared his throat, his gaze darting between Delilah's long, bared legs and Tam's chest. "I...um...we're doing a manual security check of the...of the house and grounds. Because of the power outage. It shorted the...vidmonitors."

Also what Tam had intended.

"Did the lights go out? I thought that was just the orgasm." Delilah giggled and reached up to grope one of Tam's breasts.

Tam slapped the lynx-shifter's hand away, laughing. Making a half-hearted attempt to pull her dress back up, she made sure her chest was still in view and still distracting the guard. She gave him a sheepish glance. "Our men are handling some business affairs at the party, so we decided to sneak off and handle some affairs of our own." She winked. "Drusilla said her staff would understand."

"Ah." He coughed into his fist. "Yes, well, this is a restricted area. I'm going to need to escort you out."

"Of course." Tam nodded sagely but made sure to weave drunkenly as she rose to her feet. "You'll wait out in the hall for us while we tidy ourselves up? With the door closed, if you please. Anyone could walk by, and that might be quite embarrassing for my friend's husband."

Delilah heaved a long-suffering sigh, sat up, and somehow managed to flash even more of her long legs. "We're newlyweds. He's still smitten."

"You have one minute." The guard grabbed the knob and pulled the door shut.

Delilah shoved her dress down, running for her jewel bag. "What was that about Lady Abernathy?"

"Lord and Lady Abernathy share the same mistress." Tam hauled her gown up and slid the straps over her shoulders, then went to get her own bag.

Delilah paused for a moment. "You mean a three-way or like a time-share?"

"Time-share, I think." Tam strode over to push open the window, glancing out to see if anyone was watching.

"Does she get paid overtime?"

"Hey!" The guard snapped outside the door. Tam was about to reply when she heard a low coughing sound, then the distinct thump of a body hitting the ground.

Gooseflesh rose on her flesh. "Delilah, go out the window. Now."

"Don't bother, my dear," Stefan's voice carried clearly through the door, but he wasn't the one who pushed it open.

Breck was.

Tam's blood ran cold at seeing him there. Then she got a clear view of the guard, sprawled across the carpet with a neat hole in his forehead, his eyes staring ahead sightlessly. Her stomach turned. "There was no need to kill the guard, Stefan."

"He was standing in my way." Stefan shrugged as if it meant little to him. And it did. Taking someone's life didn't rattle him at all, whereas the scent of death that curled into Tam's nose made her skin prickle with unease.

She looked to Breck, whose face was sickly pale. "Are you all right?"

A muscle flexed in his jaw, and his chin jerked down in a sharp nod. Sweat streaked down his skin, lines of pain bracketing his mouth and eyes.

"What did you do to him?" Delilah demanded.

"Nothing at all. He showed up to the gala a bit worse for the wear. I have my suspicions that he tangled with my men trying to rescue my daughter from my loving care." Stefan's eyes widened theatrically. "You wouldn't know anything about that, would you, Tam?"

"I've been here, doing your dirty work, Stefan." Her hand tightened on her bag and her mind raced. From where Stefan stood, Delilah was half-hidden behind the desk. It was possible he couldn't see that she held a bag identical to Tam's. "Why don't we get this trade over with? The Queen's Jewels for Breck, and then you just walk away and leave us alone? It's not going to be long before they find that guard outside. You don't have a lot of time, Stefan."

She hefted the bag, shaking it so the items inside jangled together. Tension stiffened her muscles, terror a living thing inside of her. Was Sophie all right? Why was Breck here and not with the girl? How had he ended up at gunpoint? How injured was he? Oh, Deus. Oh, Deus.

Greed filled Stefan's gaze as it locked on Tam's hand. "I could simply kill all of you and take what's mine."

"You think you're faster than all three of us combined?" Delilah snorted. "You're dreaming, pisswad. I'd take you down with me, just for spite."

Stefan ignored her. "Give me the jewels or I put a hole in loverboy they can't slap a nanopatch over."

"Take them." Swinging her hand, Tam threw them so they landed close to the middle of the room. Outside of Stefan's reach. She met Breck's gaze, hoping he understood that this might give him a chance to get clear of the gun. His chin dipped a mere millimeter, but it was enough.

Stefan smirked as if he knew Tam was trying to pull something. He jabbed his weapon into Breck's ribs, making him groan. "Step over there, away from both women and my treasure."

Breck walked toward the couch as he was told, and Stefan moved forward, never lowering his eyes or his gun as he dipped down to pick up the bag. "You too, Delilah. Throw the bag you're hiding over here."

"How do you know which is real?" Delilah taunted, not moving to do what he said.

"It doesn't matter if I take them both with me," he retorted, but he looked at Tam. "I told you I'd win."

Deus, she loathed him as she'd loathed nothing and no one in her life before. Hate spilled through her, dark and ugly. "The jewels aren't what matters to me. Take them and leave us alone."

"You know, I've been thinking about that. What matters to you." Stefan smiled at her. "It's not enough for you to die. I thought it would be, but it's not. I want you to lose everything you love. Sophie. Loverboy. Your freedom. I thought Constantine might deny me the pleasure when he didn't come with you tonight, but he was so accommodating. I'm going to love watching you suffer, little whore."

"Please." The word was a sob spilling from her lips. What he described was every one of her worst fears coming to life. And looking at that gun of his, the dead guard sprawled out in the hall, she could imagine it all far too clearly. "Don't hurt them."

"Begging won't help you. They're going to die. You're going to jail." He said the words as if he relished the taste of them on his tongue. "And I'll know you're out there in the world, even more miserable than I am without your mother, rotting in a cage."

"No court in the world will convict her when I'm done testifying." Delilah's eyes narrowed to angry slits, her fangs extended.

"Oh, but she killed you, too. All of you, so she could keep the jewels for herself." Innocence shone from Stefan's face as he trained his weapon on her. "Throw them to me. Now."

Helplessness spread through Tam, and tears pricked her eyes. Time slowed down, stretched out until she could feel every painful moment trickling past. Her heart beat in slow, painful thumps. She felt rooted in place, a spectator watching her world crumble. Even if they outnumbered him, he could kill at least one of them before they could take him. Delilah grabbed her bag, flipped it over the desk, and launched it at Stefan's head while she dove for the floor. He ducked and the gun went off, but Breck was already moving toward Stefan.

Sensing the threat, he turned on Breck, his finger squeezing the trigger. That snapped Tam out of her daze. No. She would not allow this to happen. *No.* She darted forward, shoving Breck out of the way. The bullet slammed into her with the force of a speeding transport, bowling her over.

A moment later, she heard the angry, piercing shriek of an eagle as Breck punched his talons through Stefan's throat. Blood sprayed everywhere, dark crimson. The look of shock on the man's face was almost comical. He really had thought himself invincible. But he'd been wrong. It was over. The monster was dead.

So was she.

She could feel the blood pumping out of her body with every beat of her heart.

"Good use of speed, Tam." Breck turned to her, relief filling his expression, but then his gaze landed on the palm she had covering her wound.

"I thought you got us both out of the way." He caught her before she slumped to the floor. He pressed all his weight down on the bullet hole.

"Deus, Tam. Deus." Delilah hauled herself upright, her eyes going wide and wild when she looked at Tam. The lynx-shifter fumbled for her bag and pulled out a palmtop to make a call. She sounded panicked, scared, but somehow her words were fuzzy and didn't quite reach Tam's ears.

"Don't you die, Tam. Don't you fucking do it."

Her head rolled against the floor and she looked at Breck. He was so handsome, so wonderful. She'd hurt him so much, shoved him out of her life, and still he was here, trying to save her. They could have been happy together—her, Breck, and Sophie. A real family. And now she'd never have the chance. She'd failed, becoming Stefan's victim one last time. But better her than Breck or Sophie.

She tried to smile at him, but it hurt. Everything hurt. Breathing hurt. There was blood everywhere, all over his hands, his clothes. Her blood. Far too much of it.

"Damn you, Tam. Why?" Fury vibrated in his every movement while he shoved down on her wound, trying to stop the bleeding, but it was a futile effort. "You were just determined to fucking die, weren't you?"

His voice broke on a sob that ripped her heart in two. She wanted to tell him that he'd been right, that she wanted to stay with him so bad she could taste it. She'd tried to find a way to stay, she really had hoped she might, but she couldn't seem to get words out past the pain. The sound that escaped her throat was a mere gurgle.

He turned his head to the side and wiped a tear off on his shoulder. "You can't die now, Tam. Not now."

She didn't want to. No, she wanted to stay. She wanted to spend her life with him, making up for everything she'd done to bring him pain. Making him happy. Mating with him. But blackness filled the edges of her vision and she blinked, trying to focus on him. Breck.

His voice turned pleading. "Please don't go, Tam. Sophie needs you. She's waiting for you to come back to her, right now. Stay for her, if you won't stay for me. Please."

She opened her mouth, needing to tell him how much she loved him, to thank him for everything while she still had the time, but nothing came out. A vise closed around her chest, the agony turning to darkness that roared up and swallowed her whole.

11

The pain of losing Tam weighed down on Breck, but he learned to live with it. He learned to breathe again and made himself get back to work. There was plenty to do from his long absence, which was a blessing. The bustle of New Chicago was a welcome balm. Home. It was good to be back. Some day it would all feel natural again, and he wouldn't turn a corner and be reminded of the precious weeks he'd had his mate in his life.

He missed her. He'd known he would, and he accepted the pain.

"Mr. Breckenridge?" One of his assistants poked her head into his office. "There's a call from Gea Crevan."

"Put her through." When his assistant disappeared, he closed his eyes, feeling a sharp stab of agony to the heart. These calls were a torment, but one he craved. He took in a breath. It would be over soon. This might be the last call.

"Breck." The woman's brown gaze was steady when she met his on the vidscreen.

"Gea." He nodded. "Any updates?"

"Yes, sir." Her voice was carefully neutral as she spoke.

"Tam's medic cleared her fully for travel, and she's taking her sister to Switzerland."

Sending Sophie back to boarding school. He shook his head. Of course. Nothing had changed, had it? He couldn't even muster any frustration, just resignation. He'd stayed in London long enough to make sure she was going to make a full recovery; then he'd forced himself to leave. He couldn't make himself look at her anymore. The woman had essentially committed suicide right before his eyes, and the horror of seeing it haunted his dreams, crept up to slam into him at quiet moments during his waking hours. He swallowed the bile that burned his throat, forcing his mind away from the memory of her bleeding out in his arms.

There had been a medic at the Abernathys' gala. It had been the only thing that saved her. Without that man, she'd be dead. Taken by a bullet that had been meant for Breck. Guilt hammered at him, but he crushed it. Just as he'd crushed any urging from the eagle within him to return to his mate. That was done. Over. He had to move on.

"Breck, did you hear me?" Gea's voice jolted him back to reality.

"Yes." He pressed his palms to his desktop, letting the smooth surface ground him. He'd hired Gea and her mate to provide security for Tam while she recovered, and to keep him apprised of her condition, but that was coming to a swift close. "If she's amenable to an escort, you and Kienan will go with her."

"Of course," she replied. "I'll offer our services to her. I think she'll take us up on it."

"Good. That's ... good." He swallowed. "And what of Leland and Nichols?"

"They've been arrested." She shook her head. "One of Kienan's many and mysterious contacts is seeing to it that those *gentlemen* never see the light of day again."

"Well ... that's good, too. It's all over, then." He let a sigh ease out. He ached to his bones, but he'd survive. What choice did he have? "Thank you, Gea. For everything."

"You're welcome." She gave him a smile that was ... sad for him, and he couldn't stand that either. He was holding together by feeling as little as possible. Someday he wouldn't be so ... empty.

"Good-bye." Tapping his fingertip against the vidscreen, he ended the call.

So, that was that. He wouldn't let himself inquire about Tam after Gea and Kienan returned to New Chicago. That way lay madness. Tam had to figure out her life with Stefan dead, and that she was sending Sophie away to school again told him all he needed to know. He stomped down on the tiny tendril of hope that emerged because she *hadn't* sent Sophie to the missionaries. So she hadn't cut the girl out of her life entirely. So what? She was still abandoning her to be raised by someone else. Tam was, as always, determined to run away from love. That was her choice. No one could force her to *want* to stay, least of all him. He'd given it his best shot, and it had ended with Tam being shot.

He pulled up a memorandum and began to read it. There was a new merger in the works, and he needed to focus on that. It was time to get on with the business of living. Every day without her would get easier. It had to.

"What did he say when you told him I got a clean bill of health?" Tam hovered outside the room where Gea had been talking to Breck.

"Not much. He never says much anymore." Gea swiveled in her chair to look at Tam, sighing. "His assistants are worried about him. They say he's not himself."

The look she pinned Tam with clearly said who's fault that was, and she couldn't argue. She needed to talk to him, but the conversation they had to have shouldn't take place through a vidscreen. So, she'd avoided it. Because she was scared.

"You need to get your ass back to New Chicago," Delilah drawled from where she lounged across a microsilk chaise.

Unlike Breck, Delilah and Hunter had stuck around to make sure Tam was all right, and she was grateful for the support. She didn't know the last time she'd had anything that resembled a friend, so she had no idea what she was doing, but she was glad they were here. That was the problem, wasn't it? She had no idea how to be in any kind of relationship, just as Breck had pointed out. She ran away from them. She hadn't given anyone a chance to reject her in decades. But that was what she'd have to do with Breck. He needed her to show up and stick around. He'd told her as much, hadn't he? Before he'd walked out of her life.

She'd drifted in and out of consciousness for days, and by the time she was truly cognizant of her surroundings, he'd already gone. That had hurt, but could she really blame him? As far as he knew, she'd been a willing lamb Stefan had led to slaughter.

"I don't know what to say to him." Tam clasped and unclasped her hands in front of her.

Delilah arched a pale brow. "Wasn't it you who told me—oh so many years ago—that men were simple creatures?"

"That was before I fell in love with one! Then I just wanted to seduce them, shag their brains out, and get them to give me things." Throwing her hands up, she paced around the main space of their suite at the Savoy. This was where Hunter had taken Sophie the night Breck and he had rescued her, so they'd decided to stay until Tam was well enough to travel. Which she was.

"Sounds like a good plan." Hunter looked up from his palmtop, where he was busy running the world. "It works for Delilah every time."

The lynx-shifter purred and leaned over to kiss him. He chuckled against her lips.

A pang went through Tam. She wanted a mating that loving. Breck had offered it to her, and she'd rejected him. Over and over again. She sighed. She didn't know how to explain this to her friends. Everything had changed. In one night, her whole world had rotated on its axis. How she looked at and treated men wasn't the same as it used to be. Breck had changed that. Hell, how she looked at and treated *herself* wasn't the same. She was still trying to find her way in this post-Stefan world. It wasn't just that he was dead—though she was glad about that— it was that he was no longer the man who defined her life. She'd let him be, and that was wrong. *That* was over.

Who she was now was still up in the air, but she'd figure it out. She wanted to figure it out with Breck by her side. And the only way to do that was to chase him down the way he'd done to her. She knew what she had to do, but she was flat out terrified. It was a huge risk, and the outcome would decide the course of her new life, one way or another.

"All right. We're going to pick up all of Sophie's things that she had to leave behind, and then we're getting our asses to New Chicago, as instructed." She tipped Delilah a nod.

"We'll escort you right to Breck's front door." Kienan spoke up from where he stood by the window. His gaze swept the room, always alert for security issues. The man was quiet, but rock-steady.

"He hasn't asked where you're going after Switzerland." Gea shrugged as she stowed her palmtop.

Tam forced a smile to her lips. "He doesn't want to know. He walked away, and he wanted to know only enough to be sure I was healthy and safe."

So like Breck. Even when he was licking his wounds and determined to cut her out of his life, he took care of her. His mate. Deus, she loved the man.

"We'll take my private transport. It's faster than a commercial carrier." Hunter waved a hand at Kienan. "And more secure."

"And less cramped with hundreds of people." Delilah gave a cat-like yawn. "I'm going to finish packing. When are we scheduled to go?"

"Dawn." Hunter grinned at her when she grimaced. "Don't worry, kitten. You can sleep on the flight."

Anxiety formed knots in Tam's stomach the closer they got to New Chicago. Picking up Sophie's belongings hadn't taken much time, but the little girl had needed some closure with the place she'd called home for years. She'd bid her friends and teachers farewell, and now she curled up beside Tam on the transport ride to America. They'd be landing soon, and Tam was as nervous as the first time Stefan had forced her to pull a heist. Only this time, there was a lot more at stake. Her heart.

She breathed in through her nose and out through her mouth, reaching for calm. She could do this. She *had* to do this.

Sophie stirred, sitting up and pushing her dark curls out of her eyes. "Are we almost there?"

"Yes, darling. Very soon now."

"I'm still tired."

"It's the jetlag. You can sleep when we get there, if you like. Breck's home has a lot of bedrooms." She hoped that was where they'd be staying.

Sophie leaned over to look out the window, but it was a cloudy night. "Breck said I could come live with him."

"What?" Tam blinked. "When did he say that?"

Her sister sat back in her chair, kicking her dangling feet. "People came for me, when they thought you wouldn't..." She swallowed, her mouth curling down. "They said since I had no one to take care of me, I had to go with them. Breck made them leave me alone. He spent a long time on the vidscreen with people, and then he said they wouldn't bother me anymore. He said I could come live with him if you didn't make it."

Her heart broke at those words. Despite everything, he'd volunteered to take Sophie and give her the life Tam had always wanted for her. She'd never loved him more. "Oh."

"He's nice. I like him a lot. Are you going to marry him?"

"I don't know, darling." She stroked her hand down the little girl's hair. "I'm not really sure of much right now. But you and I will be together from now on. I promise."

"Good." She smiled her sweet smile. "But I think you should marry him. He cried when they said you were going to . . . die. I cried, too."

Tears welled in Tam's eyes. "I'm sorry I worried you."

"You mustn't do that again." Sophie leaned close to show how serious she was.

"I will do my best to be more careful in the future." With luck, she wouldn't have to worry about that kind of danger ever again.

"Good." Sophie nodded decisively. "I'm glad not to be going back to boarding school. They're nice there, but it's not the same as family."

"I know it's not."

"We're landing." Hunter's calm voice came through the overhead intercom.

She'd had no idea when he said they were taking his private transport that it meant he'd be the pilot, but it had simplified travel plans.

It felt like no time had passed at all before they were on the ground, hugging Hunter and Delilah good-bye, gathering their things, and then the shortest transport ride of all time had Tam standing at Breck's door. She wanted a moment to compose herself, but Sophie knocked eagerly. "I can't wait to see him. He's a hero, you know. He rescued me from the bad men."

"Yes, I know." She couldn't help but smile at the girl's enthusiasm. It helped take the edge off of some of her nerves.

Breck's housekeeper answered Sophie's knock, and Tam was relieved to see it was someone she knew. The older woman's mouth dropped open. "Ms. Tamryn? I had no idea you'd be here. Mr. Breckenridge didn't say a thing to me."

"It's a surprise. A good one, I hope. May we come in?" She summoned up a smile. "This is my sister, Sophie. Sophie, this is Mrs. Hadley."

"Hello!" Sophie bounded through the door and gave the housekeeper a hug.

"Hello, dear." Mrs. Hadley laughed, then looked past Tam. "Are Ms. Crevan and Mr. Vaughn coming in, too?"

"No, we're just the escort. We need to get home." Kienan stepped forward and set Tam's and Sophie's bags inside the foyer.

He shook Tam's hand, and Gea gave her a quick hug. "Good luck."

She'd need it. "Thank you."

The wind picked up Gea's hair and she pushed it out of her face. "Tell Breck I'll call him in the morning with a full report."

Kienan caught his mate's hand. "Quill is waiting."

"Mr. Breckenridge is in his room. Why don't you go up?" Mrs. Hadley waved a hand around at the luggage. "I'll see to this and get Miss Sophie settled for the evening."

"But I want to see Breck." Sophie danced in place, beside herself with excitement.

"In the morning, dear. Let your sister talk to him, all right?" Mrs. Hadley took the girl's hand. "Do you like cinnacherry cookies? We have some in the food storage unit."

"For me?" Sophie glanced at Tam. "You'll say hello to Breck for me and tell him I'll see him as soon as I wake up?"

She bent and gave her sister a hug and kiss. "I'll make sure he knows. Good night, darling. Be good for Mrs. Hadley."

Watching them wander toward the kitchen did nothing to help Tam with her love life, but she stood there trying to gather her nerve anyway. Breck was here. Only a curving staircase away. She turned and looked up the elegant marble stairs. Breck had once told her he used to slide down the banister as a boy. This was where he'd grown up. It was nothing like *her* childhood home, but so what? Was she going to let that stand between her and the life she truly wanted?

No.

With that, she pushed herself forward, following the irresistible scent of him that beckoned her up those steps and down the hall to the double doors that led to his suite of rooms. She set her hand to the smooth wood, but heard no movements beyond. He was asleep. Was that good or bad?

She tried the knob and found it unlocked. Pushing the door inward, she saw he'd fallen asleep working, propped up in bed, a palmtop computer resting on his chest. He wore only a pair of microsilk sleep pants, his blond hair tussled. She pulled the door closed behind her and leaned back against it, letting herself take in the sight of him for a moment. Her heart squeezed tight. Please. Please let her be able to convince him to give her another chance.

"Breck," she whispered.

He stirred but didn't wake. His palmtop slid off his chest and fell to the mattress, teetering as if it might slip from the bed and hit the floor. She darted forward and caught it, setting it on the bedside table.

Deus, he was close enough to touch now. Her hands itched with the need to do just that. If this were any other time, or any other man, she'd strip naked, climb into bed with him, and awaken him with her hands and mouth on very intimate parts of his body. She'd seduce him. And despite what Hunter and Delilah had said, she couldn't do that. Not this time. She didn't want it like that with Breck. This was her mate, and she wanted him to choose to be with her, not be seduced into it.

She sat down on the edge of the bed—a bed they'd shared so many times before—her hip brushing his. "Breck, my mate. Wake up."

His eyes cracked open, and he drew in a sharp breath. Then his gaze flew to her. "Tam?"

"Yes, I'm here." She smiled at him, though her insides quaked with trepidation.

He jerked upright in bed, his hand shooting out to grasp her chin. "This isn't a dream."

"No, this is very real." More real than anything she'd ever done with any man before.

"What are you doing here?" He dropped his hand as if touching her had scalded him. "Aren't you supposed to be off dumping Sophie back into boarding school?"

"No, we went to Switzerland to collect all the things her father made her leave behind, and to give her a chance to say her farewells." She drew in a breath. "She and I talked about it and we've decided we want to live here in New Chicago. With you."

His big body went rigid, his blue eyes growing shuttered. His voice dropped to a harsh rasp. "Don't do this to me, Tam. Not again. I can't have you in my life and then watch you walk away when it gets too intense. I won't survive it."

Tears burned her eyes, and she dragged in a ragged breath. "I'm not going anywhere. You said I deserved to be happy, and that you wanted me to believe I was worthy of what I wanted most. Well, you were right. About everything. I tarred myself with the same brush as Stefan for so long that I couldn't see past what he'd made me."

"And now you can?" His expression was dubious. "Because he's dead?"

316 / Crystal Jordan

"No." She twined her fingers together in her lap, trying to hold herself together and not fumble over the words. She wanted to get this right. "Because of what you said. Because I couldn't get it out of my head. Because I looked at Stefan at the Abernathys' ball, and it hit me how I had always thought the two of us hid the badness inside behind fancy clothes and a charming smile." Tears threatened to fall again, and her voice shook a bit. "I thought I *was* what he'd turned me into. Someone awful, like him. And I hated that. I hated that I'd let him mold me into someone I couldn't face in the mirror. I know that I just did what I had to to survive, but it shamed me. All these years, every day, I was ashamed of myself. I couldn't save myself from him as a child, and I thought it was all my fault. So I deserved what I got, since I was bad like him."

He made a rough sound and moved to reach for her, but then stopped himself.

She pushed onward with her explanation. "So it struck me then, how right you were about all of it. And . . . and . . . I'm not like him. I was *never* like him. He's evil. He *was* evil. Past tense," she corrected. "Clearly, I have a conscience, even if it's a little underused and overly flexible in the legality department."

His huff of laughter gave her the courage to continue.

"I called Delilah for help because I was going to try to give the fake jewels to Stefan while she gave the real ones back to the queen. I wasn't really going to steal them. I wasn't going to let Stefan get his way, because I wanted better *for myself* than he had planned. Because I deserved better." She gave him a smile that wobbled. "Because even if I grew up on the docks, I deserve to have the kind of life I wanted for Sophie. Because even if I've done some bad things in my life, I'm not a bad person, and I deserve to have a mate as wonderful as you. You said so, and it took me a long time to get there, but I believe you now. I believe in *us,* and I want to stick around and see if I can make a relationship work. I want to see if I can be part of a real family."

The breath whooshed out of her lungs, and she waited an eternity for him to respond. Perhaps she'd hurt him too much, pushed him away too many times for him to trust her change of heart. Perhaps it was too late. Her fingers twisted together so tight they ached.

His eyes closed, and she heard him swallow hard. He shook his head, and her hope crumpled. A tear slipped down her cheek. "I love you, Breck. I . . ."

But what more could she say? That she was sorry she'd hurt him? That she wished she could have spared him? It wasn't enough. She knew it wasn't.

"How do I know you won't leave again?" The question was soft, and that very softness made it sting all the more. His eyes opened, and she saw the suffering, the doubt.

She pressed her lips together until she knew she wouldn't sob. "I never *wanted* to leave you at all. Not the night you found me at Tail, not when Stefan shot me. I always wanted to stay. I just didn't think I could or should."

"You threw yourself in front of a bullet." Guilt and shame filled his blue gaze, and that pained her, too. That he thought she loathed herself so much she'd commit suicide. Not that long ago, he might not even have been wrong. She'd been unhappy for a very long time. Dissatisfied. The thrill had gone out of conning people. Once, that had been her only power in a world that Stefan ruled, so she'd found pleasure in what she could control. But that was an empty pleasure that had stolen her soul, little by little. No more. She wanted a different life. And she wanted to share it with her mate.

"Yes, I threw myself in front of a bullet. And I would do it again. For you or Sophie, I would. Not because I don't value my life, but because I would do anything to keep the people I love safe and happy. You're the best things in my life, the best part of *me*." She met his gaze steadily, dared him to contradict her. "Wouldn't you do the same for the people you love? Risk your life and possibly die to keep us safe?"

He shook his head, turmoil in his expression. "Yes, but... you..."

Tilting her head, she arched an eyebrow. "I'm not supposed to love you as much as you love me?"

His jaw hardened. "*I'm* supposed to protect *you*."

A breathy laugh escaped her. "You saved me from myself, Breck. That's a far more difficult thing. I'll always be grateful to you for it, and for staying with me and believing in me when I couldn't. I love you."

His hand rose to touch her face, but he hesitated. She caught his fingers, kissed his palm, and cupped his hand against her jaw. When he stroked his thumb along her cheekbone, she purred. It was so good to have him pet her. She'd longed for it during the days of her recovery. She'd longed to have him near.

"Be sure, Tam." His throat worked. "I couldn't bear it if you changed your mind."

She leaned into his touch, rubbing her cheek against his palm. "I'm not sure about a lot of things, Breck. What I'm going to do with my life now that I'm not a grifter, whether or not I'll be any good at raising Sophie, but I'm absolutely certain that I love you. I want to spend my life with you. I never, ever want to leave you again."

His arms wrapped around her, dragging her down so she was pressed against every micrometer of him. She clung to him, relief making her so giddy she almost giggled. He squeezed her tight enough that she couldn't breathe, and it was just right.

"I missed you so damn much," he whispered in her ear. "I hated that you might have died because of *me*. I tried to tell myself I'd be fine without you, that you didn't want me and I couldn't force you to stay with me, but I fucking *missed* you every single second."

She pressed her hands against his chest, lifting her head to meet his gaze. "I missed you, too. I hated that I couldn't come to you right away, that I had to wait until the medics said I could travel. But I was also bloody terrified you'd tell me it was too late to make amends."

As an answer, he kissed her. It was hot and sweet and utterly perfect.

She sucked his lower lip into her mouth, scraping it with her teeth. He growled, his hands tugging at her clothes. Anticipation wound tight within her, the undeniable heat she felt whenever he was near. Now, she could revel in it. She didn't have to fight against what she wanted. She could keep it. The thought alone was enough to send desire shooting through her.

It was freeing.

She plunged her tongue into his mouth, wanting to lock the taste of him in forever, knowing this was a moment she'd never forget. Sliding her hands into his hair, she writhed against his hard length, loved the feel of his cock prodding the apex of her thighs. She parted her legs, bracing her knees against the mattress so that his erection could rub her where it would do the most good. His pants and hers frustrated her, but she rolled her hips against his, letting the excitement build to a fever pitch. Her pussy was slick with juices, and every pass of his thick cock over her clit drove her wilder.

A gasp escaped her when he flipped her over onto her back. Lust tightened his features, and a flush ran beneath his skin. He stripped her out of her clothes, his gaze burning in intensity when it touched every millimeter of her skin. She let her thighs fall open so he could see how wet he'd made her, how much she wanted him. He shucked his pants, and then they were both nude. His cock was a sharp upward curve, and she wanted to slide her tongue from base to crown and suck him hard. She reached out to run her fingers down the length of him, but he caught her hands and pressed them to the mattress on either side of her head.

He flashed his naughtiest smile. "You know what I want now."

Yes, she did. He wanted to handcuff her to the bed the way he had so many times before. His headboard was solid wood around the edges, with a basketweaving of wood and mercurite strips in the middle. At the bottom of the headboard was a bar of gleaming mercurite, which Breck had bound her hands to more than once. Probably not the function the bed's designer had had in mind, but it served the purpose so well. "You don't have to tie me down, Breck. I'm not going anywhere."

"I know," he said simply, and that faith meant so much more to her than he could ever understand. How many people had ever trusted her to keep her word and do the *right* thing? Breck and Sophie. That was probably it. He bent forward and nipped at the curve of her stomach. "But I *want* to tie you up. Because it's fun, and we both enjoy it."

She reached up and grabbed the bar. He snagged a set of cuffs out of his bedside table and used them to bind her to the mercurite. Heat pumped through her system, that same excitement of being unable to escape. "I've never let anyone but you do this to me."

"No?" His eyebrows rose, a slow grin curving his lips. "Well, you're never *going* to let anyone else but me do this to you."

She tugged against the binding, loving the sound of metal snapping against metal. No running now. She didn't want to. She wanted him to take her, hard and fast. Arching her torso toward him, she smiled at him. "Hurry."

"No, I'm going to take all the time I want." He slipped backward down the mattress on his knees, lifting one of her legs. He turned his head and kissed her ankle, her calf, the back of her knee. "We've been rushing around since I found you in London, and I want to slow down and just savor you. Because you're mine and I can."

If he hoped those words would simmer down her need, he was sadly mistaken. Her skin felt aflame, so hot with her craving she thought she might burn.

"Mine," he said, kissing the inside of her thigh. Then he kissed the other. "Mine."

Her breath caught when he dipped down to curl his tongue around her clit, and her hips lifted off the mattress. "Breck!"

The man's purr could rival any feline's. "This is mine, too."

It was a claiming. Pure possession was in his gaze when he looked over her nude form, and she reveled in it. She'd always wanted to be his, she'd just never believed it was possible. Until now.

"Yes, yours. And you're mine. Forever."

He blew a cool stream of air against her damp, overheating skin, and she choked. The cuffs around her wrists snapped tight when she tried to push her sex closer to his mouth. But he held her down and moved up to kiss the lower slope of her stomach. "Mine." Flicking his tongue into her navel made her squirm. "Mine."

His hands closed over her breasts, kneading them. Lust shot straight to her core, and her sex clenched on emptiness. She needed to be filled.

"Mine," he whispered, rubbing his thumbs over her nipples. They went tight, beading into points. She cried out when his lips closed over the tip of her breast, sucking on it, batting it with his tongue, and then shoving it against the roof of his mouth.

"Deus, *please.*" Her back bowed, her arms jerking against her bindings. A hiss spilled from her when he bit down on the other nipple. Her sex fisted, and she felt orgasm building deep within. Deus, she was going to come before he ever got inside her. "I need you, Breck. I love you. Please, please."

A shudder ran through him, and when he met her gaze, she could see how he struggled to contain the eagle within him, saw the wildness in his eyes. It called to the most feral part of her, and her fangs slid forward, claws tipping her fingers.

"I want you inside me." She licked her lips, knowing he'd see the deadly points to her teeth. "I need it."

"Yes." His talons dug into her flesh where he cupped her breasts, and he dragged the sharp claws lightly down her torso while the blunt tip of his cock pressed for entrance within her pussy.

She pushed her hips up to take all of him, moaning as he impaled her one slow micrometer at a time. The stretch made her sob on a breath. She'd missed this connection so damn much, had craved him every single heartbeat that they'd been apart. He hilted his dick inside her, rotating his pelvis to stimulate her clit.

"Mine," he groaned.

She squeezed her inner muscles around his cock, clamping down on his thick shaft. She purred when he groaned again.

"Yes, mine," she agreed.

The chuckle that rumbled out of him was a rusty sound, but he propped himself on his elbows and met her gaze while he began pistoning in and out of her pussy. The drag and glide of his flesh in hers made her shudder. Wrapping her legs around his flanks, she rocked herself into the contact. The speed and friction built, and every time he powered into her, the hair on his chest rasped against her nipples. Oh, Deus, it was beyond amazing. She writhed against the restraints, loving how they added to the overwhelming sensations.

Faster and faster, he thrust inside her, the intensity of his emotions playing over his face. He was more open to her than he had ever been before, and she let him see everything she felt. No masks, no hiding. She wanted him to know how she felt about him. Her sex began to clench with each penetration, climax beckoning irresistibly.

"I'm going to come," she whimpered, and voicing it made

the need unstoppable. She catapulted over the edge, a high feline scream breaking from her throat. Her pussy flexed on his cock, milking his thick shaft as he continued to fuck her. "Come with me."

His groan was long and loud, the sound of a human volcano erupting as his control broke. He sank deep inside her as he reached orgasm, his pelvis grinding down on her clit. His fluids pumped into her, flooding her, and her sex clenched around his cock. "Tam! My Tam."

"I love you," she whispered. "My Breck."

Emotion imploded inside her, and a tear slid from the corner of her eye, a sob hitching her breath. Her heart hammered in her ears, blood pounding through her veins. The euphoria of orgasm tangled with her love for him, and the rush carried her higher than she'd ever been before. It was so good, and it was even better because she didn't have to make herself give it up. She got to keep this for as long as she lived. She'd never allowed herself to contemplate something so sweet until now.

It was a long time before she came down from that high, before her breathing and heart rate returned to normal. His weight crushed her, and her arms were beginning to cramp, but she couldn't bring herself to protest. He groaned, pushing against the mattress to hold himself over her. Dipping forward, he pressed a quick kiss to her lips.

"Let's get these off of you." Kneeling up, he unfastened her bindings, propped her hands on his chest, and rubbed the circulation back into her shoulders and arms. A purr soughed from her throat. Satisfaction made his eyes heavy-lidded, and a lazy grin quirked his lips. He looked more relaxed and happy than she had ever seen him, and her heart turned over.

"I love you, Breck." She caught his face between her palms, locking her gaze with his. "I'm going to be here for the rest of our lives. I'm yours forever. I swear it."

"And I'm yours. I love you, Tam." He turned his face and

kissed her palm, then nipped at the base of her thumb. "My mate."

She let his love wash over her, and for the first time got to enjoy it. She didn't have to deny his feelings or hers, she didn't have to feel shamed by who she was, or guilty that he had the misfortune to be her mate. No, she could just *feel* it, absorb it, let the wonder of loving and being loved seep into her soul. She was safe and whole and happy. All the people she loved were near, and she got to keep them with her. Forever.

She'd gotten *exactly* what she deserved.